MAXIM JAKUBOWSKI was born in England but educated in France. His father was Polish and his mother British but of Russian extraction, and they met as a result of the Spanish civil war. In addition to living many years in France, he also spent several years in Italy. During a misspent youth in the food industry, he spent over ten years travelling the world, and visited most continents and remote countries.

Following a later career in publishing, he left the corporate life to open London's now famous MURDER ONE bookstore and write. He has won awards for his books in the mystery and science fiction fields. His *Mammoth Book of Erotica* was a major bestseller and he now edits the EROS PLUS imprint, when not attending film festivals here and abroad. He reviews crime in a monthly column in *Time Out* and is a contributing editor to *Mystery Scene*.

His recent books include *London Noir*, *Crime Yellow*, the two manifesto anthologies of British hardboiled writing *Fresh Blood* (w. Mike Ripley), *The Mammoth Book of Pulp Fiction* and his own highly controversial collection of interlinked erotic love stories *Life in the World of Women*. His two novels 'It's You That I Want to Kiss' and 'Because She Thought She Loved Me' have earned him the title of 'King of the Erotic Thriller' according to Crime Time.

He still favours blondes, but it shouldn't be held against him.

The Mammoth Book of

NEW EROTICA

Edited by
Maxim Jakubowski

Carroll & Graf Publishers
NEW YORK

Carroll & Graf Publishers
an imprint of Avalon Publishing Group, Inc.
161 William Street
16th Floor
New York
NY 10038–2607
www.carrollandgraf.com

First published in the UK by Robinson Publishing 1998

First Carroll & Graf edition 1998

Collection and editorial material copyright © Maxim
Jakubowski 1998

ISBN 0–7867–0535–3

Printed and bound in the United Kingdom

10 9 8 7 6 5

CONTENTS

ACKNOWLEDGEMENTS

LET ME COUNT THE TIMES by Martin Amis, © 1980 by Martin Amis. First published in Penthouse Magazine. Reproduced by permission of Peters Fraser & Dunlop Group Limited.

EMERALD by Cleo Cordell, © 1998 by Cleo Cordell. Reproduced by permission of the author and Rupert Crew Limited.

WINGED MEMORY by M. Christian, © 1998 by M. Christian. Reproduced by permission of the author.

DAY TURNS INTO NIGHT by Jules Torti, © 1998 by Jules Torti. Reproduced by permission of the author.

A FAIRY STORY by Michael Crawley, © 1998 by Michael Crawley Reproduced by permission of the author.

SPIRIT OF THE SACRED WHORE by Cree Fox, © 1998 by Cree Fox. Reproduced by permission of the author.

ROCKING HORSE by Jennifer Footman, © 1998 by Jennifer Footman. Reproduced by permission of the author.

HE'LL HAVE TO DIE by Maxim Jakubowski, © 1997 by Maxim Jakubowski. First published in Because She Thought She Loved me. Reproduced by permission of the author.

THREE OF CUPS by Cecilia Tan, © 1998 by Cecilia Tan. Reproduced by permission of the author.

INTERFACE RHAPSODIC by Alice Joanou, © 1998 by Alice Joanou. Reproduced by permission of the author.

GOVERNMENT ISSUE by Thomas S. Roche, © 1998 by Thomas S. Roche. Reproduced by permission of the author.

KISS ME by Joe Maynard, © 1997 by Joe Maynard. First published in Paramour. Reproduced by permission of the author.

EROTOPHOBIA by O'Neil De Noux, © 1998 by O'Neil De Noux. Reproduced by permission of the author.

CRAZY TIME by Noel Amos, © 1995 by Noel Amos. First published in Eroticon Fever. Reproduced by permission of the author.

THE MAGIC COCKROACH by Susan Scotto, © 1997 by Susan Scotto. First published in Pink Pages. Reproduced by permission of the author.

NEW ORLEANS by Alice Blue, © 1998 by Alice Blue. Reproduced by permission of the author.

IN THE WHITE ROOM by Michael Perkins, © 1985 by Michael Perkins. First published in Prude. Reproduced by permission of the author.

THE DRESS by Michael Hemmingson, © 1998 by Michael Hemmingson. Reproduced by permission of the author.

NIGHT SERVICE by Carol Anne Davis, © 1998 by Carol Anne Davis. Reproduced by permission of the author.

HOUSE WITH CONTENTS by Michael Crawley, © 1998 by Michael Crawley. Reproduced by permission of the author.

THE MAN WHO LOVED WOMEN by Julian Rathbone, © 1998 by Julian Rathbone. Reproduced by permission of the author.

RAPUNZEL by Sue Dyson, © 1998 by Sue Dyson. Reproduced by permission of the author.

WORTH MORE THAN A THOUSAND WORDS by Lawrence Schimel, © 1998 by Lawrence Schimel. Reproduced by permission of the author.

BLOW-OUT by Yseult Ogilvie, © 1997 by Yseult Ogilvie. First published in The London Magazine. Reproduced by permission of the author.

TRESPASS by Lunar, © 1998 by Lunar. Reproduced by permission of the author.

HACK WORK by M. Christian, © 1998 by M. Christian. Reproduced by permission of the author.

THE END OF THE RELATIONSHIP by Will Self, © 1994 by Will Self. First published in Grey Area. Reproduced by permission of Bloomsbury Publishing.

A TALE OF INNOCENCE by Cree Fox, © 1998 by Cree Fox. Reproduced by permission of the author.

ENTERTAINING MR ORTON by Poppy Z. Brite, © 1997 by Poppy Z. Brite. First published in Grave Passions. Reproduced by permission of the author.

THE HUNGRY HOUR by Lucy Taylor, © 1998 by Lucy Taylor. Reproduced by permission of the author.

THE PRESENT by J.P. Kansas, © 1998 by J.P. Kansas. Reproduced by permission of the author.

SEX IN LITERATURE by Geoff Nicholson, © 1998 by Geoff Nicholson. Reproduced by permission of the author.

INTRODUCTION

FIVE YEARS HAVE gone by since I first began work on the *The Mammoth Book of Erotica*, the first volume in what has become a highly successful series of anthologies highlighting the exciting wealth of talent and sexual imagination at work in the often maligned field of erotic writing, and the fact that the much-ignored genre can also boast of first-class writers and ideas.

This was followed by *The Mammoth Book of International Erotica* in which I sought to add a selection of fascinating foreign voices to the mix, proving that the voice of the flesh is the same in all languages, even though the tone, the sensitivity might vary while the traditional sexual positions don't . . .

In these few years, erotic writing has progressed in leaps and bounds, with countless further books being published in the field, whether in sometimes formulaic imprints or scattered discreetly amongst the forests of otherwise literary publishers' lists, and not a month goes by, it seems to me, without another important voice emerging from seemingly nowhere to add yet another twist to the pages of the literature of sex. In addition, a number of other anthologies have proven equally popular both in Britain and the United States, cementing the genre's appeal to the average reader, while an increasing number of courageous magazines are offering a breeding ground for new talents, where writers can transgress to their heart's content, experiment, innovate, explore the fertile territory where the senses prevail. Indeed, many authors first featured in these anthologies in short-story format have since graduated with brilliant results to book-length format.

This third volume in the series mostly contains stories written especially for the book, and greets a good number of previous contributors again, but also many new authors from all corners of the English-language-speaking world (including some splendid first efforts from Canada: Jules Torti and Jennifer Footman, and Australia: Cree Fox). In addition, I am particularly pleased that several authors who have established a solid literary reputation outside of the erotic field have been happy to jump on board, with particularly stimulating results. I urge you to look out for books by all the authors collected in this anthology; if you have been impressed, titillated, amused, heart-wrenched by their short stories, I know you will be blown away by their novels or collections.

Eroticism is everywhere around us. Erotic writing can be humorous, sweaty, intense, detached, literate, poetic, forceful, elegant, personal, universal, disturbing. The stories that follow are all that and more. None will leave you indifferent. Vicariously enjoy!

Maxim Jakubowski

LET ME COUNT THE TIMES

Martin Amis

VERNON MADE LOVE to his wife three and a half times a week, and this was all right.

For some reason, making love always averaged out that way. Normally – though by no means invariably – they made love every second night. On the other hand Vernon had been known to make love to his wife seven nights running; for the next seven nights they would not make love – or perhaps they would once, in which case they would make love the following week only twice, in which case they would make love four times the next week but only twice the week after that – or perhaps only once. And so on. Vernon didn't know why, but making love always averaged out that way; it seemed invariable. Occasionally – and was it any wonder? – Vernon found himself wishing that the week contained only six days, or as many as eight, to render these calculations (which were always blandly corroborative in spirit) easier to deal with.

It was, without exception, Vernon himself who initiated their conjugal acts. His wife responded every time with the same bashful alacrity. Oral foreplay was by no means unknown between them. On average – and again it always averaged out like this, and again Vernon was always the unsmiling ring master – fellatio was performed by Vernon's wife every third coupling, or 60.8333 times a year, or 1.1698717 times a week. Vernon performed cunnilingus rather less often: every fourth coupling, on average, or 45.625 times a year, or .8774038 times a week. It would also be a mistake to think that this was the extent of their variations. Vernon sodomized his wife twice a year, for instance – on his birthday, which seemed fair enough, but also, ironically (or so *he* thought), on hers. He put it down to the expensive nights out they always had on these occasions, and more particularly to the effects of champagne. Vernon always felt desperately ashamed afterwards, and would be a limp spectre of embarrassment and remorse at breakfast the next day. Vernon's wife never said anything about it, which was something. If she ever did, Vernon would probably have stopped doing it. But she never did. The same sort of thing happened when Vernon ejaculated in his wife's mouth, which on average he did 1.2 times a year. At this point they had been married for ten years. That was convenient. What would it be like when they had been married for eleven years – or thirteen? Once, and only once, Vernon had been about to ejaculate in his wife's mouth when suddenly he had got a better idea: he ejaculated all over her face instead. She didn't say anything about that either, thank God. Why he had thought it a better idea he would never know. He didn't think it was a better idea now. It distressed him greatly to reflect that his rare acts of abandonment should expose a desire to humble and degrade the loved one. And she was the loved one. Still, he had only done it once. Vernon ejaculated all over his wife's face .001923 times a week. That wasn't very often to ejaculate all over your wife's face, now was it?

Vernon was a businessman. His office contained several electronic calculators. Vernon would often run his marital frequencies through these swift, efficient, and impeccably discreet machines. They always responded brightly with the same answer, as if to say, "Yes, Vernon, that's how often you do it," or "No, Vernon, you don't do it any more often than that." Vernon would spend whole lunch-hours crooked over the calculator. And yet he knew that all these figures were in a sense approximate. Oh, Vernon knew, Vernon knew. Then one day a powerful white computer was delivered to the accounts department. Vernon saw at once that a long-nursed dream might now take flesh: leap years. "Ah, Alice, I don't want to be disturbed, do you hear?" he told the cleaning lady sternly when he let himself into the office that night. "I've got some very important calculations to do in the accounts department." Just after midnight Vernon's hot red eyes stared up wildly from the display screen, where his entire sex life lay tabulated in recurring prisms of threes and sixes, in endless series, like mirrors placed face to face.

Vernon's wife was the only woman Vernon had ever known. He loved her and he liked making love to her quite a lot; certainly he had never craved any other outlet. When Vernon made love to his wife he thought only of her pleasure and her beauty: the infrequent but highly flattering noises she made through her evenly parted teeth, the divine plasticity of her limbs, the fever, the magic, and the safety of the moment. The sense of peace that followed had only a little to do with the probability that tomorrow would be a night off. Even Vernon's dreams were monogamous: the women who strode those slipped but essentially quotidian landscapes were mere icons of the self-sufficient female kingdom, nurses, nuns, bus-conductresses, parking wardens, policewomen. Only every now and then, once a week, say, or less, or not calculably, he saw things that made him suspect that life might have room for

more inside – a luminous ribbon dappling the undercurve
of a bridge, certain cloudscapes, intent figures hurrying
through changing light.

All this, of course, was before Vernon's business trip.

It was not a particularly important business trip: Vernon's firm was not a particularly important firm. His wife
packed his smallest suitcase and drove him to the station.
On the way she observed that they had not spent a night
apart for over four years – when she had gone to stay with
her mother after that operation of hers. Vernon nodded in
surprised agreement, making a few brisk calculations in his
head. He kissed her goodbye with some passion. In the
restaurant car he had a gin and tonic. He had another gin
and tonic. As the train approached the thickening city
Vernon felt a curious lightness play through his body.
He thought of himself as a young man, alone. The city
would be full of cabs, stray people, shadows, women, things
happening.

Vernon got to his hotel at eight o'clock. The receptionist
confirmed his reservation and gave him his key. Vernon
rode the elevator to his room. He washed and changed,
selecting, after some deliberation, the more sombre of the
two ties his wife had packed. He went to the bar and
ordered a gin and tonic. The cocktail waitress brought it
to him at a table. The bar was scattered with city people:
men, women who probably did things with men fairly
often, young couples secretively chuckling. Directly opposite Vernon sat a formidable lady with a fur, a hat, and a
cigarette holder. She glanced at Vernon twice or perhaps
three times. Vernon couldn't be sure.

He dined in the hotel restaurant. With his meal he
enjoyed half a bottle of good red wine. Over coffee Vernon
toyed with the idea of going back to the bar for a crème de
menthe – or a champagne cocktail. He felt hot; his scalp
hummed; two hysterical flies looped round his head. He

rode back to his room; with a view to freshening up. Slowly, before the mirror, he removed all his clothes. His pale body was inflamed with the tranquil glow of fever. He felt deliciously raw, tingling to his touch. What's happening to me? he wondered. Then, with relief, with shame, with rapture, he keeled backwards on to the bed and did something he hadn't done for over ten years.

Vernon did it three more times that night and twice again in the morning.

Four appointments spaced out the following day. Vernon's mission was to pick the right pocket calculator for daily use by all members of his firm. Between each demonstration – the Moebius strip of figures, the repeated wink of the decimal point – Vernon took cabs back to the hotel and did it again each time. "As fast as you can, driver," he found himself saying. That night he had a light supper sent up to his room. He did it five more times – or was it six? He could no longer be absolutely sure. But he was sure he did it three more times the next morning, once before breakfast and twice after. He took the train back at noon, having done it an incredible 18 times in 36 hours: that was – what? – 84 times a week, or 4,368 times a year. Or perhaps he had done it 19 times! Vernon was exhausted, yet in a sense he had never felt stronger. And here was the train giving him an erection all the same, whether he liked it or not.

"How was it?" asked his wife at the station.

"Tiring. But successful," admitted Vernon.

"Yes, you do look a bit whacked. We'd better get you home and tuck you up in bed for a while."

Vernon's red eyes blinked. He could hardly believe his luck.

Shortly afterwards Vernon was to look back with amused disbelief at his own faint-heartedness during those trail-blazing few days. Only in bed, for instance! Now, in his total recklessness and elation, Vernon did it everywhere. He hauled himself roughly on to the bedroom floor and did it there. He did it under the impassive gaze of the bathroom's porcelain and steel. With scandalized laughter he dragged himself out protesting to the garden tool shed and did it there. He did it lying on the kitchen table. For a while he took to doing it in the open air, in windy parks, behind hoardings in the town, on churned fields; it made his knees tremble. He did it in corridorless trains. He would rent rooms in cheap hotels for an hour, for half an hour, for ten minutes (how the receptionists stared). He thought of renting a little love-nest somewhere. Confusedly and very briefly he considered running off with himself. He started doing it at work, cautiously at first, then with nihilistic abandon, as if discovery was the very thing he secretly craved. Once, giggling coquettishly before and afterwards (the danger, the danger), he did it while dictating a long and tremulous letter to the secretary he shared with two other senior managers. After this he came to his senses somewhat and resolved to try only to do it at home.

"How long will you be, dear" he would call over his shoulder as his wife opened the front door with her shopping-bags in her hands. An hour? Fine. Just a couple of minutes? Even better! He took to lingering sinuously in bed while his wife made their morning tea, deliciously sandwiched by the moist uxoriousness of the sheets. On his nights off from love-making (and these were invariable now: every other night, every other night) Vernon nearly always managed one while his wife, in the bathroom next door, calmly readied herself for sleep. She nearly caught him at it on several occasions. He found that especially exciting. At this point Vernon was still trying hectically to keep count; it was all there somewhere, gurgling away in the memory banks of the computer in the accounts department. He was averaging 3.4 times a day, or 23.8 times a week, or an insane 1,241 times a year. And his wife never suspected a thing.

Until now, Vernon's "sessions" (as he thought of them) had always been mentally structured round his wife, the only woman he had ever known – her beauty, the flattering noises she made, the fever, the safety. There were variations, naturally. A typical "session" would start with her undressing at night. She would lean out of her heavy brassière and submissively debark the tender cheeks of her panties. She would give a little gasp, half pleasure, half fear (how do you figure a woman?), as naked Vernon, obviously in sparkling form, emerged impressively from the shadows. He would mount her swiftly, perhaps even rather brutally. Her hands mimed their defencelessness as the great muscles rippled and plunged along Vernon's powerful back. "You're too big for me," he would have her say to him sometimes, or, "That hurts, but I like it." Climax would usually be synchronized with his wife's howled request for the sort of thing Vernon seldom did to her in real life. But Vernon never did the things for which she yearned, oh no. He usually just ejaculated all over her face. She loved that as well of course (the bitch), to Vernon's transient disgust.

And then the strangers came.

One summer evening Vernon returned early from the office. The car was gone: as Vernon had shrewdly anticipated, his wife was out somewhere. Hurrying into the house, he made straight for the bedroom. He lay down and lowered his trousers – and then with a sensuous moan tugged them off altogether. Things started well, with a compelling preamble that had become increasingly popular in recent weeks. Naked, primed, Vernon stood behind the half-closed bedroom door. Already he could hear his wife's preparatory truffles of shy arousal. Vernon stepped forward to swing open the door, intending to stand there menacingly for a few seconds, his restless legs planted well apart. He swung open the door and stared. At what? At his wife sweatily grappling with a huge bronzed gypsy, who turned incuriously towards Vernon and then back again to the hysteria of volition splayed out on the bed before him. Vernon ejaculated immediately. His wife returned home within a few minutes. She kissed him on the forehead. He felt very strange.

The next time he tried, he swung open the door to find his wife upside down over the headboard, doing scarcely credible things to a hairy-shouldered Turk. The time after that, she had her elbows hooked round the back of her knee-caps as a 15-stone Chinaman feasted at his leisure on her imploring sobs. The time after that, two silent, glistening negroes were doing what the hell they liked with her. The two negroes, in particular, wouldn't go away; they were quite frequently joined by the Turk, moreover. Sometimes they would even let Vernon and his wife get started before they all came thundering in on them. And did Vernon's wife mind any of this? Mind? She liked it. Like it? She *loved* it! And so did Vernon, apparently. At the office Vernon soberly searched his brain for a single neutrino of genuine desire that his wife should do these things with these people. The very idea made him shout with revulsion. Yet, one way or another, he didn't mind it really, did he? One way or another, he liked it. He loved it. But he was determined to put an end to it.

His whole approach changed. "Right, my girl," he muttered to himself, "two can play at that game." To begin with, Vernon had affairs with all his wife's friends. The longest and perhaps the most detailed was with Vera, his wife's old school chum. He sported with her bridge-partners, her co-workers in the Charity. He fooled around with all her eligible relatives – her younger sister, that nice little niece of hers. One mad morning Vernon even mounted her hated mother. "But Vernon, what about . . . ?" they would all whisper fearfully. But Vernon just shoved them on to the bed, twisting off his belt with an imperious snap. All the women out there on the edges of his wife's world – one by one, Vernon had the lot.

Meanwhile, Vernon's erotic dealings with his wife herself had continued much as before. Perhaps they had even profited in poignancy and gentleness from the pounding rumours of Vernon's nether life. With this latest development, however, Vernon was not slow to mark a new dimension, a disfavoured presence, in their bed. Oh, they still made love all right; but now there were two vital differences. Their acts of sex were no longer hermetic; the safety and the peace had gone: no longer did Vernon attempt to apply any brake to the chariot of his thoughts. Secondly – and perhaps even more crucially – their love-making was, without a doubt, *less frequent*. Six and a half times a fortnight, three times a week, five times a fortnight . . . : they were definitely losing ground. At first Vernon's mind was a chaos of back-logs, short-falls, re-structured schedules, recuperation schemes. Later he grew far more detached about the whole business. Who said he had to do it three and a half times a week? Who said that this was all right? After ten nights of chaste sleep (his record up till now) Vernon watched his wife turn sadly on her side after her diffident goodnight. He waited several minutes, propped up on an elbow, glazedly eternalized in the potent moment. Then he leaned forward and coldly kissed her neck, and smiled as he felt her body's axis turn. He went on smiling. He knew where the real action was.

For Vernon was now perfectly well aware that any woman was his for the taking, any woman at all, at a nod, at a shrug, at a single convulsive snap of his peremptory fingers. He systematically serviced every woman who caught his eye in the street, had his way with them, and tossed them aside without a second thought. All the models in his wife's fashion magazines – they all trooped through his bedroom, too, in their turn. Over the course of several months he worked his way through all the established television actresses. An equivalent period took care of the major stars of the Hollywood screen. (Vernon bought a big glossy book to help him with this project. For his money, the girls of the Golden Age were the most daring and athletic lovers: Monroe, Russell, West, Dietrich, Dors, Ekberg. Frankly, you could keep your Welches, your Dunaways, your Fondas, your Keatons.) By now the roll-call of names was astounding. Vernon's prowess with them epic, unsurpassable. All the girls were saying that he was easily the best lover they had ever had.

One afternoon he gingerly peered into the pornographic magazines that blazed from the shelves of a remote newsagent. He made a mental note of the faces and figures, and the girls were duly accorded brief membership of Vernon's thronging harem. But he was shocked; he didn't mind admitting it: why should pretty young girls take their clothes off for money like that, like *that*? Why should men want to buy pictures of them doing it? Distressed and not a little confused, Vernon conducted the first great purge of his clamorous rumpus rooms. That night he paced through the shimmering corridors and becalmed anterooms dusting his palms and looking sternly this way and that. Some girls wept openly at the loss of their friends; others smiled up at him with furtive triumph. But he stalked on, slamming the heavy doors behind him.

Vernon now looked for solace in the pages of our literature. Quality, he told himself, was what he was after – quality, quality. Here was where the high-class girls hung out. Using the literature shelves in the depleted local library, Vernon got down to work. After quick flings with Emily, Griselda, and Criseyde, and a strapping weekend with the Good Wife of Bath, Vernon cruised straight on to Shakespeare and the delightfully wide-eyed starlets of the romantic comedies. He romped giggling with Viola over the Illyrian hills, slept in a glade in Arden with the willowy Rosalind, bathed nude with Miranda in a turquoise lagoon. In a single disdainful morning he splashed his way through all four of the tragic heroines: cold Cordelia (this was a bit of a frost, actually), bitter-sweet Ophelia (again rather constricted, though he quite liked her dirty talk), the snake-eyed Lady M. (Vernon had had to watch himself there) and, best of all, that sizzling sorceress Desdemona (Othello had *her* number all right. She *stank* of sex!). Following some arduous, unhygienic yet relatively brief dalliance with Restoration drama, Vernon soldiered on through the prudent matrons of the Great Tradition. As a rule, the more sedate and respectable the girls, the nastier and more complicated were the things Vernon found himself wanting to do to them (with lapsed hussies like Maria Bertram, Becky Sharp, or Lady Dedlock, Vernon was in, out, and away, darting half-dressed over the roof-tops). Pamela had her points, but Clarissa was the one who turned out to be the true co-artist of the oeuvres; Sophie Western was good fun all right, but the pious Amelia yodelled for the humbling high points in Vernon's swelter-ing repertoire. Again he had no very serious complaints about his one-night romances with the likes of Elizabeth Bennett and Dorothea Brooke; it was adult, sanitary stuff, based on a clear understanding of his desires and his needs; they knew that such men will take what they want; they knew that they would wake the next morning and Vernon would be gone. Give him a Fanny Price, though, or better, much better, a Little Nell, and Vernon would march into the bedroom rolling up his sleeves; and Nell and Fan would soon be ruing the day they'd ever been born. Did they mind the horrible things he did to them? Mind? When he prepared to leave the next morning, solemnly buckling his belt before the tall window – how they howled!

The possibilities seemed endless. Other literatures dozed

expectantly in their dormitories. The sleeping lion of Tolstoy – Anna, Natasha, Masha, and the rest. American fiction – those girls would show even Vernon a trick or two. The sneaky Gauls–Vernon had a hunch that he and Madame Bovary, for instance, were going to get along just fine . . . One puzzled weekend, however, Vernon encountered the writings of D. H. Lawrence. Snapping *The Rainbow* shut on Sunday night, Vernon realized at once that this particular avenue of possibility – sprawling as it was, with its intricate trees and their beautiful diseases, and that distant prospect where sandy mountains loomed – had come to an abrupt and unanswerable end. He never knew women behaved like *that* . . . Vernon felt obscure relief and even a pang of theoretical desire when his wife bustled in last thing, bearing the tea-tray before her.

Vernon was now, on average, sleeping with his wife 1.15 times a week. Less than single figure love-making was obviously going to be some sort of crunch, and Vernon was making himself vigilant for whatever form the crisis might take. She hadn't, thank God, said anything about it, yet. Brooding one afternoon soon after the Lawrence débâcle, Vernon suddenly thought of something that made his heart jump. He blinked. He couldn't believe it. It was true. Not once since he had started his "sessions" had Vernon exacted from his wife any of the sly variations with which he had used to space out the weeks, the months, the years. Not once. It had simply never occurred to him. He flipped his pocket calculator on to his lap. Stunned, he tapped out the figures. She now owed him . . . Why, if he wanted, he could have an entire week of . . . They were behind with *that* to the tune of . . . Soon it would be time again for him to . . . Vernon's wife passed through the room. She blew him a kiss. Vernon resolved to shelve these figures but also to keep them up to date. They seemed to balance things out. He knew he was denying his wife something she ought to have; yet at the same time he was withholding something he ought not to give. He began to feel better about the whole business.

For it now became clear that no mere woman could satisfy him – not Vernon. His activities moved into an entirely new sphere of intensity and abstraction. Now, when the velvet curtain shot skywards, Vernon might be astride a black stallion on a marmoreal dune, his narrow eyes fixed on the caravan of defenceless Arab women straggling along beneath him; then he dug in his spurs and thundered down on them, swords twirling in either hand. Or else Vernon climbed from a wriggling human swamp of tangled naked bodies, playfully batting away the hands that clutched at him, until he was tugged down once again into the thudding mass of membrane and heat. He visited strange planets where women were metal, were flowers, were gas. Soon he became a cumulus cloud, a tidal wave, the East Wind, the boiling Earth's core, the air itself, wheeling round a terrified globe as whole tribes, races, ecologies fled and scattered under the continent-wide shadow of his approach.

It was after about a month of this new brand of skylarking that things began to go rather seriously awry.

The first hint of disaster came with sporadic attacks of *ejaculatio praecox*. Vernon would settle down for a leisurely session, would just be casting and scripting the cosmic drama about to be unfolded before him – and would look down to find his thoughts had been messily and pleasurelessly anticipated by the roguish weapon in his hands. It began to happen more frequently, sometimes quite out of the blue: Vernon wouldn't even notice until he saw the boyish, tell-tale stains on his pants last thing at night. (Amazingly, and rather hurtfully too, his wife didn't seem to detect any real difference. But he was making love to her only every ten or eleven days by that time.) Vernon made a creditable attempt to laugh the whole thing off, and, sure enough, after a while the trouble cleared itself up. What followed, however, was far worse.

To begin with, at any rate, Vernon blamed himself. He was so relieved, and so childishly delighted, by his newly recovered prowess that he teased out his "sessions" to unendurable, unprecedented lengths. Perhaps that wasn't wise . . . What was certain was that he overdid it. Within a week, and quite against his will, Vernon's "sessions" were taking between thirty and forty-five minutes; within two weeks, up to an hour and a half. It wrecked his schedules: all the lightning strikes, all the silky raids, that used to punctuate his life were reduced to dour campaigns which Vernon could perforce never truly win. "Vernon, are you ill?" his wife would say outside the bathroom door. "It's nearly *tea*-time." Vernon – slumped on the lavatory seat, panting with exhaustion – looked up wildly, his eyes startled, shrunken. He coughed until he found his voice. "I'll be straight out," he managed to say, climbing heavily to his feet.

Nothing Vernon could summon would deliver him. Massed, maddened, cart-wheeling women – some of molten pewter and fifty feet tall, others indigo and no bigger than fountain-pens – hollered at him from the four corners of the universe. No help. He gathered all the innocents and subjected them to atrocities of unimaginable proportions, committing a million murders enriched with infamous tortures. He still drew a blank. Vernon, all neutronium, a supernova, a black sun, consumed the Earth and her sisters in his dead fire, bullocking through the solar system, ejaculating the Milky Way. That didn't work either. He was obliged to fake orgasms with his wife (rather skilfully, it seemed: she didn't say anything about it). His testicles developed a mighty migraine, whose slow throbs all day timed his heartbeat with mounting frequency and power, until at night

Vernon's face was a sweating parcel of lard and his hands shimmered deliriously as he juggled the aspirins to his lips.

Then the ultimate catastrophe occurred. Paradoxically, it was heralded by a single, joyous, uncovenanted climax – again out of the blue, on a bus, one lunchtime. Throughout the afternoon at the office Vernon chuckled and gloated, convinced that finally all his troubles were at an end. It wasn't so. After a week of ceaseless experiment and scrutiny Vernon had to face the truth. The thing was dead. He was impotent.

"Oh my God," he thought, "I always knew something like this would happen to me some time." In one sense Vernon accepted the latest reverse with grim stoicism (by now the thought of his old ways filled him with the greatest disgust); in another sense, and with terror, he felt like a man suspended between two states: one is reality, perhaps, the other an unspeakable dream. And then when day comes he awakes with a moan of relief; but reality has gone and the nightmare has replaced it: the nightmare was really there all the time. Vernon looked at the house where they had lived for so long now, the five rooms through which his calm wife moved along her calm tracks, and he saw it all slipping away from him forever, all his peace, all the fever and the safety. And for what, for what?

"Perhaps it would be better if I just told her about the whole thing and made a clean breast of it," he thought wretchedly. "It wouldn't be easy, God knows, but in time she might learn to trust me again. And I really *am* finished with all that other nonsense. God, when I . . ." But then he saw his wife's face – capable, straightforward, confident – and the scar of dawning realization as he stammered out his shame. No, he could never tell her, he could never do that to her, no, not to her. She was sure to find out soon enough anyway. How could a man conceal that he had lost what made him a man? He considered suicide, but – "But I just haven't got the guts," he told himself. He would have to wait, to wait and melt in his dread.

A month passed without his wife saying anything. This had always been a make-or-break, last ditch deadline for Vernon, and he now approached the coming confrontation as a matter of nightly crisis. All day long he rehearsed his excuses. To kick off with Vernon complained of a headache, on the next night of a stomach upset. For the following two nights he stayed up virtually until dawn – "preparing the annual figures," he said. On the fifth night he simulated a long coughing fit, on the sixth a powerful fever. But on the seventh night he just helplessly lay there, sadly waiting. Thirty minutes passed, side by side. Vernon prayed for her sleep and for his death.

"Vernon?" she asked.

"Mm-hm?" he managed to say – God, what a croak it was.

"Do you want to talk about this?"

Vernon didn't say anything. He lay there, melting, dying. More minutes passed. Then he felt her hand on his thigh.

Quite a long time later, and in the posture of a cowboy on the back of a bucking steer, Vernon ejaculated all over his wife's face. During the course of the preceding two and a half hours he had done to his wife everything he could possibly think of, to such an extent that he was candidly astonished that she was still alive. They subsided, mumbling soundlessly, and slept in each other's arms.

Vernon woke up before his wife did. It took him thirty-five minutes to get out of bed, so keen was he to accomplish this feat without waking her. He made breakfast in his dressing-gown, training every cell of his concentration on the small, sacramental tasks. Every time his mind veered back to the night before, he made a low growling sound, or slid his knuckles down the cheese-grater, or caught his tongue between his teeth and pressed hard. He closed his eyes and he could see his wife crammed against the headboard with that one leg sticking up in the air; he could hear the sound her breasts made as he two-handedly slapped them practically out of alignment. Vernon steadied himself against the refrigerator. He had an image of his wife coming into the kitchen – on crutches, her face black and blue. She couldn't very well not say anything about *that*, could she? He laid the table. He heard her stir. He sat down, his knees cracking, and ducked his head behind the cereal packet.

When Vernon looked up his wife was sitting opposite him. She looked utterly normal. Her blue eyes searched for his with all their light.

"Toast?" he bluffed.

"Yes please. Oh Vernon, wasn't it lovely?"

For an instant Vernon knew beyond doubt that he would now have to murder his wife and then commit suicide – or kill her and leave the country under an assumed name, start all over again somewhere, Romania, Iceland, the Far East, the New World.

"What, you mean the –?"

"Oh yes. I'm so happy. For a while I thought that we . . . I thought you were – "

"I – "

" – Don't, darling. You needn't say anything. I understand. And now everything's all right again. Ooh," she added. "You were naughty, you know."

Vernon nearly panicked all over again. But he gulped it down and said, quite nonchalantly, "Yes, I was a bit, wasn't I?"

"Very naughty. So *rude*. Oh Vernon . . ."

She reached for his hand and stood up. Vernon got to his feet too – or became upright by some new hydraulic system especially devised for the occasion. She glanced over her shoulder as she moved up the stairs.

"You mustn't do that too often, you know."

"Oh really?" drawled Vernon. "Who says?"

"*I* say. It would take the fun out of it. Well, not *too* often, anyway."

Vernon knew one thing: he was going to stop keeping count. Pretty soon, he reckoned, things would be more or less back to normal. He'd had his kicks: it was only right that the loved one should now have hers. Vernon followed his wife into the bedroom and softly closed the door behind them.

EMERALD

Cleo Cordell

ROSA CALDIZ TOOK off her protective face mask and pushed the hard hat back from her forehead. She had been at work since first light, walking the tunnels to check the placing of jackhammers and shovels, gathering the geological data which held the information about unworked seams of emerald bearing rock.

She breathed a sigh of relief as she trudged through the ankle-deep muddy water. Ahead, showing as a distant oblong of daylight, was the entrance to the mine. Visions of a hot shower, a meal, clean clothes swam before her eyes.

Behind her a lift whined to the surface. Metal doors clanged open and the inner car disgorged a number of men. The mining crew had finished their shift. They jostled each other good-naturedly, lighting up cigarettes and exchanging jokes. Most of them wore only stained singlets on their upper bodies, their muddy overalls hanging loose at their waists.

As they drew level with Rosa, they fell into step with her, the action of their heavy nailed boots mashing the mud to a milky froth.

"Hey, Rosa."

"Finished for the day? How about coming to the bar with us, later?"

Rosa shook her head. "Not tonight, boys. I'm dead beat. Besides, I'm going to visit my aunt in Bogotá. I've taken a couple of days off to spend with her."

Rosa's slight form seemed dwarfed by the crew. They were all big men, the muscles of their chests and arms gleaming with sweat and streaked with reddish brown mud. The smell of cigarette smoke did not mask the stink of their sweat, which was peculiarly acrid as only an emerald miner's could be.

Another woman might have felt uncomfortable, even threatened, by their nearness, but Rosa was perfectly at ease. Down at the working face she was one of the boys, admired for her stamina, her self-possession and quick wit.

She knew that did not stop many of the men lusting after her. Only, most of them knew better than to try anything on.

"Hey, Rosa! You look a little tired today. Want some help scrubbing your back?"

Rosa glanced coolly at the speaker who looked her over boldly. This man was new. He'd been taken on a week ago. She had noticed him staring when she did her rounds with the other geologists and engineers. This was the first time he had spoken to her directly. Now his eyes lingered on the front of her overalls, where the bulky fabric masked, but did not wholly disguise, the swell of her breasts. He was craggy, good-looking, she noticed, and with the swaggering walk of someone who knew he was attractive to women.

One of the other men sniggered. He poked the new crew man in the ribs. "You jokin', man? Think she would look twice at a mud monkey? Our Rosa's got class."

"Oh, yeah? She's still a woman, ain't she? Just needs whadda real man can give her. Same as all the others." He rolled his eyes and clutched at his groin. "Whadda ya say, Rosa? I got what it takes. You wanna rock and roll?"

Rosa's scalp itched beneath her tightly coiled dark hair and there was a gritty taste in her mouth. She was in no mood to take any shit. Tension thickened the air. They were nearer the mine's entrance now and the guards there turned to watch the exchange. Rosa forced herself to remain calm. The other miners were waiting for her reply. She could sense their mouths twitching with humour. One or two of the older experienced men, who knew her well, shook their heads slowly. Still Rosa did not speak. She let her silence fill the cavern, waiting until the new man's step faltered and his cocky grin slipped just a little.

"You know what you've got?" she said slowly, pinning him with unblinking dark eyes. "You've got a lot to learn."

He squared his shoulders, his cheeks working at a wad of chewing gum. He moved his hand across his chest, his fingers meshing in the mat of damp curls that showed above the scooped neck of his vest. "Oh, yeah? Is that right? You gonna show me? Oh, baby. I can't wait."

Calmly she looked up him. She had to crane her neck. He topped her by at least a head. "What's your name?" she said, her voice deceptively soft.

"Ernesto," the man said, his dark fleshy lips parting on a grin. His teeth flashed white in the grainy half-light. "Ernesto Perez."

"Just so's I know," Rosa said evenly. "Sometimes I have to identify a body. You know, when there's an accident? Of course, accidents don't happen if I do my job right. And I do a good job, don't I, boys?" She glanced at the others, who were having difficulty keeping their faces straight.

"Sure you do, Rosa," one of them said.

"She looks after us real good," said another veteran. "Rosa's the best."

"You see, Ernesto," she went on, "you just never know when one of the shafts will develop a fault. Any one of you could be working there . . . bam! Down comes the rock face. Miners can get trapped, their bones smashed, masks broken, the loose dust can soak up your breath in minutes. It can be a really bad situation, difficult for the rescue crew. I have to look after you boys – even smart-arse, wet-behind -the-ears pretty boys. Make sure accidents don't happen. I watch your backs. That calls for some respect. You get my meaning?"

She watched the slow flush stain the new man's prominent cheekbones. There was muffled laughter from the other men. Ernesto looked around for moral support from them, but they shook their heads, palms held up in surrender.

"Hey man, you started this!"

"Yeah, Ernesto. You're on your own."

Rosa took a step closer to Ernesto. She raised a finger and prodded it hard into his chest. "I asked you a question," she said, her voice cold, edged with steel.

"Yes, ma'am. I hear you," Ernesto said grudgingly.

"So – we understand each other?" she said.

"Oh yeah. We sure do. Yes, ma'am."

"Good. And for your information, I don't date mine workers. I like my men without mud under their fingernails. Or anywhere else."

Rosa turned on her heel and headed for the mine entrance. The guards there had big grins pasted on their faces. They saluted as she passed them by. Behind her she heard the open laughter now, the good-natured slaps on the back as Ernesto recovered his composure. There was approval and respect in that laughter, too. But she was also well aware that, were she but to crook a finger, any one of the mining crew would fight the others for the chance to warm her bed.

The feeling of power was stimulating. It gave her an erotic charge. For a moment it distracted her from the fact that she was sweating hard beneath the thick, protective clothing. Her heart was beating with a heavy panicked rhythm. For just a second back there she had almost lost it. Oh, it wasn't Ernesto that had rattled her – she could handle his type any day of the week.

What made her hands tremble and her mouth dry was the prospect of being caught with the stolen emerald hidden on her person.

Back at the room in the low wooden house, which constituted the mine's living quarters, she stripped off her muddy boots and overalls. Underneath she wore only a practical singlet and cotton pants. She reached into the tiny pocket sewn into the inside of her pants and extracted the emerald.

The stone was a rich clear green, fully an inch across. She knew it was a remarkably good stone. That colour, unusual to be so deep. Once it had been cut, it would be magnificent. Such an emerald would fetch 25,000 dollars a carat. It was a once in a lifetime find. Pure chance that she had scraped it from near the surface of a new seam in an unworked rock face. Any one of the crew or the specialist workers could have happened upon it. But it was hers. She had not dared to hide it in the room she shared with two other women. For weeks she had carried it with her, every day dreading the threat of a random search. It was a terrible risk. She stood to lose everything. Now the danger was almost over.

The emerald was warm from her body heat. She clutched it tight, feeling the hardness of the edges bite into her hand. The stone was her passport out of here. A chance that fortune had laid within her grasp. No more gruelling hours spent in the semi-darkness, no more breathing air contaminated with rock dust. Six years it had taken to put herself through university and get to the top of her profession.

In the shower she stood with the needles of hot water lancing over her face and hair. The water trickling down her body turned reddish brown from the fine dust which got into everything. She soaped herself thoroughly, washing the mine from her skin, sluicing it from her hair.

Once she and her mother had lived in a shanty town next to a small mine. They had been hungry and skinny as wild dogs. They had been *guagueras* – emerald scavengers – digging their own tiny and dangerous tunnels into the mountainside. Fortunes could be made, her mother told her. But they found only tiny chips of the precious green stone, enough only to trade for clothes and food. The hard work had destroyed her mother's health. "Promise you'll get out of here," her mother had entreated as she lay dying. At the graveside, Rosa had vowed that she would make a life for herself, whatever it took.

She didn't feel guilty for stealing the emerald. The big mines in Colombia's highlands like Chivor, Muzo, and Cosquez were now government-owned. Private mining firms had to pay to work the mines. *Guagueras* were being gradually edged out of the market. Rosa reasoned that she had earned her payoff. She had made her employers very wealthy over the years.

After drying her body and towelling her long black hair, Rosa locked the door of the room. Then she pulled the padlocked trunk from under her bed. Inside were the clothes she had acquired over the past few months. All of them ready and waiting for the day she would leave. The designer suit, underwear, jewellery, and expensive perfume had cost everything she had. She dressed carefully, pulling on the exquisite bra, the wispy panties, and garter belt. The black lace was cobweb-fine, whispering against her skin as she moved. She fastened the lace-topped stockings, then slipped her feet into the high-heeled black courts.

She twirled in front of the mirror, scooping up the soft mass of her hair and turning this way and that to admire her reflection. Rosa loved how she looked. The full globes of her breasts were pushed together into a deep cleavage. Her prominent dark nipples were visible through the lace. The triangle of her panties covered her pubis, but the fine lace revealed the silky bush of hair at her groin. At the back, only a single, thin strand of fabric bisected her buttocks. Her legs, long and tautly muscled, looked elegant and alluring in the stockings and shoes.

She nodded with satisfaction. No one else could know what she wore next to her skin. But she knew. You had to dress the part from the inside out. It was all part of the transformation exercise. "Ramon Lopez. Are *you* in for a surprise," she said aloud, running her fingers lingeringly over her curves.

The process of making herself beautiful had aroused her. Briefly, she considered masturbating, but decided against it. She would use the contained sexual tension to give herself an extra edge during the coming meeting. She buttoned the waisted suit jacket directly over her bra. Just enough cleavage showed to tantalize. The skirt clung lovingly to her rounded hips and strong thighs. It reached to just below her knee. Perfect. She looked classy. Sexy but not too available.

From a sudden commotion outside she guessed that the bus had arrived to take the mine workers back to their villages. She was confident that the driver could be persuaded to take her to the outskirts of Bogotá. From there she would get a taxi to the hotel and the man she had arranged to meet. So as not to attract attention to herself, she packed her new shoes and the few belongings she needed into an old holdall. She then put on her flat shoes and buttoned her usual raincoat over her suit.

As the bus pulled away, she glanced one last time at the slope of the hillside, the jumble of buildings, and the mine itself. "Goodbye," she said under her breath. "And good riddance." She crossed her legs. Beneath the raincoat, her silk-clad thighs rubbed together. The surface tension clung slightly, like the friction of wet skin meeting wet skin.

Three hours later, she found herself looking onto the streets of the emerald district. Downtown Bogotá was teeming with traffic and people. Rosa directed the taxi driver to let her out near the San Francisco cathedral. As the taxi drew away she took a brief look around.

Outside the San Ramon café there was a group of young women in tight angora tops, mini-skirts, and black silk stockings. They were all young, attractive, and hungry for the good life. They gave her hostile glances, perhaps unconsciously sensing a rival, but she lifted her chin and walked past them towards the hotel. She knew these were *esmeralderas* – vendors who traded emeralds from one buyer to another. That was the way emeralds were usually sold. Women had lately carved a niche for themselves in trading the stones. But they almost never sold directly to wealthy clients. What Rosa planned to do was daring and unusual.

As she checked into the hotel, she had to make a conscious effort to steady her nerves. She must stay calm and gather her wits about her, but she was aware of a burgeoning excitement. The element of risk in meeting one of Colombia's foremost private collectors, without the security of a go-between or bodyguard, made her chest tight with panic. Ramon Lopez had a fearsome reputation.

In the hotel room, she put on subtle eye make-up and pinned her hair into a neat French pleat. She then painted her lips a clear, strong red. A change of shoes, a spray of perfume, and she was ready. Finally she slipped the emerald into a tiny silk pouch.

When she entered the hotel bar, where wealthy business men sipped expensive drinks, many heads turned. She ignored the appreciative glances, the invitation written on many of the faces. She sought only one face. Ah, there he was.

Ramon was sitting at a table by himself. She recognized him at once from the photos she had seen. The sense of relief left her weak. Only now did she realize that she had half-expected him not to keep their appointment. Everything she had planned hinged on this meeting. As Ramon stood up and smiled, her heart began beating faster. In the photos he had looked older. Nothing had prepared her for his exceptional good looks.

"Please, sit down. I've taken the liberty of ordering some drinks," Ramon said easily. His voice was deep and gravelly. It sent a shiver right through her.

She thanked him courteously and sank into a chair, confident that she appeared outwardly calm. Self-control, the schooling of emotion to her will, was one of her strengths. Even when his gaze, dark and impenetrable, swept her body, making her feel that she sat naked before him, she gave no sign that she had noticed his scrutiny.

"You do not seem surprised to see me," he said, with a disarming smile. "Were you so certain that I would be here waiting?"

"I took nothing for granted," she said carefully. "But I hoped I had been able to persuade you that it would be to our mutual advantage to meet."

His black, almond-shaped eyes gleamed. His face was narrow, every feature chiselled as if it had been carved from some fine-grained gem-stone. Against the cream linen of his suit, Ramon's skin looked like warm caramel. He wore power and sophistication as if it was an invisible cloak.

"Oh, you were very persuasive," he said. "I was intrigued by your audacity. I do not usually do business in this fashion."

"I realize that. And I'm grateful that you found time to see me. I'm sure you're a very busy man, Señor Perez."

He nodded. "That is so. Call me Ramon, please." He leaned forward and made a steeple of his slim brown fingers. "So. We understand each other. Shall we cut to the chase? You have a room here?"

For a moment she was nonplussed. His directness shocked her but it excited her too. Her control slipped just a little. She had assumed they would do business in the bar, where the presence of others offered her a degree of protection.

"But the drinks . . ." she began, before she could think better of it.

If Ramon noted her lapse, he did not react. "We'll have them sent up," he said smoothly, motioning to a waiter. "Your room number?" Rosa told him. Ramon pushed back his chair and stood up. She remained seated for a moment. Before the waiter could draw back her chair, Ramon was there ready.

His hands grasped the back of the chair. She had no choice but to rise. He was close enough for her to smell his cologne. Underlying it, she caught the scent of his body, clean and dry – faintly like almonds.

"After you," Ramon said.

As Rosa preceded him across the tiled foyer, she was aware of his eyes on her. She walked with her head held high, her shoulders squared, knowing that the high-heeled shoes caused her hips to sway provocatively. They did not speak as they rode in the lift and then walked the short distance along the corridor. Rosa was acutely aware of Ramon's nearness. It amazed her that she should be so affected by him. A few short hours ago she had been surrounded by any number of burly mine workers, but she had been more at ease in their mixed company and their boisterous maleness than with this single man.

The desire she had felt on dressing was still an insistent pressure in her belly. It had not lessened. In fact, it seemed to be building by the second. Between her legs, she felt wet and swollen. It was unnerving to be so aroused by a stranger. She must not think of the tingling in her nipples or the heavy, syrupy dampness of her sex. This was serious business. Rosa schooled herself to be calm, professional. Thoughts of pleasure must come later.

In her room, she and Ramon stood facing each other, barely inches apart. In the emerald mine, she would have found any man's closeness oppressive, an invasion of her space. And she would have dealt with the situation summarily. Yet here, with Ramon, it felt somehow natural to stand so close.

This was so strange. Rosa felt more and more unsure of herself. She prayed silently that Ramon could not divine her feelings. This was it. Her only chance. Her entire future was held in the balance. She must brazen this out. Lifting her chin, she locked eyes with him.

"Shall we get down to business?"

"You're a very beautiful woman, Rosa," Ramon said softly, unmoving, his voice low and intense. "You do realize that you're taking a considerable risk meeting me here . . . alone?"

Again those narrow eyes raked her from head to foot. Rosa did not reply. She knew the strength of silence – indeed, had often used it to her advantage. But this time, she found her favourite tactic used against her. It was a full minute before Ramon spoke again. By the time he did, perspiration had broken out all over Rosa's body. Abruptly he turned and moved away.

"You said on the phone that you found the stone yourself, yes? And no one has seen it, besides you, until now? You can vouch for the truth of both these statements?"

"That is so."

He drew in his breath. "Excellent. Such details are important to a serious collector. I collect many rare things of beauty . . . Rosa. Their provenance is always of great value to me." He paused for a moment. "Many of the *esmeralderas* are willing to sell more than emeralds," he said evenly. "What if I was to ask, even demand, these . . . special services from you? As part of our business transaction, of course."

Rosa quelled the rising excitement which pulsed in the base of her belly. God, she wanted him. Her body seemed to be running to its own rhythm. But mentally she was in complete control.

"You'd be wasting your time," she said coolly. "I do not respond to demands. And please do not insult me by offering me money. You cannot buy what is not for sale."

Ramon's expression was unreadable. "I thought not," he said softly.

Absurdly, Rosa felt disappointed. Why had she spoken so hastily, when she wanted this man more than anyone she had ever met? It would have been a bonus to fuck him. All she had needed to do was reach for him. She knew that he wanted her, too. It need not have been complicated, just shared physical pleasure, a joint release. She would have been paid generously, too. Surely a single act did not constitute prostitution? She felt puzzled. Why had Ramon not been more insistent? He was not the kind of man who denied himself anything.

The knock at the door dissolved the tension in the room. A waiter deposited the drinks. When the waiter had gone, Rosa poured the drinks, pleased to see that her hands were steady. She passed a long glass to Ramon, who had removed his jacket and now sat on the edge of the narrow hotel bed.

"Thank you." He took a long swallow. His manner was brisk now. She could almost have believed she'd imagined their earlier exchange.

"You have the stone?" he said.

She nodded. "You have the money?"

He laughed, the shadows deepening under his cheekbones. "Indeed. In cash, as you requested. Shall we conclude our business? I'd like to see the stone."

Rosa slid her fingers inside her jacket. She dipped into her damp cleavage and took the silk pouch out of her bra. Ramon watched her every movement, his dark eyes lingering on the deep "V" of bare flesh between the lapels of her jacket.

She tipped the stone into his hand, expecting him to study it at once. He barely glanced at it. Instead he caressed it with his fingertips.

"It's warm," he said huskily. "I love the way precious stones take on the temperature of the wearer's skin." Carrying the emerald to his nose, he inhaled deeply. "And it smells of you. What a pity that the stone will not retain your scent."

"The money?" Rosa said. "I'm sure you're aware that the emerald is worth the figure we agreed."

Casually, Ramon lifted his jacket, took a package from the inside pocket, and threw it on the bed. A thick wad of bills spilled onto the bed cover. "Count it if you wish. It's all there. The top rate. You won't be offered better."

"But you've hardly looked at the emerald . . ." she said as she began counting the money.

"I don't need to," he said. "I know what I have in my hand. I am never wrong when making value judgements about the things I desire. So, you are satisfied that I have not cheated you?"

She nodded. The amount of money on the bed took her breath away. It was almost over. Now he would leave and she would go on to her new life. Why, then, did she feel that the money had suddenly assumed less importance?

"Excellent. Then our transaction is completed." Ramon slid the stone back into its silk pouch and drew the drawstring tight. There was a moment of silence before he said calmly, "Take off your suit."

"What?"

"Oh, I think you heard me, Rosa." His rough voice was very soft and intense. "I can leave, right now. We can go our separate ways and never meet again. Or you can take off your suit."

It was a request. His tone was courteous, unthreatening. There was no question now of his buying her favours. She understood why he had wanted the business between them out of the way. Something, which had been tightly coiled inside her, began to unwind.

Somehow she found her fingers moving of their own

volition, unfastening each button. Slowly, she opened her
jacket. When her lace-covered breasts, slender waist and
taut belly were revealed, Ramon reached for her. One hand
slipped around her waist and drew her up hard against him.
With his other hand he cupped her breasts, moulding each
of them in turn, circling the swelling nipples with his
thumb.

The heat staining her cheeks, Rosa reached behind
herself, unzipping her skirt. The silky lining slithered
down her legs and the skirt pooled on the floor. Ramon
leaned over her, his face very close. He lifted her chin and
pressed his mouth to hers. His lips were firm and warm,
easing her mouth open until it surrendered to his will. The
kiss was deep and searching. His muscular tongue pushed
into her, tasting and exploring. As the tips of their tongues
duelled, a dart of condensed desire speared her belly. There
was a rush of slippery moisture from her sex.

She found herself pressed to the length of his lean body,
one of her thighs caught between his legs. His cock was hot
and hard against her silk-clad flesh. He rotated his hips,
pressing the big glans against the tender flesh of her inner
thigh. She could not help the soft moan breaking from her
lips. Just the thought of that moist cock-tip pressing open
the lips of her cleft and entering her wet pussy made her
weak at the knees. She imagined how his cock would look.
It would be darker than his body, the colour of toasted
caramel. How strongly it would jut out from the nest of
dark hair at his groin.

"Please . . ." she murmured against his lips. "Fuck me.
Do it now."

He laughed huskily. "Not yet. Precious things are meant
to be savoured." He urged her gently backwards, until she
was sitting on the edge of the bed. His face bound by
contained desire, he put his hand on her chest and pushed.
"Lie down, Rosa."

She allowed herself to fall backwards until her spine met

the cotton bedspread. Her high-heeled shoes were still on the floor. The position meant that her knees and legs were thrust upwards a little and her hips slightly over-hung the bed. She started to ease herself backwards, but Ramon stopped her.

"No. Stay like that. I want to look at you."

Rosa's every instinct was to reach for him, to pull him down on top of her. If only he would kiss her again; then she could lose herself in him. It made her feel so vulnerable to have him standing there, looking down at her. She was used to taking the lead in life, but Ramon somehow knew that sexually she responded to being ordered, urged into accepting pleasure.

Oh, God. How could he know so much about her? It was frightening, but so arousing. He positioned himself between her spread thighs, his hands easing her legs wide. Her back arched as he moved his hands lower and brushed the backs of his fingers over her lace-covered pubis. Now, surely, he would slide his fingers inside her panties, caress her molten heat. Her sex fluttered and pulsed. She held her breath, anticipating his touch, but he moved his hands away.

Again, he reached for her breasts. This time he eased them free of the lace. They were lifted and held out for him by the supporting strip of her bra. She closed her eyes in an agony of arousal as he pressed forward and began sucking her nipples. As he licked and pinched the tender flesh she melted and rose up against him.

Cries and groans rose in her throat. Her own sounds of pleasure astonished and shamed her, but she could not hide the desire for him, which was so demanding, so selfish. Ramon moved back until he knelt between her thighs.

"Look at me," he said huskily. "I want to see your face."

Propping herself on her elbows, she looked down. Her hair, having come free of its pins, tumbled around her shoulders. Ramon slipped a finger inside the thin side-

straps of her panties. In a swift motion he tore them free.
She barely had time to make a sound of protest, before she
felt him stroking her pouting slit. His thumb pad pressed
against her clitoris, moving in an oily, circular motion. Her
thighs trembled as he parted her labia, laying bare the
glistening folds of her sex.

"Beautiful," he breathed. "A ruby jewel."

She squirmed beneath him, horribly aware of his close
scrutiny. But despite the shame of being so intimately
exposed, she found herself reaching new heights of arousal. Never before, while making love, had she been so
wonderfully wet. Her silky moisture coated Ramon's fingers. She imagined it dripping out of her, sliding in pearly
trails down his knuckles.

"I must taste you," he murmured, burying his head
between her thighs.

As his tongue flicked against the erect bud of her clitoris,
she felt the first pulsing waves of an orgasm. She clutched
his head, meshing boneless fingers in his black hair.
Sobbing, she mashed her pubis against his mouth and
chin. As her pleasure tipped over, he thrust his tongue
deep inside her. His groans of pleasure vibrated through
her. She knew that he was relishing the internal spasms as
her vagina constricted around his buried tongue.

Barely had the final waves of her climax ebbed, before he
drew away a little. She felt his fingers pushing into her.
One, then two. He began working them back and forth.
Somewhere, deep inside, he was stroking a little pad of
flesh. There, just behind her pubic bone. Oh, God. Her
sensitized flesh quivered. She could feel another orgasm
building, but more slowly this time. Oh, God. That felt so
good.

"Don't . . . Oh, don't stop," she murmured.

She brought her hand up to her mouth, biting at her
fingers in an effort to control her groans. For a second his
fingers were withdrawn. Now he would fuck her. Ah, thank

God. She lifted her hips, longing for the thrust of his cock. She wanted to be filled by his hard flesh, to have him plunge into her again and again. She wanted his hands on her hips, his fingers digging into her buttocks as he rode her . . .

But she felt his hands on her again. No, that wasn't what she wanted. A sound of protest escaped her. What was he doing? She felt something soft being pressed against her wet vagina.

"The emerald," Ramon whispered against her mouth, covering her with his body as he pushed the little silken pouch deeply inside her. "I want it to taste of you."

His fingers remained within her, urging her to new pathways of pleasure. She surged and bucked against him. His tongue filled her mouth, pushing into her until she felt the straining root against her own tongue tip. She sucked at it, reaching desperately for the climax which was just out of reach. The thought of the little pouch, soaking up her juices, nestling against his buried, working fingers, was impossibly lewd.

"Yes," Ramon whispered, biting her neck gently. "Do it, Rosa. Break, now. Squeeze the emerald tight. Make it wet for me. I want to suck it when I come. I want to taste the milk of your desire."

His passionate words tipped her over. She climaxed again, the waves of pleasure spreading outwards from her sex. Ramon grasped the draw-strings of the pouch and drew it slowly out of her. He placed the sodden pouch onto her belly. Rosa convulsed as her orgasm flooded her entire body. At last Ramon's hips locked with hers. She felt the thick cock slide deeply into her. It was hot and bigger than she had expected. The cleated walls of her vagina closed around him, enfolding him.

"Ah," she moaned, transported to a new level of pleasure. She did not often forget herself completely. But she could no longer tell where she ended and Ramon began.

"Ah, God." He was fucking her, wonderfully, deeply. But she was also fucking him, slamming her heated flesh down onto his shaft, drawing him into the secret recesses of her body.

Arching her back, she matched him thrust for thrust. She tossed her head from side to side, her loose dark curls whipping around her face. He cupped her buttocks, driving into her while she churned beneath him. Lifting her lower body, he began pumping into her with long, slow strokes. The head of his cock was drawn almost out of her as he withdrew, so that the swollen glans nudged open her puffed-up labia. Then he pushed right into her, so that his cock-head butted against her womb.

Rosa tossed her head from side to side. She wept with pleasure, her mouth sagging open like a bawling child's. Never had she acted so shamelessly; never had she so abandoned herself for any lover. Ramon's face was intense as he lifted himself up and looked down between her spread legs.

"God, that's beautiful," he groaned, pumping his hips. He began moving faster, the sweat running down his thin, dark-gold face. "Almost . . . there . . . The pouch," he grunted. "In my mouth."

Rosa scooped the wet scrap of silk from her belly. As Ramon squeezed his eyes closed, she pushed the pouch between his lips. He sucked at it hungrily, chewing the silk, rolling the emerald within it on his tongue. Holding his upper body taut, he thrust once more, jamming his cock into her up to the root. His heavy scrotum was pressed up tight to her buttocks.

He clutched at Rosa's hips as his semen jetted from him in long aching spurts. Rosa climaxed for the third time. The pleasure was less intense, but the waves rolled though her with a sweet, aching delight. Ramon moaned loudly as her vagina clenched around his buried flesh, milking him of the last creamy drops.

A few moments later, they collapsed together, still pressed close. Both of them were breathing hard. They lay in a tangle of sweaty limbs, the smells of sex and exertion filtering into the room. Tremors, like after-shocks of pleasure, flickered over Rosa's damp skin. Ramon propped himself on his elbow and looked down at her. The silence stretched between them, heavy with possibilities.

Rosa knew that this experience had been special for them both. But what would happen next? Nothing, everything? Her emotions were held in the balance. It would be very easy to embark on a passionate affair with this man, but that depended on what he said next.

"You're a very special woman, Rosa," Ramon said in his deep, smoky voice. "A rare jewel."

His choice of words was telling. Almost she had forgotten that he was, primarily, a collector. She bent close and brushed his cheek with her lips, then rose from the bed and began pulling on her skirt. The ruined panties lay in a heap on the floor. She bent down and picked them up.

Ramon watched her dress. "You're leaving?" He sounded surprised, but not disappointed. There was a confident twist to his mouth, as if he did not really expect her to go.

Rosa knew that he relished the chase. He would want her while she remained free, but if she became his mistress his fascination and desire would fade. She threw the torn scrap of lace onto the bed. "Something to remember me by," she said coolly. "Add them to your collection."

Ramon laughed as he crushed the panties in his hand. "Delightful. But I'd rather have you."

"I'm sure you would. But I'm not available."

"Are you sure about that?" he said; his voice was light and even, offering her no special incentive. He drew a card from his jacket pocket and held it out. "Take this. Call me, any time."

Rosa took the card. She gathered up the roll of banknotes

and her few belongings. At the door she looked over her shoulder. He lay stretched out on the bed, his hands linked behind his neck. He looked like a sleek, beautiful predator. She almost faltered and went back into the room. The moment passed. She opened the door and went down the stairs.

Her heart thumped wildly. The danger was not over. Ramon could have arranged to have her followed. He had the emerald. Now he might want to retrieve his money. She hurried across the foyer and asked for a taxi to be called. It came almost immediately. "To the airport," she said. She sat in the back seat, glancing back every now and then, until she was certain that she was not being followed.

Gradually her heart-beat returned to normal. A bubble of elation rose within her. Slowly, she began to smile. She glanced down at Ramon's card, which she still held in her hand. For just a moment she wavered. She thought of the emerald, so cold and beautiful. Valued only because it was rare, not for itself, not for the simple fact that it existed.

Deliberately she tore the card into little pieces and let the scraps flutter out of the open taxi window.

WINGED MEMORY

M. Christian

IT WASN'T EASY to find. He'd have been surprised it if had been: "Industry Town, at the end of Press Street. Go to the fence, turn right. Walk between it and the building that smells like fresh lightning till you see the door," the man in the bar had said. A man with hair the color and shape of an explosion, with one eye a steel bearing, twirling a glass of smoky liquor but never drinking.

So: the rust and heavy construction of Industry Town; the narrow way of Press Street; a fence chiming from gusts of hot, dry air; the aroma of ozone (biolight recycling plant); the door – sheet steel with no knob or hinges. He approached and it swung into cool darkness.

Inside, the plastic cocoons of shipping containers: a hall of gigantic orange fingers on fat rubber tires. A gurney from what looked like an ambulance. Coils of cable. A flat-screen monitor on the floor, playing sine waves. Everything was small and portable, easily picked up and carried.

"We have a special today," a man said, stepping out from behind one of the containers, wiping his hands with an oily rag. Moving like an insect, a precise ballet of extraordinarily long arms and legs, he gently folded the rag around a brace ringing one of the containers. His face was long and narrow, pinched and tight, hair the color of old asphalt, the few white streaks of white like pebbles in a road. His name, the man in the bar had said, was many, various. "Someone's collecting virginities. Give you a hundred for losing yours," Various said.

Thinking quick about it, he thought of her instead: walking the street, eyes available red, steaming lust for rent, the defiant tension in her legs, breasts spilling from the top of a latex dress — creamy crescents under hard street-light. She offered so much more than what Mary had given him, so many years before.

"More than it's worth to me," Dusk said, stepping closer and smiling.

After a few minutes — stretching out on the gurney, Various touching the tiny aches of microdermal pick-ups to his temples — he sold Magnesium Mary and a biting cold March night behind the Autopharm™, for one hundred dollars.

"Think of it," Various said, pulling small tools and loops of flopical cable out of the bright orange industrial jumpsuit he wore, rolled at arms and legs. "Try and remember as much as you can. It'll help."

Dusk watched him move around his head, feeling the connections' pricks and gentle stabs of pain. He didn't want to nod or say anything, so he didn't. After a minute more, Various said, "Start," from behind his flat-screen panel — somewhere beyond, above Dusk's head.

Start, *right: a whistling canyon kind of cold, when simply brisk turns snapping, biting from twisting down narrow streets. Sodium lights, he remembered perfectly, crisply — how they made the street look bilious, intestinal yellow. He'd been fifteen, living with Shirley, his mother, in a yellow Datsun next to a Pornotopia store. Already he was running with the Braves but because he was small — shot up later in life — he*

*didn't get to do much except carry shit. He'd been doing just
that, thin nylon shirt packed with Speedex capsules in dirty
bubblewrap, when he'd seen Magnesium Mary.*

*To a fifteen-year-old she'd been a goddess, a spike-haired
bitch queen, dotted with the flashes of steel piercings in
eyebrows, nose, lips, and cheeks who always smoked, always
swore, and liked to change her shirt in public to give fifteen-
year-olds woodies at the sight of her middle-aged tits and metal
flashing nipples.*

*It'd been an empty night, the cops having cleared the whole
area hours before. It was just Mary, Dusk and the hard
concrete behind the Autopharm^{TM}. She said something, lost
to growing up, but the end of it was her grabbing Dusk by the
collar of his windbreaker and hauling him into the sweet-reek
of garbage alley behind the pharm. She'd fumbled with his belt,
and her words stuck, " 'bout time you grew up, fuck," as she
swallowed his scared-limp dick into her burning mouth.*

*Her suction drew it out of him in a twenty-second come:
spasms of too-young muscles plunged into steaming, moist
hotness. He blushed and felt the crashing of humiliation as
she stood up and spit his come onto the brick back of the
Autopharm^{TM}.*

*His first. Then she slammed her fist into his gut, and while
he was puking up a fast food dinner she ripped the jacket off his
back and took all the Speedex caps. When Romeo, the Braves'
chief, found out, he beat Dusk some more – eventually breaking
three of his ribs.*

Take it, man, I don't want it any more, Dusk thought as
Various clicked and clacked devices beyond his sight.

After, when the memory had faded, faded and faded so
much that he couldn't answer the musical question *How did
you lose your virginity?*, Various unclipped him and told him
to get up.

"Be glad you came to me. Someone like Gregorious, you
shouldn't trust. I'm much better than he is. I treat you
right," Various said, adding finishing touches to Dusk's

purchased memory of Magnesium Mary with pianist gestures across his glowing flat-screen. After a tattoo of his long, thin (and, Dusk noted absently, pink-painted nails) fingers he held up a tiny wafer of dull silver. "Lost virginity on a chip," he said, then took Dusk's debtcard, paid him his hundred, and sent him away.

Fifty went to back rent. It felt good, but not great, to spend some of his hundred putting off getting kicked out by another month, a little towards his debt. It felt so good, in fact, that he blew another ten getting the lights turned back on in his rack box. There was a rare satisfaction as he swiped his card through the manager terminal in the lobby that, after what seemed like months, he wouldn't have to sit in a black box. Now, for ten Revalued dollars, he could have lights for a month.

Then Dusk walked the length of Cancer Alley for three hours.

Sometime in the past, Dusk had been told, you could see the sky. Now, though, the Alley pinched upwards – buildings on one side and the other, built up generation over generation, shanty on vertical shanty – till there was nothing but cardboard, plywood, plastic truck cocoons and cheap-ass capsule hotels and no sky, never, ever.

There were stars, though. Illiterate Dusk navigated by a thousand flickers from shorting, chopped power lines and greasy cooking fires.

Cancer Alley wasn't that long – just three miles from old St. Fluke hospital (one end) to the New Deal Toxic Recycling Facility (the other) – but Dusk hadn't seen her yet, so just walked from one end to the other. It took him three hours of walking from the ghost of the old public hospital to the sound of screaming, breaking carcinogens to find her.

He'd seen her before, of course, walking up and down this narrow stretch, proudly offering her charms. Dusk knew he had been struck by her, an electric and full-voltage attraction, the first time he'd seen her, but then, walking in the always-twilight of the alley, he was hard-pressed to say why, and what, exactly, specifically, she looked like.

Then she was there and he was . . . surprised by her. He didn't know why, but he was. He also didn't know why being surprised would make him stop for a second and just stare at her – look at her – as if he was seeing her for the first time.

Which, he knew, he wasn't.

Big eyes, full of available red. She was pure lust – excitement – for rent. Her legs were packed with muscle, defiant tension, covered with the high reflective gloss of thick latex. Nasty three-inch heels. Her hair was smoke, a curly mass of black drifting strands that surrounded her elegant face like a storm cloud wrapping a strong mountain peak. Her breasts were cream, big and full, pressed in a many-buckled shiny latex top.

She looked at him and turned, not picking Dusk out of the crowd, not seeing him since he didn't seem to have money. Her back was naked, save for the lashings of her top, to the fine dip of her coccyx. On her back, the tattoo of a single wing. It was so shaded, so realized, that Dusk had to look twice to make sure it was ink in skin, and not something else.

Not knowing what kind of self-protection software she might be running in addition to her whoreware, Dusk didn't do what he wanted to – which was tap her on her strong shoulder. Instead he stepped behind her and cleared his throat.

"Yeah?" she said, voice rumbling with caution.

Dusk held up his debtcard.

She took it, slid it through the narrow plastic slot on the checker bracelet on her left wrist. Her eyes went from red to green. Sufficient credit. Thirty minutes of her was his.

"This way, lover," she said, now with tones of warmth, of moisture, of heat.

This way was into the lobby of a grand, but now sad and frightening, hotel. Its name was long gone, and even the ghostly pattern of where it had been was scrubbed clean. Three flights, past three extended families living on two stairs and one hall, and then a door. 313. She slid her thumb down the jamb and a solid bolt slammed back.

The room was sparse – the things in it a very short list: black futon on industrial rubber floor, yellow and black halogen work lamp, a bright red plastic toolbox, and a large suitcase.

She turned and smiled, a beam of pure kindness. "Make yourself comfortable, darlin'." Dusk sat down and kicked off his shoes as she walked with fluid temptation over to the toolbox and rummaged its contents. His socks went into his shoes (holes in both) as he watched her, trying to freeze the beauty of her actions in his mind. Standing, he pulled off his shirt, dropped it next to his shoes. Then belt, pants, underwear.

Naked, he stood. The room wasn't cold but he shivered anyway.

She turned, smiling comedy and lust at his hard cock. "Lay down," she said, motioning, with a quick move of her head, to the futon.

Dusk did, moving this way, that, on the lumpy surface till it felt reasonably comfortable. He noticed, absently, a huge yellow water stain on the ceiling, a curious parade of lights from something reflective on the street below. She walked, all elegance and steam, to stand next to his head. His eyes followed the fine geometry of her legs up till they reached the shadowy mystery hidden by her dress.

With a nice move, she put one foot on either side of his head, facing towards his feet. Even with the dancing lights on the ceiling, he couldn't see anything but soft shadows between her legs.

"Don't blink or you might miss me," she said, and a flash of pure white light licked up one side of her left leg and showed him (blink, blink) the pale curves of her ass, the cream contours of her mons, the gentle folds of her majora – then it was gone and there were shadows again.

She moved a bit more, and again the light flashed, and again Dusk was teased with a burst of white skin blending to pink, of gleaming moisture, of an outer opening *just so*. Darkness –

He realized that she had a small light in one hand, was using it to draw back the shaded curtain of her dress, showing herself with quick flips of a flashlight. Then he wished he hadn't realized that, understood the trick – magic explained is a little less magical.

The light again, and this time he caught the butterfly flicker of her hand, and he saw something, in addition: blood red nails on lovely frosty-white fingers covering her mons, cupping herself.

The next beat, the next pass, the light stayed – lingering on the sight of her hand between her legs, her brilliant red nails. As he watched, (not blinking, not ever) the fingers moved, a massaging ballet on her obscured cunt. His imagination got up and ran fast and far away, and he dreamed an impossible view between red-painted nails and the churning, melting folds of her. He saw, but couldn't really have, her fingers stroke and tap the big pearl of her clit, press up and part her very pink, and glistening, lips.

Then he did. Really. She parted her fingers and showed him, opening herself far above him, drawing back her majora to feast him the sight of her hot, wet inner self. Her clit was big, like one of her own red-painted nails. Her lips were fat and puffy, and her color sunset red.

His hand found his iron cock, closed around it. He was there, holding his aching self for just a pound (two?) of his pulse – long enough to feel it in a strong vein – then she said, strong but firm: "No, no – save it."

Turning, she smiled (humor, delight, steam) and carefully lowered herself down. Then, with her arms out like a laughing gymnast, she guided the flowered opening of her cunt over his nodding cock till her lips met and kissed his head. She stayed there, letting him gently tap and stroke her lips with his throbbing dick.

"Suck me?" he asked, his voice so soft and weak it scared him.

She shook her head, hair floating in the warm air. "Sorry, lover – don't do that."

She continued to rub herself, allowing him to feel the contours of her cunt with his cock head till the ache in his balls started to change, started to build. The muscles in his back, chest and groin felt knotted, bound up with a pounding tension – yet all of his attention was focused on the subtle feelings of his screaming cock-head gliding over her moist folds, gently gliding past her wet cunt. He wanted to reach up and pull her down and him into her but he held back, grabbing coarse handfuls of the futon. The torture was ecstasy.

Then she did. With that ballerina, gymnastic skill she scooped up his cock with her cunt-mouth and pushed him up inside her with one long and hot stroke. He almost came, right then and there; but, for some reason, he was able to reach down inside himself and still the straining urge.

Slowly, she withdrew again, till his head again was out in the warm air, then she pushed herself onto him again. Like that: in and out – all the way in (tap cervix) all the way out (warm air). His balls went from just yelling to maniacal screaming. His back went from knots to pulsing waves of agony. His cock was bigger than he was, taking up all of his feelings and nerves (his hands, fanatically clutching the futon, were as far away as the moon and felt as alive as it) as she slid his cock in and out of herself.

She had been looking down at his chest, concentrating on the dance she was giving his cock, but after a short while she looked up at him, locking her glowing green – *paid* – eyes at him. Smiling, she arched her back and carefully (expensive) reached down and flipped the top of her dress down, giving him a flash of her breasts, the soft slopes of her tits dotted by large, crimson, nipples.

He watched her fuck him, her big (but surprisingly not too big) tits gently lifting and falling, heavy and firm, as she did so. He watched and got lost in the feeling of her, the sight of her (green eyes).

Then, when he felt the pressure build so much that it felt far too fucking good to hold it back any longer – he came.

When his heart slowed down enough, when his legs unknotted, when he pried his claws off the bunched fabric of the futon and he could breathe without wheezing, he gained his eyesight: she had taken a little packet of medicated wipes and had gently cleaned off his dick and balls. Then she helped him get up and into his clothes.

In the hall, he cleared his throat, asked her name.

"Wing," she said, tapping one shoulder, meaning her back, the tattoo. Then her eyes CLICKED red; his time was up, the sale concluded, and she said, "Get the fuck away from me, dickhead."

Some time must have passed. He was sure of it, almost positive. Dusk would have liked to have had some pause, the knowledge that he simply hadn't stumbled downstairs and ran across town. Industry town, chainlink, ozone, Various –

But, after, he didn't really know. When he was up he knew he must have waited at least a week, a few days. When depressed, he knew – deep down and solid – that he had run there, without even waiting a handful of seconds.

Some things had stayed. He didn't know, couldn't tell you if you asked, how he'd lost his virginity. He remembered his second time, a hooker his older brother – on leave from the war – had paid for, but he knew that wasn't the first. He remembered being scared and ashamed. But for what and why there was just a hole, an ache with no context.

But Various was crystal, clear, sharp: hatchet face, piebald hair, odd accent. Legs and arms that looked stretched, too long for his body. Painted nails. He remembered the smile on his face, too, when the door opened and Dusk walked in. It was a broad and toothy smile, a *pleased to see you* smile but with a hard tinge that said that he wasn't really interested in Dusk, only the *you* that meant client, customer, *cash*.

"So glad you're back," he'd said, taking Dusk's hand and shaking it once. "So glad – thought maybe you'd gone over to that hackworker Gregorious. So what are you here to sell me today?"

Dusk hadn't smiled, didn't move. He'd stood, stock-still, trying to be iron and resolute, in charge of himself and the situation: "What're you buying?"

But Various had laughed, a wheezing, rasping laugh and his black, bushy eyebrows danced like a cartoon. "Me? I buy everything! Ask around! They'll tell you that I take whatever's around – you got it, I'll buy it."

"Fine," Dusk said, trying to relax by leaning back against one of the containers, crossing his arms.

"Got a special today. Want to sell your fifth birthday?"

For Dusk, birthdays had never been "special"; the only reason he even knew his was because it was the last six digits on the identicode tattooed on the inside of his left calf. Somewhere, though, when he was ten, he'd seen a vid or an advert or something that mentioned the concept of a birthday. He'd crawled from his bed in the front seat of the Datsun to ask Shirley about it. Maybe lucky, maybe not, she'd been straight enough to answer him: "Gave you that, dammit," she'd said, meaning the identicode – his name, genetic code, identity registered with the gov. "No one's gonna snatch and sell you if you have that. So what else you want?"

Later, when he'd been big enough to split and not look back, he'd gotten busted for selling Squeak. They'd scanned the identicode, trying to find a match to his genetic profile, check his record for being runaway, or a parole violator. The little scanner had farted an off-key bleep. "Fucker's fake," one of the cops had said of the tattoo, laughing. "No records, no match."

After thirty days in a crowded lock-down, a listing container ship in the harbor, Dusk had walked through three different kinds of bad neighborhood to find the Datsun burnt and his mother gone.

Dusk got down on the cot, closed his eyes. "Take it."

Fifty went to his landlord. Dusk watched, smiling, as he inched his way slowly towards black on the lobby monitor. A way to go, but at least not as far as he'd been before.

At least Dusk thought so – he couldn't remember exactly how much he'd owed.

It took him a while to find his coffin; they all looked alike. Lucky he was able to decipher the half-worn-off marks on his key card and was able to find his room of the last three years with little difficulty.

There he stretched out, staring at the ceiling of his capsule, trying to fathom why the pattern of stains around the broken entertainment system looked so new, so unfamiliar. After a time, as his eyes stared to droop, he tried to find the empty memory – trying to explore it like a missing tooth, working himself around the hole it had left. But he couldn't find anything: it was intangible against other yawning holes, other fragments and broken pieces.

Eventually his confusions faded in his tired mind and Dusk slept; if he dreamed he didn't remember that either.

The street had a name, but Dusk couldn't read. The signs that flicked and floated, flashed and pulsed were just colored lights to him. It didn't matter, in either case, he

was following something as intangible as their holographic
displays – a fraction of memory, a series of his own hovering
images: red eyes, smoky hair, red hooker's eyes, a single
wing on a marble back. He knew he felt something for her
(the strength in his cock and a pain somewhere in his chest)
but the contexts, the pillars of it all, were rotten with holes.
He knew he felt something for her – whatever her name was
– but he'd be damned if he knew why or for how long.

Then he saw her, and some of it came surging back up
into his consciousness: warmth, lust, affection, kindness –
he was battered with a rainbow of feelings that, without
memories to anchor them, tipped him, drunken and dis-
oriented. Almost falling, Dusk stumbled into a leper ("Jack
off, Freak!" the leper had said, or tried to say, his jaw held
in place with duct tape, as Dusk stumbled on) and managed
to cross the street.

She stood with a tiny knot of other rentable women,
standing out because of her carriage (proud and strong), her
attitude (cool and examining), and her back – which was
turned towards Dusk, showing him the graphic of her
name, her icon – through Dusk couldn't remember what
it was, exactly.

Sensing his approach, she turned, locking him with her
brilliant red FOR HIRE eyes. "What you want, fuckface?"
she snarled, hand on latex hip, eyebrows knitting hostility
at his dazed face, unsteady walk

Dusk held up his debtcard. She swiped it, coolly and
professionally, and her eyes CLICKED emerald.

Her smile in the forever shadows of Cancer Alley was a
beam of pure benevolence – as long as his credit lasted.
"Are you okay, lover?" she said, taking his arm and steering
him towards an ancient building. "Took the wrong kind of
candy?"

"I can't remember," he said honestly, allowing himself to
be towed along into the ruinous cavern of a hotel.

*   *   *

She showed him her pussy, flashing it to him with the clicks of a tiny penlight. Sprawled under her, he watched, raptured, as she flipped its detail-enhancing whiteness over her plush lips, her folds, and the tiny head of her crimson clit. His cock ached for a touch, any touch, even his own – but she forbade that, telling him to, "Save it up" with a firm, yet kind, voice.

"Suck me?" he asked, feeling childish and small, towered over by her strength and power.

She smiled, bent over and kissed him, lightly, on the tip of his nose. "I don't do that lover. But I have some other tricks up my – well, you'll have to see, won't you?"

Standing again, she carefully reached into the top of her latex dress and scooped out two handfuls of pale breast, topped by angry red nipples. She hovered above him, smiling down at him with feral lust, her cunt a foot, maybe two, away from his face and her heavy breasts above him, eclipsing the too-hard light thrown from the halogen work lamp. Looking up, he could see her nipples; large, red, tasty – *tasty*, because she lowered herself slowly down till she squatted over his bare chest, dipped them towards his mouth. "The right one first," she said, and he did: pulling it into his mouth, licking and sucking (gently at first then with greater vacuum). She responded, arching herself backwards and hissing like some kind of pressure was escaping.

"Now the other," she said, repeating the performance. Her nipple filled Dusk's mouth, getting harder and harder and bigger and bigger till he had the sudden ache to full his mouth with it, to suck her whole tit. He tried and she moaned, a deep animal sound, as she rubbed her cunt on his hairy chest.

"Enough," she giggled, standing. "You'll make me come." Turning, she lifted what little of her latex hadn't already been lifted, showing him the perfect globes of her ass, the strength in her towering thighs. As he watched, hypnotized by his throbbing cock and need, she slipped two quick fingers down to her cunt, spread her lips, and briskly circled her clit a few dozen times, moaning all the while.

"Please," slipped out of his lips, soft and small – but she heard anyway. Turning yet again, she hovered herself over his bobbing, straining cock. Then, with a still that surged memories in himself, she started to lower herself down onto him.

Memories cascaded through Dusk's fevered mind, an avalanche of sensation, emotion: *the grasp of her wet cunt as she slid over his cock, the snapshot of her face as she lowered herself down into him, the rocket of orgasm as he jetted into her – the smile on her face as he did.* Broken, fragments; they still had power, though. Even before she managed to get his cock into her, he came: an aching, quivering come and spurted cream into the folds of her cunt, still inches from even touching his cock.

She smiled and, to him, it was kind of sad. With expert moves, she cleaned his cock and herself before waiting patiently for him to get dressed.

In the hall, the door shutting behind him, he reached out of his depression, the hot blanket of sadness that was around his shoulders and asked for her name.

"Oh, sweetie," she said, touching his nose with an elegant finger, "I told you before." Then her eyes CLICKED to red and she turned and walked off, never looking back.

Things were gone, had been taken: their absence was obvious – how Dusk felt, what he saw inside himself, didn't add up to what his age should have been according to his identicode. He felt nine, ten – not thirty-eight. He didn't have the memories of someone that old.

He sat, quiet and still, on a street he didn't know, watching people walk by that he felt he should know but he simply . . . didn't.

Some things remained, but just enough to hurt – Dusk remembered the smell of his first home, the yellow Datsun (pine and the peach airspray his mother used), but he couldn't remember where it had been and when he'd seen it last. He remembered what job he'd had before being laid off (bioengine repair) but could barely remember what a bioengine looked like, needed to get fixed. He knew how the scar on the back of his hand got there (beaten by the cops after getting caught for dealing Squeak) but if you'd asked him (then and there) he wouldn't have been able to tell you when that was and how old he'd been.

Dusk didn't even know where he lived. He knew what it smelled like, what his room number was (201) but he didn't know if it was near or far – that part of his key card was worn away. He knew he owed some back rent, though – but how much was a mystery.

Some things were solid, yes, concrete, but it all floated on guesses, suppositions, and doubt.

Dusk knew, for instance, that he had wanted to come here, to the shadowy world where the buildings met high overhead and a thousand small fires created the illusion of . . . stars? He felt it, like a firm hand holding his stomach, that there was something important here, something that he wanted more than anything. He knew that it must cost, too, because he had a debtcard with a hundred on it.

He sat and watched, feeling the cool air from the far end of the street play around his ankles, chilling him. He sat and watched, taking it all in like he was drowning, trying to fill the gaps in his memory with new things: a dwarf with brilliantly-polished chrome legs selling a vat-fed catfish (on a soy bun) from a push-cart; an elegantly elongated black man who towered seven plus over the crowd, coolly checking the time on an antique gold watch surgically set into his palm; a brilliantly red woman, a flesh and bone clichéd demoness, who leaned into the widow of a plush and immaculate pocket racer and danced her muscular ass as she

bargained with the driver; a wilding of rogue school-
children, still in the threadbare remains of their Catholic
uniforms, flowed by and over a massively swollen derelict –
when they had passed Dusk noticed they had neatly stolen
his prosthetic eyes.

Dusk drank it in, trying to find something, anything, that
had meant something to him.

A trio of women, the newest generation of the oldest
profession, stood on one corner: a large black woman, her
hair a torrent of braids; a mixed-blood lanky one in a tiger-
striped poncho; and a pale Amazon, breasts all but spilling
from the top of a black latex dress.

She turned away, her eyes skipping and glancing off
Dusk and the Rent-a-Bench^{TM} he sat on as she turned.
Her back, he saw – he stared at – was bare and marble white
save for a tremendous tattoo of a single bird's wing.

Dusk watched her, trying to understand his feelings –
why he should feel a weight of sadness, a powerful lug of
desire, and the soft prickling of infatuation for her. But the
feelings were faint, lost without their context. He stood,
thinking of approaching her, offering his fat debtcard, of
trying to recapture what she must have meant to him. No,
what she must have meant to *him* – the other Dusk who
remembered.

The fury built and seemed to break him apart inside – he
wanted to get up and scream, rise and just start punching.
He wanted *something* painfully, totally – the thing that had
given him the most pleasure in . . . he couldn't remember
when. He wanted that hope and peace.

It had been something to do with her, he was sure. But he
didn't know what.

After an hour of watching her, of feeling the pain at not
knowing what to do, of how to do it, and why, he got up and
walked back over his own footsteps, stringing together a
handful of memories that slowly led him backwards.

*   *   *

Two stops first. One to a small shop that he stumbled across, something in its front window grabbing his attention and holding it. He went in and bought it, hoping he had enough experience to know how to make it work.

Then, a name – just that. But names had faces, had bodies. Dusk went to three different bars till he was able to say that name and have someone nod up and down. They knew of him, yes. They knew what he did, yes. They knew where he lived, yes.

After, with his purchase and his new sale, he let his feet lead him the rest of the way, backwards through what memories remained to him.

It was easy to find. His feet knew the way, some kind of deep, instinctual repetition. He let them take him to Industry Town (the smoke and hot metal smell of it), then to the end of Press Street. He went to the fence and turned right. The smell of ozone. The door – no handles.

It opened when he approached. The inside was familiar – and the strangeness of that feeling (of knowing) gave him a burst of strength.

"Ah, back so soon?" the man said, stepped out from behind one of the huge orange containers. "I'm glad. Always good doing business with you."

Dusk smiled as the door closed behind him. When it shut, finally, completely, he pulled out the gun, leveled it at the man – whose name he did not know.

The man froze, fear widening his eyes, clenching his teeth. He seemed on the verge, just about, to make light of it, to try and depressurize Dusk and his gun – but then he stopped, held back by the coolness, the unwavering precision, of Dusk's movements.

Stepping closer, Dusk cocked the gun, and pushed the weight of it into Various, his belly; shoving hard, smelling fear on his panting, quaking breath, Dusk felt for Various's lower rib with the muzzle.

Pinned to the wall, his eyes hunted but found nothing but Dusk's marble face, his level breathing, his unbending arms, the ache of the gun's barrel – warmer than Dusk by far.

"*Mercy*," Various whispered, the word broken and hoarse.

Dusk echoed the word: "Funny – saw someone about that. You know him. Gregorious. Bought it all."

Watching, trapped, he saw Dusk reach into a pocket, pull out something small, silver, silicon.

"Mercy?" Dusk offered, smiling cold.

DAY TURNS INTO NIGHT

Jules Torti

THERE WAS A time when I used to lie still, quietly enjoying the delicious pleasure of her touch, my body silent, my moans suppressed. My lips would remain firmly pressed together, resisting a scream of overwhelming delight, my cheeks flushing pink, my eyelids tightly shut. Was I afraid to look? Somewhat. I knew she would be there, smiling between my thighs.

I wanted to moan and groan loudly with each penetrating thrust. I wanted to beg, desperate for her to tease my clit with her deft tongue. Most of all I wanted to whisper, or maybe say aloud, *suck my clit, suck it hard*. But, to me, that didn't sound romantic at all, and I'm a romantic. I want dimmed lights, burning candles, incense, silk sheets, and a single red rose in a crystal vase beside the bed. I want Pachelbel or Bach, something classical playing in the background.

Sometimes, though, when I'm really horny, it doesn't matter so much about the surroundings. Only she matters, and if we're doing it on the hot, sticky leather seats in the back of her Explorer with Meatloaf blasting out the windows, that's okay, too. I don't have to be wined and dined all the time to be seduced; hell, a Hawaiian pizza with double cheese and a couple of cold beers suits me just fine. It doesn't even matter what we eat, because she's my aphrodisiac. It doesn't matter where we are, or when it happens ... I just need her, the center of my sexual universe.

We love to make love. I love the feel of the wide breadth of her tongue, sliding across my labia like a snake in the hot desert sand. She enjoys the sweet cream that flows uncontrollably from my insides. She tells me this as she inhales my musky scent. Her strong hands stroke, pull, squeeze and caress. I wish she could crawl right inside my cunt. I spread my legs further apart in anticipation that she would try, and then miraculously just slip right inside. One tentative hand, followed by another careful hand, arms, head, her whole body surrounded by the warm, slippery walls of my vagina. Instead she penetrates me and I feel the fullness of her clenched fist inside me, my body contracting wildly with each entry. I sit up a little, propping my elbows on the pillows behind me, so she can push in deeper. Deeper and deeper; I wish she could push the whole length of her arm into me. *I want more.*

We've done it in the snow a couple of times after soaking in the hot tub. We do it in the summer too, climbing out onto the cedar deck, finding relief in a summer's breeze before jumping on top of each other. In the winter, the lure of a blanket of snow, after hours of steam and sweat, encourages us to race from the deck to the banks below, slipping and sliding in our bare feet, unaware of the cold. Bodies numb with overwhelming desire. Strawberry lips and champagne tongues, steam rising, snow melting, hot, wet bodies ... She makes me sweat in the snow. She calls me her angel, her beautiful, sexy snow angel, and I kiss the tiny flakes of snow from her eyelashes and eyebrows.

The morning after we always chuckle, curled up together on the couch, under the navy blue afghan her grandmother gave us for Christmas. We stoke the fire and sip hot coffee with Grand Marnier, watching as the finches and chickadees squabble over the sunflower seeds in the feeder. Down the bank we can see our footprints and body prints, pressed deep in the snow where we had frolicked the night before. We are tempted to run outside again, our bodies exposed, free, nipples erect in the wintry breeze, but we decide to stay inside and crawl back into bed.

We warm fresh fat raspberry and blueberry Danishes in the oven, until the icing is soft to the touch. We carry them to the bedroom, mugs of coffee in hand, and feed each other, exchanging sugary kisses between bites. I purposely let gooey pieces of icing and raspberry fall onto her breasts so I can lick the stickiness from her milky skin. She asks me to suck on her nipples, and I do, my nipples turning hard with hers. She asks me to pull out the dildo; it's tucked under the bed, on the left side, with the purple strips of cloth that she sometimes ties me up with.

I like being tied up, a lot. My hands high above my head, suspended. My ankles firmly tied to the brass bedposts. She likes the dildo, a fat eight inches. It makes my body quiver and shake as it glides in, my lips stretching to accommodate its wide head. She likes it up the ass. Hard, rhythmic thrusts into her rectum, my hips pumping fast, watching excitedly as the dildo disappears between her wonderfully tight cheeks.

She moans and groans loudly; other times she's breathless, just panting. She asks me to rub her pussy hard with my hand. She wants three fingers in her cunt while she has the dildo inside her ass. I follow all her directions, eager to please her.

Most of the time she is on top, but when I wear the dildo she lies on her stomach, spread eagle, her anus contracting excitedly as I rub the massage oil between her buttocks with firm pressure. "Don't touch my clitoris, yet," she asks. "I want to come with you." Before, I could only come when she was on top, her pussy rubbing hard against mine, her teeth biting ferociously at my rosy nipples, her large hands squeezing my breasts, mouth sucking. Now I must fight my body, resisting the urge to come immediately, and I writhe on the bed, twisting, turning, pulling away, swallowing screams of pleasure.

She can make me come in less than a minute. Thirty seconds and I can hardly stand it; my clit is on fire, and she knows this. She smiles devilishly at me, her eyebrows arching, her hands squeezing. She continues until my body is jumping, my legs twitching uncontrollably, my heart exploding in my chest, my breath quick, responding to her vibrato, fast and furious, in and out.

I ask her to climb on top of me, so I can feel her flesh covering mine. Her pussy rubbing against mine. Her hot breath on the nape of my neck. Our nipples touching. My fingers clutching her ass, driving her mound of Venus into mine. We don't need the dildo; we only need for our vulvas to slide and glide, kissing each other. Our clits pressing, hands stroking, teeth biting.

I love loving her in all of the seasons, but especially in the summer. The smell of our aroused bodies in the humidity of the afternoon is intoxicating. Sunlight reveals a trail of glistening saliva and come on our bodies, marking the routes of our traveling tongues as they explore naked skin. We lie in the sun, tracing each other's breasts with round cubes of ice. The melted cube creates a small stream that runs into my navel, and she insists on following the stream, running the cube below my navel, in a zig zag to my moist pussy.

Mostly I like it when she doesn't use her hands, when just her tongue skates around on the surface of my skin. Finally, her tongue will race along my thighs to my waiting pussy, but sometimes she decides to cover the whole expanse of my body again before even breathing on my clit. If I begged her to touch my sweet pearl she would only ignore me and make me wait longer. And I do, patiently.

We are careful lovers, patient and sensitive. We know each other's bodies perfectly. We could make love in the dark of night, guided by the familiar curves and velvety skin of the other. I know the surface of her skin as I do the landscapes that I paint. I know the shadows, the textures, the outline, the depth, the sudden, subtle changes in the colour of her skin. When I kiss her pussy I know all of the colours her skin flushes to; I know when it pales, and I continue sucking and licking until it radiates and glows. Like the sun falling from the sky into the horizon. Her body is the sun, and together we rise and fall in the atmosphere, disappearing at night, cloaked in comforting darkness with the stars straddling the moon. We make love by candlelight, casting shadows on to the walls and ceiling of our bodies entwined.

We have sex all the time, not just at night. We do it in the daylight often because I like watching her expressions and she likes to watch me. Our gaze is uninterrupted; we find it intense, sensual. Our eyes communicate volumes, and when I flash her a smile, her eyes return it. Her gentle tongue caresses my clit, but it is her eyes that caress my soul. Her beautiful eyes, the colour of Lake Louise. We drove out west in '89 and made love on a cliff over looking Lake Louise. And in the stands of white pine. And on the soft forest floor, spongy jade green moss and little pink flowers under my back. We did it on the waterbed, on the kitchen floor covered in maple syrup, in the shower, in the back of the jeep, in the fields of purple flax and buttercups, on a picnic table, skin smeared with peanut butter and marmalade . . .

We made love under Cassiopeia and Orion, under a sliver of the silver moon, until the dancing *aurora borealis* faded with the inky sky to dawn and I kissed the entire surface of her body under the billowy clouds of day. Loving her is easy; it's like breathing.

We try different stuff all the time: different positions, toys, roles, whatever. We have handcuffs, feathers, vibrators, butt plugs, edible chocolate and strawberry massage lotion, lacy bras and red satin thongs. I like her in the black lace teddy best, when her arms and legs are tied together. I pretend to save her from the train tracks, as though she had been kidnapped and tied to the rails, a damsel in distress. I carry her in my strong arms to the bedroom wearing nothing but my cowboy boots – the pair with the silver spurs that she bought me in Texas. I undress her with my teeth but in the end I am tied up, blindfolded with her black lace teddy, and she makes love to me from behind, peppering my back with little kisses before burying her head between my legs.

I raise myself up from the mattress, wanting her tongue to wash over my clit. Instead it darts in and out of my opening, teasing me, my swollen clit throbbing, rubbing hard against the mattress with anticipation. The dark green sheets are stained with our milky womanly secretions, but this arouses us, and we fall asleep in the wonderful dampness of each other's come. The air thick with our scent.

It was when we were both blindfolded that we found a position where we could touch our clits at the same time. We were playing Twister, actually, just for fun, but somehow we ended up naked and blindfolded. I was concentrating on the game, left hand red, right foot blue . . . but she tackled me before I could balance myself on left foot green and I toppled over. The loser had to strip; I guess that was the rule, but I insisted that she be naked with me and in our twisting and turning, lying sideways a bit on the vinyl Twister sheet, kind of like scissors, I could feel her warm vulva rubbing against mine, her delicate skin folds, slippery against my own.

Then we decided to buy a double dildo and try using the vibrator at the same time. Moving in tempo, I held the vibrator between our clits and we came immediately. Her legs crossed behind my back, the steady, whirring movement of the vibrator traveling through our bodies as we held each other tightly, shivering with ecstacy. We don't use the vibrator all the time; it's just a treat. We have two: one has like a snub nose on it and a smooth rubber head that, when inserted into my vagina, its smooth flutter just about sends me to the moon. The other vibrator is an oval-shaped one, and she likes it better, especially when I guide it with my hand across her pussy.

In July, for fun, I suggested we have sex on the roof. There was a full moon rising and the shingles were still hot from the summer sun. We drank a bottle of red wine and devoured a pound of rich white chocolate almond bark that I picked up from Laura Secord's. That's her favorite. We kissed for hours, the moon rising and falling as we discovered unchartered erogenous zones, fondling, and manipulating in our simultaneous stimulation.

Friday nights are reserved for movie rentals. Hot, sexy, X-rated ones. We test ourselves, seeing how long we can resist each other. How long will it take before we abandon the bowl of buttery popcorn and M&Ms and strip down to bare flesh. The movie continues running but we create our own love scenes, steamier than the ones on film. The popcorn spills to the floor as we rearrange our bodies, rolling back and forth, prisoners of passion. We disappear behind the couch and roll into the hallway. Two hours later the credits appear on the screen and we have just begun. Should we try it standing up, outside in the refreshing rain, or on the floor, skin burning on the carpet as we chase after each other in hot pursuit?

I have fun pretending that I am trying to escape her, but I am easy prey. I put up little struggle as her naked body pins me to the floor. Why would I want to escape? Please, tie me up, torture me with your tongue. Will you punish me if I try to escape again?

She suggests that we do the John and Yoko Ono thing. "Let's stay in bed for two whole weeks." And we did. The October winds were harsh and unfriendly, the sky bitter and grey with rain. Inside our days were spent sharing sexual fantasies, exploring, discovering, and enjoying every meal by candle light. Most meals were abandoned on the tray beside the bed, eaten cold hours later when we finally gave in to hunger and exhaustion.

She likes it when we sixty-nine. We call it sixty-six, because she's a few inches shorter than me, and I have to be on the bottom because my torso's so long. But this doesn't stop us; in fact, she's just the right size. Once, when we were sixty-nining we came at the exact same time. That had never happened to me before. I always held off, making sure my partner was satisfied first, but that time I had no choice. Her wet pussy was right in my face; I was sucking her tiny clit, nibbling, my tongue flicking back and forth, as she did the same to me. Her hands grabbed my clenched buttocks, pulling my cunt closer to her mouth. Come spilled out of me like sap from a maple. That's the most incredible feeling: our bodies shaking, grinding, shivering, pulsating, rocking, both at the same time. Her body sinking into mine, her breasts pushed into my flat abdomen, her stomach pressing against my tits. My hands spreading her legs apart, her knees burning from rubbing hard against the sheets. My knees bent and spread as she clutches on to my thighs. Our bodies become one as we lick and suck and tease. Tongues fluttering and flicking, nibbling and caressing. She buries her nose deep in my cunt and I lick at her pussy, my tongue moving fast like her pumping hips. And then we come. Moaning, groaning, begging . . . and then we collapse to the side, weak in each other's arms, completely satisfied.

Hours later, when we wake from sleep, I begin licking her

vulva hungrily, still tasting traces of the Baileys I had gently poured on her earlier. Sweet, sticky Baileys, black Sambucca, butterscotch sundae topping, blackberry jam, honey, Dom Perignon . . . It didn't really matter what it was, as long as my tongue covered her smooth skin with careful attention. I like licking things off her, too. She likes it when I'm noisy about it, slurping between her legs, generous licks, finding sweetness in all her skin folds.

I like when she straddles my breasts, her pussy hovering just above my lips. My hands grab her muscular buttocks and pull her close, so I can reach my tongue deep inside her. I can penetrate her easily from here, my finger pushed up her ass as I lick her clit like a thirsty kitten lapping up warm cream. She leans forward, bracing herself against the wall behind the bed, palms open, her body becoming shaky as I continue in ardor. She likes the feel of my jawbones digging into her. I like the feel of her wet cunt, slippery on my face. When she comes, her hands slide down the wall and I wait for a minute, her throbbing clit resting on my tongue. When she catches her breath I begin sucking again until she lets her pussy glide back and forth over my chin. Her knuckles turn white as she grabs hold of the bed posts, rocking back and forth, her breasts slapping against her skin.

She likes it when I touch myself, when I make her sit in the corner of the room, her arms and legs handcuffed to the chair. I sit on the edge of the bed, sipping a chocolate martini before I begin. Soon, I allow the vibrator to pulsate along my inner thighs, circling around my vulva. I open my legs wide so she can see my body contracting, my wet lips eager for her deft tongue. Sometimes I penetrate myself, with three fingers, other times I just play with my clit. I pull back on my labia so that clitty jumps out, all pink and excited.

I know she wants to touch me, feel me, smell me. I roll over on to my stomach, sliding my fingers over my pussy.

"Go inside," she begs, but I make her wait. She enjoys the anticipation.

I find Uncle Buck under the bed and pull him out. I know she wants to strap him on and pump me like crazy, until I beg her to stop, but she is handcuffed. Instead, I place the dildo on the bed and face her on bended knees, slowly coming down on the dildo. My cunt is slippery and Uncle Buck slides in with ease, disappearing as I lower myself to the bed, enjoying the fat thickness of it inside me. I squeeze my clit between my fingers, my muscles tightening as I push down harder on the dildo. In and out, my body slurping and gasping as pockets of air are filled with Buck's eight inches.

I hold onto the dildo with two hands below my stomach, grinding wildly into the sheets, my feet in the air, pumping Buck in and out of me as she watches. She is aroused in her chair, pushing her clit down on the seat, desperate for me to let her out of the cuffs. And I do. She quickly straps on Buck and fucks me hard, my hands pulling at the sheets, reaching for the stability of the bed posts as her pelvis thrusts into mine.

Other times we do it in a different style – "Like dogs," she says. It makes me want to smoke a cigarette, and I don't even smoke. On my knees, with her shoving her fist in from behind, I stare out the bedroom window at Cypress mountain, its peak lost in the clouds. It feels good when she penetrates me from behind; I think I can make my body open up wider in this position. She likes trying new positions, and we don't always do it in our bedroom. On Sunday we did it in the woods, our naked bodies laying on the soft sphagnum, birds spying on us from their perches. I like doing it outside.

Soon I have the dildo on and she wants to sit facing each other, no space between our skin as I nuzzle and nibble on her velvety lobes. She too stares out at the mountain, beads of sweat running down her face.

After, we lie like spoons, our insides still full with the feel of each other. My clit feels numb, my thighs wet with our come, and I can taste her sweetness on my breath. Day turns into night and we begin again.

A FAIRY STORY

Michael Crawley

ONCE UPON A time there was a bright and brittle city. Its merchants traded in toys for the mind and joys for the senses; in curious artifacts, exotic essences and subtle textures. And in beauty. The City was voracious for beauty.

In that, the most beautiful and beauty-devouring city, the supreme beauty was Emerald, who, had she known compassion, would have been a woman.

Emerald had wild flame hair; startling verdant eyes; and scarlet satin lips. Her breasts were yielding, shaped to be held, with nipples hard and sharp enough to pierce palms. The cage of her ribs was a triumphant arch. She had a waist like a whip, a navel deep enough that no tongue could plumb its depths, and hips that were the vibrant crescendo in a hymn to Eros.

Her legs were poetry. When she walked, her thighs made slithery love to each other.

Emerald kept a salon in a penthouse atop the tallest spire in a city that clawed clouds. Her soirées were attended by a coterie of sycophants; tinsel men and glitter women; insipid moons brightened only by reflecting the glorious light of Emerald's splendour.

Ennui was their enemy. They combated it by playing The Game, which went like this.

When Charles Huygens the Second was introduced to Emerald, he did not gape. He did not tremble. He didn't break out in a sweat. None of those reactions would have been appropriate for the forty-seventh of forty-eight vice presidents of the City's most prestigious merchant banks.

Emerald took the fingers he'd offered her to shake and lifted them to her lush red mouth. She sucked the tip of his smallest finger and then inspected it, as if matching flavour to appearance. In a voice that an orchid might have envied, if orchids spoke, she said, "I'm so glad you could come, Charles. I hope we can become good friends."

Charles Huygens the Second forced a sound from his constricted throat.

In the course of that evening, Emerald touched Charles' shoulder twice, his forearm once and his thigh once. When he bade her goodnight, her tongue flickered and her eyelids drooped.

The next visit, she hugged him to her bosom in greeting, and her teeth nipped his earlobe. Later, her fingers brushed across his lap. When they did, she raised an eyebrow, as if in approval.

On the third evening she came to stand behind him when he was in conversation with a silver-haired waif who charged five hundred dollars an hour to loll photogenically. Charles jerked and gulped when he felt Emerald's hand slide up under the back of his jacket. When her nails prickled his spine through his shirt, he tried not to arch, but the muscles in his back went rigid.

"When the others leave, stay behind," Emerald breathed into his ear.

Once they were alone, Emerald told him, "I want to

know you better, Charles. Can we take our time? Can we learn about each other, slowly?"

Charles said, "Of course, Emerald. What would you like to know about me?"

"Show me that you are your own master, Charles. If you are, perhaps you can become mine. Would you like to master me, Charles? Would you like me to be your slave?"

"Slave? I don't . . ."

"Keep still. Don't move." She knelt before him. Long tapered fingers caressed him through the cashmere of his trousers. She drew down his zipper, very slowly.

Charles Huygens the Second clenched his jaw. His fingernails bit into his palms, but he didn't move. He still didn't move when cool fingers reached into his fly and pulled his throbbing shaft forth into the intangible air.

She held him, fevered and pulsating, on her palm. Her eyes inspected his flesh, inch by inch, as if it were an *objet d'art* that she was considering purchasing. She lifted it with the tip of one finger. Her lips pursed as she considered the thick proud vein that ran up its underside. Her eyes narrowed at the sight of a tiny clear drop of fluid that welled up from the eye of his glans.

Charles gritted his teeth, but he didn't move.

Emerald's fingertips stroked him, so softly that he almost couldn't feel it. She nodded, tucked his craving length away, zipped him up, stood, and husked, "Goodnight, Charles. Thank you. Now I'm going to my bed, to dream my obscene dreams. Why don't you go home and do the same?"

The fourth time Charles visited, Emerald greeted him with a lick down the side of his neck. She held his hand an inch from her bosom and swayed. A silk-clad nipple, proud and hard, traced electric lines across his palm. "You will be able to stay late, won't you?" she breathed.

At supper, he sat on her left. Her hand rested in his lap, cupping him. When dessert was served, two fingers pulled his fly down. One slid inside, stroked him three times, and withdrew. The hiss as she drew his fly closed was exquisite torture.

During cocktails, Emerald told him that a friend of hers, a close friend, was temporarily financially embarrassed. Could Charles, considering his position as a merchant banker, help? For just a couple of days? Nothing official, of course. Money was a topic that Emerald and her friends avoided.

Emerald's friend needed a mere ten thousand, for about forty-eight hours. Charles had eleven thousand four hundred and twelve in his personal account. With hot acid bubbling in his bowels, Charles casually wrote a cheque.

When Emerald and Charles were alone at last, she had him stand and demonstrate his self-control once more. This time she was kinder. Her strokes became longer and harder. When the long white arc jetted, she directed it into a Venetian crystal bowl that sat on an Iranian rosewood table.

Two nights later, Emerald's friend gave Charles an envelope and his thanks. When Charles retired to a sumptuous bathroom, to count, he found eleven one-thousand dollar bills. Ten per cent interest in two days is illegal, usury, but Charles hadn't charged interest; it had been given unasked. His conscience was . . . But what is a conscience, when Emerald's cunning fingers were waiting?

Her dress that evening was thin and fine and glossy. Its skirt was long but its top was backless. A soft clinging panel that was suspended from spaghetti straps draped her breasts.

When she knelt before him, she looked up at him through her lashes and said, "You remember your promise?"

"I won't move, not till you give me leave."

"I'm going to make it harder for you." She grinned a sly grin. "Both ways." She shrugged. The straps of her dress slithered. The panel fluttered to her lap. Emerald was naked to her slender waist.

Charles groaned, but he didn't move.

When Emerald had stroked him until he oozed, she touched the tip of his helmet to her nipple. Two of her fingers worked the fluid into her rigid spike as her other hand pumped him, harder and faster and harder . . . and this time his hot seed fell in a great gout across the creamy white slope of her left breast.

"The next time," she promised, "it will be even better, much better. I am very pleased with you, Charles. You give me delicious dreams."

On the next evening, another friend of Emerald's was financially embarrassed. This one needed forty thousand, much more than Charles had in private funds. Still, a little juggling would cover, and the money was secure, wasn't it? And Emerald had implied obscene promises. Charles wrote a cheque.

When the others were gone, Emerald repeated her conditions. Charles agreed once more. He didn't move, but he did groan when his love's caresses coaxed the semen from his shaft, and she opened her mouth to it, and took the full flood on the flat of her tongue.

The next day Charles squirmed and sweated as he made temporary transfers of funds between a number of accounts. He didn't exceed his authority, not as he chose to interpret it. He was, however, nagged by the thought that his superiors might place a different interpretation on his actions.

But, the following day, he was repaid, in full, plus ten per cent. That evening, when he was alone with Emerald, she dropped her dress to a pool at her feet, emerging in garter belt, hose, and a garment that was smoke caught in a cobweb. Was this to be *the* night, when she gave herself fully? No, it wasn't. But it was the night that she took him into her mouth and drew on him, not using her hands, and nodded and nodded, her tongue pressing his plum against the rippled roof of her mouth, until his very soul poured out, to be swallowed, to become her property.

The next night, one of Emerald's friends, a prince from far away, needed Charles' help. It was with supreme confidence that Charles wrote a cheque for one hundred thousand. That night Emerald had a headache. Charles left with the rest.

A hundred thousand took a lot of juggling, but Charles was becoming skilled.

On his next visit, Charles inquired about the prince. His Highness was gone, returned to far away. Almost as bad, Emerald was cold. Her warmth, her secret touches, were directed at another. When Charles insisted on talking to her and asked about the prince, that was none of Emerald's concern. Hadn't she told him that "money" was a topic she abhorred?

The merchant bank kept a loaded pistol, for security. Charles put it to his ear and pulled the trigger. When Emerald's glittering friends heard of this, they all laughed, gay and brittle laughter.

The Game had been played, once more, and Emerald had won, again. Her friends all laughed, but Emerald only smiled.

They brought a young couple to Emerald. He, John, was tall, blond, with solid shoulders and a cleft chin. She, Deborah, was ballerina-petite, dark-haired, with a wispy waist and bright eyes. They were both virgins, sworn to "save themselves" for their wedding night.

Emerald invited Deborah for tea. Over cucumber sandwiches and seedcake, Emerald congratulated Deborah on her rare purity, but . . .

. . . but the intimate side of marriage is its cement, is it not? And two innocents, fumbling? Did Deborah understand the physical side of love in theory, at least? Might a mature, experienced woman, in a spirit of sisterhood, offer a word or two of advice?

Of course she might, so Emerald explained the true nature of men. There are two types, of course, the animals and the saints. No doubt John was a saint.

Emerald moved closer on the chaise and took Deborah's hand. "A saint will be gentle," she explained. "His first kiss would likely be thus." Emerald pressed soft lips to the maiden's rose-petal cheek. "His first touch . . ." Emerald cupped a quivering young breast. "May I demonstrate a man's more familiar kiss?"

Deborah trembled but was silent. Emerald leaned closer, touched lips to lips, and slid a hesitant tongue tip. When Deborah didn't pull back, Emerald allowed the ball of her thumb to glide over the linen of Deborah's pristine white dress, where it covered her nipple.

"And so," Emerald continued, "little by little he will arouse you. Each new caress will come naturally, easily. One thing he will make sure of, that his bride reach her ultimate joy, whether or not he does the same. A good man is concerned with his love's pleasure before his own. He will kiss her here . . ." Emerald dabbed a fingertip on Deborah's nipple. "And here . . ." Her hand hovered an inch above where Deborah's dress creased between her slender, virginal, thighs.

"He will kiss me there?"

"Softly, tenderly, and for a long long time. That will be your chief delight, if he is a good man."

"And if – if he was not a good man?"

Emerald frowned. "But he will be, I am sure of it. Still, the other type, the animal type, well, he will simply ravish you, with no thought to your happiness. He will rape your virginities, all three of them."

"Three?" Deborah clutched Emerald's hand and pressed it into her lap.

Emerald touched a fingertip to Deborah's pale lower lip. "His male member will thrust . . ." She intruded her finger into Deborah's mouth, "Here. And here." She bore down with her other hand, squeezing the maiden's mound. "And . . ."

"And?"

"I hesitate to say – to shock you. There are men, beasts, who care nothing for us women except as receptacles for their unnatural lusts. John, of course, is not one of those animals, but if he were, then even your poor little, er, bottom, might not be safe." Emerald paused to let Deborah absorb her revelation.

The child-woman shuddered. "But John, as you say, is not one of those men."

"Of course not. Still, just in case, let me advise you. All newly-wed men, without exception, ask their brides how they want to be loved. There is only one proper answer. Do you know what it is?"

Deborah lowered her eyes. "No."

"You must be demure. You must give him the answer that all men desire. You will tell him, "I am yours. Do with me as you will." Then, a good man will respond to your sweet submission with the utmost gentleness."

"And – and the other sort?"

"Will brutalize you, I'm afraid. In that case there is but one defence."

Deborah wriggled on her seat. "And that is?"

"You must submit. Best, you should pretend to enjoy his attacks. That way, he will soon be done. Resist, and he will be incensed. It will go twice as badly for you. He will beat you, perhaps whip you, and still have his evil way with you." Emerald smiled a smile that started sad and then brightened. "But this is nonsense. John is a good man. He is sure to kiss you like this . . . And like this . . ."

Emerald drew back. A few chaste kisses on those sweet virgin lips would suffice, for then. "If the impossible were to happen," she whispered, "then you must come to me for feminine comfort. I will understand. There will be no need for shame."

Emerald advised John thus: "All girls, John, need to be mastered. That is their chief desire, their maidenly dream. Your lovely Deborah is doubtless aching for her ravishment."

"But she is so sweet, innocent, gentle . . ."

"A sure sign. Is not submission the complement of mastery? You must show your love for your bride by taking her, by using her. Only thus can you prove your love. She will expect to awaken the next morning stiff and bruised. Each and every purple mark adorning her pure white skin will be a proud token of your love for her."

"But . . . what if you are mistaken? What if she expects nothing but the tenderness I long to offer to her?"

"I am not wrong, John, but it is easily put to the test. On your wedding night, simply ask her, "Deborah, how do you want me to love you?" If she craves tenderness, she will tell you so. If, on the other hand, she looks at you with sweet surrender in her eyes and tells you that she is yours to use as you will, then you must tear her garments from her body. You must throw her on the bed and take her passionately, in every way, over and over, till dawn." And Emerald continued by describing, in intimate detail, every perversion that she prescribed John should visit on his bride's virginal body.

A week after the newly-weds returned from their honeymoon, a tearful Deborah came to Emerald for comfort. Emerald kissed every bruise that mottled the girl's body. She gave Deborah Sapphic consolation, proving to her, again and again, that only another woman knows how truly to love a woman.

John came to Emerald, bewildered, for though his new wife submitted to him in every way, he sensed she was not really happy. Emerald proved to John, with her own body, that brutal loving was the surest way to delight a woman.

Three months later, John and Deborah were in the divorce court.

The Game had been played once more, and Emerald had won, again. All her friends laughed, but Emerald only smiled.

It was a good year for The Game. A young clergyman was put to the test, his faith versus his suppressed lusts. After a night and a day and a second night of progressively deepening depravity with Emerald and two of her most handsome friends, the young clergyman admitted that his faith was defeated. In abject penance, he joined an order of flagellant monks and went to serve the hideously diseased in a land where white men do not live long.

And he didn't.

The Game had been played once more, and Emerald had won, again. All of her friends laughed, but Emerald only smiled.

A youthful boxer, a contender, was debauched. Weakened, he took too many blows to the head and ended up a drunken derelict.

The Game had been played once more, and Emerald had won, again. All of her friends laughed, but Emerald only smiled.

They brought her Paul, an artist in oils, untutored but a natural genius. She commissioned him to paint her portrait.

Emerald posed with naked shoulders that were wind-carved snow. The rest of her body was veiled by pink gossamer that was as concealing as a blush. After the third long sitting, she begged leave to view the work-in-progress.

"She's very beautiful," Emerald allowed, "but she isn't me."

Wounded, Paul asked, "In what way? Isn't that your hair, those your eyes, and aren't those red red lips the lips of my lovely patron?"

"True – you have a photographic likeness of me,"

Emerald said, knowing that to a true artist "photographic" is an insult.

"Doesn't my patron's kindness, her goodness, show through?" Paul protested.

"How sweet! It's very pretty. She is flawless. Is that how you see me, Paul, as 'flawless'?"

Paul fell to his knees and gazed up at his lovely subject. "I see perfection in all your parts, my muse," he sighed.

Emerald stretched an elegant leg and nudged his chest with her naked pink toe. "Perfection? How dull that word is. I am *flawed*, Paul. It is in my *im*perfections that the real me is to be found."

The corner of Paul's mouth twitched. "You – imperfect? I refuse to believe that."

"I am cruel, Paul; I tell you that to give you fair warning. I am lascivious, Paul; I tell you that as a solemn promise."

"If you are cruel, then cruelty is beautiful. If you are – lascivious, then . . ."

"Then you approve of my immorality?"

"What you are, Emerald, whatever it might be, is good and pure in my eyes."

Emerald squirmed her toe between the buttons of Paul's shirt. He flinched. She thrust. He toppled onto his back, laughing. She leapt from her chair, down to straddle his hips. Her hair fell around his head, enclosing their faces in a canopy of private shadows. "Would you like to know the real Emerald?" she sighed. Her breath was a perfumed caress on his face.

"With all my heart."

"Then you may taste my mouth."

He did. She surrendered her lips and her tongue, and captured his heart. Her hands, between their bodies, plucked his shirt open and spread it.

"You may take my dress off."

He fumbled, nervous fingers seeking some sort of fastening.

"Rip it open, fool! Don't insult me with patience."

Paul tore. Emerald sat up on him in the wispy shreds of her dress. "What do you want, Paul?" she demanded. "Are you a sadist? Do you want to hurt me? Are you a masochist?" Her nails raked his chest. "Is that what you like? Do you want me to drip molten candle wax on your nipples? Pierce you with needles? Is it pain you want? Tell me, Paul. Ask what you will of me, and it is yours. I have straps and cords and I am very flexible. Distort my body! Bind me! Make me into an erotic obscenity, if that is your whim. Make me crawl for you, beg you, grovel at your feet."

"I just want – want to love you, Emerald."

Emerald threw back her head. Her throat worked and her breasts shook, as if she laughed, but she made no sound. 'You want purity, Paul? Sweet young love? But no! I see. You want purity from me so that you may despoil it. Of course! That could be fun. Shall I dress up for you, Paul? Could you see me as a virgin schoolgirl? I can do that. I could be a very naughty girl and you could spank me till I sobbed, and then . . ."

Paul shifted beneath Emerald. "I just want to make love to you, Emerald. Normal – loving – love."

Emerald's lip curled. "Normal? 'Loving love'? Oh dear. I expected more of you, Paul. Oh well, if that's your best." She swung a leg high and off him, rolled over twice and lay spread-eagle on her back. "Very well, strip off and do it."

Uncertain, Paul stood and stripped. He kneeled over Emerald and pressed his lips to a mouth that yielded without responding. He squeezed cool breasts and laid a finger on the tip of an icy nipple. When he sighed and began to stand, Emerald snapped, "Do it!"

Paul shook his head as if bewildered, knelt between the splay of Emerald's slender perfect thighs, surreptitiously stroked himself to restore his erection, and lowered his body. When but three inches of air separated the head of his reluctant organ from its tepid goal, Emerald flipped over and knelt up. His flesh was caught between satin cushions, and, to his shamed surprise, stiffened.

Emerald wriggled. "Do it," she commanded. "Let our first union be an unnatural one or I will never see you again." She wriggled harder. "Choose, Paul. Take me this way, Paul, or you'll never have me. I warn you, Paul, refuse me now and you'll regret it for the rest of your life."

Paul swallowed, took a deep breath, and leaned into Emerald's crouched body. There was a knot of resistance. Emerald told him, "Push." He pressed harder. The knot dissolved. His stiffness sank in, and up. The constricting passage was hot, and not quite dry, and incredibly tight. Paul's entire being focussed. The intimate, the forbidden, yielded. Paul's eyes glazed. Something inside him that was not him ravened for release. He let it have its way.

When the inner beast finally slept, sated, Paul realised that Emerald's buttocks, in her portrait, lacked a certain quality that her real buttocks possessed. Naked, he took up his pallet and brushes.

At the next sitting Emerald appeared unclothed, with her hands chained behind her back and jewelled clips dangling from her nipples. Later, Paul repainted her portrait's breasts, making their peaks a little more prominent, a shade darker, and much more vulnerable.

Before each subsequent sitting, Emerald introduced Paul to a new depravity. With each obscene intimacy, the portrait revealed more of the real inner Emerald. Paul became convinced that in all the city, no one knew Emerald as he knew her. He had wallowed in her darkness. Surely no other man had been so privileged.

With the tendons in his groin aching delightfully, Paul looked up at the woman he adored. "I can't move," he groaned. "If you wanted to sneak a look at your portrait, I couldn't stop you."

"Is it finished?"

"It must be. Even after what you just did to me, I can't think of a brush-stroke I'd change."

"Then I'll be patient. Bring it to my next soirée. We'll have a grand unveiling."

"In front of your friends? I thought this was to be private. Are you sure that you want them to see you . . ."

"As I really am? You must know by now, Paul, I have no shame. And now, as you have no more work to do and I have you to myself . . ." She pulled a transparent latex glove onto her right hand.

Paul shuddered but he didn't resist.

At her soirée, Emerald served absinthe from crusted bottles, so her coterie knew that the evening was to be special. An easel was already set up. Paul arrived and set a baize-covered frame on it. The glittering crowd gathered. At a sign from Emerald, Paul stripped the baize away, revealing a fallen angel, a lamia, a succubus, Satan's personal harlot. The assembly waited on Emerald for their cue, breathless.

Her eyes narrowed. Her lip curled. "I've seen better efforts in comic books," she drawled. Emerald's arm lashed out. Absinthe splashed. Paint dissolved and drooled.

Paul turned away, plodded to the balcony, sat on the balustrade and let himself topple over.

The Game had been played once more and Emerald had won, again. All of her friends laughed, but none so gaily as Emerald herself. They turned to her in amazement.

"Why?" a thin man in a plum velvet suit asked. "Why do you laugh, Emerald? When you ruined or disgraced all the others you only smiled. Why, then, do you join in our laughter now?"

"Don't you see?" Emerald replied. "I laugh now because of all the men and women I have destroyed, for idle sport, this is the first one that I loved."

SPIRIT OF THE SACRED WHORE

Cree Fox

SHE VISITS HIM in the guise of a princess, dressed in a lustrous red satin robe, her skin sweet with the perfumes of honeysuckle, jasmine and sandalwood. She lies with him on a couch spread with the skins of bear and lion and the languid buzz of bees around them. When the sky lights at dawn, she admits her identity and he is horrified. To think he has seen the nakedness of a goddess! She makes him promise not to tell, for she is forbidden to make love with mortals. But one day he is out drinking with his friends and they ask him if he would rather sleep with so-and-so or Aphrodite herself. He boasts, for he cannot resist, that he has slept with them both.

He calls his wife. I'm lying on the lounge wondering what I'm doing here. I don't belong with this suburban furniture, the photographs of his family framed in a glass case, the pile of books for his wife's university course, a drawing of his daughter's. I belong to none of this. He comes back looking apologetic. I hate him like this, so weak, so domesticated. I want him to forget where he is. I want him to forget everything except us, our coupling, our madness.

"Do you want me to say something erotic?" he asks me, narrowing green eyes.

"Do I look as if I do?"

"Yes."

We're sitting on the floor, eating salmon and mangoes. He's looking at me, quizzically, trying to read my mind.

"There's something going on between us," I say carefully, "some kind of energy happening." I refuse to get too drawn in, not wanting to say anything I would regret.

"You seem as if you want me to say something sexy, something provocative."

"Perhaps you do."

At the door, he holds me in a long embrace that has my heart thumping wildly and my legs feeling like they're going to fold up.

"We should meet outside the office," he says, ever the ethical one. "How about next Monday?" I think I say yes, or maybe I just look at him. Right from the beginning, he can read my mind. I hear every footfall on the stairs, down, down, down, down. I hear his car door opening, thudding closed, the sound of the engine starting, the car pulling away from the crossroads. He has left a smell behind, something manly and oily and sweet.

We are sitting in a jazz club listening and not listening to a pianist, scrambling over the keys in a frenzy. We are looking and not looking at one another. We are perched on stools, arms touching all the way down, legs touching. He's tapping his foot but not to the rhythm I hear. I can hear his breathing. I wonder if he's asthmatic because his breath sounds so loud and we can barely hear each other speak in here. Speaking and not speaking.

"Do you like this music?"

"Not really, it's a bit frantic for me. I feel a bit agitated."

"Then let's go and get dessert." He sounds firm. I don't resist.

When I lean over to kiss him in the car – because it's me who makes the first tangible move – it's like opening a door. Like a hot blast of air from the desert. Like a meeting of mouths after a long absence. I've been his client for nearly five months now. This kiss is like a long-awaited greeting. Kisses are the first kind of nakedness. There are many kinds of nakedness, each one sweeter and more fragile than the last. The saddest thing is to go there alone.

We go back to his hotel. I follow him in without hesitation. It is as if the whole world has totally dissolved and it's just him, and me.

What a lover! It's hard for a woman to forget a man who has loved her well. Today I send him a Christmas card saying I would love to share dessert with him again soon, either in Sydney or in his territory. He writes back in similar vein: *I've got the ingredients, you've got the bowl. We just need somewhere to cook it.* So when he does turn up again at my front door, it's not as a professional.

He rings me one hour beforehand from the car.

"I want you to do something for me. I want you to put on some black lace underwear and wear your suit over the top. Sit on a chair in the lounge facing the sunroom and blindfold yourself. Then pleasure yourself. And leave the front door open. Ignore any sounds and do as I say."

"Yes, of course."

I'm so excited my belly is churning. I do it. I do as he says, choosing an exquisite black lace bra and g-string and my cream linen suit. I wear lace-top stockings, which he hasn't requested but I'm sure he will appreciate. I sit in the middle of the room on a chair, my legs spread gently. My fingers slide down my belly and gently around my cunt, probing, gently playing with my lips. Anticipation has moistened me. I would like to see myself, glistening, the way he will see me.

I hear someone come in; the door clicks. I feel my fear –
wondering if it's him, wondering if he's alone. And even
wondering if he will hurt me. I hardly know the man. I
know him as a professional but as a man? What kind of man
would ask me to do this for him (and what kind of woman
would do it)?

Then slowly, as I touch myself, I feel his tongue on my
thigh and his tongue joins my fingers in my cunt. He eats
me expertly and wonderfully and I, who am blindfold
with a long silk scarf, feel every sensation, every note of
pleasure in my body and he drives me wet. I come,
screaming. He keeps touching me. He has put something big and hard inside me, not his cock. It feel
enormous and spreads me wide. I keep wondering if
there's another man there. These hands on my breasts
– are they his? His hands are not yet familiar to me and I
can't be sure. He's not saying a word – and that I know is
unusual.

He wants me to face a certain way. I wonder if he
has a video camera trained on me and that excites me
more. He pushes me off the chair on to all fours and fucks
me with this huge thing. The way he manoeuvres it inside
me is perfect; I come with a thump and the walls of my
cunt throb. I want to roar like a tiger. I feel so utterly
loose.

Then he thrusts his cock in my mouth and fucks my
mouth.

"Don't move. Don't move your mouth," he orders.
"Touch yourself. Rub those puffy lips of yours, make
that clit of yours stand right up. I'm going to come in
your mouth." I can hear his soft moans, feel him thrusting
in and out of my mouth and then I taste his sperm shooting
on my lips and then he rubs his cock milk on my face, on my
neck, on my chest, and as I taste his sperm in my throat, he
shoves his tongue in my mouth and we taste it together.

"Fucking fantastic," he groans. Then he removes my

blindfold slowly and when I see him, looking so wild in his
red singlet, raw and damp with sex, I kiss him and kiss him.
We lie together on my bed, stroking and kissing for ages. I
can't believe how it feels to see him again – it's like seeing
him for the first time. My energy is seething. I still want
him. I want him to fuck me.

When we touch mouths, without actually exchanging
kisses, the energy surges between us and we both tremble
and shake. Desire rises in me like a wild snake and I shout,
"Put your fingers inside me!" And orgasm again.

"I'm at your mercy, David," I tell him.

"Is that OK?" he asks tenderly. "Did I go too far? Did I
abuse you?"

"Let's go further," I urge him. "Too far won't be far
enough with you."

We meet on top of a mountain, ten minutes from his
marital home. Although the mists are swirling around the
tops and the trees steadily dripping rain, it is dry. We are
both anxious about the weather; time is short and I'm
about to go away for two weeks. We walk into the bush
and he shows me his special place, his cave. I enjoy
walking through the bush with him, the trees shiny red
and brown and yellow from the rain, the rocks gleaming
wet, knowing we are going to his cave to make love. His
lips on mine and his murmuring tell me that is what he
wants and I always want it when I'm with him. My divine
task is to make love.

The cave is magnificent. Huge. Sheltered, high enough
to stand in, with a view of densely growing gum trees and
the blue hills beyond. It is made for us. He leans me against
a rock where I had spread a towel and kisses me with
melting lust.

"Undress. Take off everything except your stockings.
Then I want you to prowl around the cave. Prowl like a
lion."

My clothes seem to fall off me with the gravity of my lust. I undress without a murmur. Words are mostly superfluous unless they are highly specific. He lets out a low moan as I walk around the cave in my stockings and shoes, my breasts full and pointed where the breeze touches them.

"I wish I had a camera." He watches me prowl. I feel divine. Naked in the cave in the bush while the trees drip heavy raindrops. So erotic.

He is laden with lust, wild with it. His face becomes hard, twisted with it, his lips in the shape of an "o". He pushes my hands down on a stone so I'm bent in a "v".

"This is a 'fucking stone'," he says. "Hold on to it." He fucks me from behind, in, out, sometimes hard, sometimes soft, quick light thrusts, slow, melting teasing entries and retreats. My cunt feels like liquid gold. I turn around to suck his cock. I'm squatting like an animal as he plays in my cunt with his fingers and I suck him so he almost explodes between my lips.

"You fuck and suck so good," he murmurs. I come with a yell. Then he leans me over a rock and wets my arsehole enough to slip inside. I feel like his compliant boy. It doesn't hurt at all, and it feels animal, primal, basic. He comes all over my arse and cunt, rubbing the semen over my back and my buttocks. Then, without stopping, sinks his fingers into my cunt and makes me come again.

"You're so sexy. You're more than sexy. You're sensational."

Later, as we stand looking at each other in a kind of awe and wonder that often follows sex, I say, "You're the lover of all lovers."

"It's because you ignite my fire. You are my fire. You're my goddess. You're my Aphrodite." He gives me a present, some lace panties he bought in a market and hid in his sock away from his wife. "I bought them to remind you of me while you're away. It will be like taking a part of me with you."

"It will never be enough."
"That's what keeps you simmering."

Flowing like a river, my woman's essence. Deep and mysterious, light and foaming.
Shimmering, shifting, iridescent, turquoise. Ocean wave. Woman, I am.

I smell my panties, which are intoxicatingly rank with our genital smells. I need one reminder at least, of him. Something physical I can touch and sniff. The jasmine of our genitals. David is my addiction, my demonic contact with bliss.

"I want to be your slave," David tells me. "It's not that I want to be beaten; just that I want to serve you. I want to obey your every whim. I want to bathe you, to wash your hair. I want to give you everything you want."

"You are my slave," I reply. "I have chosen you." I sit back on the cushion, my legs apart, while he touches me.

"Remember me like this," I urge him. "Watch my cunt. Watch my lips, my clit, my juices. Look at me carefully. Remember that wet, slapping sound, the redness of me, remember my moans and my cries. Remember the look of my cunt as she blossoms into orgasm."

He looks. He sits there gazing at my wide open cunt like a man possessed. I come, screaming.

I run a bath for him with lemon and lime bubbles and drop frangipani flowers into the froth. I picked them up from the pathway on my way back from the beach. I imagine how lovely it would look by candlelight. In the morning sun, it looks like a cloud of flowers. When he arrives at my door, I hold him to still my quivering. I can already feel my cunt moistening and the energy of my lust dancing in my blood.

He climbs into the bath. Without thinking, I place flowers on each of his chakras, then on his nipples and in the spaces between his thumbs and his gently curled fingers. Then I slip one frangipani stem inside his foreskin so it seems like it's growing on the head of his cock, which keeps nodding and lurching with my soft touch. I breathe softly on his skin. His chest and his back are much hairier than I remember, and the hair on his head is falling almost to his shoulders.

I place one hand on his root chakra and one on his forehead. He quivers and trembles with the energy flow in his body and seems almost as if he is weeping.

"You look so beautiful," he says. "Your energy is so strong when you're near me." I know it because I'm shaking too. I can barely take my eyes off him. His eyes are piercingly blue. They seem to go on for miles inside himself. I put each frangipani in a dish of shallow water and help him out of the bath. His cock is erect. I drape the hem of my dress over it and delight in its gentle quivering. Electricity snaps between us. Then I adorn him with two necklaces, tie one stocking around his head and put my gold lace g-string over his swollen cock. I have to resist the temptation to suck him. How wonderful he looks, bulging in gold lace. Then I lead him to the place I have prepared on my futon in the corner with sarongs and scarves and a vase of roses.

"You touch me in such a deep place. I become totally raw and naked. You have a rare gift. The gift of giving yourself."

He holds me tightly, moans, looks into my eyes, clasps me as if he will never let me go. Then suddenly becomes urgent, rolls on top of me, presses his cock into my pubic hair. I want to be penetrated to my core. He presses against me, his cock growing on my lips and edging them apart, until he sinks slowly into me. I cry out from the exquisiteness of the feeling and discover my infinite wetness again.

We stay like this for a long time, lying close together, his cock inside me, thrusting or gently pushing inside me, outside me. At times, we are both on a plateau of pleasure, resting in a kind of warm bliss.

"I can't believe how stoned we get on sex," he says. Then suddenly I want him faster and deeper.

I don't know how he knows.

He says, "You want me deeper, do you? Change position!" I lie on my belly, legs spread, and he's behind me, above me and thrusting in my cunt so his balls slap on my arse. Then he retreats, rubbing the head of his cock on my lips so I nearly melt with the subtlety of it. Then he rams into me again so I cry out because the pleasure of these two sensations is so exquisite. He's breathing hard. I love it, this outpouring of fuck energy in both our bodies.

"You are such a fuck!" he cries. "Such a fuckable, fucking woman!" He shoots into me and falls on top of me, his skin hot and wet.

"I'm a fucked woman," I moan. "Now I want you to eat me."

He eats me exquisitely. I'm sitting up so he can reach me easily. His tongue traces every part of my cunt, over my clit, down my lips, into my cunt, out, flicking. I love to watch him, his eyes closed, my pubic hair covering his mouth.

"I adore your pubic hair, the texture of it. I adore your big hard clit. Your lips seem to reach out and suck me in." He hums as he eats me and it feels like a vibrator with a tongue. I open wide like a sunflower. I reach out for the mirror on the wall and place it on the bed between my legs. It's so sexy. It's such a turn-on watching his tongue on my lips and seeing the bliss on his face. I watch for ages as he licks and sucks and nibbles my cunt, as his fingers slide in. I always wanted to see my own cunt being eaten, especially by such a connoisseur. He tells me I taste delicious and I feel myself flood in his mouth, my juices running over his lips, the heat spreading like honey through my belly and I take my flavour into my mouth as I kiss him.

*   *   *

"You're so beautiful when you're in your energy. I revere you. It scares me. Your energy is so strong. You're cruel."

"How am I cruel?"

"Just being you."

"But what do I do?"

"It's the unrelentingness of your energy."

There were two goddesses who had claims on the beautiful Adonis. One had arranged his birth from a myrtle tree; the other had rescued him from a chest and made him her lover. Each was wildly jealous of the other and wild about Adonis. The courts decided that he should spend one third of the year with one goddess and one third with the other. In the last third, he should be left alone and free of their sexual demands. But the goddess Aphrodite did not play fair. As long as she wore her magic girdle, Adonis was at her mercy. Her lover, Ares, grew jealous and, disguised as a wild boar, gored Adonis to death. Anemones sprang from his blood.

Today David takes out a necklace of black and gold stones and places it around my neck. "This is what you will wear when you want to play the game. I shall be your master and you will be princess. Will you obey me?"

"Yes." I am so sure that nothing he asks me to do could ever be unpleasant. His pleasure is mine. So I wear it. He orders me and I obey.

He ties my hands to two scarves hanging down from a hook in the lounge after I have bathed myself carefully with a cool cloth. He leaves me there, my arms raised to the ceiling, and after a while they don't ache any more. It's my cunt that's aching. He comes back and I hear a toilet flushing while he's touching me. And he says, "I've got a gift for you." And I know another man is there. I am terribly excited

David explores me for his and the other man's pleasure. He talks about me.

"See what a beautiful small arse she has. Look at her long, pointed nipples and puffy red aureolae. See how easily she is aroused. See how puffy her lips are, how they're gleaming wet from where I just brushed her with my fingertips. Oh, she pleases me well!"

He bends down and eats me out to a stupendous orgasm which has me growling and pulling on the scarves like a wild bear.

"Untie her," he orders the man. "Now, suck my cock." He looks at me with such tender brown eyes. "You're so beautiful. So beautiful." I suck his cock lovingly and then kneel with my hands on the stranger's knees and David fucks me from behind. The stranger's ample cock is flicking and flopping on its own. My face is so close to it, I can smell him.

After a while, he says gruffly, "You can touch me." I caress his cock while David fucks me. His cock grows so big; it's just about in my mouth so I let my tongue slide over it. It looks so inviting. It's much different from David's – circumcised, longer, thicker, darker, much more of a mouthful. But he doesn't make a sound. Just closes his eyes and moves his hips in time with my lips, in time with my hips, in time with David's cock. After a while I get totally distracted and come. I howl like a wounded animal. David picks up the roses from the vase and rubs them on my arse, petals raining down on me in a river of red.

"I've never felt so obsessed with a woman's sexuality as I do you. You are a magnificent woman. You are so perfect, your sexuality is so rounded, so blended. You are such a perfect mixture of male and female."

"You're woman, I'm man. You're man, I'm woman. You're yin, I'm yang. Who's fucking who, David?"

"Spread your legs, open yourself wide for me!" I open my legs wider, open my arms, lift my cunt up to him. He kneels before me, shoves his fingers in me. I raise my lips to meet him. I couldn't be more open, more loose.

"I love your milk. It's like your love juices coming out

everywhere. I love the way it creeps out through the holes in the lace, all creamy." He lets his fingers find my cunt. Slowly they climb up inside me. Then suddenly he fills me utterly, so fully, so strongly with his fist. I can hardly believe the sensation of it. I cry out.

"There's nothing you won't do!" he cries. "I put my whole hand inside you. And your cunt tasted so fucking amazing today. You truly are the queen of cunts! The cunt of all cunts!"

"And I shall give you my cunt. I shall give you my cunt for ever!"

He arrives today, his hair past his shoulders, curling above his shirt. When I sink to my knees to press my face into his crotch, I can see the hair above his belly. I find his cock with my tongue and caress the soft skin of his balls, nuzzling around the insides of his thighs and licking his perineum, pressing where he likes it and feeling this warm and pleasant hollow under my tongue. He sighs gently. His cock grows under my fingers: bigger, much bigger than I remember. I tear his shirt apart to see his nipples, which are gorgeously big and red. Then I bury his cock in my mouth, suck and slurp and slide all over him, till he can't stand up any longer.

I pull my head away, catch him swooning. "The goddess looked down from above and saw you and me and thought, they need someone to play with, and she brought us together. She brought us together for pleasure."

"You are the goddess," he moans. "You have the body of a goddess. You have the cunt of a goddess. There is only one way to worship you." And he falls to his knees and buries his head between my legs and caresses my clit which has grown so big and so fat. And his tongue consumes me. We consume each other. We are mortal fire, grown immortal.

* * *

Waking up with David is so sweet. Embracing his body with mine, feeling the sexual energy rising within us. Watching his eyes turn crazy with lust. Listening to my breath quicken. Hearing him moan with the pleasure of our caresses.

"I want to be inside you."

"Yes, oh yes. I want that too." Feeling him at the edge of my lips with his cock, pressing lightly, opening me gently. Feeling him sink slowly into the wetness of me.

Waking up is so exquisite. Feeling each other's sleep-hot bodies, slowly awaking each other's desire, the feel of sleepy smooth skin. The wetness of his mouth.

There is nothing more beautiful than the two of us lost in the bliss of early morning sex. Sometimes I forget he is only a mortal.

Today I dress him in my blue bikini bottoms and a sarong, spray him with my favourite perfume. He is my man-woman. His breasts have a sweet and heavy fullness I haven't noticed before. He has a jade bracelet around his balls. He asks for a drink and a banana. As I'm peeling the banana, I get distracted and slip it gently into my cunt, then into his mouth.

"I'm going to eat this banana out of your cunt. I'm going to suck on it as if you had a cock. You watch."

I do. I watch him sucking and eating the banana till all I'm aware of is the sensation of coming against his mouth.

"I get intoxicated by your juices."

"Foxed," I say.

"Let's play foxes." And we get down on all fours, sniffing and kissing and licking each other, grunting, growling, humming with the pleasure of it, rolling around, falling into each other's crotches, eating each other's flesh. He picks me up, wraps my legs around his waist, fucks me. I'm breathing so hard I think I'm going to faint.

"One day we'll explode," he cries. "All that will be left is a bit of lace, the jade necklace and some hair. We'll spontaneously combust!" He takes me to bed, lays me down, fucks me hard so his balls bounce off me, so the whole room jerks with our fucking. He stops, sucks my breast, drinks my milk.

"Drink the poison. Drink it all and you will die."

"Your poison makes me want to fuck you," he says, and does.

I look into his eyes, which are jade like the bracelet, which he has placed around my breast so the aureola and nipple protrude. He seems to be slipping away. "Yes. You're helpless. You're in my world now."

"I'm slipping away. Away." He sounds scared. He looks quite doped up, quite drugged. I wonder if I'm hypnotizing him. I get this rush of power inside me, shooting up my spine. Yes, I can hypnotize him. I climb off him. I sit gazing out the window, watching the waves heaving and pressing on the sand. The waves are white with foam, swirling to their own moon-led rhythm. I'm down on the sand, its softness under my feet, salt stinging my nostrils, the roar of the waves in my ears. I wander out into the sea, into the foam. There is nothing but the sharp blue sky, the passionate roar of the ocean, my body floating, so light. So virginal.

He has me pinned against the wardrobe, my skirt up over my thighs, his hands under my shirt and inside my pants, exploring me slowly and firmly. I'm not allowed to touch him. I succumb. My cunt puffs up and leaks honey into his palm and slowly, I orgasm, very strongly and sweetly to his touch. He's dripping juice on his T-shirt.

"Look at your clit! It's enormous. It's like a little cock standing up to greet me."

"My little cock is standing up to fuck you, David." I look down and swear I've grown a cock. I can even see the veins standing out against the flesh.

"Let's go and eat," he teases. Before we go, he chains me. He puts a gold chain around my right nipple, pulls it tight and then joins the other end to my left nipple. He puts my black necklace around my waist, then hangs my turquoise necklace so it falls just level with my little cock. He places the necklace he gave me around my neck. Like this I am his.

We eat. I love to eat with David, knowing we will make love afterwards. My delight in him increases. He asks me to remove my panties. Somewhere between the shellfish and the coffee, I have them around my ankles, damp from where he pleasured me before.

At home he pushes me against the kitchen sink and thrusts his cock into me. I go down on him, tasting me. There is a hollow below his balls, deeper than before, and a slight bunching of skin around it. There is a muskiness to him which intoxicates me and I lick in the hollow, round and round, over the new pink skin while he moans. His cock bobs above me. I suck him greedily, slurping and moaning until he has grown so big and wet I can barely take him.

"Slow down," he says gently. I open the fridge and take out a tub of chocolate sauce. I begin to paint his cock with chocolate and slowly lick it off. The chocolate runs over his balls and into the hollow in his perineum, catches in the folds of his skin which are almost lips. I suck him mercilessly, tease him to a thundering orgasm which leaves him gasping, and I imagine, almost in tears but his eyes are closed.

"You're my goddess," David tells me. "I worship you with my body. I want to spend the night with my goddess."

The hotel is set on top of a hill and looks out for miles to the ocean and all over the city. Our room has a spa bath which has a glass wall. We pull back all the curtains.

He fucks me on the dresser and my head knocks on the mirror. "I want to fuck you in every part of this room. I want you to leave your juices everywhere so the next people who stay here will be haunted by your spirit."

He is erect during the early hours. I play with him but he is asleep. I want to climb on him but it doesn't seem right to fuck the sleeping.

In the morning the sky is clear blue and reflects in the bathroom glass. The room is bathed in gold and David is golden, his hairs dark on gold, his body warm and languid. Oh the bliss of him inside me, the sweet honey pleasure of his cock lazily moving inside my cunt, sending tremors through my body and waves of heat in my blood.

"You are my goddess. I honour you with my body. I bring you gifts of love."

We make love as only we can, with tenderness, with heat, exploration, breath and surrender. I fuck his arse with my little cock, that by day grows bigger and more useful. Then I bury my face in his cock and balls and his cunt and his lips.

"You are the best. The best. The best!" He makes me cry today, bringing me to an intense spreading orgasm where the pleasure runs so deep it touches pain.

The goddess fell in love with the winged messenger, Hermes, who was a thief and a liar, but whose eloquence and business acumen could not help but impress her. Whenever he played the lyre, she sank into a deep reverie and awoke feeling fresh and sweet. They had a child, a young man with long hair and breasts like a woman. His name was Hermaphroditus.

David rings me in a total panic. He never rings me; it is one of our rules. But his voice sounds so broken and so scared, I take pity on him.

"I'm so bloody terrified. But I swear I've got a cunt. What will my wife say? What will she say when she realizes her husband has got a cunt?

"Oh dear. Do you think she'll notice?"

"Don't be like that; of course she'll notice! I know I said we don't have that much sex, but sometimes she wants it. What's she going to say?"

"Maybe she'll like it. A new dimension to your marital pleasure."

"Don't tease me, for Christ's sake. What am I going to do?"

"Maybe if you just keep the lights off . . ."

"For Christ's sake, I'm desperate! What the fuck have you done to me?"

"Desperate problems need desperate measures, David. Please come over."

He arrives with his hair in a long plait down his back, his eyes greener than the sea. I am stunned by his beauty, the hairiness of him, and the exquisite femininity of his male body. I can't remember ever being so moved by the sight of a lover. Tears sting my eyes. I feel the stiffening in my own groin and move towards him, longing to take him, longing to penetrate him to his very centre, that protected core where he has never let me go because he has a wife.

"There's only one way, David." I touch his firm, wide chest and the hollow between his small breasts. I let my fingers run down his belly to the place where I love to stroke him, that triangle of hair that leads to his cock.

"May I suck your cunt first?" he asks.

"You don't have to ask."

"I just thought I should."

"David, with you I can't say anything but yes." He lies between my legs and lazily licks my thighs, my lips, my big clit. The laziness of a man who knows everything there is to know about cunts, a man who always knows where to go with that magical mouth of his, that expert tongue. He's not in a hurry. He wants me to open my legs wider.

"I want to bathe my face in your juices," he says. His chin and his cheeks and nose are glistening with my honey.

"I love it when you say you want to bathe your face," I moan.

"This is the way of honouring a woman. The ultimate way."

"Yes. Yes. It is."

"This is how I honour the goddess." Seeing him drunk on my juices tips me down, down, down, down to a sweet, spreading hot climax. We lie awhile, all askew, my legs apart, and he looks straight into my mouth. Later, when he fucks me, his cock feels like heaven. He is lying behind me, lazily playing at the corners of my cunt and then pushing inside me. The feeling is so intense I cry out. We both cry out again and again with the fucking; it has never been so good, so sweet, so hot. I can feel his orgasm begin, hear him lost in his own pleasure and I follow his rhythm, the penetration of me feeling deeper and darker than I have ever known.

He is in bliss. His eyes are barely focussed. He shoots into me, collapses on me.

"No words," his face says to me and he shakes his head. "You're so fucking wonderful. Fucking wonderful." At that moment I reach out for the knife and bring it swiftly down below his belly. The movement is so deft, so swift, it is as if the knife had wings.

No one really knows how Aphrodite was born. Some say that she was the child of Zeus and Dione. Others say that she rose naked from the foam which gathered around the severed genitals of Uranus and then rode on a scallop shell to Cyprus. Others say she was born in a simple terraced house in Essex. No one really knows. But whenever she bathes in the ocean, she is reborn again as a virgin.

ROCKING HORSE

Jennifer Footman

ALEX ROLLED OVER onto his side of the bed. Soon his breathing became heavier and heavier as he fell asleep. Lydia touched his face. She cursed quietly. If only . . . if only sometimes he . . . Her body boiled with unsatisfied desire. Every nerve, every cell, demanded peace. She ached to be touched, to be stroked, to be licked, to be sucked, to be used in every way a man could use a woman. She craved to have Alex inside her again, again, again.

All attempts to get him to try something more than the fast "on-off, thank you, dear, sleep," had failed. Of course she had made love to other men. Some of them were exciting, some were considerate and most made her come. She loved Alex and wanted him. She dreamed of him wanting her in the same way she hungered for him. He should be desperate for her; he should never have had enough of her; he should walk around with a hard-on thinking of her.

The rocking horse was virtually finished. She had revelled in its restoration. It had been an exquisite find, almost the size of a small horse but in appallingly bad condition. Now, with some imagination, a bit of money and a lot of time it should bring in a good profit for them. The upholsterer, Fred, had done a truly professional job of stuffing and re-covering it. He had also replaced the mane and tail and painted the base back to its original post-office-red fire.

When she had been a child she had always wanted a rocking horse. It was ironic she should have one now, the ultimate one, for sale.

In the empty shop she basked in the company of the lovely things they sold. Alex was away for a two-week auction trip and she was taking the chance of doing some of the annoying jobs which never got done. She had worked through most of her list but the horse still needed to have the tail and mane combed and ribbons attached. Final little touches would make it irresistible.

Her face glistened in the heat even though it was six o'clock. London suffocated in a July heat-wave which gave no indication of letting up. Of course she could go upstairs to their flat and open all the windows but she liked the smells and little noises here. She slid the bolt across the door, flipped over the sign to "closed", turned the main lights off, clicked on the overhead fan and pulled down the blinds.

She had never had her rocking horse; but when she was a teenager she had volunteered in a local stable and worked with living horses every weekend. At first she was only permitted to brush the horses and dress their manes and tails. She was sure that their firm flesh and hard muscle below her hands had bristled to her touch. It had been heavy work but she had tingled with satisfaction to see the horses, all loose hair gone, their coats gleaming, respond to her caresses. She would hold the curry comb and feel as one with the horse under her care.

Then, months later, she was queen as the surge of power flowed through her body when she lifted herself into a saddle. The tight tension across her thighs had made her

nearly die with bliss. Weeks later, she was taught how to
rise to the trot. She couldn't wait for Saturdays, when she
knew she would ride high on the horse, ride high and
control the up and down, up and down, yes, sometimes a
slight touch when she would just feather the saddle.

The fan hummed gently as she worked on the mane. She
slipped off her shoes and overalls. What did it matter? At
this time of the evening she was permitted some comfort to
work, and the blinds were down and the doors locked.

The new scarlet velvet used for the body glowed in the
subdued lighting. She combed the mane and tail until every
hair lay in order. The bridle had already been saddle-
soaped and waxed and was ready to put onto the horse.
She lifted it and expertly placed it on the horse's face. The
horse's head was fine tooled leather and its eyes Venetian
glass. Reins made of spun black silk dangled on the body.
Once the bridle was in place it looked alive, vital, a genuine
fantasy beast. She stood back and admired her handiwork.
Yes, a find indeed. She had only once seen a horse as
massive as this and that was at an auction in Glasgow. It
had been sold for twenty thousand pounds.

Thank God she had been able to take some of the bulkier,
lighter things up to the flat to give her room for this creature
of dreams.

God, it was hot! The atmosphere was electric, tense;
there could be a thunderstorm. The blouse and bra had to
come off. What the hell! Everything. The lot. Jeans and
panties hit the floor and she luxuriated in naked freedom.
The slow motion of the fan circulated air onto her breasts.
Frozen for one moment, she let her body respond to the
faint draught. Her nipples rose into bright russet nuggets.

She examined the saddle and lifted it into place. It was
crafted from a heavier velvet than the body but still silky,
fine, thick. Against the scarlet body the purple saddle sat
like a throne, a mystic seat. The gold tassels and fringe
trimming it shimmered and trembled. She frowned. No;

though the saddle was enchanting, somehow she preferred the horse without one. The body seemed longer, the back more sinuous. She lifted the saddle off and placed it on a chair.

When she leaned against the rocking horse there was the same solid comfortable feeling she always got when she was near a real horse. Well . . . No one was watching. Why not? She would try it. It was her duty to test it and see if it functioned as well as it looked. She placed a foot on a stool and swung her body over the horse. She tightened her thighs onto the velvet and tentatively rocked herself.

On one occasion at the stable, when no one was about, she had ridden one of the boarders in the stable bareback. It had been quite a different experience to riding with a saddle. She had felt uncivilized, wild, primitive. The horse had been in control, not she. It had been summer and, below her thin cotton shorts, hot flesh had rubbed against the flaming area between her legs, opening her, loosening her. After that ride she had found touches of blood on her shorts and had imagined that in some way the horse had been her lover.

Yes, the smell of saddle soap, rich and aromatic, rose from the bridle. A man smell. She rocked a bit harder. How strange. How very funny. She looked down to see the glowing velvet between her white, white thighs. She rocked a bit more. The velvet moulded itself to her bottom. It had a life of its own as it moved and pricked against the soft fine skin of her lips and tiny red hole. Very faint creaking noises as she rocked. Rocking, rocking, she was free for the first time in months. Gone was the stiff, formal, business-like Lydia

Yes, each fibre of velvet moved in synch with each cell of her body. Tiny needles of silk, tiny, infinitesimal bantam strokes against her bottom every time she rocked back. Her vaginal lips opened to the body of the horse; the hole in her bottom, oh the tiny hole opened and flowered, flowered into a tulip, open wide. The rhythm of the horse accelerated. She bent forward to give her body more contact with the velvet.

What? Come on . . . What was happening? The velvet soaked against her turgid full lips. She ran a hand down and felt the wetness. The reins, their silken fibre cool against her palms, slipped through her hands and lay free on her thighs. She stroked and rubbed her thighs with both hands. This was bliss. Pure ecstasy. With one hand she opened her lips and with the other teased her clit.

A crack of thunder broke the air and lightning flashed through the small gaps in the blinds. Rumbling continued up and down, distant and near. Every now and then the building shook with the violence outside.

She crushed her buttocks hard, hard against the velvet. She demanded silk, fine silk against the softest area of her body. She ground into the fibres. She leaned back and placed her hands on the horse's flanks. She was wide, wide open: open to the thunder outside and the lightning which streaked and lit the room and the horse rocking, rocking below her. She gathered up some of the loose velvet of the saddle, gathered it into a sort of glove over her finger and stroked her clit. Yes, softer then her own skin, silkier than the secret, hidden skin inside her. Secret. Hidden. Spikes of ecstasy connected her breasts, her clit, her belly, her eyes, her face, her lips, her body. She was one with the soft prickles against her downy skin; she was part of the horse; all her orifices opened to the silk, the velvet, the . . . Yes, the dark tunnel, the secret of all places welcomed her own touch, welcomed . . . Legs stretched wide open as her heels dug into the side of the horse and she was lost. She rubbed and thrust her way over the mountains, into the clouds and above the earth.

No, she wasn't addicted. Never, not Lydia. Sure she was. She doted on it, she worshipped it. She was infatuated by the secret of it. She lusted for the motion and the stroke of those tiny prickles which were, at the same time, soft: they were nails, at the same time baby-flesh. She had to have it at least once a day. It was a vital part of her life. The fact that she had put a mad, totally unrealistic price on the horse was incidental. She would not sell the horse for any amount.

Alex had just finished setting out the new acquisitions, consisting of a delightful Victorian sewing basket, a nursing chair, two sets of silver canteens, some glass and half a dozen hunting pictures.

"What the hell is that price on the horse? You must be mad."

"What do you mean?"

"Wishful thinking."

"I like it and I think it must be worth twice that."

"Come on . . . can't see why. The damned thing takes up half the shop. Who would want something like that? We can hardly move upstairs, with the stuff you put there."

"I would like it, if I were a customer," she said innocently.

"Humph." He took out the silver kit and started to polish a vase which already shone like a beacon.

"Be miserable if you like. I think we'll get the price for it. If someone wants it they'll pay anything."

They had just made love and, as usual, Alex rolled over and gave every indication of being asleep. She slid out of bed and padded down to the shop. This had been the first chance she had for two weeks. They had been stocktaking. He had been under her feet all the time and she was getting desperate. It was as if all her passion was building up inside her and she would shatter with frustration, if she didn't get comfort soon.

She breathed a sigh of relief as she sat in the saddle. This was coming home. She sat rocking and her body responded in a conditioned manner to this familiar lover. Waves of

delight were like a tide coming in and out on a flat beach.
Trickles of motion. No, she wasn't a dog to respond like
some Pavlovian victim to the food placed in front of it. She
wasn't a dog to have its saliva collected from a fistula in its
mouth. No, she wasn't just an experimental animal.

Yet, the juices did flow. The velvet was warm with her
juices. Vagina lips swelled and filled with passion. Of
course she was conditioned to this and she could not
deny it. She wet her finger and ministered to her nipples.
They stood as bright as any beacons. "Rock me baby,
rock me, rock baby, rock me over the sea, over the
ocean." A teasing, searching finger, one that didn't
seem to belong to her, burrowed into her centre of love
and found her clit.

No, bad woman. This was not permitted. She pulled the
reins and wrapped them round both wrists until they dug in
hard and sharp. No, she could not touch herself. But she
was burning, burning. She tightened the reins with her
teeth. Yes. She leaned back, the reins still being held by her
teeth. "Rock, baby, rock."

She shivered. In a mirror reflecting another mirror, dark
in reflection, she saw Alex watching her from behind a
screen at the back door. So . . . let him watch and be
amused. She would perform for him and pretend ignor-
ance of her audience. She said to herself, "Yes, I will give
the performance of my life. Never will nipples be so
tempting and aroused."

Her breasts emerged as two white mountains tipped with
red, bright red snow. Legs rested on the horse's head as she
rolled and stroked and rubbed her clit. Fingers, though her
hands were bound, moved like snakes under her command
as she moved and tilted to accommodate them. Every now
and then she would stop and lick the tips of her fingers and
run her long thin nails through the velvet, marking it,
leaving tracks in it. The taste of her juices, sweet and sour
at the same time.

Through all this performance she watched his face in the dark reflection.

Horse and she were one. They were enveloped in the occult smells of leather and wax and woman and perfume and sex. Never, never had woman come so hard, so violently, stabbing against the horse's back, swallowing velvet deep into her, she was air, nothing but air, and she swore she flew right out of the window, flying on the back of her horse, flying.

That was the first time she was sure he had been watching. Oh, she had suspected before, imagined she had heard a noise, fabricated a creak or a rustle. But now she knew.

It was his birthday and she always arranged something special for him. This time she had pretended she had forgotten. No present, no card, no special meal, nothing. Just normal dinner and bed.

Lydia stood in the carved mahogany doorway gazing at the rocking horse. The air breathed still and heavy against her naked skin. The animal glistened in the candle-light; its mane shone as if it had a life of its own and the velvet body shimmered and glowed.

She had bought some glass bangles and leather anklets with minute brass bells sewed onto them. Bells and bangles tinkled, clinked, even as she breathed. She would keep all her mysteries to herself. Tell him nothing. This was his game and he could play it.

On the cabinet beside the horse, joss-sticks burned. She had found some strange joss-sticks in a seedy little shop in Catford. The man made them himself. "Potency power, my love, they have potency power. Make him go all night. Right they will." She had lit them earlier when she had lit the candles. The air in the shop was full of patchouli, lavender, sandalwood and candle wax.

The tiles of the floor shone, icy against her bare feet. She drifted over to the horse and mounted it; all the time the bangles and bracelets orchestrated their music.

This time she knew it was a performance; it was a command performance for his birthday. She mounted the horse and heard the tell-tale creak as he came down the stairs. She rocked, rocked absently as if she were nothing but part of the horse itself.

Last weekend had been a long weekend and she had tanned herself a bit too much, so her skin glowed brown at the same time with a touch of pink blush. She wet the tip of one finger and rolled her right nipple so it stood hard, hard and bright. Then the left.

Oh, she wasn't here; she was on a beach far away and waves lapped against her toes and the sun surrounded her breasts. Velvet slicked cool against the heat between her legs; silk reins zapped every nerve in her palms; saliva sweet as honey mixed with her own sex juices.

She heard him come in and stand beside her, but didn't look down or give any indication that she knew he was there. Her voice was under tight control not to shout, not to yell, "Come up here, come up and fill me with your body, come up and ride me just as I ride this horse. Fuck me, fill me, tie me, rope me." She ached for him to feel the prickly silk velvet between her thighs; yes, he had to run the silk mane through his fingers; he must tighten his calves against the solid stuffed velvet.

Hell, she couldn't pretend any more. She looked down and held out a hand. "Let me help you up, my love; come." He was naked and the tip of his cock positioned hard and arrogant against his belly, like a glowing beacon. He ran a hand up and down her back down to her buttocks and just into her hole. Her skin opened all its pores to welcome his touch. She was nothing but that magic area between her legs, that centre of love.

The night had turned the shop into a theatre. She and Alex were alone on a stage, and the only prop was the rocking horse. He came behind her and climbed easily onto the horse. He moved slowly, so slowly, as if he was moving through oil. His warm soft hands cupped her nipples. Hard tongue licked her back and he bit hard, hard into her shoulder. She shuddered with the mixture of pain and bliss. He bit her again and she forced her bottom against his cock. She would need nothing, nothing to come, to erupt, to be spent. She was ready for him now.

Below her soaking sex the velvet resonated. She ran the reins, the fine silk cool, up and down her clit. His hand wrapped hers and took over control of her body. Silk rope wrapped round and round his finger, he gently entered and filled her with it. The pad of his thumb stroked her clit. With one finger of his other hand, at the same time, he entered her back hole, entered slowly, gently, kindly – so slick, so fine, so good.

Just as she felt herself coming, erupting, he stopped and bit her hard again. She was sure he bit right though skin. She was at that point when pain became a peak of pleasure. "Yes, again." She demanded it again and again. It drew her into him, drew her into the horse.

He ordered, "Unclip the reins. Now." She did as she was told and leaned forward, released the reins from the bridle so they hung loose. He pulled her arms round her back and crossed her wrists and tied them together with the black silk.

He started to rock her, his hands on her waist. Just a tap at first and then more force, more rhythm. She lifted up and lowered, rose and lowered. With every movement her clit bloomed against the velvet. She smelt herself and the rich oily smell of the bridle leather. Her gaping sex pulsated against the body.

"Oh . . . Yes, yes."

He moaned and raised her up so she floated above him. "You have the neatest little hole, the loveliest little bum I have ever seen. I have to lick it. Yes, lovely, lovely." He lowered her onto the saddle and tilted her forward. "Up a bit, raise yourself up onto the neck. Yes, that's good. Right up – and now I am going into you. One finger, just one finger, a wet finger right into your little hole. Yes, my love." His tongue worked round and round and in and out of her tight little hole and then his finger entered her darkness, in and out and round and round until she felt she was spread wide, wide open and there was nothing of her she couldn't see. Now it wasn't his finger but his cock. It had slid in, entered, and its movement, its river-like sinuousness, filled her from toe to head.

His voice urgent and panting, "Come on, come with me."

She would bite the mane right off. Yes, heaven, pure heaven. Faster, come on, faster; come on; more and more, she had to have him and the . . .

He pulled out of her and, with both hands on her waist, he angled her forward and lifted the rear of her body off the horse. His tongue lapped round and round and her own juices dripped against the side of the saddle.

"My love," she groaned through clenched teeth.

He tightened the reins so they cut deep into the soft skin of her wrist. "I will rock you, rock you, rock you. Move a bit . . . that's good, just a bit. Yes, very full, full enough to take a horse into you, full. Let me smell you, smell that mix of leather and you and just you."

She rode further and further away, faster, faster, faster – until she was nothing but that burning area against the saddle and him stretching, opening, licking, wetting her. So gently she felt him enter her electric pulsating vagina and she rode on him, speared on his giant cock, riding and lifting her; all the time his fingers rubbing and petting and his cock deep inside her. She was impaled on his cock. He gushed into her and she screamed deep inside her throat as she came and he thrust against her again and again: and she was full of leather and Alex and . . .

HE'LL HAVE TO DIE

Maxim Jakubowski

THE WIND WAS howling like an apprentice banshee outside
the hotel windows. The Bloomsbury pavements were wet.
It was dark and cold, a Dashiell Hammett kind of night.
Completely the wrong weather for the season.

"Are you sure you still want to do this?" Caitleen asked
me.

The warmest place would be between the sheets.

"Yes," I told her. "I haven't come this far to just stand
and shiver."

"Undress me, then," Caitleen said.

The drive through the rain had felt endless: trying to find
a hotel room for the night, parking on double yellow lines
and frantically inquiring about vacancies from bored-look-
ing duty clerks or managers, hoping all the while that back
in the dulling cocoon of the car she would not change her
mind.

Again.

As she had, once already back in July, fearful of taking
that final, decisive step that would have seen us become
lovers. Her hesitation at the final hurdle had thrown me
into despair.

But tonight, squeezed into the corner of a small unfashionable Clapham bar, she had suddenly said, "Yes, I
will."

At first, I hadn't quite understood. My mind raced back
to our aimless, low-key conversation. What was she refer-
ring to? My eyes must have betrayed my puzzlement.

"I will sleep with you," Caitleen had said.

"Really?" was all I could gracelessly say.

I had taken her hand in mine.

"Tonight. Find a place," she added quickly.

"Now?"

"Yes. I've told him I had to go to Birmingham for my job
and wouldn't be back until tomorrow. It's safe."

I had quickly asked for the bill and we'd made for the
darkness and the centre of town.

Where sinful beds were available if you had the will and
the cash.

I'm a master of fantasies. For a scene like this I would have
imagined a wonderfully emotional, magic soundtrack. Not
massed violins: more of a sensuous, sad electric guitar solo,
slide, steel or even dobro. With echoes of country. But I'd
had no time to mentally prepare. This was all too unexpected. Silence would have to do. The sound of real life
special occasions.

I moved closer to Caitleen.

Her coat was wet and heavy, but she had dried her hair
with a thin towel from the hotel room's bathroom on
arrival.

"Allow me."

I helped her out of it and draped it over the back of the
only chair in the room.

"Put the light out," she asked me.

"No," I said. "I want to see all of you."

"Must you?"

"Yes, I insist," I added.

I unbuttoned her black leather waistcoat and felt her warm breath on my cheek. Kissed her throat with all the resources of tenderness that I could summon from within the fear that rose inside me on a wave of apprehensiveness and greedy desire.

She raised her arms upwards and straightened them as I pulled the flimsy white top over her face and long tousled hair. She kicked her shoes off. I did likewise.

I kissed her again, my tongue tracing the soft contour of her lips, systematically licking away the final remnants of her lipstick, felt the jagged resistance of her teeth as I probed further. My hands tightened around her waist, pulling her towards me. Our mouths stayed joined together. Humidities mingling in another escalation of our intimacy.

So many questions assailed my mind but I tried to blank them out.

The wind kept on roaring outside, shaking the window panes with every new savage gust. Was this to be a hurricane night? A once-in-a-lifetime London twister of a storm?

Our lips separated as we gasped for air. I got down on my knees and helped her out of her jeans, her long unending legs emerging from the material as it rolled down from waist to thighs to white-socked feet.

Caitleen was now in her underwear.

I avidly drank in every scent rising from her unclad body.

I rose to my feet, gazing in awe at the whiteness of her flesh, the flimsy black bra and briefs that concealed so little.

"You're beautiful," I told her.

She loosened my trouser belt.

We kissed again.

The room around us lost its focus and the force field of our desire grew stronger with every continuing moment of physical contact.

As my hands wandered over the wondrous acres of her

unveiled skin, I relished the silken softness, familiarized myself with the outer texture of her body, mapped the topography of delicate curves, the gentle swell of her small breasts, the blinding heat that rushed through the thin material as my fingers lingered over the mound of her sex.

The indiscreet camera inside my brain recorded every detail. A beauty spot. A small scar. An imperfection. The way her eyes peered at me with curiosity and, dare I say it, love? The subtle grain of her epidermis. The cabalistic distribution of darker moles along the map of her body. I knew already that these stretched-out moments would have to last me a lifetime.

"Your shirt?" she asked.

I undid the buttons and allowed her to pull it off and away from me. She avidly buried her fingers through the streaky maze of my chest hair, as if it were a totally new experience, relishing the novelty of another man's particularities.

My own hands cupped her breasts, slipping with no resistance between them and the material of her bra. Getting drunk on the warmth of her softness; a nail grazed a nipple, and I felt it harden, lowered my lips towards it.

She moaned.

Disengaged from my tentative embrace and took a couple of steps back towards the bed that dominated the barely-furnished hotel room. Sat down on it.

"Fuck me now," Caitleen asked.

Standing there, I shed the rest of my clothes, facing her, our assorted attire in a small crumpled pile on the brown shag carpet. She brushed her hand against my growing cock. I knelt down and indicated she should raise herself slightly as I pulled her knickers down, revealing the flattened darker curls surrounding the warm territory of her cunt. Her pungent, released odour wafted towards me, and I immediately became drunk on it. I looked Caitleen in the eyes. She nodded in approval. I lowered my lips towards her.

"Oh, Jesus Christ!" she said.

So began the slow, slow story of how I die.

We made love with lingering compassion. Copulated, fucked, shagged, screwed wildly with lingering compassion well into the night and all the way through to a grey morning. Every new first time is like a rebirth, something so desperately unique it marks you forever. It was no different for us than it was for no doubt a hundred or so other couples doing the dirty that same night among the thousand and more regulation-shaped rooms of the Bloomsbury area and its countless hotels.

Caitleen.

When pleasure threatened to overtake her, she would invariably clench her teeth and mutter, "Christ, oh God!" under her breath. I soon began to measure the intensity of our lovemaking by the punctuation of her quietly blasphemous vocal interruptions. And her long drawn-out sighs as we moved in and out of each other. Of pleasure. Of guilt.

I don't think I slept at all that night.

She did. In patches. Exhausted by our frenetic gymnastics, overcome by the sexual frenzy of it all. Not much. But enough for me to lie by her side on the bed and admire with wonder the way her chest rose in her sleep and her skin silently irradiated desire, in these drawn-out minutes of leisure unbelieving the sheer beauty of her features in repose, the line of her cheekbones, the hypnotic tangle of her hair, the curve of her shoulder, all the things that made her so dear to me. Quickly, she would somehow sense that I was there, watching her in the penumbra, and her eyes would open, aware of my persistent gaze, and her lips would invite me back towards her.

An invisible request I could not disobey.

I would taste her again and soon my fingers were wandering wildly across her skin, awakening points of lust among the softness and the sweat. One touch was often enough, bringing the fire to life again as if it had never even been dimmed, and we would devour each other again, pushing ourselves to the limit, trying every geographical and anatomical position in search of greater degrees of mutual combustion. And by trial and error we somehow did everything right. There were no limits, no shame to anything we did.

Everything seemed natural. Innocently self-evident. This was how to make love: how our bodies fitted together by wonderful design.

From that first night together on, I knew we were made for each other and that my life would never be the same again.

Whatever happened.

The way she would take me deep inside her mouth, her throat and tongue joyfully cleaning away in one gulp all our joint secretions.

How she would shift to invite even deeper penetration, the shallowness of her breath welcoming just the right amount of violence and pain.

Her long fingers, her tongue exploring the deep valley where my desire was most acute, moving with excruciating slowness across the ridge of my swollen balls down to the odorous depths of my darkness.

Her lack of shame or inhibitions had my heart in instant meltdown.

Between the sex, we spoke.

Of experiences past, people, partners, things and such. But we knew that the conversation meant nothing and was just a pretext to fill the time between the fucking, while our bodies, or rather mine, accumulated enough energy to make the act possible again. At times, the thirst in the sparkle of her eyes was enough to harden me within an instant, as she looked down at the soft cock nestling between my spread thighs with gentle irony and hunger.

Bathed together, the tepid soapy water overflowing onto

the tiled floor of the narrow hotel bathroom, my wet fingers teasing her nipples into pink hardness and she moaned, "Not again."

"Yes, again," I said, raising myself from the tub and carrying her dripping from the bath, accumulating a trail of water stains across the hotel room carpet, spreading the ample form of her white body out on the bed, opening her legs at their appetising widest and digging my face into her soaking crotch. Let my mouth and tongue do the talking inside her damp warmth.

"Christ, oh God!" she said, in predictable response.

Then, quickly,

"Enough! I want you inside me. Now."

The serious talking, wives, husbands, life, would have to wait for tomorrow or another damn day.

We fumbled our way toward ecstasy.

I walked over to the windows and pulled the heavy curtain aside.

"Breakfast?" I enquired.

"You bet!" Caitleen said. "I'm famished."

"I'm not surprised," I chuckled.

"Do you think they have room service?" she asked, turning in bed toward the nearby telephone, one breast slipping out from between the white sheets, seeking a possible menu among the various hotel brochures and the Gideon Bible in the bedside drawer.

"I'm sure they do."

She found the laminated plastic sheet and examined it.

"I want the whole lot. Eggs, bacon, sausages, tomato and mushrooms," Caitleen said, with a glint of mischief in her eyes, both her breasts now peering daintily above the crumpled material of the bed sheets. "And lots of toast," she added, throwing the menu towards me.

"No kippers?"

"No. There are limits to my turpitude," she said.

"Thank goodness," I remarked, walking back towards the bed. "I would have to call the whole thing off if you'd been a kipper person, you know?"

"You bastard."

She aimed the remote at the television. A weatherman was going on at inordinate length about the freaky weather.

It was August in London. The town was full of tourists humping shopping bags and brandishing cameras. It was a Tuesday. How come I remember that so well? We had become lovers at last, and it was unforgettable.

Foolishly, I thought it could only get better.

There were good moments to come, of course, but on the whole it did get worse, Much worse.

"And cereal. And lots of milk," Caitleen asked, as I ordered breakfast over the phone, her cheeks still flushed from our earlier excesses, her mouth only inches away from my dangling cock as I stood by the bed, vainly attempting to hold my stomach in and cut a somewhat more elegant posture.

"It'll be about a quarter of an hour," I told her, putting the receiver down.

"Whatever shall we do in the meantime?" she said, her fingers extending towards my tired genitals.

"I know you'll think of something," I smiled.

"I'm quite sure I will," Caitleen said.

I drew nearer to the bed.

"When is he expecting you back?" I asked, part of my brain already back in the real world.

"Who cares?" she said brusquely.

As she brushed teasingly against my cock, a sudden urge overtook me.

"Gotta pee," I told her, moving away from the bed.

She threw the covers and the sheets aside, stepped regally from the bed, her tall frame invading my horizon. She did look truly wonderful, quite naked as she was. A natural. The object of my affection. I lingered over the spectacle of her small breasts and their gentle upward tilt, the wide, strong hips and their captivating centre of gravity, her still damp public hair, its million curls parting to reveal the dark red engorged lips through which I had ventured all night in search of unaccountable pleasure.

"I want to watch," she said.

"What? You're mad."

"I'll even hold it. Please," she pleaded.

"You're really crazy," I said. "I love you."

And I realised this was the very first time I had said the fateful words "I love you" to Caitleen. All night, even in the indescribable throes of passion, a part of me had held back, not wanting to say the words, even as I thrust relentlessly into her and sought to consume her in the rage of my passion. I knew it was too early. Not yet. Not quite yet. And now it had just slipped out. So naturally.

She followed me into the bathroom. We hadn't emptied the bath water a few hours before. She dipped a finger in it.

"It's cold," she remarked.

Then turned towards me, impishly waiting for me to urinate.

Sensing my hesitancy, she said:

"You can watch me afterwards, if you want."

I felt like a right pervert, transfixed by the quiet arc of water spurting out through the slightly wrinkled lower lips of her cunt. She kept on smiling at me, in a knowing sluttish and childish way, enjoying the sight of my embarrassment, sneakily observing the spectacle of my unavoidable excitement as my cock began to harden in response to the spectacle of such daring intimacy.

"Do you like it?" she asked me.

"I do." I could not lie. My body would only betray me.

The trickle came to a slow end.

"Lick me clean," she demanded.

I knelt down on the floor, my face entering the daring territory between her open thighs. Witnessed a last drip.

I obeyed.

"I've always wanted a man to do that to me," Caitleen said, with a sigh of satisfaction.

My tongue retreated from her half-gaping lips.

"Is there anything else you've always wanted but never could have?" I asked her. Thinking all the time of her damn husband.

"To be fucked in the arse," she calmly said.

"You've never?"

"No. He's much too conservative for that," she said, reading my thoughts. "Have you ever done it?" she enquired.

"Not very often," I admitted.

"What was it like?"

"A bit awkward," I revealed.

"Practice could make perfect," Caitleen said.

"I suppose so," I said, unsure whether this was a signal.

We didn't experiment that day. More common pleasures of the flesh were enough for us, and we had to interrupt another hectic bout of lovemaking when room service finally knocked at the door. We'd almost forgotten.

Check-out was at noon.

I suggested we stay another night.

"No, Joe, I can't," Caitleen said. "Two nights, he'd become suspicious. I don't want to take that risk. I've never been away for work more than a day before. It would feel wrong, all of a sudden."

I meekly agreed.

"We can still have lunch," she proposed.

"That would be great."

As we left the hotel and melted among the crowds of holiday makers milling around Russell Square, we each nervously looked in both directions for possible familiar faces in the vicinity. But we were quite anonymous. Sin might have been etched deeply under the skin of our bodies, but we looked quite normal on the outside.

We walked past the British Museum, uneasy. Wanting to maybe hold hands, but not able to. Feeling conspicuous in public together. Our conversation was rare and strained. We drifted into Soho and decided to eat Indian at Dean Street's Red Fort. We requested a table at the back, where no one outside could see through the street window of the restaurant.

Eating together. My mistress and me. Her lover and her.

"It was good," I said.

"Yes," Caitleen said.

"Really good . . . The sex, I mean," I added pedantically.

"I know," she nodded, perusing the menu.

"I felt so close to you, I . . . It wasn't just the sex, you see . . ." I mumbled.

"I understand," said Caitleen.

"I wanted to say that . . ."

"Don't, Joe. Don't say anything that you might regret, please. Not now." She was going to add something to the still-born conversation, but the turbaned waiter approached the table to see if we were ready to order. We were.

Most of the meal continued in relative silence. A group of Japanese businessmen occupied the table to our left, while a trio of advertising executives drank heavily on our right, arguing the respective pros and cons of the government's ban on alcopops and the direct consequences for some of their respective accounts. It was impossible not to eavesdrop on them. Another good reason for neither of us to be particularly communicative or loquacious.

We were slowly sipping our coffees.

"What now?" Caitleen asked.

"What do you mean?" I queried.

"I told them at the office I'd be away all day on research business. My train home is not for another few hours."

"Drink?"

"Yeah . . . Where? The pubs are closed and I don't think I could stand another hotel bar."

"The Groucho's down the road. I'm a member."

"Great. I've always wanted to go there."

"I want to see you again," I told Caitleen.

"Of course," she said. She had just returned from the basement toilets where she had readjusted the bright lipstick on her beestung lips. "Did you think I want things to stop? I want more, Joe, like you."

"Good."

"Next time, it'd be nice to do something normal," Caitleen remarked.

"What do you mean by something normal?" I asked, not quite sure what she meant.

"Like seeing a movie, for instance. We can't spend all our time in bed."

"Perish the thought."

"I know," she smiled at last; the first time, I reflected, since we had left the Bloomsbury hotel.

So, the following week, we caught an American indie production in a small screening room off the Tottenham Court Road, meeting up in the cinema's foyer shortly after she had left her office around six. The film was full of shattering, loud explosions, gun battles and breathless chases down unending blacktop highways and Technicolor landscapes. But neither of us could concentrate on the action, painfully aware of the other's presence and intoxicating warmth nearby, fingers surreptitiously grazing knees and thighs in the surrounding darkness.

We almost ran out of the movie house as the credits unrolled on the screen. We didn't even speak. I had the keys to my office and within a minute of locking the door behind us we were tearing at each other's clothes and embracing frantically on the thick-carpeted floor. Caitleen insisted on keeping her stockings and garter belt on as I eagerly raised her rump and entered her from behind with little in the way of foreplay. She was already soaking and my erection buried itself inside her like a well oiled drill.

We fucked.

The sound of our breath and deep sighs the only sound in the otherwise empty managerial office in which I usually processed mountains of paperwork in quiet contemplation. As I pushed still harder into her, Caitleen turned her head towards me, a bemused look on her face as she watched me labouring. What could she be thinking? I wondered, the rhythm of my thrusts assured and repetitive, shaking her body, spasms rippling all the way down from her cunt to her gently hanging breasts as she willingly accepted the metronomic movement I was imposing on her, riding the waves of pleasure, indulgent in the lust that kept us in its thrall.

I was about to come inside her.

I literally felt like screaming and as the release surged onward from the hollow of my stomach, through my innards to the tip of my warmly-embedded cock, I suddenly corkscrewed a finger into her other aperture, as its small crevice dilated slightly with every successive forward thrust of my penis below.

Caitleen shouted, "Jesus, Jeezuuuus!" but I knew it wasn't pain.

We came together and collapsed, still intimately entwined, onto the rough fabric of the industrial-issue carpeting, hastily trying to catch our breath as the room seemed to spin madly around us, as if the whole planet was out of control. It wasn't; but we were.

"Wow," Caitleen said. "That sure was intense."

I silently nodded my agreement. My throat was parched and speech felt beyond me right now.

We finally disentangled.

"Shit!" she remarked. "I've left a stain on the floor. I think my period's begun. I'm sorry, Joe; I wasn't expecting us to get it together tonight, somehow . . ."

"It's okay," I answered. "No one is going to notice or

put two and two together. The stain will fade away eventually."

There were only soft drinks in the small office fridge. I seldom entertained there. Cuddled together with our backs to the heavy oak desk, we drank slowly, lost in thought. The minutes remorselessly ticked away to the time of her last train to the suburbs.

She separated from me and rose from the floor. She began to dress. With every successive garment she slipped on, the harder my desire for her became. Never had a reverse striptease appeared so indelibly alluring to me, and a fully dressed young woman looked so sexily naked.

"I don't want you to go," I pleaded. Unconvincingly.

"I must," she answered.

"Stay longer," I asked Caitleen. "You can get a cab back later. I'll pay."

"No, Joe. It wouldn't work. He'd realize something was up. He knows the train timetables. Might actually be waiting at the station for me. There's no way I could explain it."

Caitleen returned to her husband, after we arranged another meet five days later. I caught a cab back home. Another late night entertaining clients, I explained to my wife. I don't think she believed me. But she remained silent, curiously uninquisitive. I had reached the point when I didn't care. Only Caitleen mattered.

Another evening, another fuck.

I couldn't use my office premises. Something or other going on, one of my partners in the practice, someone who worked on the necessary legitimate side of the company, having a drinks party, I think. And my office was just too close to the seldom used boardroom for our frenzied and lustful activities of the flesh to go unnoticed.

Soho Square. A wooden bench. A stolen public kiss. More frustration.

"I just can't stand this any more."

"Do you wish to break it off?"

"No, that's not what I mean. At all."

"So? Tell me."

"I want all of you. I just don't want to have to share you with him all the time. To know in my mind that he can still touch you at night in all the places that I did after you return to his bed . . ."

"To our bed. He is my husband."

"He doesn't deserve you."

It was September. The storms were but a distant memory. The weather was again oppressively warm and humid. The sky was still pale blue past nine at night. Caitleen wore a thin T-shirt and no bra. The muted curves of her breasts pressed gently against the thin material.

"Come away with me. We'll go to the South of France, to New York, I don't know, Prague, they say it's nice there. Anywhere . . ."

"I can't Joe, I can't . . ." She was almost in tears. Imagine my own state.

Pale pocked moon rising above London. Our hands gripped tight.

"What can we do?" I asked Caitleen, almost rhetorically, not even expecting an answer from this no-exit emotional road we were stumbling along, reinventing the gestures of passion and the meaning of despair as we advanced blindly.

"He won't let me go quietly," she said. "No way."

"I think my wife will," I said. 'There'll be a bloody fight. But I'll manage. Somehow or other. I'd go through with it. What about you?" I asked her.

She avoided my eyes, turned her head away and gazed at the small pavilion that formed the centre of the square.

"Then there's no alternative," Caitleen softly said.

The warmth of her body was like a pool in the advancing darkness of night.

"He'll have to die," she added.

"Yes," I heard myself saying. Sealing my fate.

THREE OF CUPS

Cecilia Tan

MAGDA BREWED CHAMOMILE tea with a touch of comfrey in it for me. I could smell it steeping from where the cup sat on the white Formica counter of her kitchenette, familiar and meant to be comforting: chamomile to help me sleep and comfrey to help clear up any bruises she might have inadvertently introduced to my flesh in the course of the evening. But tonight I sat with the comforter wrapped around me on her futon, watching her busy herself with spoons and saucers, and I wondered if, for once, she might not ask me whether I wanted to stay up, or if I wanted to *keep* those bruises. Magda and I had been together for a year now, a year come Solstice; a year of becoming familiar to each other, a year of setling. A year when, once a week, I would come to her place and submit to her touches and tickles and her whips and paddles, and she would send me off into space, into that special bliss that we worshipping masochists know. Or she would at least try to. She carried the tea over to me and sank into the covers next to me. She was brownly naked, the black gloss of her hair unbound and covering her back like a short cape. My goddess in flesh.

I took the cup and breathed the steam. It wasn't like me

to be so moody after a scene. PMS, I told myself: the universal paean.

She broke the silence, not noticing my mood. "Oh, I forgot to tell you. Those fire-dancers from Santa Cruz aren't going to make it to the meeting."

"Why?" In the year we'd been together I'd not only become a fixture in Magda's life, I'd also become Programming Chair of Leather Pagans United, her spiritual, political, and sometimes problematic family.

She shrugged and sipped her tea. "I don't know. They just said they can't, and to tell you."

"Dammit, Magda, you should have had them talk to me."

She arched her eyebrow in that High Priestess way of hers, but the way she looked at me from under her lashes suggested little girl guilt. Magda could be a contradiction sometimes. "There wasn't anything you could do."

"I could have gotten them to reschedule, maybe, and swapped someone into their place. Jesus, Magda, the meeting's only two weeks away."

Her pouty look turned to a glare at my pronunciation of the J-word.

"I'm sorry," I said automatically. I wasn't going to have another version of our long-standing argument over swear words. She was always coming out with fake-sounding stuff like "By the goddess!" whereas my theory was, swear by using a deity you *don't* like, not one you do. When I wanted to needle her, I could make up some pretty fake-sounding stuff, too, like "Satan take my bicycle!" But not tonight. Tonight, I was annoyed already. "I'll have to come up with something else."

She crossed her ankles and leaned against the perfect white of her apartment wall. "Maybe it's time to do another mutual respect workshop."

"But last month was the relationship round table."

"I know, but I think some people could use a refresher." Her dark eyes looked into her tea.

"Like who?" I blew on my tea, trying to look nonchalant.

"Like Isa," she said, puckering her lips a tiny bit. "I've been hearing some things."

I blew on my tea some more. If I waited long enough, she'd tell me. And so she did: rumors, hearsay, gossip, and dish, which amounted to a probable suspicion that Ms Isa, a Top who considered herself a mere second to the Supreme Goddess herself (hence her interest in a spiritual group like LPU) was coming down with a case of Top's disease. No one had come forward and accused her of being a lousy partner, but we hadn't been seeing as much of some folks as we used to, and rumors did get started somehow. And seeing as how Magda felt she was bucking to take the High Priestess role for herself next year, Magda wanted to know the truth. "I can't let someone who doesn't respect her tools lead the worship," she finished. "If she doesn't respect her bottoms, she's not channelling the goddess; she's just on an ego trip."

"One way to find out," I said, setting aside my cold, full cup. "One way for sure."

If I thought it was going to be difficult, if I thought I was going to have to flirt with Isa and insinuate myself like a spy, I was wrong. After the meeting Magda walked up to Isa and told her she wanted her to take me on for a night, a preliminary to a public worship next month. Isa said sure, she'd e-mail me about convenient dates.

That's how I came to be riding down the Pacific Coast Highway to Swanton on a Saturday afternoon. The music of my own anxiety and nerves played inside my helmet as my reflexes led me around the curves, sometimes making a little voice: *Come on, girl; good girl; that's the way. Nice. Keep on going; keep on moving. That's it, that's a girl* . . . and whether I was talking to myself about the ride or my destination I wasn't sure. I had a reputation with the Leather Pagans as a bottomless bottom, a tough one, like

I could stand up to anything. And, yeah, I had been through a lot, especially since coming to the Bay Area three years ago. But maybe having a rep was worse, because I wondered if that meant people would go further than they normally would. And, tough or not, I had never outgrown that special chill of anticipation when it came to a new Top, a new unknown, something new to fear.

I pulled off the highway at a tiny embankment, with five parking spaces and a weather-worn picnic table. With my helmet perched solid on the sissy bar, I swung off the bike and walked to the cliff edge. Below me, a living moon of tidepool craters glistened in the late afternoon sun. I'd taken this road all the way down to Monterey many times; I'd seen the aquarium exhibits of anemones and hermit crabs and star fish. Here they lived as they had for thousands of years. If Mother Nature could create an organism that looked like a flower but could eat a fish, it didn't seem unlikely that she'd create a person like me.

And what was Isa; did she have a poison sting, too?

She lived in a surprisingly suburban ranch-style house, like one you'd see a dozen of in different colors along any housing development east of the Mississippi. Swanton was a mixture of run-down-looking fisherman shacks and cliff-dwelling mansions with a few odd normal houses like hers. She had converted the "family room" into a full-blown dungeon with leather-padded sawhorses, a St. Andrew's cross, and a wall covered with nasty-looking implements and bondage gear. I had a quick look at it before dinner when she gave me a tour of the house.

We sat down to eat on her back patio, where we couldn't see the ocean but we could see the sun set. She'd grilled vegetables: zucchini and red peppers and huge portobella mushrooms, mushrooms that you eat like a steak, with a knife and fork with juice dribbling down your chin. It was while digging in to one of those that she remarked, "God, how I miss beef sometimes."

I kept chewing. If I couldn't chime in sympathetically, it didn't seem polite to say anything.

She raised an eyebrow at me. "Are you . . . vegetarian?"

She meant aren't you, but I shook my head. "I know, I know, I'm the sacrifice. I should have some sympathy, some kinship for the lamb. But nature, the Goddess – whoever – made me a predator, too. And I try to . . . stay true to that nature."

She smirked, a little teriyaki sauce in the corner of her lips. "Well, you know, I didn't give up meat for spiritual reasons. I saw one too many meat-packing documentaries and decided it was time to quit." Her tongue snaked out to catch the sauce and there was no doubt in my mind she was as much a predator as I. Her hair was black, too, but not the wavy cloud that Magda's was – more like a smooth helmet that covered her head and neck and shone with bright bits of red in the sunlight. She could have been anything – Hispanic, Italian, Middle Eastern – but my guess was Filipina. Which got me thinking about Roman Catholicism and stuff (did she say "God", earlier?) and wanting to talk to her about becoming pagan, what road she had traveled to arrive at that choice . . . but whatever I might have said stayed under my tongue as she stood. I felt something change, her power come to her, the subtle shift that was the scene beginning.

"Your nature," she breathed, echoing my last words. "Your nature is to serve Her. To serve Her by serving me. To submit to Her by submitting to me. To perform with me this rite, of your own choice and will."

I felt that required an answer but I did not know which to give. Amen; I do; yes, ma'am . . . I nodded silently.

She went into the house and I followed her, trying to make my mind a blank, to make myself a vessel for whatever this Priestess would pour into me. But through my mind were playing a hundred other scenes: a dozen other first times with other Tops, other women I had given myself to in the name of the Goddess. There were always patterns; there were always things to be expected. So of course I was guessing. With all that equipment I wondered if she would be the type who would immobilize me, make me feel her iron grip, and then lay into me with everything she had. Give it to me with both barrels, baby, I thought, my skin tingling. *I can do this, I can do this,* came my little voice again, the agitated music preparing me for pain. *I can do this.* In a basement off Divisadero I'd been whipped until blood was drawn. In an open field north of Muir Woods I'd been placed against a tree and whipped with freshly cut sticks. But usually I was tied to a bed, or secured with soft cuffs in a rack, while carefully-crafted leather and wood was applied.

We stood outside the dungeon door. She faced me. "If you have anything to tell me that we haven't already discussed, tell me now."

I shook my head.

She looked for a moment like maybe there was something she wanted to tell me, but then it passed and she looked away, while saying, "Take off your clothes and leave them here. Once we enter the chamber, we've begun."

I nodded. Some Tops left the bottom alone for a few minutes while they gathered their own energy, but not Isa. She turned away from me and began shedding her clothes, draping them over the back of a chair. I folded mine neatly and placed them on the floor next to the door. As I bent low to lay them down I reminded myself one last time of my purpose for being here, to find out if Isa was . . . what? Safe, okay, worthy? The real thing, or not? To see if she'd respect me as an equal. Thus far she had been exemplary.

Inside the room, the fire of the red sky mixed with the flicker of candles she lit. She indicated the open space on the vinyl padded floor and I knelt there while my still-busy mind was cataloging details: black floor, soft on the feet but easy to wash up. Where did she get it?

The sound of her chuckle brought me back to the moment. She held a single candle and stared into it, then lifted it over her head and let the wax drip down over her small firm breasts. Her chuckle became a throaty laugh that sounded nothing like the Isa I knew. She looked back at me, the candle burning twin images in her eyes. She knelt in front of me, waving the candle like a magic wand. The flame burned higher as it tipped and hot white drops of wax dotted my skin. I sat still because I did not know what else to do. Unbound, uninstructed, I reminded myself it was my duty to submit.

And then she was on me, her body on top of mine, pushing me flat against the padded floor, her wax and mine pressed together, making me think of flowers in a dictionary. I hadn't realized it at first but the instant the wax had hit me I had broken out in a sweat, and now it made my skin slick against hers. I had no idea where the candle had gone and even though I told myself it wasn't my place to worry about it, not my responsibility, the thought remained. Her hands held my head in place and her mouth sucked at mine, and without thinking, I struggled. I was used to ritual beatings with numbers called out and the solemn gathering of energy before the penetration. This wrestling was so much more like . . . sex.

She reared up, hands on my shoulders, pinning me, the gleam still in her eye not from candles but from an eager madness to devour me. This is my will, I told myself, this is my devotion; but I could not make myself sink into submission. Isa raked her claws across my cheek and I resisted, my chin up in defiance. I wanted to lie still and let her have her way. I wanted to obey, to let the Goddess ravage me, if that be her will. But something in me said, *fight*! I struggled to unseat her from me and found myself instead face down on the floor, one of her hands in my hair and one drawing lines down my back with her claws. My spine arched against that rough touch, like the tide following the moon. I tried to turn my head, but her hand held me fast. I felt her hot breath on my neck; her lips moved as she mouthed whatever incantations she wished into my skin, and then her teeth found purchase and a frisson of energy shot from the spot straight to my groin. I felt as if she had plucked a string in me, and the vibrations grew louder as I fought her, as the sensation strobed through my brain of her biting me and me bucking and her weight riding me . . .

Then her mouth was at my ear as my legs flailed for some leverage on the slippery floor and she spread herself over me like a blanket. "Did you wonder why you're not bound? Did you wonder what I would do?"

I didn't answer except to push harder against her. I wanted her to let go of me, to let me free. One side of me knew this was wrong, to resist like this, while the other side of me knew it could be no other way.

Her voice was loud and low in my ear, the spice of her breath surrounding me as tightly as any bonds, "Because I had to know your will. I had to know what you would let me do."

Obviously, I'll let you do anything, I wanted to say, because I haven't been able to stop you.

And then her weight was gone. I turned onto my back to find her standing above me, the windows behind her dark with night. "What will you let me do, eh, sister?" She knelt where she was and I pushed myself back a few inches out of instinct. "If you serve, you will not move. If you submit, you will not move."

There was power in the way she crawled toward me, jungle power, fierce and hungry. She crawled toward my cunt and licked her lips like a jaguar before she let her tongue snake out to sting my clit. She jabbed at it, parting the folds of my flesh with the sharp tip and sinking it hard against my nerves. I held still. I held my breath. I pressed my hands flat against the floor and let my head fall back, but I kept my legs as they were: knees bent, feet flat on the floor, spread wide for her, for Her. Her hands reached up for my nipples, rolling them in her fingers like two peppercorns, then pulling them like pieces of taffy. I raised my head to look and found her eyes staring at me over the horizon of my mons. Waiting, waiting. Her tongue continued to jab, the sensation building to a jolt like pain, like a shock, slow but sharp, a Chinese water torture dripping onto my clit, moment by moment.

I had never felt a pain quite like it in my life, so bad I ground my teeth; and yet I felt a flutter in my stomach like it might make me come. Now that I had nothing to struggle against, I felt shame heating up my face. Why had I fought her? Did a year with Magda teach me nothing? How could I have failed in my devotion that way? My way is to suffer. When I go to leather bars, when I go to parties or group meetings, it's so hard to explain to some of these Tops, no I'm not a slave. I'm not a servant, only to Her. I'm not submissive, only to Her. If I obey, it is because it will lead to my suffering. If I let myself be put into bonds, it is to free me to suffer for Her. Simple, really.

The pain grew excruciating. Her tongue felt like an ice pick, stabbing the nerve cluster without mercy. But mercy was one thing I never expected. I counted the jabs to myself, grouping them in sets of ten like a weightlifter, packaging the feeling to make it manageable. I had withstood worse torture than this, and I shielded myself with that thought. The goal became to make it through, to make it to the end. How long would she go on this way?

I had lost count. My breasts were on fire, her hands grabbing at hardened wax and pinching my nipples. That little voice was there, trying to tell me to keep going, but it was fading, fading as I began to slip away, to the best place of worship of all. To that place where the mind falls aside and the body becomes the empty vessel, to that place of pure existence, pure sensation. I didn't think about it happening at the time, because if I had thought of it, it would have pulled me back to the present, back into my consciousness, and ruined it.

I let myself go, my whole body rigid but resisting nothing, my fingers clutching at a floor I no longer thought about. Thinking about it now, it happened as if to someone else, like some slow motion movie. As my hands drew up to my chest and held her hands there, my hips bucked hard, pulling her forward and dragging my cunt across the full length of her tongue. My hands held her hands on my breasts as my legs closed over her head and my hips shook, wringing the orgasm out over my skin, the convulsion shaking us so hard that we came apart. And then I was on her, her head on the ground and my cunt grinding into her mouth, and then covering her, my cunt against her leg, lips spread wide as I rode her, my hands raking her body and my mouth sucking at her breasts. There was wax in my mouth but it didn't feel like my mouth; there was power radiating from between my legs; and I couldn't stop myself from making myself come.

Then suddenly the orgasms stopped and I was staring down at my fingers, woven into the straight silk of her hair behind each ear, staring into her eyes – which no longer gleamed with hunger but sparkled with awe. She tugged gently at my hands, pulled them down to her breasts. I found myself eager to return the torture of earlier, as I twirled her nipples in my fingers and listened to her moan and cry out. My mouth to her mouth, my legs wrapped around hers, my hand sank into her pubic hair, wanting to pinch her clit, to pull it like taffy. But my finger slipped right past it and went deep into her, and suddenly I had another handle to hold her down with. Her cries became more frantic and she thrashed, but not enough to break free of me, not enough to make me think she didn't want it. My thumb on her clit, I plunged my long fingers into her and watched her hips rise to meet me. Could I do this to her for as long as she had done that thing to me?

I didn't. It seemed only a moment before she was bucking hard, her hand locked on my wrist and driving it in faster, her head flailing and her teeth sinking into my too-convenient shoulder as she struggled to take back from me the power I had stolen.

But I still had her on my hand, and as the orgasm subsided and my fingers could move again, I shifted my weight to keep her from sitting up, pressed my free hand against her throat, and kept my hand moving. I flicked her clit with my thumbnail, and felt her cunt convulse. "I want you to come again," I heard my voice saying.

She whimpered very softly but did not say no.

I ground my thumb into her and her hips rose up, her legs shaking suddenly to give her that extra boost, and again she came. Again I kept my fingers inside her, and again I made her come. I made her come until I saw her face, and saw that she too had gone off to that place of pureness, that place I always sought and sometimes found.

Thinking about that brought me back to myself at last. I withdrew my hands from her and sat back on my heels, receding from her like the tide from the cliff. She lay there a moment, taking deep breaths, and then she came back to herself, as well. I saw her eyes blink as she stared at the ceiling awash with candlelight.

She sat up slowly, her face impassive, and drew a shaky breath. She shifted, until she was kneeling, too, but her body continued forward until her head touched the floor in front of me. Her hands reached blindly for me and I caught them. Her shoulders shook and I knew she was crying. She held tight to my hands like her tears might wash her away, and I squeezed back, helpless to do anything else other than berate myself.

What did you think you were doing? How could you let yourself go like that? I didn't understand what had just happened and the only person I could ask was in tears.

Eventually, she wasn't. She composed herself, and even began to smile. She wiped back stray tears from her cheeks and grinned at me. "Thank you," she said.

I wasn't sure if, "You're welcome," was the right thing to say at this juncture, not when I felt like an apology was on my lips. "I, uh, I didn't expect that to happen."

"No one ever does," she said, a wistful sound in her voice that reminded me I knew nothing of where she had come from. "Not many people can do that. You have a power, you know."

I shook my head. "No. That was, I don't know."

"Don't deny it. You felt it. I felt it. I was yours."

"Stop it." Empty words, loaded words, like guns. "That's not what I'm like. I'm not supposed to . . ."

Isa's eyes turned dark, confusion and disappointment registering on her face.

No. It had felt good. It felt as good as the day I had walked out of the Church, and as good as the day I had first been bound to a cross five years later, as good as the day I'd discovered as a child just what it was we weren't supposed to do with our hands in our panties, as good as the day I'd had my first orgasm from being whipped alone. But good didn't make it right. "Look, Isa, it doesn't mean anything." I pulled my knees up to my chest. "I don't know what it means."

She looked hurt. "You've taken me to a place I've never been. This is the first time I've known what it was like . . ."

To be the sacrifice, I thought, to be the one who gets no mercy. "I know," I said, and reached for her, cradled her head against my breast. "I know."

"I never knew I needed it this much." She was warm and the room felt cold to me now. "I never knew that this was what I was looking for. But now I do."

I just nodded. I put her into her bed with promises I'd join her in a few minutes. When she was breathing deeply, I

went back to the doorway of the dungeon and pulled on my
clothes. In the driveway, I sat for a long moment on the
bike, looking at the moonlit hills and wondering if I should
leave. Maybe she was right; maybe I had touched something deep and important in myself, something new and
vital, just as she had. Maybe I should stay and explore it
more with her.

But I didn't want to see her gaze up at me with moon-
struck eyes. I didn't want the responsibility of checking her
for bruises and making her some tea. I wasn't ready to think
that the same Goddess who moved me to give myself up had
moved me to fight and take and dominate tonight. My
world was not supposed to be so complicated.

I rolled the bike to the end of the driveway before I
started it. Perhaps in the morning everything would look
different. But now I had a dark and unfamiliar road under
me, the curves unwinding beneath the roar of wind and the
crackling of my uncertainty.

INTERFACE RHAPSODIC

Alice Joanou

DEAD DEAD DAVID'S dead, she repeated, an inward mourning, a steadying device that she hoped would anchor her through this love-making with a man she had only just met. *Dead dead David's dead David dead David's dead.* She marveled at the fact that her body could feel anything, as disaffected as her mind had become since the trouble.

The nurses come in turns. They are hushed purposefulness going about the task of removing the filth with the familiarity of mothers. The women focus their detached attention toward the cleaning of her body and the attendance of the machinery: its rhythm checked, the tubing – plastic vines carrying nourishment – arranged and rearranged. One of them spoke to her regularly.

"Come on, love, going to roll you over on your side . . . One, two . . . that's a girl."

The nurse pats the comatose patient on the cheek, taking a moment to rest her cool palm on the face of the woman as if to say, "*I'm sorry for this trouble, my dear. So sorry for all this trouble.*"

*　　*　　*

The edge of the sill was tripped by blue sky and her fingertip brushed the ledge as a reminder of her presence in the room as though her finger were the axle to reality instead of his body on top of hers. He put his lip to her breast and then pulled away, saying something precise and common, and she repeated inwardly, *David's dead dead dead David's dead* because she was supposed to be with her husband *David dead David*. She found it soothing to invoke *dead dead David's dead* and it seemed to her that the window responded with a vibrational tone as though the world were announcing itself through her jointed skeleton. The world entered her through the window. New York City flooded into her body, bringing the rest of the planet with it.

"I . . . Oh!" She responded to the tone.

"What?" Almost annoyed, he raised his head, drawn away from his urgent task. "You can come inside me. It's safe." She wasn't sure what she meant by that, but she said the words with such certainty that she surprised herself.

"OK."

In that moment, it seemed that the tone from the world outside mated with the tones of their bodies moving in concert, allowing her, compelling her, moving her toward a great and enduring.

"Yes," she said as her fingers touched the windowsill near the bed again so that she could locate her self in the middle of this calculated fit of fucking. Almost as instantly as the act had started, she thought it might have been regrettable, especially tragic in its total banality.

Of course all was going as expected – the soundtrack of their exertions, "Come on, come on," he was saying, inside the angles and contortions and bending of genital to genital.

The sensations had long since lost their novelty, but remained mysterious in their persistent, sometimes irritating allure. What prevented her from halting the momentum? What stopped them from mutually acknowledging that they didn't care for one another? What kept them from acknowledging that, in fact, they didn't know one another enough to be sure they liked each other and that their bodies were straining independently of the other, locked together only in a mechanical urge that knits the buildings of the city and the houses of the suburbs, the Third World and the First knotted together? What, finally, was this finite and hypnotic power that issues solely from the precipice of orgasm?

Just beneath all the cunning plans for *coup d'états* and the awkward seductions in bars – all have this power at their core. Being is compressed in the exchanging and the relinquishing, the conquest and the submission to this power. Finally there is the gathering of these memories of pleasure that lead us again and again to the same.

"Yes," again, implicating all in the design and locus of its immutable source.

"Yes."

She called it down. Suddenly she could embrace all of the falseness and all of the nudity of the moment. He moved his hands over her body, an awkward navigator mapping the unfamiliar terrain of her body.

"Yes."

She called it all down and he brought up his head and looked at her face and she at his and therein lay one fine, distorted moment wherein these strangers, who were seeking only to sate appetites located in a mysterious center, found themselves inside the appetite itself, knowing it effortlessly. It was a mutual exalted, but static recognition.

"Yes."

The breath and tremor passed between their hips and they were sewn in an upward motion together. There was only silence, a silence that implicates all noise and swallows it – and then together they were beyond power and its hungers. They were inside the stringing together of such silences that make symphonies, rosaries, deaths and the great clotted calling down of Being. They had the vaguest memory of never having been separate.

"Yes."

They humped past the great silence, stricken from gazing into a hugeness so unfeeling and empty.

"Oh, God."

He fell over her and she fell up into him and they rested.

"My soul doth magnify the . . ."

"What?"

"Nothing. It's something I remembered just now from when I was a little girl. *My soul doth magnify the Lord*."

"Oh, God. Poor you. A Catholic."

"A lapsed one."

"Even worse," he laughed.

And then they slept.

In this brief meeting of pelvic and person, their selves, identified as such to themselves, were stripped. Identity and all relations with the phenomenal world was ruined, and left withal but the briefest flap of the winged annunciation delivered from the clock radio – 10:10 – "Thou art blessed among women," complained a colic baby in the downstairs apartment, crying relentlessly through the machinations of love-making. The baby screamed in varying cadences with their body's movements. It seemed as though the child was hysterically battling the wakening disappointment of the world and its sharp edges and its loudness. The baby screamed beneath their mattress, giving call to the gradual awakening, the seriousness of the soul's situation. It was a siren unraveling.

The baby's crying was the sound-bed for the feeble and impossible attempts of the body to find union with the ineffable. She thought of all the mannered theatrics that persist, informed by sexual instruction largely taken from the screen, perpetually staged in clumsy pageants. Sex had become a fierce and useless plea for an end to the carnival. Such strange and particular machines, these bodies governed by codes and needs and so many nervous ticks and unmentionable hungers.

As quickly as they had met in the center, meeting in a moment where the eye notices itself, they separated alone in the remaining muscularity of the particular situation. Left alone to manage the insatiable grief and unsated hungers that drive the body graveward, they tilted down until finally sinking. The bodies dropped away from one another, fatigued from relentless efforts to stun gravity. They rested with one another, the child's cry still escaping the muffling cramp that comes with age and training. The infant called upward.

She couldn't sleep, becoming instead wholly absorbed with this child's crying, and observed the oddness of making love to the rhythm of such a sound. They lay with one another in the vacancy of politeness, middle-class upbringing disallowing them to flee. Their desire had created a vacuum of desire meant to be filled with the reassuring illusion of increase.

The child sucked in a bellyful of air, and its cry remained poised again on the window-sill, while further down the street a factory truck delivered meat by-products, a car alarm competed with a siren, and they, this couple, hung inside the silence, waiting inside the baby's lungs. They hung together from the Great Tree and blew in the wind caught in a paradoxical bipolar storm of helplessness and wilfulness and then the silence was filled again. The baby let out its cry, a continuation of the mourning while the window-sill, larynx to the world, and the great Eye observed the careening of skin and the collapsed infinity of unrequited desires and heaven heavened in the perpetual, "Oh, oh, oh," while cell became I and thou.

He did not expect to see her again except for the possibility of a casual meeting on the street. He certainly did not expect to see her on television. She smiled out at him from a picture, her arm laced around a man's neck. The man in the photograph was handsome and he felt an irrational pang of jealousy, but when he heard that this woman, this woman who he hardly knew, who he had met in a coffee shop, this woman who he had made love to ". . . had been shot in the neck and chest, her body found shortly after in Central Park. The perpetrator was apprehended and confessed immediately to arresting officers. The police are still unclear about his motives. Meanwhile, doctors at Beth Isreal have worked to stabilize the vicitim though she is in critical condition. According to hospital reports, the five-month-old fetus she carries seems to be living while the woman herself is brain-dead and currently requires life-support."

The news cut to a doctor or some administrator who said, ". . . five months pregnant and that the fetus amazingly did not naturally abort. What we have here is our first post-mortem pregnancy, and we intend on doing everything we can to bring the child to term."

And then came all the facts about her life, things that he did not know.

She had been a college professor, and she had been recently widowed. Her husband had committed suicide some seven months ago, bringing into immediate focus the paternity of the fetus still living in the body of a woman clinically dead.

He turned off the television immediately, a natural erasing reflex that had worked before. He waited for the nausea to pass because he knew. But moments later he compulsively checked his calendar. It had been almost just about five months since he had been in bed with this woman who said her name was . . . Certainly it wasn't *his* . . . He turned the television on again but the broadcast had moved on to other news.

The next morning they imitated the commonly imitated. They woke, slipping from the bed and viewed it suspiciously as a place of untoward intimacies, now denuded. They avoided looking at it at all. Bed as clinic. Bed as site for the unraveling and darning of skin, pubic hair, spit and falsified memories, retouched even as they occur. Bed and soiled linens; the obviousness embarrassed them and so they moved away from it instinctively. Avoiding the gaze of one another was the only remedy for the numbing admission that they had crashed though the seam of another being without holiness, without caution, without rite.

Midway down the stairs, he started to make caustic ironic allusions to the night's secrets.

"Let's just get some coffee."

She silenced him, not really wanting to completely dismantle the incident, but remained unwilling to embrace it. They walked together uncomfortably for half a block and then she stopped.

"I'm going to go my way."

She couldn't drag the illusion down the street behind them any more, but was aware of the impossibility of expressing to him what she had already accepted. She had peered into what was peerless. She knew. He knew.

"Are you sure you don't want to go get some breakfast?"

"Yes."

She held out her hand, and he took it.

"Can I give you my . . .?"

"No, thank you. Goodbye."

She let go.

"Please take care of yourself."

"You, too."

They parted, and wandered in their individual obscurity, quite unaware that New York had detonated itself as site specific for the great hour, a time which had already passed unnoticed as a thief in the night.

The time had passed hidden under advertisements, marriages, meat packing, the sewing of cloth and the preparation of bodies for burial and for love. All had gone on in its steady cycle of decay and dystopic renewal. The great hour had passed in a silvery corolla, unnoticed beneath the edifice of their spectacularly ordinary interface.

GOVERNMENT ISSUE

Thomas S. Roche

I FOUND THE gun before she showed it to me.

I knew it wasn't right, to be looking through her things – it was its own kind of petty betrayal, like the little white lies that fester underneath the melding flesh of lovers. But being a professional secret-stealer made me look at things differently – all things: even betrayal, even love. In terms of the number of tumblers in the lock on a file cabinet, the gentle whir of the dial on a fireproof safe. It had gotten so every secret had a price, every betrayal a counter-betrayal to prevent it, in a complex game of snakes and ladders that, through all the bullshit of my life, had become indistinguishable from, and perhaps identical to, what is sometimes called trust.

And this was the price of my trust, the door charge at the true-love carnival. That I know the texture of her secrets, smell the oil in her mechanism: forty-five caliber, blued steel, eight-shot magazine. Government issue.

Besides, it was just sitting there, in the box at the top of the closet, beside the little pillbox hat with the black fishnet veil. I had to wonder if the two were related. When I took down the box I could see that the top layer – Havanas, twelve of them – didn't quite sit even. I gathered the dozen Havanas and lifted the cardboard. I expected to find a kind of secret, – old love notes, maybe, faded photographs, decaying roses, a plane ticket never used. Anything but what I did find.

Forty-five caliber, blued steel, eight-shot magazine. Government issue.

I picked the gun up with one of Iris's stockings, turning it over in my hand. It was a criminal's weapon, the front sight clipped off to allow a quick draw from a pocket or shoulder holster. The serial number was filed off like the inconvenient segments of Iris's life – obliterated. I lifted the barrel to my nose and sniffed: powder. Not fresh, though; old, rotten, as long ago and far away as the scent on my own service revolver hanging in its cracked leather holster in the next room. The powder-smell had the stale element that spelled years of dangerous secrets, ages of loneliness spent on the run. Convenience stores, diners, motel rooms with free cable. Iris had said she left California in a hurry.

I popped out the magazine, saw that it was loaded. Put the magazine back in.

I sniffed again, drawing the scent deeper, smelling the sharpness of something else mingled with the gunpowder and the faint, dwindling smell of the Havanas. I suppose I should have figured.

I mean, she spent all those nights alone at the Travelodge in Salt Lake City. Or wherever.

I put the gun away, closed the cigar box, filed the gun under "Cooper, Iris: Secrets." Before "Detective, N.O.P.D." and immediately behind "Citation for Valor", close to the place where "Discharge, Administrative" still sizzled like a powder-burn at the base of my brain. I put the gun away – and didn't forget about it.

*   *   *

I didn't ask Iris any questions, either. Iris had her secrets, but in her own way, without knowing it, she'd paid the price of trust. I held her close to me, watching, waiting, waiting for the day she'd take the cigar box down and tell me the story. Waiting for the day I'd tell her mine. Maybe make some sense out of things. Or maybe not.

It was one of those September nights, when the Fall tang hasn't hit yet and it still feels like goddamn July, the heat stifles you and the humidity can really fuck the shit out of your brain if you let it. The fucking cockroaches are the size of toy poodles and they walk around your kitchen floor like they owned the place and when the fuck were they going to receive your rent check, asshole? But there's something more to those nights, something about the smell off the river, the way the faintest movement of the air seems like a godsend – or maybe it's just that your brain gets boiled and your body takes over. We'd made love for hours, our bodies slick with sweat, making movement effortless, like slipping on an oil spill in the driveway. The scent of our sex filled the little bedroom as the chirping of crickets came through the window, the poetry of heavy breathing with the uninvited accompaniment of a string section. After, she cuddled up against me.

That's when she looked up, her eyes moist, her expression enigmatic, forming into guilt as I held her gaze.

"*I have something to show you*," she said, and she got nothing from me, just a stare, holding her eyes.

I cannot confirm or deny that I know your secrets, Iris Cooper.

She went to the closet and brought back the cigar box. She set it down on the bed between us as she sat there cross-legged, looking hard at the box. I didn't reach for it. Iris just stared. Finally she turned the cigar box toward me, nodded.

I lifted the lid and took out the pistol, this time holding it with my bare hands, feeling the metal in my grasp. I didn't feign surprise as I turned the weapon over in my hands. Iris watched me, undoubtedly understanding that I had already known, that her secrets had been mine for longer than she knew. But there wasn't a hit of anger, as I might have expected. Instead, she just watched as I felt the weight of the thing in my hand.

It was heavier than my own revolver. I got used to the feel of it in my hand, popped out the magazine, saw that it was still loaded.

"You shouldn't store it loaded," I told her. "That's dangerous."

"*What the fuck good is it if it's not loaded?*" she snapped, reaching out to touch the smooth barrel. It took some coaxing, but with the steady pressure of her hand she guided the barrel toward her.

"Iris," I said firmly. "This isn't safe. What the fuck are you doing?"

"*Life isn't safe,*" she answered as she got onto her knees, leaning forward so she could run her tongue around the barrel.

"This is crazy," I said as Iris began to lick her way all around the end of the pistol, then to move her way down the barrel to the trigger guard. I had my thumb on the safety, making sure it was on. My trigger finger wrapped around the outside of the trigger guard. Even so, I knew this was nuts. Dangerous. It would make an ugly headline.

I felt the tip of Iris's tongue snaking its way between my finger and the trigger guard. She had put both her hands on my right hand, guiding the pistol into just the right position. She licked the trigger, the blued-steel barrel pressed against her cheek. I watched, transfixed. Her tongue grazed my fingers and each time it did I watched a little more carefully. Then she licked her way over my thumb.

I held my breath as she teased my thumb away from the

safety. It took some doing for me to let go, let her lips encompass my thumb and her tongue stroke softly against it. She nibbled the tip of my thumb, then eased her lips away and let her tongue slither down to the safety.

With a kiss, she did it. I heard the click.

"This is fucked up," I growled, pulling the gun away and thumbing the safety back on. "Fucking insane. Iris, you don't understand how common – "

"Oh, I understand," she said, her eyes full of tears as she looked up at me. *"I understand better than you could ever know."* She reached out for the pistol and took it out of my hand, which had gone limp with the sadness in her gaze – the fear, the pain, the longing. Iris clicked the safety off and leaned back onto the red pillows, guiding the gun to her mouth again.

Now there was no way I was going to reach for it, risk setting it off in her hands. I watched, telling her, "Iris, if this is some sort of fucked-up way to commit suicide – "

"No," she told me *"It's not that. It's not that at all."* And I knew it wasn't. Even with all her secrets, Iris had let me know her well enough. I knew she was as far from punching her own ticket as anyone ever is.

But was that far enough?

Iris had the barrel of the .45 wet with her spittle now, glistening. She was naked, gorgeous, her body slick with sweat so that the moonlight shimmered off her flesh. She worked the automatic down her body, barrel pointed toward her head. She held it tight, gripping it with both hands, as she parted her legs.

"Iris," I said, reaching out for her but afraid to touch her. "That fucking thing could go off any minute. Give it to me."

She just shook her head, moving the pistol down so the end of the barrel nuzzled between her lips, slick with her spittle. The front sight had been clipped and then filed down smooth, so the gun went in easy, even as Iris shuddered.

"Don't shake like that," I growled at her, finally having given up on getting her to hand me the pistol. "You'll – "

"*Be quiet*," she whispered gently, working the gun gently in and out of her. She hoisted herself onto her knees, leaning forward so she could press her body against mine. I held perfectly still, my hands at my sides – I knew that any motion could be the wrong motion, any unexpected stimulus could jostle Iris's hand to just the wrong amount – or the right –

Holding the pistol with one hand, she slipped her other hand into my hair, held my face still as she kissed me, hard, then harder, then biting my lower lip, whimpering as she worked the pistol in and out, pushing the rear sight up against her clit, rubbing her breasts against me, the nipples hard like my cock; Iris's hips moved in time with her hand and I had long since given up any hope of getting the gun away from her. This was her show, and if it was time for Iris to punch her own ticket then that's the way it was going to be. She was in charge here.

"*God*," she gasped, then bit my lip harder, pain surging through my flesh as she came. She bit until I tasted blood, and Iris's body spasmed; I closed my eyes, waiting for the muffled impact, sure I could hear the cracking bone, the erupting flesh. Knowing I could feel the heat of the flash inside her, powder-burn ripping her asunder, tearing her apart.

But she held her ground, her thumb wrapped around the trigger guard, the safety still off.

She eased the slick weapon out of her, holding it up for me so it glistened in the moonlight.

Silently, I reached out and took it from her, thumbing on the safety.

I came up behind her, much later, when it was almost daylight, almost but not quite. She stood on the back porch looking out at the river. She was wearing that thin sundress with nothing on underneath, so the light of the moon reflecting off the water shone through it and made her body into a ghostly outline, like she was a will-o-wisp made flesh, the ghost of the bayous come to haunt me, swamp gas turned first-class *femme*. Her arms were crossed in front of her breasts against the faint pre-dawn chill that had come up. I said her name so I wouldn't startle her. I embraced her from behind and she didn't flinch, didn't recoil. She reached back to touch my face and turned just enough so she could kiss me.

There was still the same sadness in her eyes. She swallowed, a little self-consciously.

"They're going to come for me some day," she told me, as if it was something I didn't know. *"They're going to find me. They'll get me for what I did. They're looking for me right now. Sometimes I think I can feel their eyes on me when I walk down the street. Some day they'll walk through that door. And when they do, I want to know that thing like it's a part of me, so I'm not the least bit afraid. They'll think I'm going to be. But when they find me, I'll know death like a lover. Better, because death doesn't change. It always feels the same. It always tastes just the same."*

I knew what it tasted like. I'd tasted it once, paid for that taste with my job. My career as a secret-stealer. I could have paid for it with my life, maybe, if I'd been just a little more prone to despair, to anguish.

Forty-five caliber. Blued steel. Eight-shot magazine.

Dawn cracked the horizon, set the roosters to crowing, lit Iris's hair on fire. She turned back toward the river, clutching my hands.

Government issue.

KISS ME

Joe Maynard

IT DOESN'T MATTER how we got there, in fact, I don't remember. I knew her vaguely through friends or something; we were drunk at a bar and then we wound up at my place. She had lovely blue eyes, full lips and soft flesh that turned red when you kissed it – and I'd been doing that for a while, here and there at the bar, and on the walk home. She was slick with sweat and remnants of my saliva. But every time I tried to kiss her mouth, she looked away and yelled, "No!"

She wanted me in her before we'd gotten our clothes off – before I'd even shut the door to my apartment. It was just, like, "Come in me, now!" As hot as it was, though, she was really pissing me off. Wasn't it the guy's job to get her wet and ready? And didn't this involve the fabulous French kiss? But when I touched her there, I realized she was ready. I savored the subtle curves of her lower back with one hand, and with the other sunk two fingers in her snatch to work her juices. This would have been a good time to kiss, but she'd have none of it.

"Just put it in," she moaned.

I wanted that explosion that would send us into some

outer astral plane together, but for me this requires a
circular current. A reciprocation between the heads, the
hearts, and the hot spots. But every time I tried to slip my
tongue in her mouth, she pulled away.

"Now!" she demanded.

There I was with my dick pulsing inside her, her leg over
my shoulder, then squeezing my hips, her nails kneading
my ass, then my back . . . I wanted that sensation of her
wetness mingled with mine, our tongues intertwined like a
couple of smelt caught in a suck-hole, the vibration of our
moans reverberating through our jaws, her hot breath
together with mine, the circle of penis to vulva and hips
to breasts to mouth to chest to penis to vulva again. I
wanted the complete circle, but she pushed my face away
with the heel of her hand.

"Kiss me," I pleaded in rhythm to our thrusts.

"No," she said.

"Kiss me."

I mean, she was naked under me, this woman in my bed,
straddling my hips, risking a disease, pregnancy. I'd been
down, and up, on her tits, armpit; even as I slipped a finger
through her sphincter I thought, damn, no mouth.

"Why?"

"No, no, no."

"Why?"

"Kissing is special."

I pulled out. "God dammit!" I yelled at the ceiling, up on
my knees, cock bobbing, both arms reaching into the air,
palms out hoping for the orgone gods to descend and
possess us, to fucking open her fucking mouth for me!
Down came my palms with a thud on her chest.

"Kiss me!" I cried with my face on her belly, my palms
beating her upper torso, "Please!"

"Nn-nn."

I opened my eyes for a second, rubbing my bristly head
into her belly, looking down across her upside-down pubis

to my veiny phallus primed to come. Come, yes! I wanted to come. I wanted to fucking get in her mouth! I rolled over on my back with my hands pulling her head over my crotch, pumping my hips into her face. She moaned loudly. She wrapped her arms around my lower torso, squeezing, twisting and bucking her head back and forth around my cock to meet my thrust. I pulled her face as hard as I could into my pubic hair. Her teeth met the base of my cock and I exploded. And exploded. I couldn't help but throw my head back till it practically hit my ass. I kept exploding and exploding until she was full and leaking around the lips and trying to swallow and take me in her throat and moan at the same time. Oh, God, it was good.

We lay next to each other for a minute or two, exhausted, panting, sober.

Finally, she rolled over onto my chest and said, "You wanna be my boyfriend?"

"What?" I said, looking down at her flushed, giggling face, her tongue playfully licking my nipples.

"We could kiss."

EROTOPHOBIA

O'Neil De Noux

SHE SHOOK OUT her long brown hair, turned her cobalt blue eyes toward me and winked as the slim Negro named Sammy began to unbutton her blouse. She was trying her best not to act nervous. Sammy's fingers shook as he moved from the top button of her green silk blouse to the second button.

I leaned my left shoulder against the brick wall of the makeshift photo studio and watched. The second floor of a defunct shoe factory, the studio was little more than an open room with a hardwood floor, worn brick walls lined with windows overlooking Claiborne Avenue and two large glass skylights above. It smelled musty and faintly of varnish.

The photographer, Sammy's older cousin Joe Cairo, snapped a picture with his 35 mm Leica. Joe was thin and light-skinned and about twenty-five. Shirtless, he wore blue jeans and no shoes. His skin was already shiny with sweat.

Sammy was also shirtless and shoeless, wearing only a pair of baggy white shorts. His skin was so black it looked like varnished mahogany against Brigid's pale neck.

Yeah, her name was Brigid. Brigid de Loup, white female, twenty-seven, five feet three inches with pouty lips and a gorgeous face. Gorgeous. With her green blouse, she wore a tight black skirt and a pair of open-toe black high heels.

She bit her lower lip as Sammy's fingers moved to the third button, the one between her breasts. She looked at him and raised her arms and put her hands behind her head. Sammy let out a high-pitched noise and moved his fingers down to the fourth button.

My name? Lucien Caye, white male, thirty, six feet even, with brown eyes and wavy brown hair in need of a haircut. I stood there with my arms folded and watched, my snub-nosed .38 Smith and Wesson in a leather holster on my right hip. I'm a private eye.

"You're going to have to pull my blouse out," Brigid told Sammy.

Sammy nodded, his gaze focused on her chest as he pulled her blouse out of her skirt and unbuttoned the final two buttons. He pushed the blouse off her shoulders and dropped it to the floor.

I loosened my black and gold tie and unbuttoned the top button of my dress white shirt, then stuck my hands in the pockets of my pleated black suit pants to straighten out my rising dick.

Brigid looked at me as she turned her back to Sammy, who fumbled with the button at the back of her skirt. Her white bra was lacy and low-cut. Jesus, her breasts looked nice.

I moved over to one of the windows and opened it and flapped my shirt as the air came in through the high branches of the oaks lining Claiborne. The spring of '48 was already a scorcher, yet the air was surprisingly cool and smelled of rain. A typical afternoon New Orleans rainstorm was coming. I could feel it.

Brigid came to me two weeks earlier, in a Cadillac, with

diamonds on her fingers and pearls around her neck, and told me she needed a bodyguard.

Yeah. Right.

"I suffer from erotophobia," she said, crossing her legs as she sat in the soft-back chair next to my desk.

"What?"

"It's the fear of erotic experiences."

Yeah. Right.

If someone had told me back when I was a cop that a luscious dish would tell me *that* one day, I'd have looked at them as if they were retarded.

She told me her doctor prescribed "shock therapy", and she needed a bodyguard.

"I want to feel erotic. But I also want to be safe."

She told me she was married and her husband approved of what she had in mind.

"What's that?" I asked.

"Sexy pictures."

Sammy finally got the button undone and unzipped her skirt.

"Go down on your knees," Joe the photographer told Sammy, repositioning himself to their side. I kept behind Joe, to keep out of the pictures.

"Now," Joe said. "Pull her skirt down."

Brigid looked back at Sammy and wiggled her ass. Sammy's hands grabbed the sides of the skirt and pulled it down over her hips, his face about four inches from the white panties covering her ass. Brigid turned, put her left hand on his shoulder and stepped out of her skirt.

"Take her stockings off next," Joe said.

Brigid lifted her left leg and told Sammy he'd need to take her shoes off first. He did, then reached up to unsnap her stockings from her lacy garter belt.

He rolled each stocking down, his sinewy fingers roaming down her legs. Brigid put her arms behind her head again and spread her feet wide for him. She bit her lower lip again.

Sammy, on his haunches now, wiped sweat from his forehead and looked back at his cousin, who told him the bra was next. I felt perspiration working its way down my back. My temples were already damp with sweat.

Brigid started to turn and Joe told her to do it face-to-face. He switched to his second Leica. Brigid gave Joe a look, a knowing look, and something passed between them. I was sure.

"If you don't mind," Joe added in a shaky voice. "It'll be sexier."

Brigid smiled shyly. "That's what I want." Her voice was husky.

Her chest rose as she took in a deep breath. Sammy stood up and reached around her. It only took him a second to unhook the bra and pull it off, freeing Brigid's nice round breasts.

Oh, God!

Her small nipples were pointed. Her breasts rose with her breathing. Sammy stared at them from less than a foot away. He blinked and said, "Wow."

Brigid looked at me and smiled and I could see a nervous tic in her cheek. She took in another deep breath, her breasts rising again.

Joe stepped up and tapped Sammy on the shoulder and told him to go down on his knees again. "Now," Joe said, "take her panties off."

Joe hurriedly set up for more shots.

Sammy tucked his fingers into the top of her panties. Brigid leaned her head back to face the skylights and closed her eyes. Joe snapped away and my dick was a diamond-cutter now.

Sammy pulled her panties down, his nose right in front of her bush. She stepped out of them, and he leaned back and stared at her thick pubic hair, a shade darker than the long hair on her pretty head. Brigid turned slowly and pointed her ass at Sammy, who reached up and unhooked her garter belt and pulled it away.

"OK. Stop," Joe said, sitting on the floor. He pulled his camera bag to him and unloaded both Leicas before loading them again.

Brigid slowly turned to face me. Her face was serious now and flushed. I moved my gaze down her body and almost came just looking at her. She winked at me when I looked back at her face and rolled her shoulders slightly, her breasts swaying with her movement.

Joe told Sammy to stand up when the cameras were loaded. He took several pictures of them standing face to face, looking at one another and then asked them to stand side by side.

"No touching," Brigid said, reminding Joe of the ground rules. He nodded and had them sit next, side by side with their legs straight out. Brigid leaned back on her hands and Sammy leered at her bush.

Then Joe had them sit cross-legged facing one another. I felt my dick stir again when she leaned back and shook out her hair and the light from the skylight seemed to illuminate her body. God, she looked so sexy with her breasts pointing and her legs open and all her bush exposed.

Joe asked Brigid to stand and put her hands on her hips and move her feet apart as Sammy remained sitting, and stared at her pussy, which was at eye-level now.

Brigid looked at Joe when he moved her, his hand on her hip. They exchanged brief warm smiles as he moved her.

Sammy let out a deep breath and Brigid laughed. I was breathing pretty heavily, myself. Jesus, what a scene. Joe moved them around in different positions and snapped furiously and switched cameras again.

He had them sit again and entwined their legs. Sammy's dark skin was in stark contrast with Brigid's fair skin. Joe moved in for close-ups of Brigid's chest and moved down to snap her bush. She looked at him and moved her knees apart as she sat.

"Yeah. Yeah," Joe said, snapping away. "Don't stop."

Joe pulled Brigid up by the hand and had her stand over Sammy, straddling his outstretched legs as he sat. Then Joe had her sit on Sammy's legs, her legs open as she faced Sammy.

"Now lean back on your hands," Joe said.

Brigid leaned back, her legs open, her pussy wide open to Sammy and Joe behind him snapping away, and me peeking at her pink slit. She was hairy. I like that in a woman. I especially liked the delicate hairs just outside her pussy.

Jesus. What a sight!

She looked at Joe for long seconds, staring at him the way a woman does when she's getting screwed. She wasn't looking at the camera, and Sammy was just a prop. She looked at Joe. The look on her face was for him. It was a subtle move, but I caught it.

Joe snapped at a furious pace.

Brigid finally climbed off Sammy, turned and walked to the bathroom and closed the door behind her. She walked purposefully, as if she had trouble moving her legs.

Sammy lay all the way down and panted, his chest slick with sweat now. Joe picked up his cameras and hurriedly reloaded both. I opened another window. The air was misty now and felt damp and cool on my face. I looked down on the avenue at the tops of the passing cars and then looked straight out at the dark branches and green leaves of the oaks.

I wondered what the passers-by would think if they knew what was going on up here.

The bathroom door opened and Brigid came out, walking more steadily. She stepped over to her purse and took out her compact, touching up her face with powder, re-applying dark red lipstick.

She smiled at Joe and said, "No pictures right now. OK?"

He nodded.

Brigid moved over to Sammy and said, "Stand up and put your hands on your head."

"Huh?"

She bent over and grabbed his right hand and pulled him up. Then she lifted his hands and put them on his head, the way we did the Krauts we took prisoner outside Rome.

She yanked Sammy's shorts down, pulled them off his feet and tossed them aside. He wore no underwear. His long thin dick stood straight up like a flag pole. Brigid smiled and looked Sammy in the eyes.

She reached down and grabbed Sammy's dick. He jumped. Slowly, she worked her hand up and down his long dick. Sammy moaned.

Brigid looked at me and said, "I don't want y'all to think I'm just a tease."

Jesus, a white woman giving a Negro a hand job. Unbe-fuckin-lievable. I figured she knew it wouldn't bother me in the way it would bother most white boys. She had me pegged from day one, I guess, from the way I treated Joe and the Negroes we'd come across during her posing sessions.

Brigid looked at Joe and it was there again, that come-hither sexy look, but only for a moment. She bent over, her legs stiff, her ass straight up, and leaned over and kissed the tip of Sammy's cock. He rocked on his feet and she increased her jerking motion until he came. She caught it with her free hand and wiped Sammy's come on his chest when he finished. Then she turned to Joe and asked if he wanted a hand job. He shook his head.

She looked at me and said, "Need some help with those blue balls?"

I shook my head slowly and watched her go back into the bathroom. She left the door open this time and washed her hands. She toweled off, left the towel and walked straight back to me. She put her hands on my chest, leaned up and gave me a fluttery kiss across my lips.

Then she went over to Joe and gave him the same fluttery kiss. I could see him squirm and then close his eyes. He smiled warmly at her when she pulled away.

"Come on," she said. "Let's finish these rolls."

Joe told Sammy to go wash off. When he returned, Joe posed them together naked. The climax of the shooting had Brigid straddling Sammy's legs again as they sat, her pussy wide open and Sammy's dick up and hard again.

When Joe ran out of film again, Brigid got up and told me, "Time to get the film, big boy. I hope you counted the rolls."

I had.

Joe unloaded both cameras and gave me the six rolls of film. We watched Brigid dress. Sammy went into the bathroom. Brigid and I left before he came out.

Sitting in my pre-war 1940 DeSoto, her legs crossed and her skirt riding high on her naked thighs, Brigid smiled at me and said, "Next time we'll shoot in a cemetery."

"Yeah?" I could smell her perfume again in the confines of the car.

"Joe knows some grave-diggers at Cypress Grove. Posing naked among the crypts, in front of a captive audience . . . alive and dead, will be so delicious."

It didn't take a fuckin' genius to figure the one thing this woman didn't have – was erotophobia. I still hadn't figured her angle.

"When did Joe tell you about the gravediggers?"

She winked at me. "When I called him yesterday. That was when he told me he had his cousin lined up for today's session."

The rain came down hard now and the windshield was fogging as I tooled the DeSoto up Claiborne, away from the Negro section called Treme toward uptown where the rich lily-whites lived in their Victorian and neo-Classical and

Greek revival homes. I cracked my window and felt the rain flutter my hair.

Brigid leaned against the passenger door and watched me. Her dress was so high I could almost see her ass the way she rolled her hips. She eye-fucked me all the way home, ogling me every time I looked her way.

Jesus, she was so fuckin' pretty and so fuckin' sexy and so fuckin' nasty. She hired me to make sure no one raped her. That was the last thing a man would do with a woman like her. At least, that was the last thing I'd do. I'd want her to come to me, wrap those legs around me and fuck me back.

"Want to come in and meet my husband?" she asked when I pulled up in front of her white Greek revival home on Audubon Boulevard.

"No, that's OK."

"He's waiting for me to tell him what it was like." She raised her purse and added, "And to develop the film." Her husband had a built-in darkroom.

She pulled a white envelope from her purse and handed it to me. Cash. She always paid me in small bills. I actually got paid to watch her get naked and pose with her legs open. Tell me America isn't a great country.

Brigid opened the door, stopped, moved across the seat and kissed me. I felt her tongue as she French-kissed me in front of her big house and I thought I would come right there.

I watched her hips as she walked away, barefoot up her front walk to the large front gallery with its nine white columns. Her high-heels dangling from her left hand, she turned back and waved at me and went in the front cut-glass door of her big house.

The rain came down in torrents that evening. Standing inside the French doors of my apartment balcony, I watched it move in sheets across Cabrini Playground on Barracks Street. The oak branches waved in the torrent.

The wind shook the thick rubbery leaves and white petals of the large magnolias. I looked beyond the playground at the slick, tilted roofs and red brick chimneys of the French Quarter. The old part of town always looked older in the rain.

I leaned against the glass door and looked down at my DeSoto parked against the curb. The glass felt cool against my cheek. The street wasn't flooded yet at least. I took a sip of Scotch, felt it burn its way down to my empty belly, and closed the drapes.

I sat back on my sofa, in front of the revolving fan, and closed my eyes and remembered the first time we went out to shoot pictures. It was in Cabrini Playground. It was a real turn-on watching Brigid sit in a tight red skirt, sit so Joe could see up her dress and take pictures of her white panties.

The second time was in City Park where she stripped down to her bra and panties to pose beneath an umbrella of oak branches. Two workers came across us and Brigid liked that. She liked an audience. Joe moved us to the back lagoon for some topless pictures, only some fishermen saw us and got pissed at the half-naked white girl with the black boy, so we had to bail out.

My dick was a diamond-cutter again as I sat on my sofa. I finished my Scotch and readjusted my hard-on, knowing the only relief I could feel would be in a hot wash rag.

I closed my eyes and remembered the two brunette whores we came across just outside Rome, the day before I was wounded. The girls were about twenty, a little on the plump side with pale white skin. They fucked the entire platoon and got up to wave good-bye to us early the next morning, when we moved out.

My doorbell rang.

I stood slowly and walked down the stairs to the door. Through the transom above the louvered front door, I saw the top of a yellow cab. I peeked out the door and Brigid was there, her hair dripping in the rain.

I opened the door and she turned and waved to the cabbie, who drove off up Barracks.

Brigid stepped past me and stood dripping in the foyer. Wearing the same clothes she had for the photo session, she shivered and cupped her hands against her chest, her head bent forward. I closed the door.

I put my hand under her chin and lifted her face and she blinked those cobalt eyes at me. They were red now with a blue semi-circle bruise under her left eye.

"Pipi hit me," she said, her lower lip quivering. "Can I come up?"

I took her right hand and brought her up and straight into my bathroom. I grabbed the box of kitchen matches from the medicine cabinet and lit the gas wall heater. Standing, I turned as Brigid dropped her bra.

"Don't leave," she said, bending over to run a bath. "You've seen it all."

I put the lid down on the commode and sat and watched her take her clothes off. She smiled weakly at me, her lips still shaking as she climbed into the tub. The water continued running as she sank back.

"How about some coffee?"

"You have any Scotch?"

I stood and looked down at her. Her eyes were closed and the water moved dreamily over her naked body and she looked so damn sexy.

I poured us each a double Johnnie Walker Red and went back in.

A silent hour and two drinks later, as well as two hard-ons, she stood up in the tub and asked me to pass her a towel. In the bright light of the bathroom, her skin looked white-pink. She dried herself and wrapped a fresh towel around her chest just above her breasts, and took my hand and led me out to the sofa where we sat.

She poured us both another Scotch, left hers on the

coffee table next to the bottle, and turned her back to me to lie across my lap as I sat straight up. I had to adjust my dick again and she knew and smiled at me.

"I'll take care of that," she said softly, and closed her eyes.

With no make-up, with her hair still damp and getting frizzy, with the bruise under her eye – she was still gorgeous. Some women are like that, plain knock-down gorgeous.

After a while she told me that Pipi – that's her husband – couldn't get it up when she came in and told him about what she'd done. She even dug out the previous pictures and went down on him, but he was as limp as a Republican's brain.

Then he hit her – punched her, actually – and kicked her out, shoved her out into the rain.

"At least he called a cab for me." She opened her cobalt blues and blinked up at me. "Guess you figured he's the one with erotophobia. Pipi's the one afraid of erotic experiences."

No shit.

She leaned up, reached over and grabbed her drink and downed it with one gulp. I got up a second and moved to the balcony doors. I didn't hear the rain anymore, so I cracked them. It was still drizzling so I left them open and went back to the sofa. I felt the coolness immediately. It was nice.

She settled her head back in my lap and closed her eyes again. The towel had risen and I could see a hint of her bush now. I reached over and picked up my drink and finished it, then put the glass back on the coffee table.

A while later, she sighed and turned her face toward me and I could see by her even breathing she was asleep. The towel opened when she turned and I looked at her body again.

I wanted to fuck her so badly. I climbed out from under her head, stood and stretched. I reached down and scooped Brigid into my arms. I took her into my bedroom and laid

her on the bed. She sighed again and I leaned over and
kissed her lips gently.

I grabbed the second pillow and went back out to the sofa
and poured myself another stiff one. I was feeling kinda
woozy by then anyway, so I lay back on the sofa and tried
some deep breathing with my eyes closed.

There was a movie I saw where a private-eye turned
Veronica Lake down because it ain't good business to sleep
with clients. Fuck that shit. Brigid won't have to ask me
again.

I pulled off my socks and gulped down the rest of my
drink and lay back on the pillow and closed my eyes. I tried
deep breathing and letting my mind float. And just as I was
drifting I realized it wasn't Veronica Lake. It was Ann
Sheridan. Or was it Barbara Stanwyck in a blonde wig?

The banging of the French doors woke me. I sat up too
quickly and felt dizzy and had to lean back on the sofa. It
was pitch outside and nearly as dark inside. Lightning
flashed and the rainy wind raised the drapes like floating
ghosts. A roll of thunder made the old building shiver.

The wind felt cool on my face. I started to rise and saw
her standing next to the sofa. I sank back as lightning
flashed again, illuminating her naked body in white light.
I felt her move up to me and felt her arms on my shoulders
as she climbed on me. She said something, but the thunder
drowned it.

I felt the weight of her body on my lap as she ripped at my
shirt. I tried to help, but she tore it and we both pulled it
off. She grabbed my belt and slapped my hand when I tried
to help. Rising, she shoved my pants and underwear down
and then sank back on me.

I felt her bush up against my dick, her mouth searching
my face for my lips. Our tongues worked against each other
as I raised my hands for those breasts.

She moved her hips up and down slowly as we kissed. I

felt the wetness between her legs. She rose high and reached down with her hand to guide my dick into her. She sank down on it and shivered and then fucked me like I've never been fucked before.

And she talked nasty.

"Oh, fuck me. Come on. Fuck me. Oh, God I love your dick. I love it. Fuck me. Yes. Yes. Oh, God."

I like it when women call me God, even if it's just for a little while.

She bounced on me. "More," she said. "More!"

Hell, there was no more. She had it all.

She screamed and I came in her in long spurts and she cried out and held on to my neck. Then she collapsed on me and it took a while for our breathing to return to normal.

I looked over her shoulder as lightning flashed again and saw the wet floor next to the open balcony doors. The wind whipped up again and felt so damn good on our hot bodies. The thunder rolled once more and sounded further away.

When I could gather enough strength, I kicked off my pants and shorts. I lifted her and carried her back into the bedroom. I climbed on her and fucked her nice and long: the way second fucks should be, deep and time-consuming.

She wrapped her legs around my waist and her arms around my neck and kissed me and kissed me. She was one great, loving kisser. She made noises, sexy noises, but didn't talk nasty. She just fucked me back in long hip-grinding pumps.

After I came I stayed in her until her gyrating hips slipped my dick out. I rolled on my back and pulled her to me and she snuggled her face in the crook of my neck, her hot body pressed against me.

Every once in a while I felt the breeze come in and try to cool us.

She was still pressed against me when the daylight woke me. I slipped out of bed, relieved myself and pulled on a fresh pair of boxers before brushing my teeth. She lay on her stomach, the sheet wrapped around her right leg, her long hair covering her face.

I went to the kitchen and started up a pot of coffee-and-chicory, then bacon and eggs. She came in just as I was putting the bacon next to the eggs on the two plates on my small white Formica table.

Naked, she walked up and planted a wet one on my lips. She leaned back and brushed her hair out of her face and said, "I used your toothbrush."

"Sit down."

I went back and put the bacon pan in the sink and poured us two cups of strong coffee.

"You don't have a barrette, do you?" She moved around the table and sat.

"Huh?"

"Left over from a previous fuck?"

"Yeah. Right." I put her coffee in front of her and sat across the table and ate my bacon and eggs and watched her breasts as she lifted her fork to eat.

OK, I looked at her face too, and stared into those turquoise eyes that glittered back at me as she ate. But mostly I looked at her tits. Round and perfectly symmetrical, they were so fuckin' pretty.

I can't explain it. Tits have a power over men we can't explain. Women will never understand. We have no fuckin' idea ourselves.

The eggs and bacon weren't bad. The coffee was nice and strong. After, we took a bath together. Soaping each other and rinsing off, we stayed in the tub until the water cooled and that felt even better than the warm water.

"Will you take me home? I don't want to go alone."

Brigid stood in the bathroom, her belly against the sink as she applied make-up to her face. In her bra and panties, she had her butt out.

I told her I'd bring her home.

"I want to pick up some things. Will you take me to my mother's, after?"

"Sure."

I finished my coffee, put the cup on the night stand and then dressed myself.

She came out and ran her hand across my shoulders as she passed behind me to pick up her skirt.

I finished tying my sky-blue tie, the one with the palm tree on it, and ran my fingers down the crease of my pleated blue suit pants.

"Nice shoes," she said when I slipped on my two-tone black and white wing tips. Women always noticed shoes.

I finished in time to watch Brigid finish. I liked watching women dress, nearly as much as watching them undress.

I grabbed my suit coat and black hat on the way out.

"You're not bringing a gun?"

"You gonna get naked in front of any strange men on the way home?"

"No."

"Then I don't need to shoot anybody, do I?"

Pipi's black Packard was in the driveway. I parked behind it and followed Brigid in. I waited in the marble-floored foyer, my hat in hand, and watched Brigid's hips as she moved up the large spiral staircase.

I figured I was about to meet old Pipi, the fuckin' wife-beater himself. I hate men that hit women. Hate 'em.

Just as I peeked in at the Audubon prints on the walls of the study, Brigid screamed upstairs. I took the stairs three at a time and followed the screams up to a large bedroom with giant flamingo lamps, blond furniture and a huge round bed with the body of a man on it. The man's head lay in a pool of blood.

Brigid had her back pressed up against a large chifforobe in the right corner of the room, next to the drapes. She covered her face with her hands and screamed again.

The man lay on his side. I leaned over to look at his face. I recognized Pipi de Loup from the society page, even with the unmistakable dull look of death on his waxen face and his eyes blackened from the concussion of the bullet. The back of his head was a mass of dyed black hair and brain tissue.

Brigid turned around and started crying.

I looked at the mirror above the long dresser, looked into my own eyes and felt my stomach bottom out. I saw the word "sap" written across my face.

I moved over and grabbed Brigid's hand and led her out of the bedroom and down the stairs and out to my car. I opened the passenger door and told her to sit. Then I went next door and called the police.

Brigid was still crying when I got back to the DeSoto. I leaned against the rear fender and waited. Two patrolmen arrived first. I knew neither. I pointed at the house. The taller went in, the other took out his note book and asked me my name.

A half hour and fifty questions later, Lieutenant Frenchy Capdeville pulled his black prowl car behind my car. He stepped out and shook his head at me, took off his brown suit coat and tossed it back in the prowl car.

Short and wiry, with curly black hair and a pencil-thin moustache, Capdeville looked like Zorro – with a flat Cajun nose. He waltzed past me and stood next to the open door of my car and looked at Brigid's crossed legs. He pulled the ever-present cigarette from his mouth, flicked ashes on the driveway and looked at me.

"You stay put."

He reached his hand in and asked Brigid to step into the house with him. He left a rookie patrolman with an Irish name to guard me while other detectives arrived, one with a camera case, and went into the mansion.

I looked up at the magnolia tree and tried counting the

white blossoms, but lost count after twenty. At least the big tree, along with the two even larger oaks, kept the sun off me as I waited. I looked around at the neighbors who came out periodically to sneak a peek at the side show.

A detective arrived and waved at me on the way in. He was in my class at the academy. He was the only white boy I ever knew named Spade.

Willie Spade came out of the house an hour later and offered me a cigarette.

"I don't smoke."

"I forgot." He shrugged and lit up with his Zippo. About an inch smaller than me, with short carrot-red hair and too many freckles to count, Spade had deep-set brown eyes.

"I need to search your car. OK?"

He meant, Do I have your consent?

I told him, "Sure, go ahead," but didn't expect him to pat me down first.

"No offense," he said.

"No problem," I said.

While he was digging in my back seat he said we needed to go to the office for my statement.

"I'd like to drive," I said. "I'd rather not leave my car here."

Spade turned and wiped sweat from his brow. "You can drive us both."

"No," I said. "I didn't touch a fuckin' thing in the house. She opened the door and I didn't touch the railing on the way up the stairs. The only thing I touched was her arm, when I dragged her out."

Spade narrowed his deep-set eyes. "You touched more of her than her arm."

I nodded and leaned back in the hardwood folding chair in the small interview room. I looked out the lone window at the old wooden buildings across South White Street from the Detective Bureau Office on the second floor of the concrete Criminal Courts Building at Tulane and Broad. A gray pigeon landed on the window ledge and blinked at me.

"We found the murder weapon on the floor next to the bed."

"Yeah?"

"A Colt. 38. The missus says it's Pipi's gun. He kept it in the nightstand next to the bed. The drawer was open."

"I didn't notice." I picked up the cup of coffee on the small table and took a sip. Cold.

"The doors and windows were all locked," Spade said, watching me carefully for a reaction.

"What time did the doctor say he died?"

"Between two and four a.m. Give or take an hour."

I nodded.

Spade leaned back in his chair and put his arms behind his head and I saw perspiration marks on his yellow dress shirt. His brown tie was loosened.

"So you're her alibi and she's yours," he said.

I nodded again and felt that hollow kick in my stomach.

There was a knock on the door and a hand reached in and waved Spade out. A couple minutes later Spade returned with a fresh cup of Java, along with my wing-tips. He dropped my shoes on the floor and put the coffee in front of me. He pulled my keys out and put them on the table before sitting himself.

"Find anything?" I said as I leaned down and pulled my shoes on.

"Nope." Spade didn't sound disappointed. He sounded a little relieved. He put his elbows up on the table and told me how they knew the killer came in the kitchen door. It rained last night. The killer came in through the back with muddy shoes, wiped them on the kitchen mat and still tracked mud all the way up to the bedroom, then tracked mud right back out.

"That's why we had to search your pad and office," he

explained the obvious. They had to check out all my shoes, and everything else in my fuckin' life.

"Let himself in with a key?" I asked when I sat up.

"Or." Spade shrugged. "The door was unlocked and the killer flipped the latch on his way out, locking it. We have some prints, but smudges mostly."

I nodded.

Spade let out a tired sigh and said, "You know the score. Whoever finds the body is automatically the first suspect."

"Until you prove they didn't do it. I know."

I didn't say – especially when it's the wife and the man who's fuckin' the wife.

"I'll be right back," Spade said, and left me with my fresh coffee and my view of South White Street.

A while later, just as I was thinking how an interview room would be better for the police without a window, the door opened and Frenchy Capdeville walked in with Spade. Capdeville took the chair. Spade leaned against the wall.

Capdeville smiled at me and asked if I knew anything about the pictures they found in Mr. de Loup's darkroom. I told them everything. Fuck, they knew it anyway.

I ended with a question. "Did your men sniff my sheets?"

Capdeville smiled again. "Who found the photographer?"

I waited.

"You come up with a nigger photographer for her, or did she?"

"She told me Pipi found him."

Capdeville blew smoke in my face and gave me a speech, the usual one. I could leave for now, but they weren't finished with me yet. They'd be back with more questions, he said, flicking ashes on the dirty floor. He made a point to tell me they weren't finished with Mrs de Loup by a long shot. Her lawyer was on his way and they expected a long interview.

"One more thing," Capdeville said, looking me in the eyes. "You have any idea who did it?"

"Nope," I lied, looking back at him with no expression in my eyes.

They let me go.

I drove around until dark, checking so many times to see if I was followed, I got a neck ache. I meandered through the narrow streets of the Quarter, through the twisting streets of the Faubourg Marigny and over to Treme where I parked the DeSoto on Dumaine Street.

I jumped a fence and moved through back yards, jumping two more fences to come up on Joe Cairo's studio from the rear. As I moved up the back stairs, I thought how much this reminded me of a bad detective movie. Easy to figure and hard to forget.

I knocked on the back door. A yellow light came on and Joe's face appeared behind the glass top of the wooden door. His jaw dropped. It actually dropped.

"Come on, open up," I told him. "You don't have much time."

He opened the door and gave me a real innocent look, and I knew for sure he did it. I breezed past him, telling him to lock the door. I followed the lights to a back room bed with a suitcase and camera case on it.

"Going somewhere?" I sat in the only chair in the room, a worn green sofa.

Joe stood in the doorway. He looked around the room but not at me.

I put my hands behind my head and watched him carefully as I said, "She's gonna roll over on you."

Joe looked around the room again, his fingers twitching.

"If I figured it out, you know Homicide will. They're a lot better at this."

Joe started bouncing on his toes, his hands at his sides.

"They found the pictures. She'll bat those big blue eyes

at them, roll a tear down those pretty cheeks and tell them, 'Look at the evil things my husband made me do . . . with a nigger'."

Joe stopped bouncing and glared at me.

"Don't be a sap," I told him. "She'll tie you up in a neat package. Cops like neat packages, cases tied up in a bow. Get out now. Leave. Go to Calaifornia or Mexico. Just leave, or you'll be in the electric chair before you know it."

Joe leaned his left shoulder against the door frame. "There's nothing for her to tell."

"OK." I stood up. "Wait here. They'll be here soon." I looked at the half-packed suitcase and said, "Don't tell me you thought she was gonna run off with you."

Joe puffed out his cheeks.

"Look around. Look how you live. You saw how she lived." I stepped up to his face. "She used you, just like she used me."

Joe squinted at me. "What you mean, she used you?"

"She came over last night."

Joe shook his head. "She went to her mama's."

"Come on, wise up. She fucked us both. Only you're gonna take the hot squat."

Joe balled his hands into fists.

I looked him hard in the eyes. "What's the matter with you? You killed a fuckin' white man. You're history."

He blinked.

"Forget her, man."

I could see the wheels turning behind his eyes. He opened his mouth, shut it, then said, "He beat his wife."

"I know." That was the thing that tipped the scales, that brought me to Treme, instead of just going home. I hate wife beaters. I lowered my voice. "You killed a white man. You're in a world of shit, man."

"How . . . how did you . . . know?"

How? It was a gut feeling. It was the way Brigid looked at him, the way he looked back. It was that look of intimacy.

Joe was the obvious killer, so obvious it was obscene.

"It had to be you," I told him, "because it wasn't me."

Joe blinked and I could see his eyes were wet.

"You willing to turn her in? You willing to tell the cops she was in on it?"

He looked at me and shook his head. "I'd never do that."

"Then you better beat feet. Go to California. Change your name. But get out now."

Joe looked hesitatingly at his suitcase.

"Forget her," I said forcefully.

"Forget her?"

"Like a bad dream."

I stepped past him. I knew if I was caught here, I'd be in a world of shit too.

Joe grabbed my arm, but let go as soon as I turned. He looked down at my feet, said, "Why you helpin' me?"

"Because I'm more like you than I'm like them."

I'm not sure it registered, not completely.

"You're not getting rid of me to keep her for yourself," he said in a voice that told me he didn't believe that.

"She's done with both of us, man."

I went out the way I came, my heart pounding in my chest as I jumped the fences. I slipped behind the wheel of the DeSoto and looked around before starting it.

I took the long way home.

It's night again. The French doors of my balcony are open, but there is no breeze. I'm on my fourth Scotch, or is it my fifth? I'm waiting for Capdeville and Spade.

They'll be here soon, asking about Joe Cairo, wondering where the fuck he went.

I'll tell them I drove around and went to Cairo's on a hunch. Figuring someone must have seen a white man jumping fences, I'll tell them I tried to sneak up on Cairo, but he was gone.

They'll do a lot of yelling, a lot of guessing, but won't be able to pin anything on me. After all, I didn't do it. I was too busy fucking the wife at the time of the murder.

I close my eyes for a moment and the Scotch has me thinking that maybe, just maybe she'll come. But I know better.

Rising from the sofa, I take my drink into the bedroom and look at the messed-up bed.

God, she was so fuckin' beautiful, it hurt.

I sit on the edge of my bed. It still smells like sex. I'm sure, if I look hard, I'll find some of her public hair scattered in the sheets. That's all I have left – the debris of sex, the memories, and the fuckin' heartache.

CRAZY TIME

Noel Amos

I'M WAITING IN my office just this side of midnight with my feet up on the desk. I've got sparkling lights in my peripheral vision due to an unwise selection of cocktails earlier in the evening and a numb right ear on account of the extended phone conversation I am engaged in. It is a one-sided exchange of views. My client, Mrs Marilyn Mountjoy, is not a happy woman. She's not happy in general because she thinks her husband is fooling around. And right now she's not happy in particular because someone has fucked up the operation to catch him. In her opinion that someone is me.

"Everything's cool, Marilyn," I say to her. "I'm sure there's a good reason Bella is a little late. Give her another ten minutes. She's gonna come walking through the door with all the evidence we need."

"And if she doesn't?" Marilyn says, and I blather a bit because, to be honest, there's nothing I can do. We're both in the hands of some ditzy Italian broad with legs up to here and tits out to there and brains nowhere – probably. But we mustn't prejudge the issue. That's what I say to Mrs Mountjoy. "Fuck you, Raymond

Fielding," is what she says to me, "I wish I never saw
you on TV." And hangs up.

Which is all part of the job, I remind myself. There's the
glamour side – the TV stuff and the *Hammondsville Clarion*
profile – and the other side. Which includes hiding in a
garbage bag while one of my assistants tries to break into a
man's bedroom wearing nothing but a black lace teddy and
six-inch spike heels. When she falls off the ladder we both
end up at the local hospital. Me with a broken rib. I
laughted till I cried, as they say.

I told that story on the Winona Walsingham TV show
and the studio audience cracked up. Afterwards Winona
took my card and said she'd tack it to her kitchen notice-
board so her husband could see it over breakfast and think
twice the next time he came on to some fluff bunny in a
hotel bar. They way she said it I half expected to pick up a
little business in that direction, but not so far.

However, I did get Marilyn Mountjoy, who is an over-
groomed blonde with well-oiled hips and pouty lips that go
all tight when she talks about her husband, Clyde. Clyde
has the kind of job that entails lots of trips to lunch and
planning sessions round the pool and breakfast meetings in
cities a plane-ride away. At the same time, his role as a key
trouble-shooting exec means his working hours are apt to
be extended at short notice. He can never be relied on to fit
into Marilyn's extensive social calendar. He can't guarantee
that, ten minutes into the opera or the Rockerheim cocktail
party or the Guild fund-raiser, his bleeper won't summon
him to do something very important somewhere else. In
short, Marilyn can't ever count on the schmuck to be
around.

When she first came to see me it was obvious this state of
affairs was eating her alive. There were worry lines tugging
down her mouth and furrowing up her smooth brow. They
put years on her which, of course, was making her worry
more.

"I'm sure he's seeing someone. More than one, maybe. He's never home; he could be porking half of Hammonds-ville for all I know. You catch him, Mr Fielding, like you said on TV. You dangle some babe in front of him and get it all on tape. Then I'll chase the asshole through the divorce court till I've got enough to buy my own stable of live-in studs."

"Are you sure you want to do this, Mrs Mountjoy? Some- times it can be best not to know the truth, If you and your husband have a comfortable *modus vivendi* – "

"Modus what? Don't talk crap, Fielding. Do you want to make some money or not?"

Well, of course I did. As badly as she wanted to find out if Clyde was a rat, one way or another. We shook hands on the deal.

Which is why I'm sitting here, wondering what in hell has happened to Bella.

Bella is without doubt the horniest woman I've ever been in the same room with. She oozes pussy. Which is not a delicate way of putting it but it's true.

Every little thing about her you could look at on its own and say it's not perfect. She's got thick honey-brown curls that hang in a tangle, like she can never be bothered to find a hair-brush. Her eyes bug out slightly, they're so big, and one's not quite the same shade of burnt sugar as the other; it's got flecks in it. Her nose is probably too long and her lips too thick and her tits are definitely too heavy for such a slender build. But . . .

But she looks half the time like she's just climbed out of bed with a lover and the other half like she can't wait to climb back in with a new one. You. The first time I met her, she tripped at the door and I caught her arm. She had this tiny dress, a flimsy summer thing with straps, and I found myself holding her bare arm up high with the back of my hand in the hair of her armpit. The smell of her was in my face, part perfume, part woman smell – ripe peaches, bare skin, scented sweat.

I'm used to American females, every square inch of them exfoliated, deodorized and sanitized. Suddenly I had my hands on a real woman, not a Barbie doll. I pulled my hand from her armpit like I'd accidentally touched her snatch.

Though I knew I was going to use her, even if only to make sure I was going to meet up with her again, I had misgivings. I wasn't convinced she understood everything I said about my procedures and there were things every other girl I used always picked up on and she never did. Like the money. I told her what I'd pay her, with a bonus if it all worked out, and she never blinked or pulled a face or said you gotta be kidding, like most of them did.

Mrs Mountjoy – Marilyn, by now, because we'd had lots of tearful should-I-shouldn't-I? conversations and I was up there in her pantheon of father confessors, along with her shrink and her gynaecologist – Marilyn had said Clyde was a sucker for European women and big breasts. So, despite my worries about Bella – her lack of experience in the world of subterfuge and surveillance etc. – I decided to hire her. After all, I thought, she may not know a damn thing about the divorce laws or how to bug a phone but I'd bet a doughnut to a diamond pinkie ring that she's had a *lot* of experience at listening to guys in bars.

Which is all I want her to do. Cosy up to this bar where I've discovered Clyde sometimes goes after work and let her phenomenal body work its magic. If he's in the habit of hitting on babes then he won't pass on this one. And she'll have a microphone in her purse and get all his schmooze on tape. Or maybe he's a monk and he'll ignore the bait. We'll see.

I went through all this with Bella and showed her Clyde's photo. She held it close to her face as if she were memorizing it. Then she turned her wet, toffee eyes on me.

"I love dark men," she said.

I blushed. I'm a dark-haired guy myself.

I'm not blushing now, though I bet my cheeks are a shade on the red side. Red as in angry. Bella is sashaying into my office in a black cocktail dress cut high on the thigh and low on the chest which looks as if it's spent the evening crumpled up under a bed some place. She gives me a big beam like she knows I'm going to be delighted to see her and throws herself into the chair facing my desk. Having failed to meet me in the Piccadilly Pot Roast parking lot as agreed, and not having rung in on the half hour as also agreed, she is approximately two and a half hours late.

I try to control my righteous ire.

"Where the *fuck* have you been, you mindless Italian fruitcake? I've been waiting for you half the night. I'm in deep shit with Marilyn Mountjoy."

"What you mean, 'fruitcake?'" she says, an adorable little wrinkle appearing on the bridge of her nose. Her long long legs stretch carelessly in front of her. The way her thighs gleam hurts my eyes.

"I am seriously pissed off with you, Bella."

"Are you all right, Mr Raymond?" she says.

"No. I just told you, I'm not all right. I am very displeased. I – "

"Ssh!" she says, jumping up and coming round to my side of the desk. "I see you are ill. Your head is hurting, yes?"

The next thing is she's leading me to the couch and making me lie down. It's true, I *am* feeling ill. The head-ache has got worse, The lights are flashing on and off and everything on the edge of my sight is fractured. I feel like I want to pull a big black blanket over my head and bury myself in the dark for ever.

Bella takes off my shoes and lays me out with my head on her lap. It's soft like a pillow, yet warm and alive. Her face is suspended over mine, the curtain of her hair falling down to envelop us both, and she's rubbing some kind of lemony lotion into my temples. The effect is instantaneous. Those slender little Italian fingers are smoothing the hurt and anger right out of me.

But not all of it. I have to know what she got up to. Marilyn will be on the phone again at any minute. In fact, I'm surprised it isn't ringing right now.

"Bella, please," I say, "what happened?"

She smiles down at me. From this angle her breasts are like the Dolomites. "You are going to be pleased with me, Mr Raymond. I've got your tape."

"You did?" Somehow I assumed she'd be too much of an airhead to actually record anything.

"Listen," she says and slips the recorder out of her purse. Then she goes back to massaging my forehead. I am mollified. This, I think, is more like it.

Voices fill the room through a tinny hiss of background chatter and clatter. The sound is not too good but what the hell, this recording is not destined for public release. A male voice comes through loud and clear.

"Hey, babe whachoo drinkin?"

"Go away."

"Say, you're a hell of a looker. Why ain't choo bin in here before?"

"Leave me alone, you don't want to know me – "

"You're wrong there, honey."

" – because I got a bad sexual disease."

"Hey, now . . ."

"It's true. I'm here to meet my doctor. Please go; it's not safe to be seen with me. Not if you have other girlfriends."

"Well, I don't see what harm one little drink – "

"I'm not joking, mister. You stick your penis in me and you'll shoot pus for months."

I look up at Bella and she's grinning from ear to ear. I

already know this isn't Clyde on the tape because I've bugged a few of his conversations already and I know his voice.

"All the guys kept trying it on," she says. "I got fed up."

"Where the fuck is Clyde?" I say, certain she's started a brawl or something and spent the evening being interviewed by the cops. However, it's hard to stay mad at her with those magic fingers massaging my brow and her perfumed thighs cradling my head.

"Ssh," she says, and puts a finger on my lips. "He comes to buy a drink now."

"Miller Lite," says a different man's voice. Sure enough, that's Clyde.

"Put it on my tab." That's her.

"Do I know you?" he says. He sounds suspicious.

"I'm sorry, but I told those guys over there you know me very well."

"Are they hassling you"

"They are trying to pick me up. I don't like it."

"I see." He sounds friendlier. He's probably got a better look at her by now. "What did you tell them about me?"

"I said I was meeting my doctor here. You look a bit like a doctor. Handsome, healthy, smart."

"All the doctors I know look like shit."

"You don't mind, do you? If we just talk for ten minutes then they'll leave me alone and I won't feel so bad about being stood up."

"Aha." It sounds like he's finally sussed things out. The damsel is in distress and fate has selected him to be the knight in shining armour. It strikes me, as the last shreds of my headache are banished by her touch, that the damsel is not as dumb as I'd supposed.

"So who's this person who's stood you up?" says Clyde.

"My ex-fiancé."

"Ex?"

"We just called it off."

"Poor you."

"I don't care now. The thought of settling down with one man – well, I don't know. It's terrible of me, I guess."

"What's terrible?"

"I can't tell you. I'm embarrassed."

"Sure you can tell me. I'm your doctor, remember?"

"It's just the thought of making love to only one guy for the rest of my life. I don't think I can do it."

"If you love someone enough, you can."

"It's not about love. It's lust."

"Lust?"

"Yes, I have too much lust. I lust after men all the time and sometimes I've just got to have them. Even if I don't know them well. Is that very bad?"

"No. That's how guys feel about women."

"Is it? Really? I never knew that."

There's a pause in the conversation. I raise my eyebrows at Bella and she shrugs, sending a shudder through her delightful superstructure.

"What's your name?" says Clyde.

"Maria."

"You're some woman, Maria. My name's Jack."

Bingo, I think, that's lie number one.

"Are you married, Jack?"

"No."

That's number two. It should be plain sailing from here on.

"Why not"

"Like you, Maria, I have too much lust. There's too many gorgeous women out there to tie myself to just one. It wouldn't be fair on my wife."

It's not, you slimeball, I think. Boy, is Marilyn going to throw some kind of shit-fit when she hears this!

"I know what you mean," says Bella. "It's like with Tony, my ex. When I first met him I thought he was everything I would ever want in a man. It was funny how I met him. He won me in a fight,"

"What?" That gets his attention. It gets mine, too. I look up at Bella and she just gives me her trust-me smile. She's pulled off my necktie by now and loosened my collar so she can massage my neck. I don't trust her one bit but right now I'm not complaining. I settle back to listen.

"I was going with this other guy – Roy. He was a gambler. Sometimes he'd have money and sometimes he'd be broke. He never wanted me around when he went to the track but this one time I went along. I finally nagged him into it, I guess. Well, he lost on the first race and decided I was bad luck so he parked me in the clubhouse restaurant. I didn't mind. I ordered a lobster salad and white wine and I thought I'd play the horses myself. The only thing was, I wasn't sure what to do."

"Don't tell me," says Clyde. "Tony showed up and lent a helping hand."

"How do you know? That's exactly what happened. Except it was me who asked him because he was at the window making this bet and I thought he looked, you know, *simpatico*. So when he'd finished I asked him how to do it and he showed me."

"I bet he did."

Bella giggles. "You have a filthy mind, Jack. It wasn't like that at first. Sure, I picked him, I suppose, because he was tall and looked smart. He had thick black hair like you. I like that. It makes me want to run my fingers through it."

"You're some sexy witch, aren't you?"

More giggles. "Don't you want to hear the rest of my story?"

"Sure. Go on."

"Well, Tony showed me how to do all these funny bets – exactas and trios and things – and I lost most of my money. Then the fifth race came along and I won. I won a lot because, so Tony said, it was a pretty stupid bet. Anyhow it came off and I was holding about five hundred dollars when

Roy came storming up. He didn't see Tony, just me and the money. I could tell he'd been losing because his eyes were all beady and hard. He said, 'How the hell did a dumb cunt like you pick a winner?' and he took the notes out of my hand. Tony was behind him and said, 'Give the lady her money back, mister,' and Roy grinned and hit him in the face. Then they went at each other right there in the foyer of the first-class restaurant. By the time the manager rounded up a couple of waiters Roy was laid out on the floor.

"I left with Tony after the manager questioned us. He was going to call the police but all the witnesses said Roy got what he deserved. Anyway, he wasn't hurt that much. The funny thing is, I didn't bother to take my money back. I left it with Roy. I was so hot for Tony, I didn't care."

"It turned you on, huh?"

"It did, Jack. We must have fucked for twenty-four hours straight. I'm sorry."

"What for?"

"For saying fuck. Now you won't think I'm a lady."

"I think you're a magnificent horny woman, Maria. I wish half the women I know were as honest about the way they feel. Did you really fuck for twenty-four hours?"

"Well . . . maybe not quite that long. But he had me in his car in the car park during the seventh race."

"Really?"

"Yes. He had his hand on my ass as he pushed me towards this big Caddy and we were almost running. He just shoved me in the back and pushed my skirt up round my waist."

"What happened then?"

"Jack! Don't tell me you want the naughty details."

"You bet I do. Did he jump on you?"

"Well, he wanted to go down on me first. He put his head between my legs and sucked me through my panties but I didn't want that. I undid his trousers and made him put his cock in me."

"You *made* him?"

"I had to have him at once. I pulled his head up by the hair and tugged him between my legs. He ripped my panties off me and pushed it inside, right up, all in one go. It was wonderful. He had his eyes shut and there was blood on his cheek from the fight and he was going 'uh, uh, uh' from deep in his chest as he gave it to me. All the time I was coming, I had the taste of his blood in my mouth. It was wild. Have you got an erection, Jack?"

If he's anything like me, I think, he's got a pole in his pants.

"Is any of this true?" I say to Bella, but she just shrugs in a kind of who-cares fashion and puts her hand on my trouser buckle and begins to undo it. So help me, she's going to run a flag up my pole and I don't intend doing a damn thing to stop her.

"I've got a little place round the corner," Clyde is saying on the tape. "Let's go back there for another drink." Even as Bella's warm hand is fishing in my fly I'm thinking, what little place?

"Not yet," says Bella to Clyde, "it's your turn to tell me a story."

"I can do that at my place."

"Here's more fun. I like to sit in a bar while a man with a stiff penis tells me naughty stories. It turns me on."

"Are you sure you're not just a pricktease?" says Clyde. Suspicion has returned to his voice.

If she is, she's damn good at it, I think as she circles my shaft with her fingers and squeezes. She's got my whole tackle, balls and all, outside my pants now, and I can tell I'm in the hands of an expert.

"Come on, Jack. Isn't talking sexy to me right here exciting enough for you? Tell me a story. Tell me about a horny time you had."

"Well, let me think." He sounds embarrassed, which is a laugh. "Uh, OK. There's this woman in my office. She

heads up the computer support system for the whole
building so she's no bimbo. In fact, she's got a department
of about a dozen people who maintain and train staff on the
computers."

"What's her name?"

"Francine."

Now, this is very interesting, I think. Clyde could be
making this up, but far more likely, given that his brains are
currently residing in his pecker, he's about to spill some real
juice. In any case, it will be easy to check. I blow Bella a kiss
as her fingers ever-so-gently juggle my balls and she bends
over and places her lips on mine. I am taken by surprise but,
on instant reflection, don't see why I should be. This night
has already spiralled off into fantasy. As she and I explore
each other's tonsils, we listen to Clyde's little tale.

"Francine's been at the company for years. Longer than
me. Sometimes I see her around downtown on the weekends, shopping with her kids. She looks a little different
then to how she appears at work. She wears these dark suits
to the office, cut tight across the ass and bust. She's big, but
in proportion if you know what I mean. She's five nine or
ten and wears heels and her hair up. You can't miss her.
And the way she comes on to her staff, she's like the wicked
governess. Whack! Six of the best and all of that. You can
see some of those young assistants almost wetting their
pants when she gets going

"However, she's sweet as pie to me, since I'm about two
levels up the ladder from her. In fact, the guy she reports to
reports to me. About the end of last year he had to go into
hospital and she started to come into my office regularly.
The more I saw of her, the more I liked her. It turned out
she had a sense of humour. She knew the impression she
created around the place, everybody thinking she was some
kind of dragon, but she didn't care. In fact, it was good
camouflage for what she was really like. When she told me
what she did for a hobby I nearly fell off my chair."

"What does she do?"

"Invents porno computer games. She told me it had started as a joke but she now had some interest from a software manufacturer and she asked me what the company's attitude would be if she did a deal with them. I said I thought the company wouldn't give a damn what she got up to in her own time. Then she told me about Check Mate – that's her game – and my jaw hit the floor.

"Of course, I wanted to see it. So, one evening after everyone else had gone, I went to her office and she let me give it a whirl. First off, if you're a man playing the game, you have to invent a woman and there's all these choices you've got – long legs/short legs, big ass/small ass etc. – but refined to the point where you can specify thirty-four C-cup breasts with pink upturned nipples or a boyish bum with apple cheeks dusted with blonde downy hairs. That precise. But the point of the game is that you have a certain amount of money to spend on seducing your fantasy mate and every little detail costs you. You could end up blowing your stash creating the girl of your dreams but then you wouldn't be able to take her out and buy her dinner. I'm sorry, Maria; this kind of stuff fascinates me, so tell me if I'm boring you."

There's a small silence punctuated by a wet, sticky sound as of two people kissing. A magical sound, I reflect, as Bella and I reproduce it in the here and now.

On the tape, Bella says, "Just cut to the sexy bits, Jack, before I wet my pants."

"OK. Francine ran me through the whole set-up and of course asked me if I wanted to play. I said yes and she said it would speed the whole thing up if I had a ready-made female to seduce. She tapped in an instruction and, bingo, I got this image of a fabulous naked woman. She was a tall brunette with thick dark hair that fell to just above the most incredible tits – big low-slung melons with pointy brown nipples. The waist was small, which made the breasts look even bigger, and it flared out into wide rounded hips. The legs were long and solid and there was a strip of chestnut pubic hair that was shaved around the pussy split. And when you chased her round the bedroom her big square ass winked at you. I mean, it wasn't the woman I would have created but she was stupendous.

" 'She looks familiar,' " I said. " 'She should be,' " said Francine, " 'I modelled her on me' " She let that thought sink in and then she said, " 'And I based this guy on you.' " Up on screen suddenly there was another figure, a naked man, and I looked at it more closely than I've ever looked at anything, I swear. Sure enough, it did look like me: same hair, same eye colour, same build. There was just one thing different."

There's a pause on the tape. The sound of people ordering drinks and swapping yarns further down the bar can be heard quite clearly.

Then Bella's voice says, "I think I can guess. Was it his cock?"

"You bet. He had a joint like a baseball bat. It looked like a cannon sticking up from between his legs. I was speechless. 'You're not offended, are you?' she said. 'I mean, I know I've probably got a few details wrong.'

"What did you say?"

"I said, 'Art improves on life every time, Francine',"

Bella laughs, a real down-and-dirty chuckle, before she says, "Did you show her the real thing?"

"About two seconds later. We had lust, as you say, all over her office till about midnight. It's about the weirdest bit of fucking I've ever done because she made these two little figures on the screen go at it too. She'd turned off the lights so there was just this flickering from the terminal while we got down to it on her office couch. Every time I'd look up there was me and her screwing hammer and tongs on screen. I give dynamite computer sex, I tell you."

Back in the real world, as it were, I have my hands on

Bella's breasts through the material of her dress. She's not wearing a bra and the tits are hot and heavy. I can feel every ridge and crinkle of the areolae. I pull her bazookas into the open. The nubs are swollen, like someone has been sucking on them already. The thought excites me as I feed a big nipple into my mouth.

"What about Francine? She must have been hot for you."

"Sure."

"Was she good?"

"Oh yeah, she's a passionate lady."

"So you still see her?"

"Do you always ask so many questions, Maria?"

"Only about sex. I like to know what people do. That way you can learn new things. I bet Francine taught you things."

"Well, I guess."

"You see? Tell me."

"Maria, please! We hardly know one another. We just met. We haven't even, you know . . ."

"That's OK, Jack. I'm only joking. You are a nice man not to say everything you do with this Francine with the big titties. Did she let you put your penis between them? I love it when a man does that to me. Or maybe she let you put it up her ass. That's so dirty but sometimes it's just what a girl feels like – ow!"

There's a sudden yelp and Bella cries, "Hey, Jack, let go of me!"

Clyde's whisper is hoarse and urgent. "You're leaving with me right now, you little pricktease, or I'll drill you right here, so help me!"

"OK," says Bella, "just pass me my purse," and there's a rattling noise and the tape goes dead.

I'm lying across Bella's lap in a state of torment. Above me sway those fantastic breasts now gleaming with my spittle.

"You didn't go with him, did you?" I say. That's the most important rule in the book. No matter how sexy my operatives behave to get the goods, they never, ever, take it further. Even if they want to. It is forbidden. "You didn't go back with him, did you?" I repeat, but I know the answer already. Where else has she been for half the night? It's obvious.

She shrugs her shoulders. Her big titties shrug too, right in my face. You can imagine the effect.

"Why?" I say. "We've got enough on the bastard to divorce him twice over. You didn't need to go with him."

"I didn't want to give the wrong impression," she says. "People call me many things but nobody calls me a pricktease."

I laugh and there's a touch of hysteria in it. She shuts me up by pushing her tongue down my throat and speeding up her fingers on my prick. She's been keeping me on the brink for hours, it seems, and now I can't hold it any longer. My hands close on those creamy globes above me as I'm ravished by her lips and she works me in her hands like putty. Stiff, aching, trembling putty. I spunk over the pair of us like a teenager on a hot date.

Two minutes later we're cleaning up when the office door crashes open and Marilyn Mountjoy walks in. Her pretty face is drawn in tight ugly despair. My first thought is, thank God I got my handjob before she showed.

"Hey, Marilyn," I say as casually as I can, "guess who turned up? This is Bella."

"So I see," she says, slamming the door shut behind her with her foot.

"Have a seat. Relax. We've got some great material for you . . ."

"Just tell me," she says, her eyes like chips of ice, "has this tramp slept with my husband?"

"Of course not," I say. "But I'm afraid we have gathered

incriminating evidence about his behaviour which confirms your – "

"Have you?" she hisses, stepping closer and speaking directly to Bella, who gazes back at her with wide-eyed innocence.

"Don't get excited, Marilyn," I say, interposing my body between the two of them. Sometimes clients get a little heated in these situations and take it out on my operatives. "Bella was only doing her job."

"Slut!" cries Marilyn.

"Hey, Marilyn," I say. "Don't shoot the messenger." Which is a phrase I often use because it seems to fit the bill, but right now it's a big mistake.

"Why the fuck not?" says Marilyn, and takes a pistol out of her purse.

Uh oh! I think as the room goes deathly quiet. Behind me I hear Bella's breath coming in little raggedy gulps. Apart from that you could hear a mouse fart.

"Get out of the way," says Marilyn to me, "or I'll plug you."

"Don't be ridiculous, Marilyn. You don't want to shoot her, she's on your side. We both are."

"I'll count to three. If you don't move I'll kill you too. *One.*"

Her eyes are full of tears, I can see, and her voice is all wobbly. But the gun is steady. It's a great big mother and she holds it in both hands. She can't miss.

"They got a death penalty in this state, you know," I say. "*Two.*"

"You'll fry, Marilyn, and Clyde will be out there screwing around. What good will that do?"

"*Three!*"

I close my eyes. Behind me I hear Bella muttering some kind of prayer beneath her breath. The gun does not go off.

"Shit!" says Marilyn.

I open my eyes and see her knuckles whitening as she

squeezes on the trigger. I step forward and take the gun out of her hands.

She looks me in the eye and says, "The fucking thing doesn't work."

"Not if you don't take the safety off," I reply, and she falls into my arms and begins to blub into my shoulder.

Bella removes the gun from me and locks it in the top drawer of my desk. Her face is drawn but she's in control. How come I ever thought she was dumb?

She looks up at me and says, over Marilyn's howls, "She would have shot us dead."

It's my turn to shrug. "So much for the death penalty as a deterrent. I always knew it was a crock of shit."

Marilyn is now inconsolable. The tears have done their work and she's cried all her anger into my shirt. We sit her down and press a glass of Scotch into her hand. Bella wets a handkerchief and swabs Marilyn's throat and forehead. Marilyn clings on to her free hand.

"I'm sorry, I'm sorry," she says over and over. "I could have killed you. I'm sorry."

Bella says it's OK and gives Marilyn a hug that starts the tears up again. She holds her till they stop and then Marilyn looks normal again.

"I want to hear the tape," she says.

I say I think she should go home and we'll discuss it in the morning.

"Are you crazy?" she says, which is a bit rich, since she was the one waving a gun in my face ten minutes back. "I can't wait till tomorrow. Put it on now."

I'm prepared to debate this further but Bella is switching on the tape machine. She sits next to Marilyn and takes her hand. I think, What the hell? and take her other hand and sit on the other side of her. Thank God I got a big couch.

"Do you live here all alone?" That's Bella's voice.

"Sure do. It's all a single guy needs." That's Clyde.

I realize Bella has put on tape two but refrain from explaining the scenario to Marilyn. I doubt she'll need an interpreter.

"Now where were we?" says Clyde, and we go into sticky-kissy mode. In the background Mark Knopfler doodles a solo. At least Clyde's got decent taste in humping music.

Marilyn's little pointed jaw is set firm and she's holding it steady. Her fingers are digging into mine, though, as we digest the slithering sound of clothes being rearranged.

"Man!" breathes Clyde. "Oh brother, these are the most fabulous titties I've ever . . ." The words tail off as he puts his mouth to other uses. I can picture his lips closing on a puckered brown saucer of areola and a big chocolate-dark nipple filling his mouth. I guess Marilyn can picture it too because her fingernails are about to draw blood.

"Oh Maria, Maria. God, Maria, I love your tits . . ." The words are punctuated by sucking and slobbering as Clyde goes ape over Bella's balcony fittings. And who could blame him? I reflect. It's a silly question, sitting as I am right next to his wife.

"He's always thought mine were too small," says Marilyn, in a matter-of-fact voice.

"Men are stupid like that," says Bella.

"God, Maria," goes Clyde, "I've just got to, you know . . ."

"Do you think mine are too small?" says Marilyn.

"Don't be ridiculous," I say, "they're everything a guy could want."

"I wasn't talking to you," she snaps, and pulls her hand from mine, for which I'm grateful.

"Ooh!" that's Bella squealing on the tape.

"I'm sorry, Maria," says Clyde, "but first I've got to fuck your tits."

To my amazement, Marilyn doesn't turn a hair. She's too busy unbuttoning her blouse.

"What do you think?" she says to Bella, pulling a peach silk camisole up high over two shivering pink-and-cream titties like small perfect pears.

"Oh my," says Bella. "They're gorgeous."

"Uh, uh, uh," goes Clyde in the background.

Marilyn ignores him. "Do you really think so?"

"Fabulous," says Bella, and touches one tiny raspberry nipple with her forefinger. I rub my eyes. I can't be seeing this.

"Oh yes, yes!" moans Clyde. "Lick it, yes – that's it. Oh, my God . . ."

"Show me yours," says Marilyn, tossing the camisole onto the floor on top of her blouse.

I hold my breath as Bella gets her tits out again. The olive-skinned globes dwarf Marilyn's pink pears. The two women look at each other closely as if I'm not there.

"I can see why he liked you," says Marilyn. "He's a greedy pig."

"He's foolish," says Bella, and places Marilyn's hand on her big left breast.

"He's a man," says Marilyn, and lowers her head to Bella's tit.

"Uh, uh, uh," continues Clyde like a blissed-out soul singer in the background as Bella strokes Marilyn's spun-sugar hair. Her hands rove down the woman's dimpled back, soothing and comforting, like she's trying to smooth out the creases. I can see Marilyn responding to her touch, relaxing into her arms. Just before they kiss, Bella shoots me a glance over Marilyn's shoulder. It says, *Leave this to me*. As if I were capable of doing anything else.

"Oh God, oh God!" mumbles Clyde, heading into his short strokes from the sound of it.

Marilyn and Bella are mouth to mouth and tit to tit. From the side I can see Marilyn's sharp little nips digging into the smooth enveloping flesh of Bella's round jugs. I'm almost as far gone as Clyde and there's only one thing that stops me coming in my pants. The thought that, for the first time in my career, I've completely lost control of an investigation.

Bella has her hand up Marilyn's skirt as the two of them

wrestle around. Marilyn's got great thighs, smooth and slim and silky from years of leg-wax, I can tell. She does her bikini line too, that's now clear. The skirt's up to her waist and Bella's walking her fingers all over her little blue panties. The cotton's so wet it's sticking to the cleft. Marilyn's not a natural blonde – I can see that from the dark shadow beneath the blue.

"I gotta put it in – I gotta!" It's a shock to hear Clyde still jabbering. I'm getting carried away with events right here on the couch.

"Oh, you're so big," says Bella on the tape. "I don't think I can take all that."

Who says the guys have a monopoly on the dumb lines? I reflect as I watch Bella yank Mrs Mountjoy's panties to her knees. I lend a hand and whisk them down her legs and off her feet. She's not going to notice – not with Bella's fingers combing out her bush. As I thought, her legs are smooth as silk.

"Oh yes!"

"Put it in!"

"Oh God!"

"Quick, quick!"

I'm getting confused here. Marilyn is muttering out loud as Bella finds her clit and the on-tape Bella is making with the boudoir dialogue. The room is filled with oohs and aahs and grunt-moan sounds and I can't deny it's having an effect. So much so that I miss what Bella is saying to me. She says it again.

"Have you got a hard-on?" she hisses, kind of impatient, like she wants to add, Pay attention, asshole.

I don't know how to answer this question. There are two half-naked women sitting beside me on the couch, one's got her hand up the other's twat and there's a soundtrack of a man and a woman fucking like they just got out of jail. I haven't just got a hard-on – I've got a prick made out of tempered steel.

I nod my head.

"So take it out and fuck her," she orders.

Marilyn's eyes bug open.

I stare at Bella like she's a madwoman.

"It's what you need," says Bella to Marilyn. "Listen –
Clyde's getting his. You deserve it too."

Marilyn kind of moans. Like she wants to protest and it's
stuck in her throat. But her sweet little pelvis is jerking on
the seat as Bella handles her pussy and the juice is flowing.

"Get it out," Bella repeats, this time to me. "This girl's
in distress."

Who am I to say no? I think as I unbutton my pants. So
what if it breaks my sworn vow never to touch a client? This
is crazy time. Anyway, this woman held a gun on me. She
owes me a piece of her pretty pink pussy.

And Marilyn's not complaining. "Take off your
clothes," she says. "Show me what you got."

I don't want to boast but I know I don't look bad. I keep
in shape and I've got muscles. I kick off my shoes and socks
and drop my pants to the floor. My cock is straining in my
shorts and I drop them too. The women are looking at me
with eyes like shiny new quarters.

"Yummy," says Marilyn, and reaches out her hand. I
step between the vee of her legs as she sprawls on the couch
and let her explore my cock and balls. She does it with the
hand that held the pistol on me. I don't care about that now.
She leans forward and looks close at the red head of my
dick. She smiles and slips it into her mouth. Jesus, it's hot
in that little furnace. Flames lick down my root and up my
belly. As she sucks me in and gobbles I thank my stars that
Bella brought me off already in her hand. Else I'd be
emptying my balls down Marilyn's throat right now.

She lifts her head, her lips are red and moist and very full.

"Please," she says, and I sink to my knees between her
legs.

With her on the couch and me on the floor, her cunt's just

at the right height for ease of entry. I put my cock at the gate of her pussy and slide right in.

Bella has primed Marilyn for me. She's on the edge, wound up so tight that when I hit bottom, as you might say, she goes off the rails. Her upper body flails and those cute little tits shiver and bounce and she gives out with a string of "Oh-yes-oh-God-that's-great-you-big-fucker-oh," etc. till I shut her up with a kiss. I wrap my arms around her and hold my cock still till she calms a bit. I'm aware that the fucking noises on the tape have come to an end. I'm aware too of Bella, so close to us, watching everything.

I get Marilyn into a proper fucking rhythm, easing my dick in and out of her in a steady pump, and she spreads her legs and takes it. She's got her eyes closed and her mouth shut, thank the Lord, and she just lies back in Bella's arms and I fuck her like a doll. This is fantastic.

Now it's a silent serious business. Marilyn's cunt is like a warm glove around my cock, massaging every inch. It's an incredible sensation and I feel like I could go on all night. I'm kneeling up, shafting between her legs, fondling her thighs, watching my dick as it stretches her sweet little puss. For the first time in the whole messy business I'm in control and I'm loving it.

Then Marilyn starts to come. She's lying back across Bella's lap and jerking like a landed fish. Strangled sounds are coming from her throat and she's got her fingers in the dark thatch at the top of her crack, diddling herself. She's got a big clit, a wine-red peg sticking right up, and I watch the way she goes at it. She pinches and jabs herself in a way I'd never dare. Whatever she's doing it works, for she's in freefall, way off somewhere else, flopping and moaning and squealing on my cock.

Her orgasm seems to go on forever. I'm not exactly detached about it but I'm wondering what the hell is going through her head as she bounces on my dick. Is this a weird revenge on her two-timing husband? Some kind of hysteria? Or is she always this hot?

There's another noise mixed in with Marilyn's squeals, a long sigh that sends a shiver through me. I look at Bella. She's biting her lip but she can't hold the sound back. Her wonderful tits are shaking and her left arm is half hidden behind Marilyn, but I can tell from the way she's sitting that her hand is between her legs.

I think to myself that the moment Marilyn is finished I'm going to push her off my cock and sink it between the luscious olive thighs of my new associate. I look into Bella's big wet eyes and she knows what I'm thinking. She nods her head and smiles.

Then, though I don't want to, the blood starts to rush in my veins and I feel the sap rise in my balls. I grab Marilyn's butter-soft hips and thrust into her. I can't help myself. As I come I hear the sound of Marilyn moaning and Bella sighing and I hear myself shout, "Oh fuck!"

Bella and I take Marilyn home. She's almost comatose, won't open her eyes, and we have to carry her to the car. As we pull up at her house she snaps out of it.

"I'm fine," she says, and vanishes indoors without saying goodnight.

Clyde's car is in the drive so we wait for ructions, but all seems peaceful. Lights come on at the bedroom window then go out again.

After half an hour, during which Bella and I say nothing but think plenty, we drive off. I ask Bella to come back to my place but she says she's pooped. So am I, to tell the truth.

The next day Marilyn rings to say she and Clyde are solid so forget the whole investigation. She'll put a cheque in the post.

Bella comes in at four in the afternoon. I go to kiss her and she tells me to back off. I go to pay her and she says "Put it on my account. I'm hiring you to check out my husband."

I lift an eyebrow. Is she kidding? This is the first I've heard of a husband.

"I'm serious," she says. "I'm married three years and I know my guy is running around with other women."

"But don't you need the money? I thought you owed the bank."

"Sure, but how else can I afford you?"

I grin and pull some notes out of my wallet.

"Here's your money, sweetheart," I say. "You can pay my bill some other way."

She gives me a look as she picks up her dough. One of the complicated kind.

"Will it be very expensive?" she says.

I just nod my head, my voice frozen in the back of my throat as I watch her fingers undo the pearl buttons on the front of her bulging blouse . . .

THE MAGIC COCKROACH

Susan Scotto

UPON HEARING THE story I am about to tell, you may insist that I am mad, that the fantastic events described herein could not possibly have occurred. But I beg of you, before condemning me, consider my words carefully. For he does exist, and he is indeed magic. I am fully aware that nine out of ten of you, if asked, would readily reveal your hatred of cockroaches. I, however, am the one out of ten who is an amateur of these amazing insects, or rather, of one particular cockroach I had the great good fortune to meet. But it was only after the event I am about to relate to you that I came to feel this way about roaches.

Some years ago I had as my residence a deteriorating sixth floor walk-up in 112th St and Broadway, several blocks distant from Columbia University. Although rent-controlled, my two-room flat was not cockroach-controlled. I had just arrived in New York from the Middle West of our country, where sow bugs abound but roaches are scarce. At this time, the mere sight of a roach was enough to send me screaming from the room. Smashing them with a shoe seemed contact too intimate for my delicate constitution. Thus, after consultation with friends and coworkers, I chose to employ the services of an aloof gecko I named Tim.

Ours was an easy partnership. Tim kept the cockroach population well in check, and I made sure he had a tiny dish of milk in the cabinet under the sink. Tim's presence was a comfort, especially at night. As I sat curled on the settee reading, or smoking as I worked until the wee hours on a new story, I would hear his nails scratch as he raced across the floor or the counter after his prey. If he was nearby, I might even detect the crunch as a roach met its well-deserved end. The sound never failed to send a shiver down my spine, a shiver of sadistic pleasure. But, sad to say, not even Tim was able to totally eradicate the six-legged pests. This became abundantly clear one hot summer night.

My air conditioner had broken, so I lay nude on my bed with a fan pointed directly at me. Already dozing as I indolently masturbated, I fell into a fitful sleep, but was roused some time after midnight by the feeling that my inner thigh was being simultaneously scraped and tickled. In that shifting state between slumber and wakefulness, I opened my eyes. I noted nothing suspicious, but still I felt the odd sensation, further up on my leg now. Light from the streetlight outside fell in a beam across the bare wooden planks of my floor and up onto my bed, illuminating the very part of my anatomy whence emanated the strange feeling I have described.

Still groggy – could I have been still asleep? – I made out a dark, ovoid form approximately four inches in length. I looked more closely, squinting, and then my eyes widened in terror: moving slowly up my inner leg was a gigantic cockroach. I opened my mouth to loose an inhuman scream but nothing would come out. Wishing to brush the roach off, to jump up, to shake it away, I found myself frozen to the spot. I had no choice but to watch, mute and paralyzed by terror, as the hideous insect tap, tap, tapped its way higher and higher, tickling my leg with its antennae. How I wished at that moment that all was but a nightmare, but now I was fully and undeniably awake.

When it reached the very top of my leg, the nefarious insect halted and raised its head. It seemed to me that the cursed thing was actually winking at me. Horrified, I shut my eyes tight, willing my muscles and my vocal chords to act. In vain. As I lay there, hoping against hope that when I opened my eyes once more the beast would be gone, I felt the terrifying tickle once more, but now it seemed more bearable, somehow, and was centered between my legs.

As the minutes went by, this sensation grew surprisingly pleasant. Although afraid of what I might see, I nonetheless opened one eye. Yes, the roach was still there. Having braced his tiny appendages against my two legs, his head was moving furiously up and down, back and forth. His antennae waved wildly. Lost in the pleasing sensation, I knew not how long I lay that way, but when I glanced next at him, the black bug was already in shadow; the street-light's beam now crossed my breast. Again I attempted to scream, and scream I did, but not out of fear. No, it was a scream born of billowing surges of pleasure which coursed through my body as a result of the roach's attentions. It was an intense sexual release, unlike any I had ever felt. My eyes closed, and I lay still, exhausted, covered in sweat. Soon, I found I could speak once more, but only murmured expressions of endearment and then, of gratitude, passed my lips.

Opening my eyes only by great effort, I addressed the cockroach. "Who are you? Are you real?"

"Quite real," came the reply, in a man's voice which bore traces of a European accent.

"Do you have a name?" I asked.

"Casanova," he whispered.

"You certainly . . . are . . . a Casanova," I said.

"No," he objected. "I am . . . the . . . Casanova."

"How could you be?" I was sitting upright now, with the

bug perched on my knee. "Casanova lived in the eighteenth century. What's more, he was a human."

"All true," the roach confirmed. "And yet, you see before you Jacques Casanova."

"Jacques the roach?"

"Yes, *mon ange*," he confirmed. "Many cuckolded husbands called me such during my lifetime, and through a cruel trick of fate I was condemned to roam the earth in insect form."

"But surely not all cockroaches can do . . . what you do!" I exclaimed.

The roach assumed a haughty pose. He even appeared to frown. "Precisely, *mademoiselle*. My skill is unique among crawling forms of life. In the nearly two centuries since my death, I have perfected my technique."

I only nodded silently.

"And now, to make up for the sins of my human life, for the reckless abandon with which I treated each female I loved, I travel the globe, bringing pleasure to hundreds of thousands of women like yourself."

"But surely you have not inhabited the same body for all this time, unless you have been granted immortality?"

"Indeed, *ma chérie*," he replied. "I live the life of the roach, with all its risks. I cannot count the times I have been crushed."

"But how do you come back?" I queried.

"Upon leaving one body, I move immediately into another. But I never know where I shall turn up next. That is not within my control. In this life, I am a cockroach in New York. My next may find me a taraquan in Saint Petersburg, or a cucaracha in Madrid. It is a difficult existence to be sure."

Suddenly I felt something resembling pity for the gleaming black bug before me. "But must you roam forever?"

He shook his head. "I will be free when my tally reaches one million."

"How many do you have to go?" I inquired.

"Ten," he replied.

"I'm at your service," I replied sincerely, opening my legs once more for him. "Be my guest."

He smiled, if it is possible for a roach to smile. "Ah, my dear, I would be glad to oblige, but the terms of my sentence require one million different women."

I leaned forward and gazed deep into his eyes. Behind the proud gaze of this amorous cockroach I glimpsed the soul of the tortured bug within.

"Let me help you," I said to him. "I'll invite some friends over this evening, we'll have a party, and you can reach your total in one night, without ever leaving the apartment."

Jacques the roach scurried up my arm and planted a tiny kiss on my cheek. "I shall eagerly await the occasion," he replied with a bow. "And now, my pet, lie back, and I shall offer you a token of my thanks."

I did as he bade, and watched fondly as he made his way over my breasts and hip, and back between my legs.

Once more the blessed bug brought me to heights of ecstasy. Then I drifted off to sleep. The room still lay in darkness when I next came to, awakened by the sensation of scraping upon my inner thigh. My first thought was that Jacques was intending to thrill me once more with his gifted tongue, even as I rested, spent, on my bed. But, upon raising my eyelids, I was met with a horrifying sight. The scraping had been produced not by my amorous friend, who was asleep on my thigh, tongue lolling out of the side of his mouth. What I now saw struck such terror into my heart as I have never known.

So exhausted that I was unable even to rise up on my elbows, I could only shriek. And shriek I did.

"Tim! Don't!" But it was too late. In a flash, Tim fell upon Jacques and seized the roach's head with his razor-sharp jaws. Involuntarily, I shut my eyes, unable to watch the demise of my beloved. When finally I was able to bring myself to survey the carnage, I began to weep, for there, on my thigh, lay the now headless cockroach, his life essence oozing out in a yellowish stream. Tim was perched triumphantly on Jacques' back. One antenna protruded grotesquely from his mouth. He looked to me for approval, but I swept him violently off me and took Jacques' carcass in my palm.

"Darling Jacques," I sobbed, "forgive me. It is I who is the selfish one. If I had not been thinking only of my own pleasure, I could have saved you."

But then I recalled the roach's words. Of course! He had perished here tonight, but as surely as the sun would rise and set again tomorrow, Jacques the roach would appear once more, somewhere on this cursed earth. That means, I realized as I stroked his lifeless exoskeleton, there is still hope for Jacques . . . and for me, if ever I can find him.

Since that fateful night I have roamed the world in search of the reincarnated roach of my dreams. Having long ago left my job, I subsist on interest from an inheritance which fortuitously came my way upon the death of a wealthy aunt. This provides but a pittance, so that I must dwell in the most shabby of apartments and cheap hotels – a situation quite to my liking, in fact, since it provides me easy access to the insects I seek. Ah, how many seedy rooms have I seen since that night long ago? Into how many blank cockroach eyes have I stared? How many times have I begun nighttime conversations with roaches of all descriptions, only to be answered with silence? I have lost count. Friends who see me say I have changed. They are horrified by my pale visage and the crazed intensity of my gaze.

Although I fear I am no closer to completing my search than I was when it began twenty years ago, still I do not despair. I look with hope upon each roach I find. For I cannot say when or where I will find my dear Jacques. But find him I shall, if it is the last thing I do.

Perhaps you are unconvinced of my tale and think me mad. But I beg of you, take care before crushing the next roach who makes his way quietly over your bedclothes in the dark of night. He may be the very roach I have described. And please, if you do find him, inform me immediately by registered post, for he is a very fine bug, indeed.

NEW ORLEANS

Alice Blue

DAPPLED SUNLIGHT MADE hot spots on my tummy. Leaves
flickered and twirled above me; the flashes of their revolu-
tions making my eyes ache. A coupla beers and a shot of
Jack Daniels boiled me. I was grumpy. I was twisted and
mean with the forces of worked dykehood. I was leather
without lace, twisted with spirits. I was one of three bitchin'
dykes and two flaming fags set to bruise our knuckles on no
one in particular, but too tired and hot to move.

The party was only an echo: a hot sun and aquarium
weather had bleached Mardi Gras into nothing but die hard
drunks and pathetic cruisers. Our kingdom was a sad
willow and the porch of our sad cottage with the thumpa-
thumpa of pre-Columbian disco leaking to us from a bar next
door. Through the narrow slats in the fence we could see the
flashes of the milling, aimless Them and their funny hats,
clever T-shirts "Show us your tits!" and vomit. We were
invisible behind our fence, a wall of hostility and heavy, tired
flowers that smelled like very cheap wine. Among us,
nothing moved but the flies. Nothing doin' anything except
feeling the sun on my warm tummy.

Downy and I shared the nest (a pile of leather jackets on

the complaining porch) with a cute girl (Sal?) I let in because she reminded me of Dixie and a pair of Jack's friends – a bleached blond ornament and a leather and Crisco-greased Chicago boy. All of us, the boys and the girls, lay in the hot undersea air and watched the world flicker by through a flowers-and-wine-choked fence.

It was hard to say where the undersea climate ended and the penis began. But there it was, round and white like a short slug, on the side of one of the Chicago boys' leather pants. "What do you use that thing for?" Downy asked, feeling it, running fingers over the sticky skin, ringing the head, gently flicking the tight vein underneath.

"Some guys like it sucked. Some like fucking with it," Chicago said in a heat-drunken voice, a rum-drunk voice. He watched the dyke play with his dick – drunk and hypnotized by her fascination, her brown-eyed wonder of it.

"Little boys?" Sal (I think her name was) asked from her sprawl on her back. The cock was almost hard now. She stared at it: amazed, disgusted and drunk.

"Big boys, too," he said, smiling too wide and too pleased.

The cock got hard. Downy looked at us, her sisters. A *What do I do with it now?* flickered across her face. Hot day, rum and harder, boredom, comfort – I don't know. Sure, I was there, that day, but I wasn't her, wasn't Downy. I didn't know what was tripping through her head, I was just watching – as she took the unlubed condom (blue, I noticed) that he offered, rolled it down, then started to suck the Chicago boy's cock.

"Watch me be a boy," Downy said, pulling away for a second to speak.

The sun blinked down on them: the dyke sucking cock, the leatherboy with girl-lip on his meat. It blinked down and made everything hotter. As the haze of the Louisiana afternoon settled down over my brain and wrapped everything in an undersea bed, I found myself slowly, geologically, rolled over and lifted up so I was on hands and knees. It took some work, and I didn't help, to get my leather pants down, but it happened. Sudden air, slightly cooler air on my sweaty ass. "You know straights, how do they do it?" asked another girl-girl voice, a smiling voice, a playful voice, a *festive* voice – Sal's voice – from behind me.

"I think I can figure it out," the pretty boy said from behind me, and above.

Sal stroked my pussy from behind, coaxing me open with girl fingertips, knowing the buttons to press, the silk to stroke. I felt myself yawn, a falling feeling under my warm tummy.

"You big enough, girl?" Downy said, taking her lips from Chicago's cock, concern sprinkled over her words, silver spit threads going from cock to her mouth – or was it the other way around?

I can't remember if I nodded or I just gave permission with silence. Either way, I was committed – my ass was naked in the hot daylight and I heard the sound of something tearing open and, "Never done this to a real one before," from Sal as, I knew later, she rolled a condom onto pretty boy's cock.

A real one – I'd never thought of it like that before. I'd played with his rubber kin, his silicone brethren, but never one of the real thing – or, at least, the flesh and blood thing. Then, there on that porch, though, I was saying *ah!* with my other mouth and, before even I knew it, I was full.

Boy, was I full! At the end, when I felt his furry thighs press against my ass, and his cock tapped me deep inside, I thought I was going to unzip from the pressure, that overwhelming *filling*. But then he pulled back, and it faded – only to come back again with the next stroke.

"Tsk – tsk," Downy said, absently stroking Chicago's blue-covered cock, "what will the girls say?"

I put my hot forehead down onto the coat I'd been stretched on, breathing in black leather, boy armpit stink and spilled beer. In and out in and out was all I could really think about – not what I was doing, what Downy was doing, what tomorrow would be like, what even tonight would be like (let alone in a hour or two). In and out in and out in (ouch!) and out (ooooh!) was all that easily moving boy-cock managed to let into my brain.

I didn't try to come – didn't really want to. I was trying something new, that's all, and the newness was all I really wanted to feel (in and out in and out). I was being doggy-humped on black leather by a pretty boy – that was quite enough. My clit was tight, yeah, and hard (yeah!) but I didn't feel like stroking it, touching myself or even having Sal or Downy down there with hands, lips, whatever, doing it for me (even though they'd both done the same and worse). I was just then, there, getting fucked by a boy and that was quite enough.

I didn't plan on coming, but that's what happened. I didn't try, but I came, the coming came, and I did. It was weird, unusual – deep and pressurized, not lightning-bolt like fingers and lips and whatever else on throbbing clit. When it came it boiled up from my cunt, building like a can of beer casually shook and shook and shook then popped open.

I popped, that's for damned sure.

One minute I was just fucking, just being fucked, and then, like the filling overflowed, I was coming – grunting like a pig into the leather jacket, biting it: tasting polish, dust, and my own stale breath. I must have collapsed after, falling down into the warm porch, the hot leather. Must have, but don't remember doing so.

Then someone was speaking. I blinked away the sparkles and the heavy exhaustion that had fallen on top of me and ground my head to the left.

Dancing green eyes; a spotlight, toothy smile – Downy's cheeks creased with warm laughter: "So, little one, get fucked by girls and you get fucked by boys – so what are you?"

I closed my eyes, feeling the weight again. I don't know how long I had them closed, maybe a blink, maybe a much longer blink. When I opened them again the sun was passing behind the fence and the world was becoming deeper colors.

"Tired," I said to Downy's naked back as a bar across the street flashed its first neon of the night, "and happy."

IN THE WHITE ROOM

Michael Perkins

IN EASTHAMPTON, MAURICE was our host, a jealous, thorough man.

However shocking (or perhaps just plain curious) it may seem, when I saw Mora naked with Charles and Vy it wasn't jealousy that I felt. It was lust that grew in my belly like a sapling putting down roots. I knew the voyeur's stunned delight in achieving erotic perspective. Our nakedness created the illusion that we had entered another dimension, a counter world of the id, where our apprehensions were removed with our clothes and past and future ceased to exist.

Vy's bedroom was white, but by no means chaste. White walls, white sheepskin rugs on the parquet floor, huge antique mirrors, white vases filled with daisies, and a platform bed on which the three of them sat as if on a tongue sticking out of fluffy clouds, for the silk spread was white, but the sheets underneath were crimson. Satin.

I sauntered around the room sipping a brandy and looking at things, conscious of the cool night air on my bare skin. I studied four large framed photographs of Vy on one gleaming white wall, two of them by young fashion photographers I knew. In the portraits she was elegant, stylish, with formidable cheekbones and a frosty gaze; I didn't see the woman I'd watched kneeling before Charles on the beach.

When I walked over to the bed, Mora and Vy were lying on each side of Charles like houris, watching him stroke himself. His tongue moistened his dry lips, his strong hands moved slowly from his knees up his firm thighs to his rounded belly. His breath came in shallow gasps. His chest swelled and his nipples pointed. I shivered.

We drew matches and Charles won. He asked that Vy and Mora stretch out between his thighs and handed me the Polaroid. I was happy to hide behind it, because I felt flushed and my ears were ringing.

It was the first time I'd seen Mora hesitant about lovemaking; her touch was tentative at first and she followed Vy's lead. Charles's swollen flesh glowed wetly in the soft light of a bedside candle. From my new perspective as voyeur I saw that what was exciting about oral sex was not the mechanics of one person satisfying another, but the selfless art of it, the submission of ego to pleasure. The women's tongues and fingers worked gently and assiduously; Charles groaned. The phrases that broke from his lips were the mutterings of gratified desire. I wanted until they had forgotten the camera before I snapped a picture.

They all blinked and looked around dazedly when the flash went off. Once again; and then it was time to draw matches. Mora's turn. I was surprised when she moved toward Vy instead of Charles, but when she touched Vy's breasts, Vy turned her long body to the side.

"Not yet," she said huskily. "Let me warm up first."

Mora smiled as if she'd expected the rebuff, and crawled to Charles, climbing atop him, swiveling her hips to claim his hardness. The two of them flowed into each other.

For a moment it hurt like hell. I remembered every time Mora and I had made love, the heat and wetness, our nerves rushing to release, our ragged romantic promises, the closeness we'd found sexually during times when we couldn't even speak to each other. I was drawn to her; I handed Vy the camera and knelt beside them, kissing Mora and stroking her taut breasts, placing my fingertips on her pubic mound to feel the movement of Charles's flesh inside her beneath the soft maiden hair.

The room melted, contracting so that only the bed existed. My hands moved over their bodies, urging them together, teaching Charles about Mora's responses, sculpting them. When the flashbulb went off it fell like a lightning bolt on us.

It was Vy's turn. "*Whoo*, boy," she exclaimed. "This is most extraordinary. Hot, hot, hot."

"Tell us what you want before things get out of hand."

"I want to take Richard into the next room."

"No pictures?"

"Just the two of us, no silly cameras."

I was scared of Vy. Shyness, I suppose, and the fact that I was attracted to her. The room she took me to was obviously a guest room. Rattan furniture in the shadows, a colorful handsewn quilt on a large brass bed, summer moonlight making patterns on a faded Chinese rug.

We didn't make it to the bed. I reached for her but she slipped away, onto her knees, and took my limp flesh into her warm mouth. I thought my knees would fold, and my hands went to her shoulders for support while fire raced up and down my spine. It was over before I could take a deep reluctant breath, while my fingers were still caressing her silky hair and finding the secret places of her delicate skull.

I was shaking all over. "*Whew!*" I breathed after a moment spent looking up for my head, which had shot like a rocket to the ceiling. "That was too fast."

She chuckled appreciatively, licking her lips like a cat over a saucer of milk. She rose gracefully and shrugged her square shoulders into her caftan. "That calls for a drink," she said, going into the next room for the brandy. I was aware of a steady, rhythmic thumping through the wall and wondered for a minute if she'd return. I lighted a hurricane lamp next to the bed and waited. She reappeared with the bottle and two glasses, looking younger and more vulnerable in the flickering light.

"So the doors of marriage creak open," she said.

"I think you oiled the hinges with that one."

"Well, I'm good at what I do. I enjoy the power of doing that. It wasn't until I saw men from that perspective – on my knees in absolute control of them – that I realized they weren't omnipotent."

She was too glib. It had bothered me since our first conversation.

"I was born this way. No illusions. I look at things in black and white. It's like not having eyelids."

I wanted to hold her, to press my body against hers, to feel the length of her thighs on mine, but she sat away from me, smoking one of her cigarettes. Her sharp profile cut through the aromatic blue haze that distanced us.

"I wish I didn't love Charles so much, that I could turn it on and off."

I lifted my glass. "Here's to marriage."

She sniffled. She was squinting and her eyes were wet, but that might have been the smoke.

"Marriage? That's for victims. I don't intend to be a victim ever again. That's why I stay with Maurice, even though I know it drives Charles crazy."

"What have you got against marriage?"

"His name is James Lee Tait. My used-to-be. Three years of holy wedlock made a sorrowful woman of me. He promised everything – he had the gift of promise, you know? But in the end it was the same old song and dance."

"So you divorced him."

"Not without a lot of turmoil. A woman gets attached to

you creatures, and a divorce is like losing . . . your past, maybe your future."

I wanted to understand. "Do you hate him?"

"No, not really. Let's just say I envy his get-up-and-gall. I suffered over that. He's a singer, and I waited in the wings of his career and let mine slide; I had my own ambitions."

"You make marriage sound like a mine field."

"It's no picnic. It's probably the most dangerous relationship you can have."

"And Charles? How does he fit in?"

"He doesn't believe in marriage, and he lets me do what I want to do. We have a pact: no apologies. Jimmy was the kind of man who was always saying 'I'm sorry' while he was stepping on my feet – but I could have twisted his balls into a daisy chain. Charles, on the other hand, makes no bones about being exactly who he is, and he never apologizes. I don't expect anything from him, so I'm never disappointed."

I stretched out in the bed, thinking about marriage, and Mora and Charles in the next room.

"Sorry. I'm rattling on, and I know you're thinking about Mora. She's so restless."

I told her about my first wife, wishing that the scars were visible so I could show her. I tried to explain about Mora. "Sometimes I feel like she's only mine on loan, that nothing will ever satisfy her."

"She's vibrating like a spinning top. Nothing will slow her down, she's like a natural force. Take it from another woman."

"I love her. You love Charles. We're crazy."

"Charles says two plus two equals twelve."

"Charles is crazy."

"I know."

"But you'd rather be with him right now, wouldn't you?"

"Well? Wouldn't you rather be with Mora?"

"That's not what's happening."

"You're evading the question. I mean, what if Charles fucks her better than you ever did? He's very good."

Check. I couldn't bear any more conversation. I wanted to make love to Vy. It was the only answer I had.

"I can't," she protested when I touched her. I put my hand through the opening in her kimono onto her cool stomach. "I absolutely cannot. I'm sorry."

"I don't understand."

"Charles and I made love while you were off looking for Mora before dinner. He's big, and I'm sore. It's my background," she sighed expansively, theatrically. "Fair-skinned mothers. Delicate skin. Look here, I'll show you."

She opened the kimono and spread her white thighs. "You see the blood?"

The lips of her vulva were irritated and swollen, and there was a tiny drop of blood on her clitoris. Imagine the center of a rose with a drop of blood on a petal . . .

I found cotton and peroxide in a bathroom medicine cabinet and brought them back without looking in on Charles and Mora. I heard them talking through the closed door and I wanted to eavesdrop, but I wanted to make love to Vy more.

"Your hands are so gentle," Vy told me when I wiped away the drop of blood and covered her soreness with Vaseline. The glistening petals of her sex opened beneath my fingers.

"I'll stop. I promise you. If it hurts, I'll stop."

She squirmed evasively when I penetrated her. I stopped, moving again only when she opened to receive me. She whispered hotly in my ear and licked it with the point of her tongue.

"I trust you. No reason, but I do. I know you'll stop – but *please* don't stop now."

I cupped the plump weight of her strong buttocks in my palms and let myself be swallowed by her womanness. We rocked together in the dialogue of bodies, questioning and

answering, alone on a gently rolling sea in the blackest
night.

She pulled a yellow popper out of the darkness and
crushed it between her fingers, holding the amyl nitrate
to my nose and then to her own. We both inhaled deeply
and felt our hearts rush to where our genitals were, riding
on the cloudy, pungent chemical high like surfers on a
wave.

"*Ooooo!*" she cried out, as if in a dream. I heard someone
wailing without realizing it was me. Each wave that took us
was bigger than the last, and we were no longer rocking
gently but struggling together to stay afloat.

I heard tapping on the floor and looked down to see my
fingers doing a fast dance on the wide boards. I was half off
the bed and sweat was pouring from me. Vy's body was
arched so she looked like a dying swan. There was a roaring
in my ears like the ocean at the same time. I heard knocking
on the door, and then I hit the last, biggest wave and was
dragged head over heels into shore. In love. Vy's whole
body clenched and she followed me, digging her nails into
the backs of my arms. A high thin noise came from her
throat.

When I opened my eyes Charles was standing over us,
naked, grinning, scratching his chest. "Birds would give up
a winter's feed to hit that note," he said, while Vy shuddered and I navigated the reentry to consciousness.

"What time is it?"

"Half past four. You two make a lot of noise."

Mora moved from the shadows to stand beside him, her
hand on his shoulder. Her hair was matted and wet and she
looked ragged around the edges. They looked like weasels
who've been in the chicken coop. There were feathers
hanging from their swollen mouths.

"I won't be able to explain this away tomorrow morning," Charles said. "I won't believe it. It was so incredibly
high at times. So intense."

"I guess we did it after all," Mora smiled tiredly, shaking her head in happy disbelief.

"I don't know what could be bad about this," I said.

Vy sat up and stretched, reaching for Charles's hand and pulling it to her breast. "It was divine, and I love you all, and I don't know what to say. I've got to think of something, though. Maurice will want to hear all about it."

"Tell him nothing happened," I suggested.

She snorted and put my hand on her other breast. "Nothing of a sexual nature goes on in his house that Maurice isn't aware of. He's been known to chart the amorous activities of mice. Be prepared for an interrogation."

Charles yawned and rubbed his eyes sleepily. Mora came to sit next to me on the rumpled bed that smelled of sex and poppers and cigarettes.

"You can sleep here," Vy said. "A Filipino houseboy will pound on your door at nine to call you to breakfast. You can ignore him, but he'll be back for you in half an hour. Maurice likes company at breakfast."

We kissed goodnight with the gentle tiredness of exhausted lovers, and Mora and I curled up spoon fashion on the bed. She was mine again, for a few hours.

THE DRESS

Michael Hemmingson

Finding the Dress

THIS IS THE season for Christmas parties – the big one for us is my wife's office party, thrown by the publisher for all the employees; from the head honchos, VPs, marketing, editorial, publicity, right down to the janitors and interns. It was usually attended by somewhere between fifty and a hundred people. We'd gone for a number of years now. Time was when Ashley was conscious of her role as a member of the publicity department, so she arranged herself conservatively, in subdued colors and dress lengths ending at or perhaps just slightly above the knee. All very tasteful and dignified – and pretty. A few years ago, one of the editors, a woman, appeared at the Christmas party in a short red dress with spaghetti straps that had everyone's eyes flying out their sockets like cannonball dare-devils in a circus. According to my wife, people talked about her and that dress until the *next* Christmas party. Last year, I suggested to Ashley that the pleasant reception the hot dress received should indicate she need not be so concerned about her "station" in the company; and she could attire herself a bit more – *creatively*. I persuaded her on one of my favorites from her wardrobe; it would be sufficiently conservative in terms of coverage to satisfy the stodgier types, but by its constitution eye-catching. This was a red leather ensemble: short leather jacket with long sleeves and a modest mini-length leather skirt ending a few inches above the knee. Both zipped up the side. Under this she wore a lace bodysuit without a bra, so the jacket worn open would allow anyone, who cared to notice, to observe she was braless, without showing her breasts. That outfit worked fine. No one blanched, but a number of the women employees whispered compliments about how great she looked. Ashley liked that a lot.

In anticipation of the upcoming party, I looked through her wardrobe again, to see what kind of interesting attire I might suggest she wear. I found that without repeating the leather ensemble there was nothing of comparable excitement.

So I went shopping.

I shopped a long time before latching onto what I thought was the perfect choice. It was a slinky floor-length sheath made of a glittery silver stretch fabric. I could tell it would gently cling to her curves from shoulders to hips, then fall in a straight line to the floor. The cling would be enough to show panty lines, easy to persuade her to go *sans* underwear. Then, besides cutting a dazzling figure for everyone else to look at, I could enjoy the extra closeness of her oh-so-thinly clad skin as we danced. I also bought this other dress, but The Other Dress is different from The Dress.

And as I was ready to declare victory and head for home, I saw it – The Dress.

I stared at it a long time, like a gawker's first sight of human gore on a bad freeway accident. But I left the store, thinking it was too much for the party. Halfway out the mall, I said to myself, the hell with it; she may not want it, but I *have* to see her in it.

I went back. I looked at it a long time. I was preparing myself for worship. It was close fitting at the neck, and had simple short sleeves. No fancy cut-outs or anything like that. Just brazenly bold looking, and *so very short*. I got out my mental measuring tape and moved close to it. I knew it measured out a full inch shorter than the shortest dress in her wardrobe, a dress she would wear only under a long coat until we were safely away from our conservative neighborhood. The possibilities were wonderful. It was made of a slightly stretchy but strong festooning fabric with a rather open weave and decorated with fine vertical bands of black. It was unlined, but looked opaque. Actually it was not *opaque* – more a bit like those tan-thru swim suits. Those suits are actually fairly transparent, but they are printed with bold patterns to confuse the eye. If you saw someone in a plain, unpatterned tan-thru suit, you would clearly see all their worldly goods. Same here. The fabric was *not* thin, but the weave was sufficiently open that if it were not so boldly spangled, you'd be able to see through it with relative ease.

I *had* to see her in it, so I bought it and put it with my other items, and went home – for my private fashion show.

That night, I sat down with Ashley and explained my thoughts on her existing wardrobe and the upcoming party, and that as sort of an advance Christmas present I'd bought a number of dresses for her to try. Everything returnable, no fragile male egos on the line – I just wanted to do something nice for her. We were in our nice mode these days, looking for alternatives from ennui and stupid arguments contained in many marriages five years down the line and older. The night we both brought up divorce was the night we decided our lives had to be different. We were becoming boring and old, and neither Ashley nor myself wanted that.

She said she appreciated that and proceeded to strip. It's almost a rule that clothes I buy for her are intended to be worn without underwear, so these occasional modeling sessions begin with her getting naked. We began with a flouncy little mini I'd purchased just for fun. She liked it. We moved to the floor-length silver-spangled gown that slid onto her very nicely. She looked great in it. She liked it.

Of The Other Dress, she just said, "And *where* am I supposed to wear *that?*"

Then I brought out The Dress, smiling, feeling anxious. She asked, "Where's the rest of it?" and "You bought this for the *party?*"

I explained how I'd been so enthralled I *had* to get it; she could keep it or not, wear it or not as she wished.

She nodded and put it on. I could see immediately – see it in her eyes – that she liked the feel of it. It fit her like a queen who knows her head was made for the jeweled crown of her sovereignty.

She looked at me; I looked at her. I was smiling with wantonness; she was smiling self-absorbedly, smoothing The Dress to her body. She started swaying her hips a little, side to side; licked her finger, touched her ass and said; "*TSSSSsssssssssssssstt.*" Hot indeed. She started walking around the room, laying her hands on different parts of herself; her sides, her tummy, her hips. She walked to the patio door and studied her reflection there, the mirror image. She turned to me and said, "It's kinda short."

I later checked out more carefully just how short it was. In the front it stopped eight inches above the top of her kneecap (yes, I measured this time with a tape, not my mind). In back it was a little more difficult to ascertain; I'd say it stopped about an inch and a half below the thigh-buttock crease; short enough that if she raised her arms over her head in a good early-morning stretch, her whole cunt and half her derrière were exposed. She continued turning this way and that, then turned to me again.

She said "I could wear this."

I thought we might keep it for one of our risqué private dates. I didn't think she'd actually wear it to the corporate Christmas party. We practiced slow dancing, sitting and standing, et cetera. With her arms around my neck in slow-dance position, The Dress rode up high enough that the bottom edge of her ass was exposed. Sitting, she remained decent if she tugged on the hem as she sat and got up again; if she forgot, she sat bare-assed on the chair with daylight on her cunt, so that crossing her legs couldn't extinguish this, and getting up again flashed more cotton-tail.

We both agreed that as hot as this dress was without underwear, for the corporate party she would need panty hose. But we also agreed to inaugurate The Dress properly (i.e. butt naked underneath) in a more private date very soon.

The next day we re-modeled in the strong morning sun, just to be sure that things still looked cool. There was an added bonus I hadn't noticed before. The fabric of The Dress had some properties, as I had noted previously, similar to tan-thru suits. That didn't really matter much because The Dress clung so nicely to all her curves *except* the space between her legs. In the bright sun, if she were standing at the right angle, the actual transparency of the material made itself apparent, revealing a shadowy but unmistakable view of her twat, with just enough definition to define the furrow between her labia, and a tousling of blonde pubic hair.

The Other Dress

The Other Dress is one of the three I bought for Ashley to try. I ended up returning the spangly floor-length number because it didn't go well with her skin tone. The appeal of The Other Dress takes a little explaining because it is somewhat subtle.

I find that the *artistry* in barely-acceptable exhibitionism lies in revealing without appearing to be revealing, or in *not* being revealing when appearances suggest otherwise; what I mean is playing with people's minds. The trick is to be subtle enough so in the interval of time one has passing encounters with strangers, the unsuspecting stranger is left uncertain as to whether s/he has been treated to a peek or not. And, if possible, those who *do* realize they are seeing something forbidden should be left thinking not that they've been flashed, but they, the observers, have some-how invaded the privacy of the exhibitant; their own sense of decorum and social order can be used against them, leading them into a kind of denial; thus, they ignore the "bare" facts of what they see (Orwellian doublethink, you see) – and in fact become conspirators in the act.

Part of this artistry lies in playing with light. For example, in choosing garments such that in the typical low light of a bar or other night spots not much is seen; but in this or that pocket of bright light a sight emerges to behold. Another aspect lies in the sense of touch, or what I like to think of as *virtual touch*. I liked Ashley to go without underwear – not so much to flash her privates, which was not in her comfort zone, but to smooth the look and feel of her body through her clothes. This enhances the degree to which her clothes fit her body, so as we danced, for example, I could let my hands follow the smooth contours of her body more closely and without interruption. As I did this, it also encouraged observers to follow those contours with their eyes and minds – and wonder.

The Other Dress played on these themes. To see it on her from some moderate distance, it looked little out of the mainstream, not really remarkable. It was solid black without any pattern, cut-outs, or other decoration; and pulled over her head without any buttons, hooks, what-ever. It fit closely at the neck and was sleeveless, falling in a smooth line from her neck all the way to her ankles, with a

walking slit in back from the ankle up to a few inches below
the knee. It was sufficiently clingy, if you are inclined to
think that way, to remind you a bit of Morticia of the
Addams Family; even more so because Ashley has such fine
pale skin. It also occurred to me that it would look
wonderful with her elbow-length black evening gloves.

Part of the beauty of this dress was that it had an
unusually flat finish, in the sense of flat versus glossy.
Although clingy, even where the fabric was stretched over
her various curves, the fabric did not become shiny; it
absorbed virtually all light that struck it, making it hard
for the eye to make out the detail of her underlying shape.
This effect confused the eye even at close range, so that
without rather obviously inspecting distinctive parts, such
as her breasts, it was difficult to tell whether one was seeing
anything through the fabric or not. Going without underwear helped greatly in achieving this effect – although it is,
in truth, more revealing: we tend to expect the outlines of
undergarments, and when we don't obviously see them, we
tend to assume the outer garment to be more substantial
than it is, ironically creating a "less-is-more" situation.

The Other Dress was somewhat diaphanous; in adequate
light and on careful inspection you *could* see through it to
enjoy the view of her breasts, but this was unlikely to make
itself apparent to the casual observer in typical evening
lighting. In fact, the visual effect was a little like those
quasi-holographic prints that require you to stare long and
hard at a somewhat bizarre-looking scene while crossing
your eyes until suddenly (if you're lucky) a 3-D image
appears. Because the image of the underlying breast was
well filtered by the fabric, and the flat black of the fabric
withheld visual clues such as the variations of shadow that
we are unconsciously used to seeing, it was possible to stare
right at her nipples for some time before realizing what you
were seeing was *not* the variation of shadow but was the
breast itself. Like the holographic print, once you see it, you

see it, and it's hard to go back to *not* seeing it. The impact of this sudden realization was as if she stripped off her clothes right in front of you when she had actually done nothing but stand there.

However confounding The Other Dress was to even close observation, being so black it created a very sharp silhouette against almost any background; although the eye was confused by looking directly at her, there was no confusion about her profile. This created the unusual situation of seeing more by looking *past* her than by looking directly *at* her – affording more sensuous views to the peripheral observer than those engaging in casual social intercourse.

To look at The Other Dress and heft the fabric in your hands it appeared and felt like extra-thick hosiery material – say about three, maybe four times the density. But hosiery, of course, is made to stretch taut; this fabric looked like it should do that, but did not. Rather than being of a tight strong weave, like hosiery, this fabric had an extraordinary suppleness, giving easily to the slightest pressure. As a result, it practically melted onto her body, adapting readily to the slightest curve. We've all seen form-fitting dresses made of Spandex-like fabrics – they tend to be fairly thick fabrics; and, although form-fitting, they also tend to smooth out certain contours like the curves under the breasts. Even though they can easily reveal an un-shielded nipple, that tends to be smoothed out some-what. Not so with this fabric. Somehow this fabric followed the contour of her breasts deep into the curves on the underside; nearly invisible when you looked directly at them, in profile the silhouetted shape of her breasts was as plain as if she were standing nude, right down to the full detail of her nipples and areolae. The only contours of her body missed were between her legs. Even the cleft of her buttocks got resolved to some degree, almost in defiance of the laws of physics. This visual definition was aided by the fact that this is the one place where there is enough stretch in the fabric to create a little extra transparency, so the globes of her buttocks showed slightly less black than the cleft, creating an illusion of deeper penetration into the cleft. It is not *obvious* – of course, that is what is going on. I could well imagine someone studying her shape from behind and slowly coming to this comprehension: they are actually seeing the bare skin of her ass; and then following the lines of the dress up and down from there to gradually apprehend she is standing there completely naked except for this wispy-thin second skin. The bottom line is: this fabric almost disappeared, coating her body like flat black paint. It felt that way to touch; it felt like nothing at all.

So where could she wear this dress? This was not something to don for a casual night out, like most of what I got her. It was too formal-looking. But: it *was* the kind of thing to wear for more ceremonious nights out, such as going to the theater, opera, or ballet. Imagine it – moving about practically naked yet fully clothed among the high-brow set in their gowns and furs and tails. Walking in and out of the glare of street lights, moving from the twilight of early evening into the bright light of the theater lobby, and again into the twilight of the main hall for the show; milling through crowds of hundreds at intermission, brushing closely with men and women alike left wondering, *who was that barely masked woman?*

Thinking only about dress length, Ashley suggested maybe she should wear The Other Dress to the big party rather than The Dress. I thought otherwise. Although The Dress was devastatingly short, it was *just* short, and by being short only *threatened* to reveal forbidden fruits; decorum could be maintained by giving care to her posture and revealing only as much or as little as she wished, and only when she wished. On the other hand, The Other Dress, although covering her from neck to ankle, was actually more revealing once you were hit by its full impact, and no amount of tugging at hemlines or demure positioning could undo that revelation. Despite its much greater length, The Other Dress left very little hidden and nowhere to hide it. In the course of a long evening among friends and co-workers, as the big party promised to be, there could be little doubt that *everyone* would discover the barely hidden truth by the time the night was over. There was also the strong possibility that someone other than myself would ask her to dance.

It would be apparent enough to anyone dancing with her in The Dress that she was braless and wearing very little indeed, but anyone who'd dance with her in The Other Dress would be treated to the marvelous but scandalous tactile illusion of holding her naked.

I didn't think the publishing company crowd was ready for that.

White And Flouncy

I had also bought her a short, white and flouncy one-piece dress made of a light sweater-like material that was mostly opaque but had just enough sheerness to make you wonder if you really saw what you thought you saw. It hung on her loosely by itself, and was made to be belted at the waist. This belting created a skirt portion that followed the contours of her hips rather well and then fell loosely, ending a little above mid-thigh.

On the particular night she first wore it, she was meeting me at a designated restaurant after work, and we were then just going to wander the mall, hitting a couple of clothing shops. She arrived at the restaurant, not realizing she had forgotten the belt; the belt actually helped the dress behave itself. Without the belt, it tended to slide around in ways that one might not anticipate, and, by allowing the dress to hang away from her body more than was intended, allowed the ambient light to play with the sheerness of the fabric

and show more of the shadowy outline of her body underneath. Under optimal conditions of lighting and position,
more underlying detail could be seen now and then.

Of course, I enjoyed this very much. After dinner, as we
walked through the mall, she found she'd brought the
wrong shoes; the ones she wore hurt her feet. So she
kicked them off and we carried them in a shopping bag.
So there she was, wearing a moderately sheer white flouncy
dress, little more than a T-shirt in size, and nothing else,
padding around barefoot in the most public of places. The
mall was interesting, too, in having spots that had particularly strong lighting in which she looked practically nude,
at least in silhouette. Having no undergarments for modesty, trying on outfits proved interesting as she modeled
them in the generally bright light of the dressing areas of
various shops.

Just as the night was ending for us, we came across a
once-a-year shoe sale at an upscale store and, being in need
of good quality shoes, she decided to try it out.

Now, I quickly put two and two together, realizing the
exhibition potential of this situation: Ashley in a very short
flimsy thing without underwear, trying on shoes with some
salesman in position to get an eyeful; and, without the belt,
her dress shifting about somewhat unpredictably . . .

I hung out some fifteen feet in front of her, in position to
catch a piece of whatever display she might present. Sure
enough, after picking out a few pairs to try on, she sat down
on one of those little stools and brought up one foot, letting
a knee fall wide to one side. As a result, her dress slid to
where the hemline was no longer on her leg but in her lap.
Her cunt was visible not only to the salesman on his knees,
but just about anyone within ten feet or so to either side of
where I stood. She didn't appear to grasp this and finished
putting that shoe on; she stood up and walked around a bit,
sat down again, and went through exactly the same motions
with the next pair of shoes. Easily half a dozen times she got

up and down, nonchalantly flashing cunt to half the shoe department.

She ended up not finding any shoes she wanted to buy. I don't think the salesman minded.

She didn't act like she knew what she had done.

We went home and had dinner and I told her about it. Ashley blushed and said, "You could see my pussy?"

"Of course," I said.

"The salesman saw it?"

"I'm sure he did," I said. "You had to know this."

"All I could think about were my aching feet," she said. I nodded.

"But it *was* in the back of my mind." She smiled.

I nodded and said, "I had this scenario in my head. Maybe I'm not there. The two of you are alone. You're flashing him your cunt. He loses control. He grabs you, starts to eat your cunt out. Right there in the middle of the store. You don't care, because you're caught up in the heat of the situation. He makes you come. He stands; his cock is out, in front of your face. He says, "Suck me." You take him. He comes all over your face, scooping his come onto his fingers, making you lick his fingers clean."

Ashley took in a deep breath. She said, "Would you like to see me with another man?"

"I think about these things," I said.

"You would watch?"

"I'd watch," I said, "because I like to watch things."

"We did say we'd try everything," she said. "I wouldn't mind seeing you – watching you – with another woman," she said.

Unveiling The Dress

Let your fantasies run away with you, and you'll get in trouble.

My wife, Ashley, and I illustrated the point.

She was usually conservative and conscious of propriety – that she indulged me was a very deep gesture of affection on her part, and further indicated she was serious about inserting excitement and risk into our lives; something to be respected, I must say. It was easy when playing close to the line like this to trip over it, or to create situations in which the momentum of a moment may threaten to carry you across it. This was complicated by the fact that it was a *moving* line, a function not only of the fixed social mores of others but of both your states of mind. That's why Nicole came into our lives as she did, and changed our lives in a way we never thought possible. But I'm getting ahead of myself. This isn't about Nicole, *not yet* – but it leads up to how we met Nicole, how that line we made crossed with the lines *she* was making.

There were two instances in our evening in which we blundered into this line. In neither case did anything unfortunate happen – not yet, anyway – and in each case we were in circumstances similar to those of other inter-ludes; the difference in these two moments was in our joint constitution, and subtle miscues or misreadings of mood. Never underestimate the importance of communication, communication, and more *communication*.

A small dinner party at the publisher's house a few days before the company-wide party. I enjoyed imagining how a "trophy" wife or two in all their regalia would feel slam-dunked when Ashley walked into the big party wearing The Dress. After this dinner soirée, I thought how, in this context, *I* was kind of a trophy *husband*. Considering how dolled-up Ashley was going to be, and how critical eyes would be on us all night, I took stock of my own wardrobe and realized what I had assumed I would wear, just by default, was not anywhere in the same class as The Dress. Giving it some thought, and of the more limited options open to men (a leather G-string and muscle shirt just wouldn't cut it), I concluded I finally needed to spring for a tuxedo, something I have never owned in my life. There were several aspects to this idea that were relevant. One was simply that a tux would add an extra touch of class and glamor to my wife's presence; which, of course, was what a good "trophy" husband should do. Another was that a tux is a stand-out kind of outfit; my dressing this way would help attract more attention to Ashley. Another, but more subtle, mien had to do with the magician's technique for creating illusion; a magician will often use misdirection, focusing his audience's attention one place while the real action is happening somewhere else. By wearing a tux I would (while there would be more attention to Ashley) help diffuse close scrutiny by causing attention to both of us.

I decided to go for it, yet keep it a surprise, so I could just appear, like magic, completely decked like James Bond at his best for the night of The Big Do. (As a little surprise for her to find later, I wore a black thong under my pants instead of my usual Fruit-of-the-Looms.)

I figured we should plan for a late arrival, so as to gain the maximum effect from our entrance; however, Ashley knew me to be an early bird by habit, and so would be expecting us to get there more or less on time. In order to defeat this expectation, I arranged to be delayed at work; I got home later than she expected. She was pretty much ready, keeping a snack warm for us to share (we would eat at the party, but that would be unusually late for us). We had our few bites together; then, as I hoped, she took to pottering around with dinner dishes while I went back to dress. This gave me the time I needed to get all put together before she would have a chance to see me.

I was just finishing as she hollered for me to hurry my ass up. I took a position near the bedroom door where she finally saw me. Surprised, to be sure, and pleased, was she. With all the build-up for this party being focused on her, and as exposed as she felt in The Dress, she was glad to see I was going all out too. We almost fucked then and there, but that was for later.

I must say that we looked dapper together, her all in black and silver spangles, me in the classic all-black tux, complete with bow tie, studs, cummerbund – the works. I had hoped to get her away from the house without a wrap, thinking that she could use my tux jacket for getting to and from the car – it was too nippy for her to contemplate that. I was pleased she did not opt for the calf-length overcoat, and instead chose a shorter, poncho-like wrap that draped a little elegantly over each arm in front rather than being tied or buttoned; a bit like an unusually large stole, I guess, but of a dense natural wool. Of course, I feared that once at the party she might not let go of the wrap, clutching it closed in front of herself in a final rejection of what we had planned.

The night began with what I considered a good omen. I expected Ashley would have a tendency either to over-compensate in moments of self-consciousness and tug unmercifully at the hem of The Dress, or in moments of self-unconsciousness forget about decorum and let fly with some titillating views. As we got in our car, I held the door for her and she stepped in. In the course of this maneuver, she ended up flashing a rather wide view of Heaven's Gate as she adjusted her legs, and because of the contortions involved and the friction of The Dress against her wrap, she missed the tail completely when she first sat down, sitting butt-to-carseat before realizing her rather displayed condition and tugging herself back to something approaching decency.

I kept the heater on high as we drove to the party. This didn't do me any good under all of my layers, but kept her mind off the cold. We arrived at the hotel that had been rented for the evening and began the search for a good parking place. We had to enter through one of those little gates with a uniformed gnome sitting inside, issuing passes and taking money. Once through, not fifteen feet from the little gnome's hut, was what most people would consider the perfect space: as close as possible to the entrance/exit, right by the occupied gnome booth and under a bright streetlight for added security.

Ashley said, "There!"

I have an instinct to do as I'm told in a parking lot. If I don't get the space she believes is best, there's grouse to live down. Without thinking, without even being aware of it in real time, I cut the wheel and with a screech we were parked. She was sitting smugly, proud of herself for once again having found the best parking space in the whole lot. I recovered from my instinctive behavior, and sat there looking dejected.

"What's the matter?" she asked.

I said, "Oh, it's a great parking spot, all right. High-traffic area, in easy view of the parking attendant, well lit, very secure."

"Yeah," she said, touching her leg.

"I was planning on driving around a bit to find us a nice secluded spot," I said. "You know – for later."

"Oh," she said, but smiling, "I forgot."

I didn't believe her for a minute.

She said, "That's OK, we'll go somewhere else afterwards."

We sat there for a bit, soaking up just a little more heat, then I leaned over and gave her a *kiss for luck* and stepped out. I rounded to her side and opened her door, whereupon I was blessed with another view of the Promised Land as she unfolded from the car. She realized it this time and, on standing up, started to pull her hemline toward her knees, which didn't do much good. I reminded her of what we had practiced: that as long as she was standing up she did not need to tug on things in order to know that she was technically decent. Simply smoothing out any wrinkles would assure that everything else fell into place. More-

over, the act of running her hands over herself to smooth
them out had a rather sensuous look to it, as opposed to the
rather awkward, self-conscious appearance tugging on her
hemline telegraphed.

"Just stay close to me," she whispered.

"Hell couldn't tear me away," I said.

It was a fairly long walk to the ballroom. On the way, I kept
replaying the roster of all the faces and names I could
remember, and the various ways I'd imagined our entrance
would work out. It didn't happen any of those ways – I had
been imagining our entrance as being dramatic, letting The
Dress have its full and immediate impact. But since she
wore a wrap, and kept it on for some time, the jolt of The
Dress was smoothed out over a considerable period, until
we eventually claimed our seats for dinner. For example, I
had imagined the various senior editors and other execitives
to be standing in a stuffy huddle when we walked up; I
looked forward to seeing the steam rise from their collars as
they looked her up and down, not quite knowing what to
make of her new appearance; but no such melodramatic
episodes occurred.

I was reminded of how much camaraderie there is within
the publishing company. Furthermore, it seemed the
employees felt closer to my wife and the other female
workmates than they did with the males, so we were
constantly engaged by people of all strata. More, there's
a history in this company of the social barriers tumbling to
dust by the time the annual Christmas party has run its
course, so I expected things to get pretty loose by the time
the night was over.

It reminded me of a humorous incident: the first of these
parties we attended some years ago. It was my first chance
to meet almost everyone in the company, and so I was
almost completely unknown to everyone else. We had had
to leave rather early and Ashley waited for me while I

visited the john. Returning, I saw one of the male junior editors come up to my wife, slip his arm around her and whisper a few sentences into an ear. She answered with something, then he whispered again.

Now, apparently he had just asked her something about *me*. About that time I'd arrived to stand right next to the guy, on the side away from my wife. She looked at me and lifted one hand in a genteel gesture of introduction. The poor fellow had the shit scared out of him like he had seen a gray alien wanting to do unspeakable medical experiments on him. He yanked his arm away from her shoulder like a culprit caught, jumped back a foot or two, and stammered, "H-H-hello, Sir!" I extended my hand and introduced myself. He quickly walked away. Ashley and I left, sharing a good chuckle. But my notions proved wrong.

"Was he hitting on you?" I asked.

"No," Ashley said. "He likes you. He wants to fuck you. I mean, he probably wants you to fuck him. He has a nice ass; what do you think?"

She gave me a wink.

After a bit of schmoozing, I made a bar run; I figured Ashley would be a little more at ease after a glass of wine. I was a little afraid she would feel the need to hold something for security, and if it wasn't the wine, she might hold that damn wrap all night. So I traded her the wrap for a glass. Not being quite ready to let it go, she watched longingly after it as I used it to save a couple of seats for dinner.

The Dress was now on unobstructed display for the first time since we came in the door. It was not long before the attention started to pile up. As we stood near the bar, for example, we chanced upon one of a handful of openly lesbian women in the company, together with her girl-friend. She caught sight of my wife and did a little double-take, obviously not connecting Ashley with The Dress at first gleam. She turned to us and called Ashley by name, taking Ashley's free hand (the one without the wine) and holding it away from her body, taking a good look at The Dress.

"What a *sexy* dress!" this woman said. "What closet did *you* come out of?"

The obvious joke was on the mark. Ashley had always been curious about the lesbian experience, and had always felt a connection with these women; I think they sensed this at some level. What did I know? In fact, what did *she* know?

We continued milling, enjoying the appreciative comments of men and women alike. A couple of the partners and their spouses made a point of greeting us *again*.

Ashley, at first a little embarrassed by all the attention, quickly answered the incoming compliments by saying *I* had bought everything for her – thinking this, of course, an excuse for her uncommonly daring appearance. She and I both were a little unprepared for the even higher and more envious praise we received in response; wives envious because their husbands would never exercise such thoughtfulness, husbands shuffling a little because they knew this to be true. Two of them in particular, at different times, spoke to me in low tones, "*You* bought her that?"

"Yes," I said, watching their faces as they stole glances back at Ashley, their demeanor betraying envy of several different stripes; then, self-consciously and with just a hint of personal shame muttering, "I just can't shop for my wife."

Another gulp of a highball and then on to more mingling.

One of the men whom I knew was gay came up to her, and, lifting both of her arms upward and outward in front of her; he looked her up and down, telling her The Dress was simply to *die* for.

We were getting hungry, and found ourselves hanging out with a couple of the marketing directors and their wives near the seats we had chosen for dinner. One of these men had the most party-doll-like trophy wife of them all.

Bouffant blonde with enormous cleavage barely contained in her dress, drippy jewelry, teetering heels, and one of the most annoyingly snobbish nasal voices I've heard outside of a situation comedy. She looked a little green around the eyes to me, and the way she interacted with my wife, placing herself between Ashley and her own husband, suggested to me that the cat in her was flexing its claws.

I'd noted The Dress was so short that she'd need to wear some kind of panty hose to stay on the responsible side of the publishing company's moral clause (it would've been *something* to have her bare butt pop out in front of the CEO). We'd found some black, glittered panty hose, giving the ensemble a nice dashing "Emma Peel" sort of look. I was a little disappointed that the only suitable pair we could find had a dense black panty at the top, rather than being uniform to the waist. I would've preferred the color to continue; were The Dress to ride up at all, the image of her legs would persevere smoothly across the divide. As Ashley had practiced various movements in The Dress and panty hose, I found the black panty had an interesting and unanticipated effect, the same as seeing the tops of thigh-high or gartered hose peeking out from under a more demure accouter.

There had been a small dinner party the prior night, for the publicists and their spouses. I had the idea Ashley ought to use this smaller affair as a warm-up to the big party, and attire in something flattering but not so daring as The Dress. She thought most of my suggestions were too much for her boss's house; I could see her point.

She had not yet decided what to wear to this dinner party when she came out from our bedroom Sunday morning, in a charcoal gray catsuit and a brief blazer. I was a little surprised by this, since I've always thought the catsuit displayed her body rather well and I had no idea she would think it appropriate for a simple dinner. This was tasteful – muted soft cotton blend that tapered without clinging from stirrups at the feet all the way to the curves of her hips, following her torso and arms closely, without fitting too tightly. The most suggestive thing was a nice definition to her ass; and, when worn alone, it invited the eyes to wander up and down. The blazer broke up that wandering eye effect, but allowed her ass to show nicely. I suggested that this outfit would probably work better at the dinner party than any others we'd discussed.

The dinner party was uneventful, by the way. The other women were tastefully dressed, some casual, some in high-end fashions and teetering heels. None bore the subtle hint of daring Ashley had. The effect was mostly in her mind and mine. Once, during a little break in the cocktail chatter, I caught her eye; I licked a finger and touched her butt, mouthing, "*Tsssssssst*." She grinned and swatted my hand away playfully, saying, "Don't embarrass me!"

Soon we were called to dinner. I sat beside Ashley, and the aforementioned trophy wife sat on her other side – to be sure her *husband* didn't sit there. This was Ashley's first sit-down of the evening, and she sat priggishly, giving a gentle tug on her hem that *just* kept The Dress from riding up without unnaturally distorting things. Even so, she sat, for the most part, directly *on* the chair, showing a wedge of the black panty, growing from nothing above her thigh to about three-quarters of an inch below. I got a kick out of this – it'd make the trophy wife squirm; it also meant she was sitting with her pussy in contact with the chair. Continuing her sedate behavior, Ashley acquired her napkin and placed it on her lap, conveniently covering the triangular shaped tunnel.

As dinner wore on, the patch of black panty to be seen was gradual, as the natural movements associated with sitting a long time caused The Dress to creep. I inspected this progression as indifferently as I could. I had anticipated this, yet the creeping continued well beyond the point which I expected her to re-compile herself and restore The Dress to its intended position. Two things made her unaware of this – she often wore leggings, stretch pants and the like, and was used to the feeling of sitting in them (I suspected the panty hose had a similar feel); and that damn napkin: she didn't notice her hemline was trailing so. It delighted me to note the trophy wife was also seeing what I was seeing; more than once I noticed her glancing down and getting this uncomfortable look on her face, tinged with disbelief. I found it hard to believe, too. The creeping continued higher and higher until none of The Dress was left between her and the chair. This extreme condition didn't last long. Ashley soon realized she'd come rather undone and moved to put herself back together. She laid the napkin aside, which then showed her hemline to be not down on her thighs where she had left it, but to have gathered in the crease of her pelvis, leaving the totality of her crotch on display. She was a little flustered, but one quick tug and she was normal.

After a delicious dinner, dessert, and a little more wine, everything was cleared away. The conversation and drinks had loosened the atmosphere. The music started and people began to dance. Ashley and I decided to wait, let the dance floor fill up, let people relax before venturing out. It wasn't long before the DJ switched to a particular swing I enjoyed, and I had to drag Ashley out, ready or not. We made our way to the dance floor hand in hand; she was smoothing The Dress over her hips and butt as we walked.

Just about everyone was on the floor for this one, which was fine, since Ashley felt less exposed in the middle of the crowd. She made sure we didn't stop until we got to the most hidden point of the dance floor. For the first couple of songs, one or the other of her hands tugged on her hemline about every eighth beat. I tried to tell her she didn't need to do that, and she eased up as she got into the mood. The

Dress had a tendency to rise a bit as she danced, but this was the panty hose; had she been butt-naked, The Dress would've behaved better, sliding on her hips.

Soon the music slowed down and we got a chance to get touchy-feely. We'd practiced this in front of a mirror that morning, so we knew exactly what would occur. She placed her forearms loosely on my shoulders, lightly folding her fingers together behind my neck, keeping her elbows at a level just below my collarbone. This was sort of a modest half-stretch that'd raise her hemline just about exactly even with the bottom of her black panty, allowing a peek to those far enough away to enjoy the right angle, but otherwise kept decent. If I chose to, I could manipulate this, drawing her extra close, or unobtrusively pressing The Dress into the small of her back as I held her, both of which caused The Dress to slide up more, assuring that somebody, somewhere, would catch a glimpse.

Being a good boy, however, whenever I let her come a little undone that way, I would soon shift position and smooth her out. This must've looked pretty interesting as well: it meant sliding my hands down her back and across her ass in a rather intimate manner.

I had to answer nature's call. It turned out this place was not very well equipped in the outhouse department; the only lavatories for the ballroom floor were halfway back into the lobby. I got to the men's room and, being a man, walked right in. At the wash basins were two men and one woman. And a beautiful one at that. The men were washing hands, straightening ties, whatever; she was freshening her makeup. She looked at me in the mirror, I acknowledged her with a polite hello, and went to my business. I assumed the position at one of the urinals.

As much as I needed to go, the thought of this peculiar and resplendent woman standing at the mirror a few feet away complicated matters by rendering me, shall we say, a little less than flaccid. About this time, she said something to someone else in the stalls, and a feminine voice answered, talking about having on one of those snap-crotch bodysuits, and the fact she was having trouble getting the snaps to close.

Soon there was a flush, and out stepped a leggy blonde, still not quite put together, adjusting what I would say had to be the #3 dress of the evening. She stood there for a couple moments, just a few feet to my left, fumbling with the closure around her neck. I could see in the reflection of the polished marble tile on the wall that she was taking in a relaxed view of my not very relaxed cock.

She finally succeeded in getting her dress closed, smoothed herself, and started to walk by, still looking at my poor cock that by now was showing unmistakable interest in something other than taking a piss. She looked up just in time to say hi as she passed me. I said, "Hi." They were gone. My bladder was still struggling to empty, the flow so abruptly interrupted. On the way back to the ballroom I saw these ladies in the hall, and acknowledged them with a polite, "Hello, again." They smiled and nodded. And that was that.

The DJ tried to cater to everyone, and eventually a few big band tunes came on. That cleared the floor pretty quick, but if you like ballroom dancing, that's exactly what you want. Ashley and I were fond of ballroom dance in college (where we met), especially swing. Glen Miller's "*In the Mood*" came on. Poor Ashley: she puts up with a lot from me. During "*In the Mood*" she was whirled and twirled and twisted and rocked and bopped and who knows what with nary a moment to regain her equilibrium until the thing was over. This also meant she was rather indisposed to maintain control of her hemline; although we missed a couple of moves because her catch hand was tugging instead of catching, she lost the battle. We were dancing so vigorously, Ashley found it impossible to keep her hemline within the bounds of propriety.

There were a couple of combination twirl-and-clutch moves that were especially revealing. There was one where we were hand-in-hand facing each other, then passed each other raising hands over heads (hemline going *way* up), then extended and returned to a closed position with my arm around her waist (bringing the hemline up still more). This is actually a simple maneuver, but one of my favorites; it looked good and we did it well. Consequently, I threw her into it a number of times during this one song.

As the song progressed, we had an increasing difficulty with it. This particular move left her hemline somewhere around mid-butt. Ashley was trying to make me aware of this, and was valiantly trying to regain control of her attire. I suspect it is safe to say about a third to a half of the company got a good view of about a third to a half of her pantied butt.

This proved the wisdom of the panty hose.

On that note, we collected ourselves and left. We unraveled the long walk back to our car, saying assorted good-byes and Merry Christmases to those we met along the way. We found our way back to the car, safe and secure under that bright street light, various people and the occasional car going by. At least the uniformed gnome was gone from the hut. This was far too conspicuous a place to get carried away, and the risk of any passers-by being company people was great. Still, it was tough to just walk away from an event like this without a little gratuitous foreplay. I opened the driver's door and dropped a couple of items inside, then rounded to her side, the side away from the worst of the traffic, and opened her door. We held each other for a while, enjoying warm kisses betraying the heat growing within us both. I told her that wherever we were going, and whatever we were going to do, she wouldn't need the panty hose any more; so while we stood there together, I was going to strip them off her. She said, "Okay."

I slipped my hands under her wrap, let my hands drop to her hemline and slid them under The Dress, raising it ever so slowly as we kissed, continuing until The Dress was in a wad around her breasts. I slid my hands down again to the top of her panty hose, hooked them with my thumbs, and began to peel them off with surgical precision. I worked them down to about the end of her wrap, so that it would not yet be obvious to passers-by what was going on, and restored The Dress to its proper position.

Taking one last nibble on her lips, I glided down her body and finished peeling the hose off each leg. I pulled the wrap off her and put it in the car, enjoying a few moments of The Dress in its bare-assed glory. We exchanged a few last kisses; for a second, I slipped my hands under The Dress once again, raising it over hips, exposing her nether cheeks to the nip of the December air. One squeeze each and we were on our way.

I drove us toward the shore, to a place we'd visited once or twice last summer. It was a small beach set among the rocks. Not really good for swimming or sunning; the surf too rough, not much sand. It was popular with the surfers. I reasoned that this time of night, and this time of year, it'd be deserted; except for local traffic on the access road and the houses overlooking the beach. It'd be pretty quiet too. Besides the natural beauty of this spot, and the prospect for solitude, it was also quite picturesque. Set into the rocks, just above high tide, were four heavy wooden poles supporting a lattice roof in good repair, which was overlaid with palm fronds that made a sort of Tahitian gazebo.

We arrived at the beach, and things were as I'd hoped. There were less than two dozen parking spaces, and the couple of cars looked like they belonged to dwellers rather than visitors. We secured our car, and walked carefully down the sand and rocks to the gazebo, taking care that

Ashley did not lose her footing due to the inappropriateness of heels to this terrain.

We'd never actually visited the gazebo before. It provided token shelter from the surrounding houses and elements – more in concept than fact; the streetlights still fell on us, and I faced the ocean in what followed and knew we were in the plain view of the nearby street and houses. Our real cover was night itself. The little gazebo provided mood, like that of a well-chosen picture frame, adding romantic flavor to an already beautiful scene. The tide was high, with the waves broke just a few feet from where we stood. Ashley liked it.

I leaned against one of the four posts and opened my arms, inviting her in. She came and stood in front of me, gave me a kiss, and began to unfasten my trousers; they were new and it took her a little while to figure out how they fastened, but soon she had them open and coyly, slowly, lowered my zipper. She pushed her hands inside my waistband, stroking my hips and working her hands up under my shirt. Her next motion was intended to drag my usual banal underwear down, but as she got to the waistband of my thong underwear, she stopped short, smiling and saying, "And what's *this*?"

She lifted my shirt-tail and inspected approvingly, but paused only a moment before continuing on and dragging these down mid-thigh.

Having liberated me, she cupped my cock and balls in both hands and stepped into me, pressing her pussy against them. By this time I was eager to return the favor and, reaching under her wrap, I slid my hands under The Dress once more, this time raising it as high as it'd go, baring her from her breasts down to tiny heels. She pressed into me harder now, both out of a visceral urgency and a need to shield us both from the cold. I roamed over her body like it was the very first time, taking in every curve and deeply massaging every sensuous tumescence from her breasts to her supple sides to her hips to the globes of her exquisite ass.

Meanwhile, she stroked me to maximum rigidity, and guided me into her very core. We merged. She lifted one leg over one of my arms, and I took her cheeks in my hands, letting her relax her full weight onto her pussy for maximum stimulation. We slow danced – me slowly driving into her, lifting her off the ground by her pussy at the crest of my stroke, her relaxing into me at the trough, over and over and over in an agonizingly wonderful bump and grind. She was biting her lips, now lifting, now sinking, her head lolling this way and that as she dissolved into me. She opened her eyes for a moment and I whispered to her one word "*Now*."

Now is a simple word with a deep meaning. For us, in our intimate familiarity, our knowledge of each other's ways and wants, *now* had a special meaning. *Now* was the time to culminate all the preparation, the weeks of anticipation, the hours of titillation. *Now* was the nexus of this drama that we had staged and were playing out there between the land and the sea. *Now*. She knew.

She let go of me and leaned back, looking me in the eye, watching for the expressions she knew well, but that still remain a mystery to me. Meeting each agonizing thrust, she rocked back and forth like a ship rolling on the waves. She lifted her hands to her shoulders, and began slowly pushing her wrap aside until gravity took over and it fell to the ground. She grasped The Dress, already bundled into a ring between her breasts and shoulders, and, giving me a little look that said *here we go*, lifted it over her head and let it, too, fall to the ground.

It was an electric moment as she stood there looking like Botticelli's Venus, in total nudity, total sexuality, impaling herself on and being impaled by my cock, waves crashing into the rocks as waves of passion overtook us. The sensations of being stripped totally bare and taken in this wonderfully open place quickly became too much for her; despite the cold that had hardened her nipples into rocks she lost touch with anything but the fire that welled up within her. She took me again by the neck and threw her other leg over my other arm, literally mounting me, her only connection to this world being my grip on her thighs and the repeated pounding of her loins against mine.

She bucked up and down as if in one moment struggling to escape and, in the next, disintegrating into submission. Over and over in ethereal agony. Unrelenting, unforgiving, unconceding. Her loss of control infected me, and I soon felt a warmth that grew in intensity with every heave and thrust like a bellows blowing blast after blast of life-giving air, warming the dull ember to a brilliant red and then suddenly into open flame. The warmth within me suddenly turned to fire and I pumped blast after blast of come deep into her, driving her from passion's trance into spasms of resolution, tensing her every muscle, sending her clawing the air, gasping guttural animal-like cries over the pounding of the surf.

She lay atop me, legs over my arms, arms over my shoulders, head down, quaking, shaking, without the strength or control for voluntary movement. I took us down slowly, continuing a slow and gentle rhythmic penetration that eased us back into the world, the world of thoughts and consciousness.

Another day, we would have stayed in that moment for the duration of passion, savoring the going as we savored the coming; but the cold proved too much for us and we soon had to make our way to real shelter and real warmth.

I eased her down to the ground and she slowly shifted her weight off of her cunt and onto her feet, disengaging from me. She took a deep breath, and with one body-racking shiver was suddenly possessed by the chilling cold that in our passion we had managed to ignore. Another shiver shook her frame as she looked about for The Dress and her wrap. Since her first priority was to warm up, and The Dress would not help much in this regard, she just picked up The Dress without putting it on. Instead, she placed her wrap about her and urged me to get her to the warmth of the car a.s.a.p.

We made our way back and I saw that her wrap didn't cover her adequately. I said that she should probably put The Dress back on, for decorum's sake. She cared little for conventionality at this point, being more concerned about getting warm.

We made our way over the rocks, back to the parking area. Two surfer-looking guys arrived in a VW van, parked next to the trail head, where we'd have to pass. They were cracking open a couple of beers, tailgating on the little seawall, using parking lights for illumination. We had to walk right by them, and I found myself ill-advisedly muttering, "*See?*"

Ashley was too cold to care by this time and just grabbed my hand harder, saying, "*Let's just go!*"

We continued walking gingerly up the rocks, me in my tuxedo, she in heels and a wrap. She had one hand in mine for support and the other, holding The Dress, was stretched out to her other side for balance, leaving her wrap wide open, giving our two spectators a full-frontal view of her body. There was no way to be inconspicuous in passing, so we walked causally by, exchanging "hi's" and "good evenings". Once on the solid, flat ground of the parking lot, she let go of me and clutched her wrap shut, folding her arms over her chest; she strode determinedly towards our car, looking just a little bit steamed.

I must've given her one of those I-told-you-so looks; by the time we got to the car and I unlocked her door, she seethed "Okay, I'll put it on. You happy, now?"

She took off her wrap and laid it over the open door, standing naked on the public street for a few moments as she fumbled with The Dress and shimmied back into it. She put her wrap back on and said sharply, "Now, let's get this heater back on!"

The whole interlude at the beach had not taken long enough for the engine to cool down much, so very soon the car was toasty and Ashley relaxed. She apologized. She said, "I'm sorry . . . I just got too cold!"

I said, "Yeah, it was pretty chilly."

"Nice to be here, now," she said of the car.

"We'll have to come back some time," I said.

"In the summer," she said, and laughed.

I laughed too.

An hour passed by the time we completed the drive home and prepared to sleep for the night. I was still riding high from the whole evening's experience; rather than get into my nightclothes, I placed them by my pillow and remained naked, readying myself for bed. I slipped under the covers, not particularly conscious of sex; as we warmed each other under the covers, Ashley took my cock in her hand, much as she had there on the beach, giving me the sweetest, slow, soft caresses with her slender fingers – and brought me to full erection. She gave me a little peck on the lips, then slid down the bed, pausing here and there to plant a kiss on my chest and another on my stomach. She snuggled in close, lying on her side, and after a few introductory kisses and licks, took my cock into her mouth.

Oral sex was not easy for her; for oral sex to be comfortable, penetration of her mouth had to remain relatively shallow. Sometimes, as my own spasms racked my frame, this line was crossed accidentally, sending her gagging and retching. She would simulate a deeper penetration by sliding her hands along my cock in sync with her sucking, and this was what she was doing now.

We were both feeling pretty easy, relaxing in the glow of a truly remarkable night together, with the aura of our beach-front lovemaking still above us. It was almost as if we'd picked up where we left off when the cold had over-whelmed. I'd been easing us back from our climax by continuing my penetrations in a very slow and gentle mode, rhythmically caressing her from within, just as I might stroke her cheek from without; it was that kind of motion we settled into.

She lay still with her hands about the basal half of my cock as I slowly executed shallow penetrations into her mouth. We often did this rather vigorously, in what might crudely be called a face-fuck. She seemed to be expecting this, and was gripping me somewhat tightly with both hands and mouth as she usually did on these occasions. I was in a much more pliable mood, and asked her to ease and relax. She did, and in a few minutes became sufficiently relaxed that she shifted position and lay her hands behind me, caressing the cleft of my ass, letting her mouth do all the work. Her mouth relaxed, too, and I noticed a subtle and unfamiliar change.

It's funny how two people can know each other so well that such a subtlety can be detected. It was there. I knew her mouth. I knew her style. I knew her way of forming a pocket to receive me, and knew its shape and depth. It was different. As I continued my slow and steady probing, the nature of this change took shape in my mind, and I realized she was relaxing the blind end of that pocket, inviting me to penetrate her deeply. I did so cautiously, only the smallest fraction of a millimeter with each stroke, until I filled out this new, elongated pocket, really only a speck of an inch longer than the old one. But my cock knew the difference; it knew where her teeth came to rest on each stroke, and it knew this was new turf.

The changes continued. Again, I detected the boundary of this pocket receding shrewdly, and it seemed to subside more this time than before. Once I was sure, I again let my stroke elongate to meet it, and my consciousness was overtaken by an altogether new sensation that it took some time to shape in my mind. As the image came together, I dared not believe it, but as I continued the agonizingly slow penetrations, I knew it to be real; she had relaxed her mouth enough so my glans slipped past the base of her tongue and entered her throat. The realization went through me like a bomb from a terrorist blast, yet I managed to maintain control over my entrance to avoid any untoward movement which might disturb the unfolding miracle.

The changes continued still. She showed no signs of discomfort; I no longer could discern the existence of the familiar pocket, took it from the causal lay of her hands across my body without the slightest tension; she was inviting me to continue forward. This I did, ever so slowly. Agonizingly unhurried, maintaining the same speed, just gradually lengthening each stroke.

I was increasingly threatened with physical incapacitation as the new sensations were quickly overwhelming my ability to control my movements, but I maintained enough of it to stay the course and continue the long easy rhythm, nearly withdrawing from her mouth, then sliding in again, deeper and deeper, past the base of her tongue, into her throat, heading for her toes. The crescendo of deeper and deeper penetrations continued to build until I felt her nose nestled in my public hair and her lips against my balls for the first time in this life.

I erupted. Like Vesuvius. Like Krakatoa. Like Mount St. Helens. My hands behind her head; her face pressed against my body; hot come boomed deep into her throat. The sleeping gag-reflex awoke in all the commotion, but did nothing more than grip my cock all the harder, and catapult me over a peak I'd never really hoped to scale. Sounds boiled out of me I'd never heard before: pitiful timbres of a man reduced to a whimpering, helpless, and quivering collapse.

She pulled back for a moment, to grab some air, and then slid gently back onto me – one long, smooth, unimaginable stroke from Earth and all the way to Heaven. When I felt her face press into me again, my body reacted of its own accord, convulsing as tsunami surged outward from my epicenter, laying waste to any conscious thought, as I dissolved into pure sensation.

She pulled back, and, as at the beach, I eased us back into the world with slow, gentle strokes, caressing her from within; she now eased me from the out-of-body experience, coaxing my soul back into my body, with a series of ever more shallow strokes, ending her relaxation back into our familiar shallow pocket, where she held me motionless for some minutes, as I slowly softened in her mouth.

She released me, pressing a parting kiss deep into my pubic hair, then joined me face to face on our pillow. We kissed; I tasted myself. I babbled incoherently. She pressed a finger to my lips and we lay in silence, each in our own thoughts, as, slowly, sleep overtook us – like guards over prisoners.

Inauguration of the Dress: *sans* Underwear

The Dress was but a piece of cloth.

After numerous false starts, Ashley and I finally got it together to give The Dress its bare-assed inauguration.

I almost didn't believe it would happen; each time we'd attempted (three times) had fallen through. I was patient with Ashley's dubiety.

It was just before the New Year; we made up for it by resolving to spend New Year's Eve lounging in our open-air spa. For fun, we decided to do a little photography – something we do now and then, just for ourselves. Unfortunately, my good camera was on the fritz, so we had to use one of those point-and-shoot things I hate, but are necessary in times of sudden need. Even under optimal conditions, the pictures are of a lesser quality than is possible with the other camera; and, being auto-everything, it's tough to be creative. We were shooting outdoors in minimal light and adverse conditions, with a choice of no flash or full flash, and no control over the exposure.

I had her model The Dress *sans* underwear, standing on the edge of the spa where I could get a good angle of her ass, using spa light as background illumination. Later, I tried to get a shot from a more normal height, which would catch the spa light between her legs, giving some indication of the confusing semi-transparency of The Dress.

After squeezing off a few shots in this manner, we stripped and got into the spa, spending a couple of hours sipping martinis (stirred, not shaken) and talking. Once we rang in the New Year, we decided to call it a day, *and* a year, and finished off with a few in-spa shots of her fully-exposed body. I was not much of a photographer, and she wasn't a professional model, but I liked doing this and she liked the fact that I like it.

Where to go for this Risqué Night Out – it presented some problems. Since Ashley would barely be clothed, wearing only The Dress and shoes – no panties, no bra, no slip, no panty hose, no nothing – she'd feel exposed and vulnerable. I could relate to her reservations, despite my stirring. One important criteria: she should not feel in danger of recognizition; we could not go to any of our usual haunts, or places where other people we knew could be. The possibility made her touchy.

This would require heading out of town. We also needed a place that was relatively busy, allowing her to feel invisible – yet have quiet, dark corners where we could feel free to *feel* free. There'd have to be a bar so I could relax her with a few drinks. And, with less than usual to shield her body from the cold we'd already had an experience with, the establishment needed to be reasonably warm.

I considered all these factors and ended up settling on a place without much investigation. It was far enough from the city and impractical to check it out ahead of time. I just played a hunch on suitability, which was unlike me. Most places like this start to pick up around 9 P.M.; I planned to have us there well before, so we could get a decent pick of seats and still have a chance to go somewhere else if the venue turned out to be inappropriate.

As the appointed date and time approached, I grew restless with apprehension – we were *actually* getting it together this time. Ashley, recognizing this as well, became skittish. As she had before, she'd work off her perturbation by half-amusedly, half-seriously attempting to negotiate a way back into more a demure attire. But, having had things fall through three times, I was in no mood to barter. This was *our marriage*; this adventure was what we had *agreed* upon.

I pulled her onto my lap before we left, and looked into her eyes, and told her not only would I insist she wear *nothing but* The Dress and shoes, but my poor libido had been so jerked around anticipating this night I would also insist she submit herself completely to my desires: *whenever, wherever, whatever*. She sat still for a moment, then half-grinned and said, "*Oh, yes sir!*"

My one difference was to allow her to wear the long overcoat for coming and going; for warmth, yes, and as a security blanket. Also, anticipating she might be sitting with her bare ass on a cold chair in the night club, I thought having her coat to drape over the chair would make her feel more comfortable and less self-conscious; she was not so brazen an exhibitionist that she'd take any delight in having her exposed cunt slickening a plastic seat cover that Bubba and his buddies might've been blasting with chili-farts an indeterminate time earlier.

So many details for just a few precious moments.

It was enough to drive you crazy.

The time finally came to go. We approached our car like misfits of Eros. I unlocked the passenger door. Before opening it, I took her in my arms for a little pep talk. I kissed her, and held her face in my hands, looking into her eyes.

"Now," I said, "you're going to feel deliberate tonight, as you probably should. Your naked body is just barely concealed, and I have every intention of taking full advantage of that. People will look at you, but you will ignore them and look at *me*. Your sole interest tonight is to relax and place yourself pliably in my hands . . . *Okay?*"

"I'm putty," she said.

We arrived without incident, and found the establishment nearly empty; only twenty or so customers were scattered about the multi-tier club, which had a capacity of several hundred. It was early. This worked out very well. We found two bar stool seats in a far corner of the club, well shielded. Our backs were to two walls (sort of); our front was safeguarded pretty well by an elbow-high bar-like wall overlooking the lower levels and the dance floor. There was one open side where the bar continued across the back of the club. Ashley sat next to the far wall, and I sat between her and the rest of the bar.

It was not quite that simple, as nothing ever is. The wall opposite her side was the front of the DJ's booth; the wall behind us had a little walkway for coming and going to said DJ's booth. What made things considerably more interesting was the front of the booth, covered with mirrors down to a couple of feet off the floor; and the wall ended just a little above her standing height, opening the rest of the way to the ceiling, where the DJ pottered around. In their normal doings, the DJ and others who happened to occupy the booth were not in a position to see low enough to catch any interesting views, but there was always the possibility that one of them might come close enough to the edge to see something, *if* there was anything to see. The mirrors were another matter. Although I effectively secured Ashley from any direct observation by others further down the bar, the mirror made it possible for glimpses to be had from quite a distance away. It was a question of whether someone was in the suitable line of sight and, of course, whether there was anything to see.

When we first sat down – and for close to an hour after that – we were the only patrons choosing to perch at this long bar. Most who came in sat at one of the many tables on the next tier or gathered around the serving bar on the other side of the club. I bought drinks, which we quickly downed, and then went for more.

By the time we were halfway through the third round, Ashley had acclimatized to the place and, owing to the near absence of anyone in our section, was being quite receptive to my taking advantage of her barely clad state. I induced her to stand next to me, which, owing to the height of the bar stools, placed her head at a particularly comfortable height for kissing, and her butt at a particularly comfortable height for fondling. Not coincidentally, her cunt was at just the right height to press into my cock as she stood between my open legs.

I could've fucked her there, in public. (I wanted to do this with her, one day: the ultimate exhibition.)

We kissed. We pressed.

It was one of those nice long kisses. When she was in the mood, she had no problem closing her eyes and ignoring the rest of the world: kissing me like we were alone on a deserted beach. I sensed her slipping into this mood, and let my hands caress her body through the thin veil of The Dress. I reveled in the delicious contours of her hips, the inviting cleft of her buttocks, as I stood there quaffing her fusillade.

I could no longer contain myself, nor could I let her be contained in The Dress. My caress wandered off the bottom edge of The Dress and onto the warm flesh of her thighs; I brought my fingers together in that enigmatic void where cheek meets cheek, thigh meets thigh. I gave her a two-handed squeeze, the kind that lifts and separates.

Our kiss continued without a discernible break in mood; if anything, our long connection became a little sloppy. I released my grip on the bottom of her bottom, and slowly let my hands glide upward, only this time keeping my hands in full contact with her bare flesh, carrying the hem of The Dress higher and higher, angled on my thumbs.

I hiked The Dress up, inch by cautious inch, until it was around her waist; I had free rein to roam over the full expanse of her naked ass. We continued to kiss as I continued to caress her bottom, until she yanked The Dress down to a more constrained disposition. For the first time, one of the waitresses had appeared out of nowhere to take our spent glasses away. Her approach took us by surprise, and our reactions were too late. Thanks to the mirrored wall, the waitress had gotten an eyeful. She was stoic about it – just took our glasses and asked if we needed anything.

"No," I said, "not just now."

Shortly after this, Ashley, flustered, suggested we take a stroll around the club. I'd mentioned that I'd noticed a couple of pool tables on the opposite side. The vision that leapt through my mind, like a possessing demon, of her leaning over a pool table in The Dress, was enough to make me run, not walk, to the tables. When we got there, the tables were occupied by regulars – you could tell by the way they handled themselves they were regulars; and I've learned in the past one doesn't butt in on *regulars* unless one is serious about the game. We walked on by; I was somewhat disappointed.

Ashley whispered, "People are looking at me."

We returned to our places and, except for more bar runs, we remained planted there all night. We could've danced, but we didn't feel particularly moved by the music; and we were having so much fun with each other that we just *hung out*. We spent about half of the time in a kind of sit/stand/

prance combination, with me sitting on my stool and she standing between my open legs, wiggling to the music, constantly rubbing part of her body against my constantly stiff cock.

In this position, I could keep one hand permanently forged in her mysterious void, maintaining a couple inches of her bottom to peek from under the hem invariably. Every once in a while we'd kiss and I'd give her a two-handed butt hug, briefly exposing more rear, and just a few times (the viewing pleasure crowds and those foreign eyes) hiking the dress to her waist again for a particularly *satisfying* feel.

As the dance floor filled out and the evening began, people would earnestly come up every once in a while to the walkway behind us and make requests to the DJ. Except for the occasional guy who'd lean against the back wall of the club, making use of the mirrors from some distance, this trickle of traffic constituted the main audience for our cautious exhibition. Ashley did not take meticulous note of these people (as long as I was not getting too far out of line) and, the way she stood, she wasn't in position to heed any reactions. I, on the other hand, was. There were numerous evident times that the bit of bottom I kept exposed was heeded, and with it the fact that my hand was in firm contact with said resource.

The mirror abetted considerably in this regard.

One case in particular – there were several young women in their early twenties hanging out in a clutch somewhere below us; I'd seen them on the dance floor. One of them came up to make a request, and seemed to notice our intimacy; she did so discreetly, out of the corner of her eye, granting us a degree of public privacy.

What followed, however, was rather different. Apparently, these girls were acquaintances of the DJ. Shortly after this young woman returned to her crew, all three returned and entered the DJ's booth. Rather than talk to the DJ, they came over to the edge of the booth right above us and struck apparently nonchalant positions. One of them sat with her hip on the edge of the booth, while another leaned with both elbows on the edge. The third stood behind the two. The two in front, at least, had a clear view of our interactions.

It was clear enough to me why they were there, so I took that moment to snag a kiss from Ashley and cop one of the bigger feels of the evening. We kissed and I ran my hands down her back, hooking The Dress on my thumbs at the upstroke; I retraced my steps up to the small of her back, giving her ass a nice firm squeeze on the way, then letting The Dress fall back into place. I didn't dare watch these young women as I did this; but as soon as we broke our kiss, the trio immediately returned to their seats, confirming in my mind, at least, I'd given them what they came for.

Let your fantasies run away with you . . .

And perhaps it was all bullshit and they didn't see anything, and they didn't care one iota about us.

Among the rest of the house was a trio who'd caught our eye for most of the evening: two women in striking red dresses hanging out with one guy. At first we thought they might be two lesbians, the way they were intimate, but they never danced with each other; they took turns dancing with this guy, and occasionally all three danced together, never with anybody else. The dresses were pleasing to the eye: they were skin-tight with deep scoops in the back, laced together. And identical. Eerie. One of the two women danced more than the other, and had a tantalizing way of dancing with her feet rather spread apart so her dress would creep higher and higher as she danced. She would let her hem creep right up to her butt and pull it down to mid-thigh again. A nice tease, I thought, and it all added to another mystery. Eventually the other of these two women came up to the DJ's booth to make a request. I took the opportunity to ask her what the story was with the two identical dresses. Her answer was a shrug, a pucker of lips.

"Name?" I asked.

"Nicole," she said.

While we talked, she clearly looked my wife up and down, with just a little heat behind the eyeballs. She then went into the DJ's booth. From my position I could see her doings in there, and I knew that when she came out she'd be in perfect position to get a direct view of my wife's ass. I pulled Ashley to me for one more deep kiss of the evening, raising The Dress to her waist as I watched with one eye for our mystery woman to head for the door. Sure enough, here she came, just in time to see Ashley naked from the waist down. I quickly dropped The Dress on seeing her appear, but just a fraction of a second too late to avoid flashing her.

By the end of the night, my mind turned seriously toward capping off of the evening. When we arrived, I'd scouted out the parking lot for a nice secluded spot, but the lot did not lend itself to this at all. It was well lit, all spaces in easy view of the bouncers; and it was off a major street with plenty traffic. It was also very cold.

We bundled ourselves in our coats and headed for the door.

"Who's driving?" she asked, because we were both fairly buzzed.

"I am," I said. "You are going to be otherwise occupied, *my dear*."

"I am; oh?" – wicked grin from her.

"You are," I said.

We made our way to the car, and took up our familiar position on her side of the vehicle, me leaning against it, her leaning against me. We both looked around for a while without saying anything, then I broke the silence.

I said, "Here's the deal. I'm going to go around to my side of the car, start the engine, and get the heater going. Then we're just going to stand here for a while, let things warm up. Then we're going to stand here a little longer and wait for an opportune moment. Then we're going to open

the car door and put your coat inside. Then, when you feel
the coast is clear, I'm going to strip The Dress off you and
let you get into the car naked.

She didn't say anything, just looked around.

I didn't say anything, just looked at her.

"Mmmmnnnnn," she went, "okay . . ."

I started the car and let it warm. We passed the time
kissing; she huddled close to me and I wrapped my coat
around her as far as I could. So we waited, and people came
and went from the club; a car or two near us left; another
came and parked. Two bouncers and the doorman milled
about the club entrance in easy view, and a jobber was
making rounds of all the cars, putting little fliers under the
windshield wipers.

Enough time passed that I expected the interior to be
warm; I checked, and it was. Now – a matter of opportunity. The jobber was starting to work his way back toward
us. The three club employees continued meandering. Two
people were getting into a car about three spaces away.
What to do? With no improvement in the situation evident,
the deciding factor was the jobber getting closer. Ashley
finally said, "Oh, let's just do it!"

I opened the door; she threw her coat inside. Without a
second look, she slipped The Dress over her head and threw
it inside as well. One very quick naked peck and hug, and
she dove in behind her fabric. I ran to my door and also got
in. In the twilight of the car's interior, she looked flushed.

Head to toe.

In preparation for the ride home; we pushed our seats
back as far as they'd go; I had her recline her seat back to
forty-five degrees. Then I took my liberties. She resisted
some, suggesting we should get on the road, being a little
concerned about spending too much time naked in an active
parking lot; besides, the jobber might make it to our car. I
agreed, but pointed out that, on the road, I'd have to keep
both hands on the steering wheel, and I wanted to spend a

little time enjoying her predicament. She understood and laid herself open to me as I let my hands and lips roam uninhibitedly over her body – *for a minute*.

Then we moved out.

The traffic light at the main road was red. I loosened my own clothing, allowing my cock to breathe. The light changed, and as I merged onto the main road my naked wife took my naked cock in her naked hand.

We were on surface streets for a while before reaching the highway; this meant a certain amount of starting and stopping and turning on well-lit streets. She pumped me softly until we settled into the steady ride on the main stretch of dark highway that'd take us most of the way home. On that dark road, I settled into a comfortable, legal speed, putting on the speed control, and let her know I was ready for her. She adjusted herself into a semi-fetal recline across the front seat, head in my lap. She gave me a couple of teasing kisses, then took my cock into her mouth.

To receive this from my wife, her body buck-naked like that, was inspiring. I was in no particular hurry. I drove quite a while, enjoying the experience.

I wanted to bring things to a conclusion before exiting the highway. She sensed my progression; we escalated matters together. As a precaution I slowed a bit, enough so traffic overtook us. When I could see a stretch of empty highway behind us, I began to progress more vigorously toward my climax. The coordination of driving and getting head is a little distracting to the libido; thus I proceeded steadily. More traffic was beginning to gain on us. I could tell the next patch of vehicles was led by two pickup trucks; one which would pass us on the left, the other on the right. By the speed of their approach, I knew I could probably reach climax just about the time they would pass.

I had a *brilliant* idea.

I turned on the interior light.

I could now see my wife's naked form illuminated in all

her glory, her head bobbing up and down. I knew very well the occupants of these two pickups would also see everything Ashley and I had to show them. They gained on us slowly, the difference in our speed not that great. I watched their progress in my rear view, and managed to time my climax so I was pumping semen into Ashley's mouth during the entire interval these two trucks passed.

It is not possible they did *not* see everything. And I mean *everything*.

Once I was drained, I turned the interior light off. I encouraged Ashley to stay in my lap, letting me go soft in her mouth. When she finally sat up, the headlights of oncoming traffic showed her face to be glistening with a mixture of saliva and come. As she slowly wiped her cheeks and chin clean, eating the come off her fingers with a glance my way, I couldn't help but notice her soft expression: a happy, privately contented, self-reflective kind of look not really meant to be seen by others. I soon felt myself falling in love all over again, the lights of the freeway on her face. Our marriage is saved, I thought.

She remained naked as we drove home, putting on her coat when she left the car. We walked to our front door; she was huddled under my arm.

She asked me why I had turned on the interior light.

"Because I wanted to *see* you," I said, kissing her hair.

Little Black Thing

What struck me first about Little Black Thing – it was made out of exactly the same ultra-thin, clingy, jet-black fabric as The Other Dress, and it measured exactly the same length as The Dress. Like both, Little Black Thing fit closely at the neck, yet had sleeves to the wrist, attaching like a full-body leotard from the hips up. And, like The Other Dress, Little Black Thing provided a delectable definition to the silhouette of Ashley's breasts, yet flared just a touch at the hips; so rather than clinging to her lower cheeks, this one floated, playfully brushing her curves, rather than grasping.

Like The Dress, Little Black Thing ended a tad below the edge of her butt; and unlike The Dress, the hemline was free to flit loosely about. Although The Dress fit close enough so the fabric had a tendency to ride up now and then, its hemline was pretty much captive to the movements of her legs, hugging closely; the only unintentional view granted by The Dress were peeks associated with sitting and standing, or unprepared creeping.

On the other hand, the hemline of Little Black Thing floated freely, and did not threaten to trail up. The fact it could swing loosely allowed casual motions and afforded occasional glimpses of still higher ground; for example, twirling on a dance floor, casual grazes with her chair or other people, static cling, and so on.

The fabric was transparent to a small degree, yet opaque enough so this subtle transparency was not apparent to casual observation. Whereas The Other Dress was at its most diaphanous across her ass, that mild transparency was due to the slight stretching of the fabric which was greatest around her hips. This was not so with Little Black Thing; its fabric was somewhat loose about the hips; the bit of transparency was subtle. In normal light, it appeared to be murky; however, against a bright backlight, the looseness of the fabric at her hips allowed the outline of her form to stand out clearly, causing a greater sense of transparency had the fabric clung closely to her frame.

Impulses. I came across Little Black Thing by chance and purchased it on impulse, not having any particular immediate plans, designs, or scenarios. It also happened by chance that I found a great place to summon it for a début.

It was a hotel. A grand hotel. A colossal building, with a cavernous two-storey lobby, Romanesque and Gothic, slightly French provincial furnishings and statuary in alcoves for just a scanty Grecian touch. If it were not for the massive square columns in two rows down the center, the lobby would've been a large open space, almost the size of a basketball court; however, the columns broke down that space into smaller elements with a slightly more intimate feel. Opposite the entrance, at the far end of the lobby, was a wide staircase making its way up to the first floor. In between, about a third of the way through the lobby, sat a grand piano. In any other room this piano would appear to be a massive fixture, but under those mammoth columns it looked lonely.

The overall lighting in this place was variegated, depending on the schedule of events. When parties or conferences were scheduled, the lobby chandeliers were brightly lit, bringing off a bustling, rather palatial air. On off nights, the lights were kept low, invoking a darker (and erotic) mood.

On one side of the lobby was a passage to conference-sized chambers; on the other side, passages to smaller rooms, a bar, and a small restaurant. Five-star, I heard. The theme of dark light and colors continued in these lesser side chambers. The tavern was saturated in dark wood, with a long, horseshoe-like bar dominating the center of the room. It was surrounded by high black leather stools and a few towering tables. The street side of the bar was café-like, with a few ordinary tables and chairs in front of extremely tall windows, statuesque lengths of glass teetering on their sills like Amazonian legs in stiletto pumps, appropriately under-dressed in short café-type curtains that do little to shield the bar's patrons from inquisitive streetwalkers.

Walking in was like taking a step into *film noir*.

The brightest spot in the room highlighted a pool table in the corner. In a perfect scene, this light would be thrown off by a stained-glass fixture hanging just a few feet above the table, creating sharp boundaries between a central stage and peripheral shadows – shadows the imagination could envision filled with unseen faces scrutinizing each player's moves and strokes. Instead, floodlights in the ceiling high above created a more diffuse light that, though still some-what conical, left little in the way of intimation to shelter either player or voyeur.

Yes. A lonely pool table in a rather upscale locale frequented more by weary travelers than locals. I was tingling.

The time came to get ready. Ashley put on Little Black Thing for the first time since the traditional modeling session a week before. She adjusted the sleeves and smoothed the fabric to her body. She looked in the mirror and observed, predictably, "I need hose."

I tried to look crestfallen and said, "You wouldn't do that to me, now, would you?"

"I know," she said, "but look at me – my legs are so white."

At least her first concern was not about Little Black Thing being too short. But the eye *was*, I noted, naturally drawn to that sharp boundary between the whiteness and blackness, naturally drawn to that daringly flirtatious line.

I tried for the wounded puppy look. "Well, yeah," I said, "uh, the contrast with that jet-black *is* pretty strong. But hose would really dampen the sizzle – maybe not for other people – but – you know – I've really had my sights set on taking you out just like – *this*."

She stood quietly for a while. I wanted into her thoughts. I knew she was thinking back to the company Christmas party, her hose the only thing that saved her. She smiled at me and grabbed Little Black Thing by its hem and tugged it down several inches further than the manufacturer (and I) ever intended. I had been afraid of something like that – another night of hemline tuggery. But another idea came to me as I observed . . .

I'm not sure whether she noticed it – I would guess not – but that demure tug born of modesty produced a delight-fully immodest effect. Since Little Black Thing was pretty much one sinuous piece of wispy and elastic fabric, the tension introduced by that tug spread more or less instantly from her hemline all the way up to her shoulders, dilating the weave of the already somewhat gauzy material just enough to cause a marked increase in its transparency. Whereas the relaxed fabric offered barely more than a subliminal image of her charms, that tug revealed an image of hidden treasures, walloped into the cognizant, her breasts especially shining through.

Prior to this, I'd worried the tug reflex might take some of the fun out of the evening, but I could see Little Black Thing would silently conspire with me to frustrate her modest instincts, at all times revealing either a dazzling expanse of leg seeking ever higher ground, or an immodest image of breasts shining through a gossamer smokescreen. I lauded at the subtle ironies, looking forward to noticing which of the possibilities would actually rule the evening. I reminded her, as I often do, that it does little good to fight the natural equivocate of a dress such as this – she would ultimately be more comfortable by relaxing and letting it *do what it wants*.

As we pottered around getting ready, Little Black Thing did indeed work itself back to its natural place, and the vitreous image of her breasts dimmed to a mirage. It struck me, out of the corner of my eye, that Little Black Thing seemed to be just a bit shorter than The Dress. Puzzling, since I knew they measured out to exactly the same length – hanging in the closet, at least. This was a poignant thought, since The Dress was, until then, the shortest thing in her wardrobe by about one full inch. I mused idly that it must be a pleasant illusion, one whose study I would have to defer till later.

The weather still being on the cool side, she donned her long overcoat on the way out but, as is her habit, rather than buttoning it, she just cinched it loosely about her waist with the sash. There seemed to be a startling amount of leg showing through the opening of the coat. In retrospect, I think the effect was just one of color contrast – white leg from well-turned ankle to high-on-the-thigh, topped by jet-black – made her legs stand out. The long slit created by the overcoat helped.

We made our way – finally – to the hotel and cruised around to park. I had inquired by phone where and how we should park, hoping for a structure that might afford a little transient seclusion. Indeed, there was such a structure adjacent to the hotel, and I had been instructed on its use. Valet parking was offered, but that would put the damper on certain potential adventures; it was explained to me how I could self-park in the same structure. That seemed to be the appropriate choice for this occasion.

When we got to the hotel, however, the parking structure had been commandeered by some kind of *event* and was unavailable. We had to drive around the downtown area and park on the street near the hotel, amid traffic, passers-by and panhandlers.

I had tried to paint a mental picture of this place for Ashley, but verbal words often elude me, unlike putting them to paper. In order to present it to her in the best light, I took her to the front of the hotel; we entered through the main entrance and to the lobby. This particular night there appeared to be a conference, a convention, something. The place was bustling, and the lobby lights were high. We stopped a few feet from the grand piano and stood for a moment. She looked around and soaked up the atmosphere.

"This is the piano I was telling you about," I said, adding, "Wouldn't this be a great spot for a nude photo?"

"You have to be kidding," she giggled, whispered. "With all these *people* around? Right in front of the *door*? On the main street?"

"I don't mean under conditions like this," I said. "I mean on an off day, when things are quiet."

"It'd better be *pretty damn quiet*," Ashley said.

"Well, like I told you at home," I said, "when I've been

in here before, at off hours, this place has been virtually empty – and the lights are usually kept much lower."

"Still," she said, "it's right off the main street – "

I said, "We could drive up, stroll in, take the shot, stroll out, and drive off before anyone would know what happened."

"So . . . I'd come in – in my coat, and just throw the coat aside when you're ready?"

"Exactly."

"I don't know," Ashley said. "I don't see myself laid out across a grand piano."

I said, "I was thinking more in terms of having you sitting at the piano as if playing, taking a wide angle shot of the whole lobby. You know, contrasting the formal elegance of this backdrop with the intimate image of your bare-ass naked body."

She smiled at that and said, "It'd still have to be pretty quiet."

We moved to the side of the lobby, to the restaurant and bar. We confirmed our reservation, time and table; and then went next door to the bar.

Like the rest of the hotel, the bar was relatively busy. Just by chance, the pool table was being vacated as we walked in, so we claimed it and I went for drinks. By the time I returned, she had racked up the balls, and was sitting pretty, *waiting for me*. She sat with that long coat cinched around her, crossed bare legs sticking out. I swear she looked naked from the waist down.

I handed her a drink and said, "You gonna wear that coat all night?"

She smiled, "Maybe."

She took a sip, and then stepped out of her coat into the swanky light that gave just a hint of pool-hall atmosphere to this corner of the otherwise upscale bar.

I had to take a deep breath. I still couldn't tell whether it was an illusion or not, but Little Black Thing seemed just breathtakingly short, topping a jarringly long expanse of leg with a tousled skirt edge.

We each picked a pool cue and looked stupidly at each other. I had been so long since we'd played pool; neither one of us remembered the rules. We started playing anyway, and within a few shots it was coming back. We both sucked. We were having fun.

We were no more than six to eight shots into the game when we came to a point where Ashley had an awkward cross-table shot. She asked for the bridge.

I handed it to her but didn't let go. "Don't use this too often," I said.

"What?"

"Don't use this too often," I said, and reminded her this whole evening had been contrived so I could admire her figure bent over the pool table.

We both held on to the bridge for a few seconds, staring. I doubt whether more than a single muscle cell flinched in her face, but her countenance shifted subtly during that brief shared gaze, from one of simple social pleasure to one laced with sultry mischief.

I eased my grip, releasing the bridge to her, and she took it slowly, letting her eyes linger on mine just a bit longer than necessary. She took her shot, missing as wildly with the aid of the bridge as she would've without it.

Since we had not been playing very long, I hadn't really noted anything significant in her behavior one way or another, but as we continued playing it seemed to me she was acting less self-consciously than I might've expected. For example, with all the bending over, I might've expected her to be tugging herself more than she was, which was essentially not at all. I was, in fact, curious to see the effect her tugging might produce in this situation, but that effect never materialized. Instead, the atmosphere was rarefied by the high altitudes through which Little Black Thing flitted. Whether she quashed her modest instincts in

deference to me or not I don't know. I didn't ask. I just
enjoyed the scene.

Eventually, Ashley found herself with another bungling
cross-table shot that clearly called for the bridge. This one
was made awkward by the fact she would have to make the
shot with her back to the open area of the busy bar. She
looked at the shot, looked at the patrons and, rather than
asking for the bridge, whispered, "Stand behind me."

I looked about the bar, partly in that quick, involuntary,
self-conscious way we all do in public when we do the
unexpected – which may draw the attention of others; but
this quick scan was also in a practical mode. I was just one
person. I did not expect to be much of a screen; the people
in the bar were too scattered about, and I'd have to stand
back a few paces from her to avoid interfering with her shot.
Obviously, she didn't take this into account and turned to
the table, already starting to lean over. "Oh well," I mused
with a grin, and took about three paces back.

She lined up her shot, leaned in far, a stretch that raised
the hemline of Little Black Thing well past the edge of her
ass, unveiling several inches of her bare, creamy cheeks and
the mysterious void nestled below. She was no more than
five seconds thus, lining up and taking her shot, but it was
one of those delightful moments that seem to proceed in
slow motion.

After that high point, things seemed a little different, a
little more charged. I was perplexed; something was different. It was some time before my attention returned to the
thought that kept flowing through the evening like a sensual
fugue – Little Black Thing was shorter than The Dress. As
I studied this again, it finally occurred to me what was
different – an effect I had not anticipated.

The Dress is form-fitting; it is not really clingy. One
consequence of this is when Ashley wore it sans-underwear,
The Dress slid well on her skin, generally behaving itself.
Little Black Thing, however, was clingy everywhere except

in the skirt. I was faced with a consequence of that cling I'd never thought about. With all of her bending and standing, bending and standing, the fabric of Little Black Thing had been subject to a lot of flexing in a kind of a breathing motion: stretching, relaxing, stretching, relaxing.

Another fabric would've shown a wrinkle or two as a result of this, but with every stretch relax cycle this fabric seemed to adjust itself in such a way that the bit of slack which crept in was evenly distributed over her torso, so no wrinkles were evident. The result of this activity was Little Black Thing had shrunk by about an inch over the course of the game. The hemline of Little Black Thing no longer fell an inch below the edge of her butt, but precisely *at* the edge of her butt.

I watched her closely for a while to confirm this conclusion. There was no doubt about it. Most every shot from this point onward showed cheek. And some showed a *lot*.

I was on edge for the rest of the game. My eyes and mind were obsessed with her ass. She had to realize the state she was in. Yet, not once did she tug herself toward a more modest condition. Her face continued to reflect just a hint of mischieviousness, her countenance remarkably cool. She displayed no self-consciousness whatsoever in her shots. She didn't asked for the bridge again. She didn't avoid deep bends when conditions called for it. In fact, she seemed to be bending more than necessary. Her hemline rose so high toward the end of the game, that not only did every shot show a bit of cheek, but on her tougher shots I could have cupped a healthy handful of her luscious behind without touching fabric. I kept picturing myself grabbing each cheek, right here, spreading them, finding the pink pucker of her asshole and exposing it to the bar.

Our game came to an ignominious end about the time we were supposed to take our table in the restaurant. We stowed our cues and left the bar. She walked smugly; I walked stiffly. No one seemed to notice us. I think I was

disappointed. There are so many little worlds in the world,
it amazes – sometimes.

We didn't really need a reservation. The restaurant was
less than a quarter full. I had expected this; when I'd
checked the place out before, there'd been *no one* in
restaurant except the service staff. When I walked in,
they'd all jumped to their feet and assumed positions.
Although a reservation was not necessary, I made one
because I wanted a particular table. By many standards,
the table I chose would not be considered the best. Like
most of the tables here, this was a booth; it was next to the
kitchen, so the service traffic passed between it and the rest
of the dining room. Its orientation was such that we faced
the open area of the restaurant and would have this parade
of traffic right in front of us. For me, this negative was more
than balanced out since this was the most dimly lit table,
furthest from the entrance, a bit around a corner from the
main part of the dining room: quite private, quite intimate,
quite romantic, perfect for a devious turn of the hand.

Except for the service traffic, of course.

Waiters, stewards, maître d's – all are members of a cadre
who know the value of discretion, particularly the fact that
greater discretion is often rewarded with higher tips. The
situation presented by this dark little alcove was perfect for
intimate nuzzling, while savoring a few culinary delights.

We announced ourselves and were shown to *our* table.

We settled into the plush leather. I coaxed Ashley back
out of her coat so I could enjoy our closeness more than had
been possible in the bar. We were given menus, which
revealed right off why this was a five-star restaurant.
Fortunately for us, there was a commoner's special, still
somewhat steep by my standards, but a worthy compro-
mise. We both chose that, and settled in for the wait.

We sat quietly, enjoying the setting and each other's
company. Too many people, I feel, don't know how to
enjoy silence. My wife sat to my left, so I let my left hand

slide smoothly over those wonderful legs, up one thigh, following the fold of her thigh and across her cunt, grazing pubic hair, following the other fold onto her other thigh and down again. Nice, easy, absent-minded caresses. Back and forth.

The net effect of a few of these gliding touches was to get us both nicely relaxed, and to leave her sitting with Little Black Thing pulled up around her waist. I gently lifted her right leg over my left; her legs parted in a relaxed carriage that kept her cunt open for me. It was the kind of position that would have easily allowed me to stimulate her, had we both been in that kind of mood, but our mood was more casual. Maybe another time.

Our dinner proved to be truly splendid, albeit rather expensive; it was well worth it. I, at least, was moaning over almost every mouthful. Positively decadent. Our commoner's special included dessert, which I had forgotten until Ashley mentioned it as we neared the end of the meal. I told my wife how I would like to have *her* for dessert, at which she just smiled, and offered herself up for a particularly deep kiss. "Your ass," I said to her, "I'd like your ass for desert."

"Why that in particular?" she asked, batting her eyes.

"I had to drool at it in the bar," I said. "The pool table. You had to know."

"I knew," she said.

"Now all I have is your ass on my mind," I said to her. "That's what I'd like for desert. A mouthful of ass. My tongue deep in that."

She snuggled closer. She held her glass of white wine and said, "As we ate dinner, I imagined that you had come in this glass, and I was drinking your warm come with this wonderful food."

The nuance of our dessert discussion grew increasingly sexual, frustrating me to no end, since I knew we would not be acting on any of our suggestiveness until we got home.

We finally collected ourselves to go. I tipped the waiter well for his discretion. We exited the hotel and approached our car. I cursed myself for not being able to find a more secluded parking place; I could see myself in the back seat with Ashley lying face down on the leather, my face buried between her butt. We leaned against the car in front of passers-by and several lanes of traffic. I opened her coat, taking her in my arms from the inside.

I pulled her to me for a final kiss and, as we kissed, I slid my hands under Little Black Thing, raising it up enough so between the two of us, at least, she was as naked as circumstances would allow. I stroked her flesh as far as my hands could reach, caressing her buttocks, stroking her, pressing her breasts into me. We finished our kiss, I restored her to decency, and we drove home.

The safety of our own house; there is no better feeling.

We undressed and got into bed.

"I thought I'd suck you," she said. "All that talk during dessert got me in the mood for sucking." She asked, "What do you want?"

"To eat your ass," I said.

"Let me suck you off," she said, "then you can lick me to your heart's desire."

I loved our silly talk. I laid back as she took me into her mouth. She was rather rough, and while the penetration of her mouth was shallow, her roughness with me brought me to quick excitement. I was surprised at how fast I came. She hummed, swallowing, and lay next to me.

"I could sleep now," she said.

I was rubbing her back with one hand, that hand moving down to her ass. I ran the images of her bent over the pool table, a head-movie I would come to again and again the next few days. The excitement was still there.

I kissed her on the mouth, twisting her neck back to do so, strands of her hair between us. I kissed her hair, her neck, down her back. I kissed each buttock, taking a moment to admire the contours of this flesh, and spread them with my hands, getting a view of her sweet asshole. I tasted it, and it was as sweet as it always was, as I anticipated it to be, as I dreamt and desired and knew.

I started off slow and gentle, running my tongue around the perimeter of her sphincter. She responded appropriately, arching her butt, emitting small sounds of approval. With one finger, I opened her asshole so my tongue could slide in. My entire universe, at that moment, consisted of her ass and my tongue. I took her in, mouth and soul full of her, and felt high. I was hard again. With my free hand I stroked myself to a complete erection. I told her I wanted her and she said yes. I got up, went to the bathroom, came back with the tube of K-Y, applying a healthy portion first to my cock, and then her ass. I slid my middle finger in and she gasped. I tongued her some more, put more K-Y on my cock, and positioned myself. I got the head of my cock in, then stopped, asking if she was okay.

"Just fuck me," she said, and as I went in she kept saying, "Fuck me, fuck me, dammit, fuck me," and I did.

Her ass juiced around my cock. I began slowly, and built a fast friction. She began to slam her ass up, to meet my thrusts, and a loud slap was heard when our flesh met. I though I could go on all night – forever – like this. I came in her ass and stayed still for a minute, removing my flesh from hers. I lay next to her.

"I could sleep now," I said.

Ashley looked at me. The make-up was smeared around her eyes. She sat up, taking my hand. She kissed my mouth, kissed my neck, my chest, my stomach. She kissed me and I could taste myself on her. "I can sleep now," she said, and we did, in each other's arms.

I woke up twice that night, because she was awake, sitting up, looking out the window.

"What's wrong?" I asked.

She turned to me and was quiet for a moment. "I really enjoyed tonight," she said.

"So did I," I said.

"I enjoyed every minute."

"It was nice," I said.

"It's going to work, isn't it?" Ashley said. "Our marriage won't fall apart, after all. We needed this."

I moved to her and said, "Yes."

"I want more," she said. "I want to do more perverted things. With you. And out in public, I want to wear more provocative clothes."

"That can be arranged." I said.

"I want us to try everything," she said, and we went back to sleep.

The second time was close to morning. She was looking at the ceiling. I held her close to me. She closed her eyes and I closed mine.

Red Leather

Let your fantasies run away with you, and you'll get in trouble.

Ashley and I –

Of course, we had to take The Dress back into the world. One time wasn't enough; the very thought of it was addictive. I have to admit I was having dreams of this, and all the various, enticing scenarios we could find ourselves in as a result.

We go about our everyday lives in an everyday way; we get up, we shower, we dress, we grab something to eat, we go to work, we do what we do in the world and make money so we can subsist; and we come home. I wanted more and Ashley wanted more – there had to be *more* to our lives. Some sort of adventure we couldn't correctly pinpoint – like it was at the tip of our tongues, yet memory failed us.

We thought we were looking for danger, I suppose, but we were merely playing head games and *maybe*, maybe, we didn't have a clue how to fully live the lives we thought we wanted.

After we made love, she caressed my face; she said, "I want to go back there again."

"You want to open yourself," I said.

"Yes," she said.

She meant the club outside the city, where we met Nicole. Again.

It was almost like we were repeating ourselves. Two weeks ago we'd been here, and it was the same night, and Ashley had The Dress on, and, before leaving, she had twinges of second thought.

"Tell me," she said.

So by the car I held her close to me. I looked into her eyes. I told her, "You'll feel exposed."

"I want to be exposed," she said.

I didn't have to tell her anything else. We got into the car, put the heater on, and drove to the club. We arrived pretty much the same time we'd arrived before, and found the two bar-stools behind the DJ's booth. It was almost as if two weeks hadn't gone by. I got us drinks, and we drank, and I got us more, and we kissed, and I pulled The Dress up from behind with my thumbs, glancing at her perfect white ass in the mirror behind us. I thought, she can suck me off in the car when we go home, and I'll put on the interior light, and a truck will pass by, and some stranger will get a glimpse.

"Look," Ashley said.

I relieved The Dress from my grip. Ashley smoothed it out, and I turned to where she had nodded her head. Across the dance floor were the same two women and man we'd seen before, in the red dresses with the scooped backs. The two women were in red again, yes, but red leather this time: red leather mini-skirts and fishnet stockings with small red leather jackets exposing breasts barely covered by satin red bras. I have to admit the sight was amazing, as both their red minis were, perhaps, just millimeters shorter than The Dress, and one slight move could, I knew, uncloak something quite interesting. The three were looking at us as we were looking at them. As if on cue, the two women got up, strode across the dance floor, and went to the DJ's booth. I knew they were going to look down at us. I took this opportunity to draw Ashley close to me for a long kiss, and a pull at The Dress.

"Hey," Ashley said.

"They want a peek," I said. "Let's give them one."

Ashley, embarrassed, hid her face in my shoulder as I lifted The Dress, looked up, and saw both red-leather-clad women glancing down. I watched them descend from the steps; I tried to get a peek under their skirts, but it was too dark. There was music. The women got on the dance floor and their male companion joined them. Ashley and I watched. I suggested we should dance but Ashley didn't want to move. After a few songs, the trio went back to their table and refreshed their drinks. One of the women, the one (I'm sure) I'd talked to last time (they both had dark cropped hair, though), continued to glance our way. At one point, I raised my drink and smiled. Ashley slapped my hand.

I said, "Just being friendly."

"We don't need to be friendly," Ashley said, then, "Oops."

Oops was that the women in the splendid red leather was walking our way. She wasn't going to the DJ's booth because her direction and eyes were straight for us. Ashley self-consciously adjusted the hem of The Dress and tried, demurely, to cross her legs – to no no avail. The woman carried her drink, which looked like a vodka martini. She put the drink on our table; there wasn't a third chair so she stood.

"Hello," she said.

"Nicole," I said.

"You have a good memory," she said.

I introduced Ashley and myself.

"Hope I'm not too forward," Nicole said, "but what the hell, I'm always forward. Forward is my middle name, and my last name. I thought I should come over here. You were here a couple of weeks ago."

"You have a good memory," I said.

She explained that she and her friends came here almost every night of the week, including Sundays and Mondays when it was often dead (it hadn't picked up yet, this night, but she assured us it would). She also said we were a couple hard to forget – especially that *dress*, she said. "It's a nice dress."

Ashley didn't know what to do. "Thank you," she said.

"Provocative," Nicole said.

"I'd say the same for your outfit," I said.

"Well," Nicole said, "*I'm* wearing underwear."

Under the table, Ashley gripped my knee. She was flustered and embarrassed and doing a damn good job not showing it toward this stranger.

"Don't get me wrong," Nicole said with a smile. "I mean, it's all more effective without underwear. There are some good snapshots you've been giving us and other people around here tonight, and before, too. Last time, when you left, you were quite the conversation piece. But I suspect that's what you wanted. People do certain things – people do *most* things – intentionally. You're very beautiful," she said to Ashley.

"Oh," Ashley said, "thank you."

Nicole looked at our hands. "Married?" she asked.

"Yes," I said.

"Can I tell you something about your wife?" Nicole asked me.

"Sure," I said.

Nicole said, "Sitting over there, getting a crotch shot now and then, all I could think about was burying my face into your pretty wife's beautiful cunt."

That set Ashley off. She was red in the face now; she uncrossed and crossed her legs; she pulled at the hemline; she said, "Oh, well . . ."

Nicole laughed, reaching over and patting Ashley's hand, saying, "Hang on just a minute." She went back to her friends. Intentionally, Nicole put a sway to her walk, touched her red leather mini, pulling it up some, showing us the thong underwear creased between her ass cheeks.

Ashley finished her drink, quickly, and said, "Maybe we should leave."

"Do you really want to?"

"I don't know."

We saw that Nicole's entourage was leaving. Nicole turned and walked back, smoothing out the red leather skirt and smiling all the time. She sat back down. We'd had our chance to escape but failed to make that move.

"So," Nicole said, "I'm free."

It would be pointless to record some of the mundane details of conversation and silence, both of which were dull, helped on by another round of drinks. Nicole suggested the three of us dance. I looked at Ashley and she got up from her stool. I must admit I felt rather lucky in the company of these two resplendent women on the dance floor, both with hemlines so short that the moves we made to the music (a little too fast and modern for my tastes) certainly bared something now and then – something which I tried to get a look at, but they were both moving so quickly, gyrating, that I only caught glimpses at what may have been hints of real flesh or just my imagination. I was intrigued that Ashley was able to loosen up so quickly – I wasn't sure if this was caused by our drinking or Nicole's warm gestures of friendship. Either way, my wife took a quick liking to Nicole. I had to stand back a moment as we danced, and watch the two of them, knowing there was erotic exchange both obvious and alien.

We returned to our table. Nicole was close to Ashley. They smiled at me and I smiled back. Nicole touched my wife's bare knee and said, looking at me, "You know, my friends are gone and I don't have a ride home."

Ashley and I were more drunk than we usually were after leaving a bar or club. I am often nervous about drinking and driving – I was quite over the legal limit here – but that night, I didn't give a damn. It was one of those nights. Nicole was in the back seat, and we were taking her home; somewhere between drinks and dances and chatting, Nicole managed to get us to invite her back to our house. Nicole leaned forward and said, "*Drive faster.*"

I did.

Ashley and Nicole were in a giddy and giggling mood. Ashley said, "Do you want to know something?" and laughed.

Nicole ran her hands through Ashley's hair.

Ashley laughed again.

"What?" Nicole said.

"The last time," my wife said, "the last time we were here, that one time, when we drove home, I sucked him off as he drove, and I was naked, and he had the light on, so people in passing cars could see me."

I looked at her. She knew. I smiled. She was insidious; I wondered what else she knew.

"That's nice," Nicole said. "I like that," she said. "Would you do it again?" she said to my wife. "Would you suck him so I can watch?"

Ashley giggled. She looked at Nicole and realized Nicole was serious. "Well," Ashley said, "okay." She looked at me.

Nicole ran her fingers through my hair this time and said, "Relax, it's okay. Drive faster."

I didn't drive faster.

Ashley was pulling The Dress off her body. She was having trouble in the cramped confines of the seat, and being drunk didn't help.

"What are you doing?" I asked.

"It has to just be like last time," she said. "Don't you want to?"

Of course I wanted to. As with all new experiences, I was nervous and excited. Our exhibitionism had always been at a safe distance, viewed by those we never talked to or were themselves discreet enough to play the game of secrets and surprises; we'd never had an active participant, watching so close. Still, my cock was hard and I had it out of my pants, looking at my naked wife and the road, catching quick glances of Nicole in the rearview mirror. Ashley said, "Here goes nothing," and she moved her head into my lap. Nicole reached up and turned on the interior light, like she could read my mind, like she knew exactly what to do. Nicole moved closer so she could watch Ashley.

"Drive faster," Nicole said again, almost in my ear.

"I can't drive *too* fast," I said.

"Just a *little* bit faster."

I drove a little bit faster.

"Sizzle," Nicole said.

Inside our house, I made all three of us a drink. I didn't know what was going to happen, but I had a good idea, and I was hoping, and I was scared at the same time. We were drunk – Ashley was drunk – and how were we going to both feel tomorrow? Looking at the two women in my home, I told myself, *what does tomorrow matter? You're always thinking about tomorrow. Live for the moment.* Living for the moment was what I planned to do. The three of us were in the living room: I was leaning against a wall, Nicole was standing in the middle (as if she stood before mirrors to get that stance: legs apart, drink in hand, one hand on hip, oblique smile, skirt riding high) and Ashley was sitting on the couch, slumped, The Dress bunched up (she had quickly put it back on before we came inside) and pubic hair visible.

"Spread your legs for me," Nicole said.

"Okay," Ashley said. There was only a moment of indecision, then she slowly opened her legs. I could see, from where I was, that my wife was very wet.

Nicole turned to me and said, "I want some of her." I nodded. Nicole walked over to Ashley and stood above her. Ashley looked up, and looked at me, titillation and vacillation on her face. I thought about my come that had been in her mouth, and how she'd shown Nicole this in the car (at Nicole's request): opening her mouth to Nicole, my come on her tongue, her teeth, the roof of her mouth. Nicole finished her drink, put it down on the coffee table, and knelt before Ashley. She touched Ashley's face, neck; she said, "You turn me on."

Ashley's hand was shaking when she put her drink to her mouth; she drank quickly. Nicole took the glass from her, placing it next to the other glass. I moved near to watch. My wife closed her eyes when Nicole lightly kissed her on the lips, hands on my wife's breasts, hips, bunching The Dress up more, spreading Ashley's legs just a little wider and moving to kiss around Ashley's vagina.

Nicole took a patch of blonde pubic hair and gently chewed on it, which received a favorable response from Ashley. I could smell Ashley's musk from where I stood, and where I stood was a good place: a wonderful view of Nicole's ass perched upward, her own skirt pulled taut so that I got a good view of her black thong underwear. At this point, Nicole had spread Ashley's cunt open with two hands and was licking all over. Ashley shuddered and immediately came, and Nicole continued to lick, and suck at Ashley's clit. I knew what I had to do, and I was quick about it. I rushed to the bathroom, opened the cabinet, and for a dreaded moment I thought they were gone. No, no:

they were there. Three packaged condoms. They'd been there for over two years but I knew they still had to be good.

When I returned to the living room, Ashley's body was in the throes of spasm and she was moaning loudly; Nicole had her face pressed deeply into my wife's cunt. I moved behind Nicole and got on my knees. Nicole briefly looked back at me and smiled, telling me it was okay. Ashley also looked at me, briefly, and closed her eyes again, caught in her own delectation. I pushed the red leather mini higher, out of the way, squeaking new leather sound at my palms. Nicole's fishnets were held up by black lace garters, which probably gave me more of an instant erection than the proximity of this woman's ass to my flesh.

I pulled on the thong, first forward so the material would, I hoped, stimulate both her cunt and asshole. Then I pulled it back and down, leaving them near her knees. Nicole's response was to eat my wife's cunt faster and harder, making Ashley come again. I was amazed at Ashley's intensity and orgasm, her back curvature, her face sweating, her breath so hard I thought she might hyperventilate. It was a combination of the alcohol and the thrill of this situation; all the times Ashley had expressed an interest to be with a woman, and she was finally doing it. My cock was out and I had two fingers in Nicole's cunt.

"Come on and fuck me," Nicole said, her words muffled from a mouthful of Ashley's cunt. I quickly put the condom on and shoved myself into Nicole. It was amazing. I had been monogmous with Ashley for years and *only* knew Ashley; and suddenly, after so long, to be inside another woman, and realize that women are not alike in any way, they're all so different – they feel and taste and smell different.

Nicole's ass, for instance, was rounder, plumper than Ashley's; Nicole's cunt wasn't as tight as Ashley's, but seemed warmer, wetter. The way Nicole pressed her ass against my thrusts was different than the way Ashley did.

Furthermore, the condom added another dimension — I hadn't worn one in over ten years (in fact, we had the condoms at the house anticipating something like this might happen in our wayward dream-lives) and I knew that the latex was inhibiting my experiencing Nicole fully.

I grabbed at Nicole's ass and squeezed. I spread the cheeks to look at her asshole and was delighted to see it opened rather widely, much more so than Ashley's. I might be able to stick myself up her ass tonight, or some other night, and that made me very happy. I had an urge to reach down and stick my tongue in her ass but knew this wouldn't be a healthy idea.

My plunging into Nicole increased as Ashley's cries grew louder, and Nicole began to cry out too, and it seemed both the women climaxed simultaneously. Having come recently in the car, I wasn't anywhere near there myself, and anticipated more fucking.

"I can't take any more," Ashley said gently, looking at us. Nicole sat up; my cock slipped out of her. She turned and kissed me and I tasted my wife's cunt on her lips and tongue. It was a long, deep kiss. She broke away, two thick strands of saliva and cunt juice dangling. "Fuck her," Nicole told me. "I want to watch."

Ashley, her legs spread wide, touching her cunt, said, "Fuck me."

I went to my wife and kissed her, smoothly. She touched my hair and face.

"Take the rubber off," Nicole said, standing over us. "She *is* your wife."

She had a point. I removed the condom, which was soaked with Nicole's own cunt. I placed Ashley's legs on my shoulders and entered her. Ashley breathed, "Slow, slow," and I was slow, but started to pick up speed.

Nicole, standing next to us, was touching herself, watching, going, "Yes, yes; fuck her; fuck that cunt."

I was delirious, delirious with fuck and the desire to be

bad. I turned Ashley over immediately. Ashley gasped, stiffened, and then relaxed. Nicole seemed to like this, saying "*Yes,*" breathing hard, observing with angular, horny eyes. I turned to Nicole and said, "I want you this way, too."

"You want a lot, little boy," she answered.

I came inside my wife.

When we went upstairs to the bedroom, we were all naked and lying in semi-darkness, touching and kissing one another. Ashley said she wanted to go down on Nicole and Nicole said she would like that. "But," Ashley said, "I've never done it before."

"You know what you like and feels good," Nicole told her. "Just do me like my pussy is yours – you know what your pussy likes."

My head was spinning with lechery and all the new possibilities. Nicole lay on the bed, legs up and spread, pillow under her head. Ashley positioned herself. At first, Ashley just looked and touched Nicole's cunt, tracing the trim of hair, tracing the lips. She bent down once, tongue out, for a quick taste, and stopped. Nicole told her it was okay.

Ashley went back down, timid for a minute, then she started to get into it. I watched with a smile on my face, for I was finally seeing it (how many times had I fantasized about this?) – Ashley's tongue and mouth meeting another woman's sex. And it seemed natural; it seemed Ashley should've been doing this all along. I noticed Ashley had reached between her legs, turned on by this.

To my delight, I had another erection. Normally, at my age now, the best I can do, on a really good night, is two erections per occasion, which I had already had; but this was something else and I was wanting. I got behind Ashley, lifted her ass, and entered her cunt. We went like this for a while, and Nicole came, and she said it was good, and

Ashley turned around and sucked me off and I came in her mouth. Then we went to sleep.

Sometime in the early hours of the morning, Nicole left. She must've called a cab. Normally, I'm a light sleeper, and I probably would've awakened at her getting up. I had fallen deeply, nicely asleep wedged between my wife and our . . . lover. We didn't wake up until close to noon anyway. The sun was bright in the bedroom and my head – and Ashley's as well, I'm certain – was hazy with a slight hangover. We looked at each other with what I thought was a sense of disbelief, curiosity, and fear. I held her close to me.

Okay, maybe it was a dream. Maybe one of my fantasies had manifested itself in my head and seemed real. But I could smell her, I could smell Nicole – on the bed, on Ashley. We didn't say anything to each other. Evidence of last night was in the living room: Nicole's thong panties were on the couch. I smiled, thinking of her getting into a cab, in public, short red mini and naked underneath.

Ashley made a big breakfast. We were both starving. Those hash browns, eggs, and bacon never looked so good.

"Honey," she said.

I said, "What?"

"What do you think?"

"The food is good," I said.

"About me," Ashley said. "What must you think of me."

"It's okay," I said, taking her hand.

"Is it okay?" she asked.

I said, "Yes."

She said, "Did you like it?"

I said, "Yes," and: "Did you like it?"

She said, "Yes. I liked it when you fucked her. I liked watching."

"I liked watching you and her," I said.

She blushed and said, "Why did I wait?"

"You liked it?"

"I loved it."

"It's okay," I said.

"Yes," she said.

Later that day, Nicole called. I answered the phone.

"Hey there," she said.

"Hey," I said, and looked at Ashley.

Ashley, sitting on the couch (in the very same spot where Nicole had gone into her cunt), reading a book, whispered, "What?"

"Nicole," I mouthed.

Ashley's eyes widened.

"What's up?" Nicole asked.

"Nothing," I said. "We're just sitting around."

"How boring," she said. "Look," she said, "I'm sorry I split, but I had to go, and you both looked so cute, snoring away there, so I didn't want to wake you."

"It's okay," I told her. "What did you do? Call a cab?"

"No; I stole your car. Didn't you notice?" she laughed. "Look, why don't you guys meet me tonight?"

"Oh," I said.

"Something wrong?"

"No."

"I'd like to spend some more time between your wife's legs," she said in a voice that gave me a semi-erection.

"I'd like that," I said.

"I *know* you would," she said. "You going to meet me tonight?"

"Where?"

We met Nicole at the same club around nine. Ashley was wearing Little Black Thing this time; we both agreed it'd pleasantly surprise our lover. ("Our lover" – how foreign it was to come off my mouth.) We were the ones surprised, however, sitting at the same table underneath the DJ's booth (the place was pretty deserted) when Nicole walked in wearing The Dress. She ambled in, proud, swaying, looking around, and when she saw us, she smiled, and sauntered our way, quickly pulling this dress up – just a tad – to reveal that she, this time, was without underwear (that quick flash of dark trimmed pubic hair I remembered well from last night).

It was interesting to view, since Nicole's hips were wider than Ashley's, which stretched the fabric and, with each step Nicole took, gave the slightest hint that maybe one was still seeing some pube. My wife and I just looked at each other.

"Hello," Nicole said. First, she reached to touch Ashley's face, then kissed her on the lips. There was a strand of saliva between their lips, which broke as Nicole moved to me, gave me a quick kiss and grab at my crotch.

"So," she said, and to Ashley, "I like the outfit."

Ashley said, "It's my Little Black Thing."

"Cute," Nicole said.

"So's your dress," I said. "Remarkable. Where did you find it?"

Nicole shook her head and laughed. She said, "I didn't find it. I borrowed it. Didn't you notice it was missing?"

I turned to my wife and she had this *I don't know* look, a slight shrug. The last I remembered, The Dress was left on the couch, as the three of us proceeded up to the bedroom – naked and giggling and drunk and ecstatic. The Dress never came to mind – it was Ashley's and I figured she took care of it. I could tell by the look on Ashley's face that she, too, hadn't given it any thought.

Nicole made a tsk-tsk sound and said, "I didn't get you *that* drunk."

I had to laugh.

"I like it," Nicole said, making a half-twirl and smoothing her hands over the length of The Dress. She said, "I hope you don't mind."

"Well," Ashley said, thinking: no.

"I couldn't help myself," Nicole said.

I said, "It has that effect on you."

"Still," Nicole said to me, "I think it looks better on your wife."

To Ashley she said, "What do you think? I'm more into bright bold things that are, umm, leather, velvet. I like what you're wearing. Here, let me get a good look at you."

Nicole took Ashley's hand, made Ashley turn in a circle for her. Still holding her hand, she guided Ashley out to the dance floor. "Come on," Nicole said to me. I didn't move. I wanted to watch them, my two barely clad women. I wondered how I got here. Hadn't I always fantasized a scenario such as this, never thinking it would come true?

Let your fantasies run away with you . . .

Nicole lost interest trying to get me to join them. They were caught up in their own world together, alone on the dance floor, and the few people here couldn't help but watch them as well – I'm sure because now and then there was a glimpse of flesh. It was the kiss that did it for me.

Out there in public view, Nicole kissing my wife for an extended moment on the mouth, touching my wife's back and derrière during this kiss, I thought: people could mistake them for lesbian lovers. But they *were* lovers. They were *my* lovers. I was very close to screaming and running out there and tearing their clothes away and having them right there on the floor. It took a lot of effort to sip at my drink, and wait for the song to end and their imminent return.

We stayed for a few drinks, but the club was dead, and Nicole convinced us there was more sensation elsewhere. It wasn't hard to convince us. Nicole had her car; she said she wanted to drive this time. She said she wanted to take us home. She had a loft downtown; she said we'd like it and it'd be fun. I didn't have any doubts. What happened at the loft you can guess, and I knew that Ashley and I had found the adventure we were waiting all this time for.

Or I had, anyway.

Yellow Leather

Nicole disclosed that the one color she liked to see on a woman – the color that *really* got her going – was yellow. She said not all women went well with yellow but she thought Ashley would look wonderful in this color. I had to disagree. Nicole, of course, wanted to prove me wrong, and she showed up at our house one night (her visits were starting to become quite frequent) with a present for my wife (and for me): a yellow leather mini-skirt.

The moment Nicole took it out from the small bag she was carrying I smelled that new smell of leather, which always got *me* going, but I was still skeptical. This yellow leather mini zipped in the front, and from what my eyes could see was just as short as either The Dress or Little Black Thing. Okay, I had to admit, I was curious, and I wanted to see her in it.

Ashley didn't hesitate to strip at that moment, take the skirt, and slip it on. It was a very tight fit, and hugged her hips nicely. She didn't look right standing there in the skirt and nothing else (not to say she didn't look *enticing*); Nicole said the same. Nicole took Ashley by the hand and they went up to the bedroom. "You stay here," Nicole told me. I did as I was told.

The two women returned, Ashley wearing black heels with a matching black sweater that showed just a hint of her midriff: Nicole paraded my wife down as if she were a prize, as if I were a gentleman in a brothel and she was trying to sell me on one of her "girls."

"Turn around for him," Nicole said, and Ashley did this.

I had to take a closer look. Ashley in yellow leather was something I needed to ponder, to scrutinize. There was no doubt about it, Ashley was hot to behold, but I wasn't completely sold on yellow. I had Ashley bend over, and as she did this, the mini-skirt rode up high and revealed her ass cheeks and the opening of the crack and a hint of pubic hair. This I liked – the tightness of the skirt didn't allow for any elasticity, and when she stood up, her ass still hung out, and it was difficult for her to tug it back down to a "respectable" shape.

I confessed the tiny leather skirt was enthralling but I was still dubious about yellow. If we got the same skirt in black, I said, or blue . . .

"I happen to like yellow," Nicole said. She smiled, grabbed my wife, and kissed her. Ashley was startled for a moment – Nicole always the impulsive one, seizing a person when they least expected it – but she promptly relaxed and returned our lover's smooch.

"How far do you want to go?" Nicole asked, and we told her we wanted to go all the way.

"How far can you *really* go?" she asked, and we said we could go all the way.

"You'll be frightened, you'll be scared," Nicole said. "You'll stop just when things get a little *too* dangerous; you won't cross the line when we get there," she added with a laugh.

"Not us," we said, "not us."

A strange thing happened that night. The three of us were at the club where we met. It was our favorite place, for all the obvious reasons, although Nicole was hinting that we should probably find a better place to hang out.

I marveled at the fact we'd been in each other's company for almost a month now. Things were going by fast, yet Ashley and I seemed to find a comfortable niche for Nicole to be in our lives. We had no idea what Nicole did for a living, and she seemed to live rather well; we had no idea what she did when she wasn't with us. Whenever we'd ask, Nicole would change the subject – our life together was surrounded by sex, and there was a *lot* of sex.

However new this was for Ashley and myself, it seemed par for the course to Nicole. That night at the club, we spotted a man and a woman, and I recognized them: they were the couple Nicole had been with when we first set eyes on her (or vice versa, depending on whose version of the story you were inclined to believe). The couple seemed – I don't know – startled to see Nicole. Nicole sighed, sipping her drink, and said, "Wait a sec," and went over to this couple. There was an exchange of words, and the woman seemed upset. Nicole returned.

"Is everything okay?" Ashley asked.

"It's nothing," Nicole said, "let's dance."

I wasn't invited, I guess. Nicole took Ashley's hand and led my wife onto the floor. I wasn't in the mood anyway – I needed another drink or two. The place was pretty full. I regarded the couple looking at Ashley and Nicole. The woman got up, said something to the man, and went to the women's restroom.

My eyes wandered back to my wife and our lover, who – as always – made an exquisite pairing. Ashley was in her white and flouncy sweater thing with a red belt tightening and keeping it in place. She didn't have on any underwear, of course, because it would be a sin to return to this place with any. As certain lights from the roof struck her, I could make out Ashley's naked form and I was pretty damn pleased.

Nicole was wearing The Dress, believe it or not; she'd become quite fond of it. I'd tried to find another dress just like it, going back to the same store, without any luck. Nicole didn't mind borrowing The Dress now and then – she said she had too many clothes anyway; and Ashley didn't mind her wearing it. Nicole wasn't shy about any flashes of ass or cunt that occurred as she danced; once she pulled Ashley for a hug, Ashley gripped The Dress just at the waist and pulled, giving a quick flaunting to anyone who noticed Nicole's consummate derrière. Finally, Ashley was on the other side of things in the world of display, and I believed she enjoyed it.

It was then I noticed the man from across the club walking my way. He was about five years younger and three inches taller than me, as well as twenty pounds lighter. There wasn't any malevolence in his stride, although I couldn't help feeling he wasn't pleased with me. I tried to play it as nonchalant as possible, like I didn't recognize him from anywhere.

"I was you once," he said.

"What?" I said.

"We were you once," he said over the music, and, "Just watch out. She'll break your heart and kill you."

With that, he left. His companion returned from the ladies room and the two departed the club.

When I told Nicole about this, she laughed.

There were occasions I photographed Nicole, having cameras on hand. I took pictures of her modeling The Dress and other outfits, both hers and Ashley's. I took pictures of the two of them together, dressed, semi-nude, naked, kissing. Nicole wasn't impressed with the quality of the photographs and I explained to her that I was the amateur of amateurs.

"Do you have a video camera?" she said.

"No," I said.

The next time Nicole came over, she had a video camera. She wanted me to use this. It took me a while to get a feel for the instrument, but once I did, I enjoyed it. Ashley and Nicole modeled clothes, they stripped, they kissed, and I came in for a close-up of Nicole with her face between my wife's legs.

Nicole called me at work one day. It was a pleasant surprise. She said I should take the day off tomorrow and we could go around town with both the still and video cameras and take risqué exhibitionist shots of her in various places in the city.

I told her this was a good idea but I didn't know if Ashley could get tomorrow off. "This is really short notice," I said.

"Ashley doesn't need to be there," Nicole said. "It'll just be you and me. We'll get some great shots and surprise Ashley with them. Think how amazed she'll be!"

I had to agree, but for the wrong reasons. I hadn't been alone with Nicole once.

I was a little too excited by the prospect. I wanted to tell Ashley. I was vigorous with my wife that night, fucking her hard. She said, "Where'd you get all the energy?"

I told her I didn't know. I had a hard time sleeping. I felt guilty in the morning, as if I were lying: acting like I was heading for work when I had plans with another woman. I'd never been unfaithful to Ashley – not since we met in college, lived together, and got married. Yet this wasn't like having an affair, this wasn't a secret rendezvous *per se* – Nicole was our lover, *ours*, and I was just going to be with her alone for a while, and we were only going to take some lewd shots around town for Ashley's later enjoyment.

I met Nicole at her loft. She was ready, with a bag of assorted clothes, wearing the yellow mini she'd gotten Ashley and a thin, white, virtually see-through button-up top. (Since I still didn't care much for yellow on Ashley, Nicole had decided to adopt the skirt.) Yellow looked good with Nicole's darker complexion and dark hair. I had my still camera and she had her video camera. I asked what was in the bag and she told me just a few items that might come in use.

We left and got into my car. I started to drive but I didn't have any idea where we were going.

"Where are we going?" I asked.

"Where do you want to go?" she said.

Nicole reclined her seat back; she pulled the yellow leather mini-skirt up, showing me a delight: she'd shaved most of her pubic hair, except for a tiny, tantalizing mohawk.

"Do you like?" she said.

"I like," I said.

"Can you," she said, "finger-fuck me while you drive?"

I failed to mention that Nicole had a craving and desire for fast food. Ashley and I, always conscious of our health and dietary intake, never affected Nicole with the food we made when she came to our house. When we visited her loft, she never had a scrap of nourishment in the fridge or cabinets, and always suggested Jack in the Box, McDonalds – or her favorite, Burger King. I wondered how she maintained such a fine figure, eating like that; maybe one day it'd catch up on her. (I have to admit I liked the occasional sloppy hamburger, much to Ashley's chagrin.) Nicole also liked hot dogs from Der Wienerschnitzel, but there were very few of those around. Anyway, as we drove, my fingers in Nicole's cunt, Nicole said, "Let's go and take some photos. I'm hungry, too."

I wasn't sure what she had in mind. We went to the fast food place in question, parked the car, and got out. I had the equipment with me. We stood at the counter and looked at the menu before us. Nothing seemed all that enticing, but I was a little hungry and knew I'd need some energy for whatever this day had to offer. I asked what she wanted.

Nicole took my arm in hers and batted her eyes and said, "Well, I don't know; what do you want?"

I figured I could stomach an order of hash browns and some milk.

"What I want," Nicole said to the teenager at the register, "is a big fat bacon cheeseburger, dripping with melted cheese, and a large order of fries, and a vanilla milk shake."

The teenager nodded, his pimpled face flushed; he glanced nervously at Nicole's exposed, long brown legs popping out from the yellow skirt.

At this time of day, the fast food joint was unoccupied. Nicole and I sat down with our meal. The hash browns were rather salty and greasy, but I liked the milk. Nicole devoured her food. She held a French fry before my face like some thin phallus and said, "Here." I opened my mouth and took it.

We were alone in the area we sat; the morning sun shining through was good. Nicole made sure I was aware of this. It was time to take some pictures. I got up, took the lens off the camera, and found a good position to get Nicole in the booth. She turned to me, a fry in mouth, and I took a shot. She grabbed the milk shake, drank from the straw, and I took a shot. She spurted some of the vanilla shake, thick white fluid on her lips and chin, and I took a shot.

I stepped back some. Nicole leaned into the booth, spread her legs, pushed up the yellow leather, and showed me her shaved cunt. I snapped. She reached to open her cunt, and I snapped. She smiled, and I snapped. Just then, I was aware of someone coming into the area with a tray – a man with frizzy hair and wild eyes. I gathered myself and sat down. Nicole looked at him, made a sound, and composed herself. The man looked lost in his own thoughts, and had no idea what Nicole and I were up to. Damn – and I was hoping to use the video camera.

I used the video camera outside. We left the building, and by the parked car was a three-foot high brick wall. Nicole had an idea; I got the camera ready. She got on hands and knees on the wall, taking her blazer off first, so that as I got behind her, I had a great shot of her ass and cunt. She crawled along the wall and I videoed her. She looked back with a few puckered kisses. She tried to reach back to her flesh and almost fell; the wall was too thin. A Chevy pulled into the parking lot. Two young men got out, and imme-

diately took notice of Nicole. Nicole got off the wall, and I
don't think they caught a flash of anything. They stood
watching her, until we both got into my car and left.

I'll run down what we did that day.

There was a small park nearby the fast food place. Nicole
said, "Stop here." She leaned against a pole on the walkway, hiked up the yellow leather, and bent over. This time,
she used her hands to spread her cheeks and show me her
beautiful puckering brown and pink asshole.

"Hey," she said, "you want a taste of this?" God, did I;
but when I had the nerve to go for it, Nicole, wiggling butt,
quickly moved away and giggled. She got on a bench,
leaned back, and spread. She got on the ground, ass
high, and spread her cheeks again. There was a playground. She sat in a swing – too small for her really –
and spread her legs, and began to urinate in the sand.

We found a busy street corner, where she took a spot to
stand and occasionally stoop down for undetermined reasons other than to beam someone going by. I was in the
parked car, catching this on video and stills. Some people
noticed her, others didn't. Nicole took various positions
opportune for a flash, both standing and sitting. She was
approached by a man in a suit, who left a few moments
later. When I asked her what the man said, she said he
wanted to take her to lunch and she told him to fuck off.

We discovered a construction site while driving around,
seven men working on the roof of a partially finished house.
Nicole told me to let her off at the beginning of the block,
drive up to the end, and get the camera ready. I did this.
Nicole started walking down the block, and of course the
construction workers immediately took notice and began to
whistle and call out to her, like construction workers are
known to do. She feigned dropping her purse, and bent
backwards so as she did so she was flaunting her bare ass at
these poor unsuspecting laborers. They started to wail and
scream even more; Nicole acted like she didn't notice them.

As she got close to the car, she turned to the men, pulled up the yellow leather skirt, and gave them a view of her mohawk cunt. The men started clamoring down the house. Nicole quickly ran to the car and said, "Go!"

We stopped somewhere secluded, and Nicole got out and bent over the hood of the car. I taped her, but couldn't help myself – and fell face down into her ass, licking her, but she pushed me away. She told me to just shoot; she reached into the car, opened her bag, and took out a fat and long dildo. She spat on the rubber cock, bent back over the hood, and tried to shove it up her ass. She got the head in but no further. She told me to do it, told me not to worry about hurting her, told me to video it. I held the dildo in my hand and felt a little weird. Nicole spread her cheeks with both hands, like a captive under orders. With camera in one hand and phony-dick in the other, I stuck it in her. I took heed of her request and was not gentle: I got past the the rubber head and penetrated her asshole deeply.

In the bag, she had a black coat. After I fucked her with the dildo, she stood up, removed her blouse and blazer, then the skirt, and stood naked before me. I stepped back to get this on tape. She opened the bag and took out the coat, which she put on, buttoning it up slowly, and throwing me a kiss.

I had, at some point, told Nicole about the hotel with the grand piano, and she wanted to go there. We drove there. Nicole seemed to almost know her way around, and found the grand piano by herself. There was nobody here and there was good light. I was excited because I knew what she had in mind – at the same time, I had this dismal sensation that all Nicole wanted to do was show me (and my wife) that she could go beyond Ashley.

I didn't care at that moment. Quickly, Nicole dropped the coat and stood there in the foyer totally nude. She leaned against the piano. I took a few still shots of her, then switched to video. Nicole threw a kiss, leaned forward, threw another kiss, turned, bent over the grand, spread her ass and wiggled. She next sat at the piano, looking at me with big brown eyes. I thought – I *thought* I'd never seen anything so perfect, her hair over her face, her breasts firm, her skin glowing in the semi-sunlight.

It was at this moment I realized she was playing an actual song, something in the classical mode, which the audio of the video caught. Nicole knew piano! Just as we were both aware someone was going to notice this, Nicole quickly grabbed her coat and put it on, wrapping herself into decency as I put the camera down and someone from the hotel front desk peeked around the corner and looked at us –

"Tell me something," Nicole said in the car, three of my fingers in her cunt.

"Okay," I said.

"What's the story with you and Ashley? I know you get off on women flashing themselves; you get off on the visual shit of it. I think Ashley does in a way, too, but it's not really in her. It's like you've talked her into it."

"I did talk her into it," I said.

"But it's not really in her," Nicole said, "not like it's in me."

"Like I'm in you right now?" I smiled.

She stretched and said, "What you do now, it wasn't part of your marriage before."

"We had the greatest marriage," I said. "We still do. But something happened along the way. I don't know what. Our lives were dull. So dull, in fact, that we considered divorce, although neither of us wanted that. What we needed was excitement."

"Excitement," Nicole said. "I've heard that before."

"What do you mean?"

"Are you both sincere?" she asked. "To what extent are you willing to go to find this excitement?"

"I feel like you're always testing us," I said.

"I am," she said.

Nicole was telling me, too, as we drove, that Ashley was simply going to adore this video tape, and the subsequent photos. I had to agree – I couldn't wait to show her. We went to Nicole's loft, at her request, and here's a rundown of the video from there on.

She stood in the middle of the main area of the loft, sun shining through the skylights, in the yellow mini and see-through white satin shirt, legs spread apart, hands on hips, and I started the video recorder. The light from above played well across her body; her dark-nippled breasts were visible under the fabric. Her hands wandered from her hips to her breasts, gently gliding up, then to her neck, her face, her hair; she stretched upward, as if she were trying to touch the light, causing the yellow mini to stretch as well, where I went for a close-up and caught her cunt peeking out.

I zoomed back as she began to unbutton the blouse, slowly, one at a time, her eyes peering into the camera with alien intent. She removed the blouse and let it fall to the floor, sticking her chest out, standing sideways, pulling at her nipples to cause them to be more tense. The bag was on the floor near her feet, and she looked at it.

She said, "I didn't show you what else I have in my little bag of tricks."

She bent down to the bag; I quickly went around and stopped behind her to zoom into that bend-over shot and the view of her ass. She turned, abruptly, holding two red clothes-pins.

She said, "Get this." I zoomed in to one of the clothes-pins, followed it as she carefully placed it on her left nipple. She hissed, smiled. She put the other one on her right nipple. She kicked off her heels. She massaged her breasts around the nipples. I wanted to ask if the pins hurt, but it was a dumb question, because I knew they hurt, and she wanted them to hurt.

She took another dildo out from the bag – this one was

normal-sized, regular, made of some sort of rubbery white plastic. "This is Lola," she said, "my friend." She put the dildo in her mouth, taking the whole thing down, releasing it full of saliva. She walked toward the couch and I followed, where she got on her knees on the couch, crouched over, ass out, and reached under herself to put the dildo into her cunt.

"Do it for me again," she said; and again, camera in one hand, I took the dildo with my free hand and proceeded to fuck her with it as she rubbed her clit. I moved the dildo from her cunt to her ass, where she easily opened to accommodate.

What followed was a fairly long dildo-ass fucking as she masturbated and brought herself to orgasm three times. My hand was getting tired. Finally, she turned over, took the dildo from me, and sucked on it. It was clean but smelled that erotic aroma of ass.

She said, "Sit down." I sat down, camera still on her: she stood before me, yellow leather bunched up, nipples red-white from the pressure of the pins. She bent down, into my lap, and started to unbutton my pants.

"Wait," I said.

She looked up and said, "What do you mean, wait? Ashley will enjoy seeing this."

I nodded and agreed (although still uncertain) and that brief moment of distressed hesitation passed – lust always wins in these situations, and my cock had been hard for a good forty minutes from all this observation. She pulled my pants and underwear off my legs so that I was free and naked and ready for her touch, her kiss, her engulf.

She managed a few deep-throat maneuvers, but her penetration was pretty much the same as Ashley's, although with Nicole, there was a lot of saliva. She spat gobs of saliva on my cock, sucked, pulled away, thick strands from her lips to the head of my cock. Saliva gooed down onto my balls, where she quickly lapped it up, and spat it back out. She did the same with my semen, when I came: she held my expulsion in her mouth, slowly spitting it out into a white puddle in the palm of her hand, then applying it all over my penis, making it sticky and wet. She started to suck on it again, half-erect, getting my come back into her mouth, where she proceeded to spit it back out and play with it on my flesh.

It was something to watch from the viewfinder, and I found myself anticipating when I (and Ashley) could see it on a TV screen. I was flaccid, but she continued to suck and kiss.

Nicole

Nicole told us about a different club, one she liked better than our usual haunt, which was downtown and closer to her loft. She wanted Ashley to wear The Dress there. By this point, Ashley was less concerned with running into anyone we knew, or from her work, and was even less worried about going out into public with The Dress – that is, I didn't need to give her any pep talks. I sort of missed them.

She was eager to see Nicole, as was I, although I sensed anxiety. I still wasn't sure what Ashley thought of the video tape. When we first showed it to my wife, she was delighted; over the next few days, however, Ashley seemed distant, contemplative, and one time incensed when responding to me. On a particular night, when I attempted to make love to her, she was cold at my touch, but took me anyway, lying there. I asked her what was wrong and she said it was nothing, she said there was a lot of pressure at work right now with the Spring list coming out. I felt there was something else, and asked if it were the tape.

"No," she said, "no."

"Are you sure?" I said. "You didn't mind me being alone with Nicole that day?"

"No," she said. "Just tell me, next time."

I'm not sure how truthful she was being, but I hoped this wasn't the case – fearful of those little angry feelings kept hidden, exploding later. This is what happened when we almost separated, and I didn't want to go through it again. Communication, that was the important thing; *communication*.

The club was smaller and darker than the other, with only two tiers. The crowd was younger as well, and the music louder. Nicole called out to us from a large, U-shaped leather booth, where she sat with two people – a muscular man with swarthy skin, uncommonly handsome, and an Asian woman. Nicole was wearing a black lace bodysuit and leather jacket, more make-up on than usual. Her hair was also spiked with jell. As we approached the table, Nicole stopped us before we sat and said to the people she was with, "This is the dress I told you about." To Ashley, she said, "Can you turn around and show them what you got?"

Ashley was hesitant, but a glare from Nicole prompted her, and she turned around like an item on display. The couple nodded their heads with approval. Ashley and I sat in the booth, Ashley next to Nicole; the couple were across from us.

The man's name was Serge, he was Italian, in a tight t-shirt and tight black slacks. The woman was Tina, Eurasian with a slight accent, and she wore a flower-print mini-dress cut low in back. They were old friends of Nicole's, apparently, or new friends, I wasn't quite clear on the status. They made me nervous, and at the same time aroused: they were a beautiful young couple (I'd say in their mid-twenties). Tina had the most piercing small, slanted black eyes, and I sensed pure decadence from within her. Serge appeared the happy-go-lucky type.

Nicole introduced us like this. "They're the couple I've been fucking lately."

Ashley flinched. I liked her crude description; when you got right down to it, this was the essential truth.

"Ahh," Serge said, "and sometimes she fucks us, too."

"You ever get the feeling," Nicole said, "that I fuck everybody?"

"Or everybody fucks you," Tina said.

"I want to fuck the world," Nicole said, kissing Ashley on the cheek. "How about you, baby?"

"I don't know about the world," Ashley said, "but maybe just you."

"Don't limit yourself," Nicole said.

A waitress came by and took our drink orders. Nicole, Tina, and Serge were ahead of us by two drinks. We made small talk. Like Nicole, it was hard to pinpoint what Tina and Serge did for a living – seemed like they just had fun.

"If you cannot have fun," Serge said in that Italian accent, "if you cannot sit back and relax, then what is life worth living for?"

Serge asked Tina for a dance; the two of them went out to the floor and we watched them. Tina's dress was cut so low that the beginning of her ass showed; and cut so short at the thigh, her ass was hanging just a tad as well. She was very thin, however, and had a thin rear-end, the kind that looks well on Asian women.

"So," Nicole said with a wide smile, "what do you think of them?"

"They're very attractive," I said (feeling like a shark).

"They're sexy all right," she said, and, to Ashley, "What do you think of Serge?"

"He's sexy," Ashley said.

"He's hung like a fuck," Nicole said.

The two started kissing. The waitress came back; she didn't pay any attention to the women. I ordered another round of drinks. When the waitress returned, Ashley and Nicole stopped their smooching to take a drink.

"Hope you don't feel left out," Nicole told me.

I said, "Not at all, I like watching."

"Yes, you do," Nicole said, and to Ashley, "Sometimes I have wayward designs on you. Sometimes I just want you to be my slave."

"I'll be your slave," Ashley said.

"You have to *really* be my slave," Nicole said. "You have to do *exactly* what I tell you, no matter what. If I told you to strip and walk around here naked with a dildo up your ass, you'd do it. You have to be my little fuck-slut slave."

Ashley said she would be.

"Tell me," Nicole said. "Tell me that you want to be my little fuck-slut slave."

"I want to be your little fuck-slut slave," she said.

"Tell it to him," Nicole said.

Ashley turned, fire in her eyes. Nicole leaned close to her. My wife said, "I'm her little fuck-slut slave."

"Have you ever thought about Ashley being with another man?" Nicole asked me. I told her I had. Nicole said I was getting the best of it all: two women. It was time, she thought, that Ashley make it with another man and I watch. "After all," Nicole said, "she watches us fuck."

"I wouldn't mind seeing that," I said. "In fact, I'd like it."

"Would you like it?" Nicole asked my wife, and Ashley nodded.

Nicole sipped her drink and said, "If I wanted you to suck off Serge right here, would you?"

Ashley and I both looked around. The club was very dark and smoky now, especially where we sat.

Ashley said, "Yes."

I whispered, "Yes."

Nicole laughed and leaned back. She said, "I don't believe you."

"You say that a lot," Ashley said.

"Maybe this life isn't for you, really."

"What life?"

"Oh, come here," Nicole said, kissing my wife.

I looked for Serge and Tina but I couldn't make out any of the dancing opaque shapes.

"Do you trust me?" Nicole said.

"Yes," Ashley said.

"Do you love me?" Nicole said.

"Yes," Ashley said.

Serge and Tina emerged from the smoke and blackness, a little sweaty and glowing, and sat down. They were happy to have refills on their drinks.

"Serge," Nicole said, "Ashley would like to blow you."

"Really?" Serge said. "How nice."

"There's room enough under the table," Nicole told Ashley. "Don't worry, I've done it before. Plenty of room, and it's dark."

Tina lit a cigarette, Ashley gulped down the rest of her drink, then turned my way. I nodded. Slowly, Ashley slid under the table. I felt her brush by my feet, going towards Serge. The music seemed to get louder. Tina stared at me. I thought, then, about protection – we didn't know these people. But I didn't say anything; I didn't stop her. This was all part of the adventure – taking chances, taking guesses, moving on impulse. By the look on Serge's face, I could tell Ashley had his cock out and was working on it.

"Hey," Nicole said, sliding over to me, placing a hand in my crotch. She whispered in my ear, "This is very hot."

I touched Nicole on the lips and went, "*Tsssssssst.*"

Tina put her cigarette out.

Serge seemed to breathe almost in rhythm to the music. He leaned back, sliding down just a bit. I could detect motions under the table: Ashley moving her body to a better position, her head going up and down. Serge started to moan, and let out one long grunt, his body shuddering. He caught his breath, letting out a little laugh, and said to me, "Hey, I just came in your wife's mouth."

Up until that moment, I was aroused by this, the idea of

Ashley unseen but so close and another man's cock in her mouth. The way Serge put it, however, brought me back to the reality of the situation, and I started feeling perplexed, wondering if Ashley really *did* want to do this. I was erect and Nicole was freeing it from my pants, and to my surprise Ashley had turned around under the table and was taking me in her mouth.

I looked down but could barely make out her face because it was so unlit. The waitress returned again for more refills and didn't have the slightest idea what was happening under the table; or if she did, there was no recognition in her bland expression. I, too, came in my wife's mouth, just before the waitress returned, but my orgasm wasn't as strong – or as uninhibited – as Serge's. I put my cock in my pants and saw that Ashley was trying to come back up, on the other side of Nicole, but Nicole leaned down and I heard her say, "Go and do Tina, too. Little fuck-slut slave."

Ashley bumped against our feet and legs as she made her way to Tina. Tina lit another smoke, leaned down some, and spread her legs.

"Ummn," Tina said. "Nice."

Later, I had to ask Ashley what it was like; it was too much to *not* want to know. Several things went through my head, like she felt disgusted with herself, she felt disgusted with me for letting her do this. But what she told me was that she liked it very much – she felt like dirt, she was Nicole's slave and did whatever Nicole's will warranted. *Little fuck-slut.* She lost herself down there, she said, brought down to a mere sex instrument for everyone's pleasure. "I felt used," she said, "and it was liberating."

Ashley told me, "When I was in high school, I wanted to be a slut. I wanted to sleep around with a lot of boys, like some girls I knew. They had bad reputations, but who cares?

They were having fun. I had to play on the more decent side, the good student, the girl with glasses who read books, the girl who kept only one boyfriend. But in my fantasy life, I was something else."

At Nicole's loft, Ashley and Nicole hid away in the bedroom and I was left out front with Serge and Tina. Tina didn't waste any time stepping out of her dress. There was an intricate tattoo of a snake on her belly. She was very thin and almost flat-chested, but breathtaking. Serge wanted me to fuck her, and I took her on the floor. Tina's cunt was tight, and we fucked in several positions; then I lay on my back and she got on top of me. (I was wearing a condom, of course.)

Serge was naked now, and he came up to Tina to put his cock in her mouth. I was stunned, and felt threatened for a brief instant. I've never been one to compare my cock to the size of other men, but Serge must've been a good four inches longer than me, a tad thicker, his body a taut roadway of well-defined muscles. I immediately thought of Ashley sucking him off under the table, and wondered how she managed to take this man's penis in her mouth when she had enough difficulty with mine.

This *wasn't* the time to think about this. Serge and I fucked Tina every which way we could, and then some, and for the first time I found myself in a sandwich, my cock in Tina's ass as she took Serge in her cunt, and I could feel Serge between the thin veil of flesh that separates cunt and ass. This went on for a good two hours and was for the most part uneventful: just sex.

Serge and Tina collected themselves and said they needed to be at some other party; they asked if I wanted to go but I said I was going to stay here. They told me to tell Nicole and Ashley good-bye. Naked, I went up to Nicole's bedroom. The door was ajar and it was dark and quiet, except for a dimly lit candle. The room was musky with sex and perfume. Ashley and Nicole were lying on the bed, legs entwined, their bodies effulgent with perspiration.

"I want to stay here tonight," Ashley said, feeble and rasping.

"Okay," I said, and started toward the bed.

Nicole sat up and said, "Ah-ah. We want to be alone. You have to let her have some time with me, too."

I nodded, turned, and left. I hurried and tried to catch Serge and Tina, but their car was just leaving. I shrugged. I dressed, and went home alone – for the first time in my life with Ashley.

On rare occasions, my job requires that I leave town for a few days, usually when an emergency situation arises. The following week, such a situation came up, and I was gone for two days. I tried calling Ashley at home both nights, but she wasn't there. I called Nicole's, and got the answering machine. I knew my wife was with our lover. I wasn't exactly sure how I felt about this. On the one hand, it excited me; on the other, I was uneasy, knowing the lengths Nicole could go, and where she wanted to take Ashley (and me, I hoped). I was obsessed about it, and couldn't wait to return home. Ashley was there, reading in bed. We kissed. I asked what she did while I was gone and she told me, yes, she was indeed with Nicole for two nights.

"We made a video tape too," she said.

I put the tape in, and my wife sat next to me, to watch my reaction, as I had done with her. First, I saw Nicole on the screen. "Hello," she said, "this tape is for you."

It switched to shots outside of Ashley flashing herself in various public places, wearing The Dress, wearing Little Black Thing, even wearing the yellow mini. The camera switched back and forth between Nicole and Ashley. In one, Nicole fucked Ashley with the big dildo.

The inside of the club, Ashley in Little Black Thing,

Nicole wearing The Dress. It was too dark to really tell what was going on.

Nicole holding the camera down; a good shot of Ashley sucking on Nicole's cunt.

Then Ashley standing, in The Other Dress, sleek and black, in the middle of Nicole's loft. "Hello," she said to me. "Here's something I think you'll really like." Serge and another man, with longish blond hair, came into the screen.

"Hello," said Serge, "it is me and my friend Eric and we are going to fuck your wife." (Ashley was watching my expression, which I tried to conceal.) What I watched, for the next three hours, was Ashley ravished by these two men.

They were rough with her, guided by Nicole's unseen voice, "*C'mon, tigers*," and shit like that. They peeled The Other Dress off her, like trappers skinning their prey; they made her suck both their cocks; one fucked her as she sucked on the other. They fucked her mouth, her cunt, and her ass; they came on her face. There wasn't a sandwich situation, though. These guys didn't have any problems getting it up again and again.

Nicole went in for close-ups as my wife sucked these men off and they came in her mouth. Serge bent over and Ashley reamed him. After this, I was hard, and Ashley was sucking on me, and Nicole's face appeared. She said, "Hope you liked it."

I liked it, but I didn't like it. I was inveigled, seeing my wife like that with two men, but I was also repelled. I was jealous that she spent this sort of time with Nicole and I wasn't there. I knew how Ashley must've felt when I did it. Was she trying to get back at me? I didn't know if I wanted to see this video again.

Ashley asked me how I felt, what I was thinking. I told her I didn't know. "This is all part of the jeopardy," I said. "This comes with the territory. We want to be swingers, and we have to follow what we want. Did you," I asked, "like being with those two men?"

"Yes," she said. "I did."

"Did you feel dirty?"

"I felt dirty but I liked feeling dirty. I feel dirty now watching myself. I've never seen myself screw."

"What was it like," I said, "to fuck two men like that?"

"What do you mean what was it like?" she said. "It was like doing two men. Nicole thinks I should do more than two."

"Would you?"

"I don't know," she said. "I like the idea."

She asked me how I felt again.

"I wish I was there," I said.

"You should've been there," she said.

I kept thinking about the scene where Ashley was giving Nicole head, and the sound of Nicole's orgasm, and Ashley reaching up to kiss Nicole, and Ashley saying, "I love you."

Why couldn't I tell Nicole the same? I wanted to. I could've been lying if I said something like that. I loved Ashley. I loved Nicole. My wife was becoming a sex machine – didn't I always want this? She was becoming less indifferent, more audacious – isn't this what I wanted all along?

We went to Nicole's that weekend and Serge was there, without Tina. He greeted Ashley with a kiss on the mouth, which she returned. I looked away.

"So you saw the tape?" Serge said to me.

"Yes," I said.

"It was something nice," he said. "And now tonight, we will fuck your wife together."

I was looking forward to it.

"I have some surprises," Nicole said, kissing Ashley. "Are you ready to get really wild?"

"More than ready," Ashley said.

We immediately started to get drunk, and Serge had

cocaine. I passed, but was shocked to see Ashley snort a line. Was she high when they made the tape?

"We should get started," I said.

"Not yet," Nicole said." Just be patient, we have all night."

Okay, okay. I had a consuming urge, now, to fuck Ashley with another man. I wanted to see her to do this in the flesh, *in corpo*, as Serge might say, not on camera. Nicole's doorbell rang. She answered it, and let in five men. They were all around Serge's age, and one was the blond from the video. Ashley went visibly rigid. I knew what Nicole had in mind here.

Nicole took us both aside for a little . . . pep talk.

"We don't have to do this," she said. "I thought maybe you wanted to do it." Nicole explained she'd invited these men over for a gang bang, and Ashley was going to be the recipient. "You told me," she said to my wife, "that you thought you'd like to fuck a lot of men at once."

Ashley nodded.

"What about you?" Nicole said to me. "You want to see her get royally fucked? Fucked like the little fuck-slut tramp she is? You want to see her get fucked by six men – seven, if you include yourself?"

"Yes," I said. "Yes, I do."

Nicole had her camera ready. I sat back and watched. The men started to converge on Ashley, started to peel her clothes off, started to wave their cocks her way.

"No, wait, stop," Ashley said. "Stop."

"Stop?" Nicole said.

"I can't do this," Ashley said. She started to cry. "I'm sorry," she said, "I can't do this."

"Hey, baby," one of the men said, "you just can't stop like this."

"We came all this way," another said.

They grabbed at her. Ashley cried out, and they backed away.

"Okay, stop," I said, stepping towards my wife.

"Fuck you, man," one of them said to my face.

"Enough!" Nicole yelled. "Enough. If she doesn't want to do it, then fuck her; she doesn't have to do it. Just get out of my house, you hear me?"

Nicole grabbed Ashley's clothes and threw them at her.

"Get out!" Nicole screamed, furious.

She pushed both Ashley and myself toward the door. "You're both fucked," she said. "I *knew* you'd chicken out when it got to be too much! You're *afraid* to go all the way! Go back to your *fucking* quiet safe little marriage and home! You don't belong here!"

We stood outside.

Nicole was seething. "Now I have to take care of these fuckers," she said, and slammed the door.

In the car, Ashley spurted tears. I held her. She kept saying she was sorry. I told her it was okay, there was nothing to be sorry about.

"I didn't really want to do it," she said, wiping at her eyes. "I didn't even want to do it with Serge and Eric. I only did it because Nicole wanted me to. She said it'd excite you. I just wanted to please her. But I only wanted to be with *her*. And *you*. Not those men. I feel so fucking filthy. I didn't want this."

Driving, Ashley confessed she was in love with Nicole and she didn't know what to do.

"Really in love?" I asked.

"Yes," she said, and I said I was too.

She held on to me the whole way home.

The Dress Recovered

The Dress was but a piece of cloth, and it was no longer with us. Nicole had it.

Nicole wouldn't answer our phone calls the next week. We called every day. Finally, she phoned and said to stop.

She said it was over. She said she didn't want to see us again. This only made Ashley cry.

"There's something missing in me," Ashley said. She stayed in bed all Saturday.

It wasn't Nicole that was missing. I had to get it back for her. Sunday, I went to Nicole's loft, alone. The door was unlocked. I went in and called her name. I went up to the bedroom. No one there. I looked through her clothes. I came down, and Nicole was standing under the light from the ceiling, wearing The Dress.

"What are you doing here?" she said.

"I had to come," I said.

"You broke into my place."

"It was unlocked."

"Leave," she said. She smiled, and said, "Let your fantasies run away with you . . . and you wind up fucked. I'm tired of playing with people who can't play the game for real."

"The Dress," I said, "doesn't belong to you."

"Oh?" She walked around like she was modeling the fabric. "This dress?" she said. "It doesn't belong to me? Is this what you came back here for? Why? So *poor* little Ashley can parade her legs and ass around in it for you? So you can get off having other men *look* at her? You like it when they *look* at her, don't you? But you don't like it if they have her. *Look, but don't touch.* You're such a fucking hypocrite, you know that?"

"I'm not leaving without it," I said.

"Fine, fine," she said. She pulled The Dress up and off her, and she was naked. She held The Dress out. "Come on," she said, "and take it."

I went to her, cautious; she had something planned. She was smiling. Just as I reached out for it, she let it go. I bent down to pick it up. Nicole put a foot on my shoulder.

"Just for the hell of it," she said. "Just for old times' sake, since we'll never see each other again, you want to fuck the shit out of me?"

In a more noble story, where I was a more noble man, I would have walked away. I would have laughed. I would have hit her. But, looking up at her in splendid nudity, my libido, once again, called the shots. I grabbed at her. I took her on the floor. I fucked her in a demented vehemence. I slapped her across the face. I pulled at her hair. I bit at her neck and back and face. I shoved myself up her ass. I came in her.

Spent, I lay on the floor. Nicole got up, catching her breath, her face streaked with red marks, smeared make-up, her breasts, neck, and back clawed from my bites and lacerations. "Goddamn you," she said, "God-fucking-damn-you," and she ran toward her bedroom. I glanced up, and standing above me were Serge and Tina. Had they been here all this time? Did they watch? Serge started to slowly clap his hands. Tina blew smoke my way from a small cigar.

"Bravo, my man," Serge said, "but I think it is time you leave."

"We're next," Tina said.

Ashley was still in bed when I came home. I'm sure there were telltale signs on my skin of that last union with Nicole. I resigned myself to the fact that I'd have to tell Ashley what happened and hoped she understand. My wife had a drink in her hand. She'd been crying more. The phone was off the hook. She wouldn't look at me, only out the window.

I held out The Dress. "I got it back," I said.

She wouldn't look at me.

I crawled on the bed, holding The Dress to her. "Here," I said, "here, take it, please. I got it back."

She only touched it. I placed it next to her.

"Please put it on," I said.

She took a drink.

I started to cry myself. I said, "Ashley, *please*, put The Dress on; I want to see you in it."

I must have sounded pathetic. I felt pathetic. I felt like shit. I *was* shit. I wasn't anything. I just needed her to – *goddammit*, I needed my wife to forgive me.

She touched The Dress. Her fingers examined the rigid fabric. The Dress, I realized then, smelled of Nicole, and sex. She stared at me for a long moment. There was nothing in her eyes. I knew there were scratches on my face.

"Please," I said.

"Get on your fucking knees and beg," she said.

NIGHT SERVICE

Carol Anne Davis

STRANGERS ON A train was one thing – but strangers in a sleeper berth was quite another. Shelley stared at the tall dark-haired man with the backpack. "A male and female sharing the same set of bunkbeds? There must be some mistake."

The man nodded. His voice, when he spoke, was reassuring, well rounded, "My Christian name's Carl. When I booked this berth by phone I gave the prefix *Mr* – but the clerkess obviously wasn't concentrating one hundred per cent."

"So much for *we're getting there!*" They smiled at each other across the narrow cabin doorway.

Carl swung his bag back over his shoulder. "There's supposed to be a stewardess we can ask."

"D'you want to do that now? I was about to grab a drink from the lounge car," said Shelley.

"Mind if I join you? I had a forty-minute walk to get here, so I've built up quite a thirst."

He'd built up quite a lot of muscle, too, Shelley realized as she took her seat across from him in the meals on wheels carriage. His blue checked plaid shirt was rolled up above the elbows, revealing sunkissed forearms with strokable golden hairs. Strong wrists led on to long firm fingers, none of which were fettered by a wedding band. Fingers which could . . .

"So, what are you planning to do once you reach London?"

She blinked at him: here he was making small talk, when she'd been thinking about large climaxes. "I'll stay with my sister, take in a few shows, eat out a lot."

"Pleasure rather than business?" he queried softly.

"Uh huh. If it was business I'd have a sleeper to myself – I'd be travelling first class!"

He grimaced in sympathy, and she grimaced inside at her words. They'd sounded unfriendly. As if she hated the idea of sharing with him, when in truth the notion was seeming less and less bad.

"Can I help you?" The dining assistant smiled at Carl, and went on smiling.

"I'll have a scotch on the rocks," Shelley said firmly.

"Make that two."

"So, Carl, what does London hold for you?"

"Work at The National, I hope. I'm an actor, just wired up to a new London agency. I'm going to see them tomorrow. After that . . ?"

"Maybe resting, huh?" He looked too good to be resting overmuch. She'd love to see him in action.

"No; I do modelling work for the clothing magazines. It's not too bad."

X-rated flesh in Y-fronts: it made an appealing picture. Just sliding your hand in and down until you found . . .

"Your drink, sir, madam," the dining assistant purred.

"Let me," said Carl.

"No, we'll go Dutch – more egalitarian." Dutch treat. Amber liquid and crystal ice. Her lips burned lightly. "Have you been on the sleeper before?" she asked.

"Yeah – all the time. Means you turn up *compos mentis* for

auditions, whereas when you take the overnight coach . . ."

"Yeah, that bus is the pits! There was this time I was going to a Greenpeace rally . . ." Her funniest anecdotes. His dramatic ones. Pupils and lower petals widening as she saw and sensed.

"Same again, please."

"Here's to travelling!" The second whisky was going down more slowly, warming brain to breast.

By midnight most of the lounge car occupants had slipped sleepily away, leaving the usual rugby-playing trio surrounded by dead and dying beer cans. "Better make a move and find this steward," Carl said.

"I guess so. She'll know if they've got empty cabins." Shelley felt a sudden sense of loss.

A train-swayed stroll, a whisky walk, hugely aware of his presence right behind her. She stalled slightly as she stepped from one carriage to another, felt his hard belly collide with her arse.

"Oops – sorry!" he muttered.

She pulled away, from habit rather than from choice.

"There she is." They peered inside the steward's open doorway, then Carl gave a low laugh and shook his head. "Looks like she's really on the job!"

The sleeper stewardess with her head on her arms, sleeping soundly.

"We could . . . share, after all. Just leave her," Shelley said.

"You don't mind?"

"Uh uh." Her head swum with tales of the unexpected.

"In that case, let's unpack," Carl murmured, tiptoing away from the steward's tiny room.

Bunk beds. A portable ladder. A sink. A mirror. Wall-bound coat hangers. "Cute," said Shelley, eyes fixed on Carl's arse as he stowed his backpack below the lower bed. "I'll go on top," she added, then couldn't quite meet his gaze as her sex pulsed and swelled.

"How do you want to handle getting undressed?"

Shelley bit back a provocative reply. "You sit on your bunk and I'll get changed up here on mine. Then I'll put the main light off and you can get ready by the small light beside *your* bed."

"Sounds foolproof! Sure you haven't done this before?" She wished!

Clothes off, nightie on; she was ridiculously glad that it was a thigh-skimming lemon silk one. Did he sleep in the nude? She got into her solo bunk, listening to the rustle of his shirt, the clunk of the belt from his jeans. Would he hint that he fancied her? Ask to meet her in London? She winced as the cabin was plunged into black.

"Goodnight, Shelley."

"Goodnight, Carl. See you in the morning." *See you in my dreams.*

Firm round hips, heavy balls – she could almost picture them: *just close your eyes and you're there*. Shelley slid her fingers down, down, down, found the soft liquid promise of her labia. Gently parted the lips and transferred some of the wetness up to her eager clit.

The train shuddered slightly. There was an almost rhythmic clicking sound. "Damn," said Carl. "That noise is enough to keep us awake."

She sure wasn't sleeping.

"Mind if I investigate?"

She pulled her fingers back from her pudenda. "No, go ahead."

Lights. Action. She risked a peek. Nice black briefs that clung to his arse without cutting off his circulation. Strong hirsute thighs.

"It's the coathangers," Carl said.

"What about them?"

"There's nothing on them so they're moving about."

"Uh, my coat's in my suitcase." Her suitcase was on the shelf near the roof. She crawled out of bed and opened the lock, got out the garment and started to hand it down.

Her hands touched Carl's. His eyes were in line with the full dark hollow between her breasts. He looked up at her face, his lips close to her lips. She brought hers nearer, nearer still. Their mouths parted slightly, then opened, hungering. Tongues teased, tasted. Her fingers dropped the coat and concentrated on finger-combing his hair. His hands moved round to cup the back of her head, then traced down her neckline; it was a long time before she reluctantly moved away.

"I'm in danger of falling off this thing." She swayed on her narrow top bunk, and he held out his strong arms towards her.

"Let me help you."

She felt too vulnerable to go down backwards with her micro-sized nightie, so she put one foot on the sink top and the other on the ladder, facing out into the room.

"Now what?" he murmured, after he'd swung her on to the cabin floor. He gazed down, his pupils dark and wide and wanting.

"Use your imagination, actor man."

There wasn't room to swing a cat in here, but he'd have to find space to pleasure her pussy.

"Oh, I'm very imaginative." Carl ran his hands down her back to her buttocks and stroked them through the silk covering till she moaned. "I can imagine your breasts . . ." He tautened the material across them until the nipples poked out, longing to be gently nuzzled. He caressed the heavy warm underside of both soft globes while she nibbled his ears and stroked his hair and kissed his neck.

"What else can you imagine?"

"How wet you'll get." He slid his right hand down and curved it up under her nightie. He caressed her warm belly while she reached for and grasped his small high hips. He had a great arse – muscular but not overworked, with a compellingly hirsute furrow which tightened as she ran an exploratory finger down its length.

"Jesus, Shelley!" They stood there, pressed together, his urgency more and more pressing.

"Quite like that, huh?" She did it again, feeling his prick rubbing against her waist. She wasn't going to waste it. "I'm just travelling light . . ." Her light fingers found his arsehole and rimmed round. Some men came as soon as you pushed a digit in. She'd had this boyfriend . . . Instant karma every time.

"Too much! If you do that I can't hold back."

"I thought good actors had control?"

"I'm good – but I'm still human."

"Once I see your performance," she whispered teasingly, "I can judge for myself." She felt sexy and assured, stroking him in this swaying cabin with the window shutter down, the door shut, the sleeping steward. Strangers shafting into the small hours on a train.

The wall mirror was at the wrong height for voyeuristic fun, but she saw the reflection of their shared lust in his eyes as she grasped his manhood. Men liked to have their pricks held in the early stages of foreplay. She'd read that somewhere.

"God, I love that!" He pulled her down onto the lower bunk, rolled on top of her. He took some of his weight on his elbows, not crushing but keeping close. Kissing, licking, gently biting. Nipple to nipple, mouth to mouth, hand to arse. He fondled her buttocks and she cupped his, bellies cleaving together, each stroke sending a new surge of cells awash with lust.

She edged his briefs down and he kicked them off. His bum looked as good as it felt: naked oval firmness.

"Time we did the same with your nightie." She lifted her arms high to help him and he gazed appreciatively at her full pink-tipped breasts. "Pretty in pink."

"And lemon?"

"And everything."

"And nothing," she said, sliding her palm across his

groin for a second, before moving it up to trace the hard
young strength of his spine.

Aroused by his weight, his voice, his scent, his caresses,
her nubile nook opened down below, saying *fill me, fill me,
fill me soon.* Her right palm edged down to explore his chest,
his stomach; it slid over his prick to find his scrotum. She
held it gently, brushing the sensitive undersides; his eyes
closed as she probed sensitive inch by inch.

"Got to . . . " He lifted off her, scrabbled on the floor for
his jeans, thus came back holding a sheath in a bright scarlet
wrapper.

"Planning to paint the town red, were we?"

"Well, hoping. I never dreamed . . ."

"Maybe the station clerk planned this. Maybe she gets
off on imagining." Imagining her helping him to roll the
rubber down his thick hard length.

When he had his protection on she smiled over at him
and said, "It's woman on top time." She pushed him down
on his back and teased him some more.

"Shell . . . please!"

She raised herself up on her left palm and both soles,
used her right hand to rearrange her labial lips, then put her
tunnel against his night train: welcome in.

His head connected with her tail, and for a moment she
thought he was too big for her to enjoy fully. Then he raised
his hips slightly and she bore down gingerly and suddenly
her sex was stretching, taking, holding tight.

"You feel gorgeous," he whispered, opening his eyes and
smiling up at her.

"You, too."

The topmost third of her breasts felt swollen with desire.
Her groin was surging need. Each upward thrust of his cock
sent sensation singing. She whimpered as his large male
hands reached for her breasts and held them firmly, thumbs
brushing the areolae with soft insistent rhythm.

She bore down, raised up, finding her pace; his plush

hardness slid its way to her cervix. Then half out, triggering the sensitive area just inside her mons. He put a finger to her clit and she cried out, knowing no one would hear them. That the moaning thrashing ecstasy of their bodies was overshadowed by the *sh-sh-sh-sh-sh* of the train.

"What's this?" He teased with his voice, teased her clit. She pushed down against his cock and rubbed against his fingers.

"It's the emergency button."

"Do you want me to stop?"

Christ, no. "See what happens when you rub . . . " Her entire mount was swollen now; signals went off in her lower belly, the rush of rapture nearing. "Just keep doing it like that."

Carl started thrusting harder, raising his hips from the bed. His hand slipped from her clit and she grabbed it and held it in place; she moved against it, against him. Sensation stampeding: going, going, almost gone. Pleasure building, surging, softening her belly and tightening her thighs and widening something high and hot inside her. She breathed in and held, felt that momentary stillness when her body seemed to stop functioning, then she came and came and came.

"Ah ah! Ah ah!" Lids down, mouth open, voice guttural as she rocked herself against him. "Ah ah! Ah ah! Ah ah!"

His bucking was almost too much for her now. She closed her legs fast to create a closer fit, and he groaned loudly.

"You're so hot, so wet . . ." He slid out, rolled her onto her back. Thrust in again.

"Man on top – is this sexual politics?"

"Got to . . ." Bucking, bucking, movements beyond a joke. She put her fingers to the backs of his thighs and played them exquisitely. "Got to . . ." he gasped again. Rammed forward and groaned. Sap rising, peaking . . . She pushed a finger against his arsehole and he let himself erupt. "Uh. Uuuuuh!" Hips plunging forward against her, making a low bass sound deep in his throat which lasted as long as his joyous, thigh-tensed strain.

"Journey's end?" she whispered, kissing his nose, his eyes, a neck that tasted of salt and shaving essence.

"End of the first fare stage only," he grinned, flopping down beside her and holding the saturated sheath out of the way.

"Promises, promises."

They lay there, holding and half-dozing for almost an hour, lulled by the sound of the train, the movement of the carriage. Then she burrowed more closely in to him and her nipples brushed his chest. And suddenly she was hugely, hungrily aware of each millimetre of her breasts, took his hands and placed them over her needy breasts. "I think they're begging for attention," she whispered, nibbling his lobes, then putting tongue-tip to teeth tops. His thumbs skimmed each bud.

"What kind of attention?" He held one in each hand.

"Mm, just like that."

"What else do you need?"

"You – inside me." She was still soaked from before, everything re-opening and expanding as she explored his broad chest, his strong firm arms.

They stroked, held, side by side. At last she moaned. "I want it now."

"Where?"

Shelley grinned. "Seems a shame to waste the ladder."

"You mean . . .?" He stared at the metal flight, supposed to convey the top bunk sleeper to their wooden bed.

"Mm. I'll stand up and face it, lean against it. You stand behind me and . . ." And find Eden, the Pleasure Dome, Paradise Regained.

"Stairway to heaven," he smiled.

Stairway to her G-spot, she hoped. She moved, naked, to the steps, putting on the dimmed light so that he could only just see her. She gripped the ladder and he gripped her breasts and she opened her legs until she felt his fingers find her entrance. She heard the rustle of a sheath wrapper, then the slick sound of satisfaction as he slid in.

"So hard, thick . . ." His belly brushed against the steps, her bum against his stomach; his maleness began to thrust inside her. *We're getting there.* Weren't they just? Her lower lips were still sensitive from before, lengthening, widening. Building, building. Oh yes, yes, yes, yes, yes!

His hands slid down her waist; his tongue licked at her ear, her neck, kisses on her backbone. His cock moved harder, faster, deeper. His breathing speeded up. Do the locomotion: her body signalling as it responded to his testicular timetable. "Keep doing it like that, like that! Just there!"

Eight minutes, nine minutes, ten: straining back against him to take in every last inch, the pleasure starting up inside and spreading up and flooding out. Weakly she clung to the ladder as her climax livened her mount of Venus, her belly, her brain.

Cabin fever. She felt his own heated rush drawing near, sensed it in his plunging shaft as he drove in and in and in to her welcoming entrance. Hands held on to her tits as if they were handles, his balls moving at their own rhythm against her arse.

"Wonder if the stewardess will come round to make sure we've settled in nicely?" she teased him. "Wonder what she'll think when she sees your moving arse?"

"She'll maybe want . . ." The voyeuristic fantasy seemed to overwhelm him. He thrust forward and cried out and held the end of his sheath inside her as he emptied his pleasure sac.

Breakfast on board. They woke to the knock. She watched Carl scramble over her and out of the bed, smiled sleepily as he pulled on his briefs and tried to hide his morning erection. "Coming!" he shouted to the stewardess in the corridor.

"Again?" Shelley laughed. She saw him open the door, accept the two small trays.

"Our complimentary tea and shortbread."

"What more can we want?" she asked, nibbling at the golden sweetness which immediately took the sourness of sleep from her mouth.

"What more, indeed?" They eyed each other as they sipped their tea, as they washed at the minuscule sink and rinsed their hair with the help of the plastic mineral water glass. Watched each other slide into undergarments and overgarments, slip on shoes.

"Want to come with me to my audition, then go on for lunch?" he asked hopefully.

"No, but I'll meet you this evening, if you like."

"Of course I'd like."

"Good." They kissed. The train was stationary now.

"What time is it anyway?"

"Mm? Almost seven."

"That early?" She looked round the shadowy promise of their sex chamber. "We don't have to disembark till eight."

She got off on the idea: a standing train, the rest of the world hurrying by their door with heavy suitcases. The two of them licking, sucking, fucking behind the shuttered window as porters sauntered past.

"I mean, even with a standard fare, you want to get your money's worth," Shelley whispered.

"Mm – we guarantee good value with our morning service," Carl smiled as she slowly unzipped his jeans.

HOUSE WITH CONTENTS

Michael Crawley

I SAID, "WHY don't we start at the top and work our way down?" I was putting off showing her the basement. I still wasn't sure how I was going to handle that.

Her hips swayed. She looked up at me through the curved sweep of unnaturally long lashes. "Bedrooms first; is that it?" she purred.

She'd been like that since I'd picked her up at the airport that morning, coyly flirtatious. A lot of women come on like that when shown homes. I've heard of guys getting ideas, laying a hand on a hip they think they've been offered, and wham! Sexual harassment.

I said, "I'm not being forward, Mrs Eddase, I promise you."

I must have sounded a bit stiff, because she laid a finger on my arm and said, "I'm sure that a lady is completely safe alone with you."

That was a back-handed compliment if ever I'd heard one. It made a difference to how I'd deal with the situation in the basement. If she was going to be a bitch I didn't have to be so concerned for her feelings.

She preceded me up the stairs, which softened my

resentment at her remark. Her dress was a button-through slithery, clinging silk jersey, in dark green. It came to mid-calf, an inch above her matching suede high-heeled boots. Some dresses reveal what they conceal, and that was one. It clung to her haunches in a way that dried my mouth. I couldn't detect a pantie line. That didn't mean a lot. The way they make lingerie these days, the only way you can tell it's on is that the more intimate details underneath are blurred.

"Come on, Markie," she said, "Don't be a slowpoke."

"I prefer 'Mark'," I gritted.

"Whatever."

Of course she had to bounce her bum on the bed in the master bedroom. When she did, her breasts bounced as well. They weren't particularly big. It was her slimness that gave them the illusion of being over-sized. They were high and round though. They looked quite resilient.

She leaned back on her hands, which pushed her shoulders forward. You *know* what that does to breasts. I swallowed.

"A four-poster, huh?" she said. "I've always wanted a four-poster."

"The listing includes all the contents."

"Even that naughty picture on the wall?"

It wasn't that "naughty", just a coy nude from the back, looking over her shoulder at you. A side curve of one breast was the most intimate part she showed.

"Even that," I told her.

The vendors must have been a very romantic couple. The *en suite* bathroom had a heart-shaped tub for two, with gold-plated swan taps and a ledge with candelabra.

"All it needs is a magnum of champagne on ice and the right man," she said.

"I'm sure that Mr Eddase would be delighted to join his lovely wife in enjoying this – er – setting."

She flicked her fingers. "Him? Perhaps. Or perhaps I'll

find a younger man to take my bath with – one with more staying power."

The woman really was *too* much. Another man would have been tempted, I was sure. She was just asking for it; then, once the action got hot, she'd be screaming, "No!" and where would the poor devil be, then? She was a very attractive woman. I certainly fancied her, but I wouldn't lay a finger on her – at least, not until I was sure she wasn't going to cry "Rape!"

Or wasn't able to? That was an interesting thought, considering what was in the basement.

She didn't show much interest in the other four bedrooms or baths. In the kitchen she seemed fascinated by the view from the window over the sink. She leaned over to get her face as close to the glass as she could. I was more interested in my view of her. Leaning angled at the hips like that did lovely things for her breasts. It tightened the silk across her rear and her thighs. Then she bent a leg at the knee, lifting one foot high, the way girls used to in movies when they were kissed. The bitch was deliberately posing to tempt me. Well, I *was* tempted – to smack my palm across her bottom. I resisted the urge.

"There's a fully finished basement?"

"This way."

The furniture down there was heavy and leather, two couches and two armchairs, arranged in a semicircle around a sixty-inch TV. I showed her through the archway to the spa. The tub was big enough for six. She toyed with the controls – heat, jets, bubbles and so on. "They partied a lot, did they?" she asked, an eyebrow arched.

"I wouldn't know."

"You never met them?"

"No."

"I thought perhaps you'd been down here before."

"Only to preview the home."

"If my husband and I buy this place, we'd throw a house-warming down here. You'd come."

It wasn't a question and she'd emphasized "come".

"There's a sauna through here."

"Only one? Unisex? Naked sweaty bodies, men's and women's, together?"

"So – what do you think of the home, Mrs Eddase?"

She dented her lush lower lip with the point of one nail. "I think I'd like to see the rest."

"The rest? The utilities?"

"No – the rest. It's supposed to have a fully finished basement. This . . ." She waved an arm. ". . . can only be about half. What's in the other half?"

I cleared my throat. "Just a – a sort of . . ."

"Sort of what?"

"Um – some equipment."

"A games room? An exercise room?"

"Sort of, I suppose."

She stretched and smoothed her palms from under her breasts down to her hips. "I like to keep in shape. Show me."

"If you insist . . ."

"I do."

"Okay." I led her back through the TV room to the bookshelves on the far wall. There was a catch behind some leather-bound books by some dead Frenchman. A tug opened the shelves like a door.

She clapped her hands. "A secret room! How delicious!"

It wasn't exactly a "room", more a wood-lined dungeon. Being shown it would have embarrassed most women, but not Mrs Eddase.

"Fascinating! What are all these gadgets for? How would you use . . .? Oh, someone forgot something."

The chair was like an executioner's electric one, but without the skullcap. There were canvas straps for wrists and ankles and to go around the body. On the flat hard seat there was a gift-wrapped box.

"Would it be all right for me to look inside the box?" she asked me.

"The home comes with all its contents. Technically speaking, that includes that box."

Taking my words for assent, she ripped paper and ribbons. "Oh! Boots! And brand new. What heels! Mine are four inches . . ." She lifted a foot behind her to show me her heels – as if I hadn't noticed. I'm a sucker for high heels. ". . . but these are much higher. Hardly the heels for a stroll around the grounds." She peered inside one. "And in my size. What a coincidence. Markie . . ." I winced. ". . . I love boots that button. I like suede. Would it be all right if I tried them on, do you think?"

"If you'd like."

"Then you must help me." She swept the wrappings to the floor, tossed the boots at me and plopped herself into the chair.

I counted to ten. It would have been so easy to strap her in and then I could have shown the arrogant bitch what was what. Instead, I knelt at her dainty little feet and started to undo the buttons on the boots she was wearing. As I worked, she drew her dress up to above her nylon-glossy knees – to hold it out of my way? Yeah. I believed that. I believed it even more when her hem rose higher, to rest mid-thigh. She was deliberately tantalizing me.

I eased her boots off her feet. They were pretty feet, small neat toes, high arches, taut insteps in straining bows. Kissable feet. Suckable toes.

She pointed the delicious toes of her right foot. I picked up a boot and inserted them. The fit was too snug. I wriggled the foot of the boot but couldn't work her toes all the way in.

"Here!" she snapped. Her foot snatched out of my grasp. She set the boot flat to the floor and thrust down. Her foot plopped in. "Now the other."

The process was repeated.

"Now do them up."

The buttons were covered and tiny. Instead of button
holes, there were little loops. It was fiddly work. From time
to time she twitched the other foot impatiently. I did the
best I could but it was a delicate job, just fingertips, and my
hands are quite big.

The finished effect was worth the effort. It wasn't until
she had them on that I realized that their crank was so
severe that where their toes touched the ground was just
about an inch in front of the heels' metal tips. How she
could wear them was beyond me. The strain on her insteps
must have been intense. She was virtually *en pointe*, like a
ballerina.

"What's that on your palm?" she asked me.

I turned my hand over. Quick as a cobra, her foot stabbed
down, toes on the heel of my hand, sharp heel pressing hard
into my palm.

"*I like* these boots," she said. "A woman could keep a
man under her control with boots like these on."

I wrapped a fist around her slender ankle and lifted her
foot. "Perhaps, but not *this* man."

"My mistake," she said in a meek little voice.

"Yes, it was." I stood and brushed my hands. "Have you
seen enough of this area, Mrs Eddase?"

She brightened. "Oh no. I want you to explain to me
what all these things are for."

"Can't you guess?"

She minced on those impossible heels to a wooden post
set in the center of the room. A pair of fur-lined leather
cuffs dangled from it, about six and a half feet high. "I can
guess this one," she whispered. She stretched up to it,
wrapped the cuffs loosely around her wrists and turned to
lean her back against the post. "Like this, right?"

I crossed to her and held her wrists with one hand.
"Exactly, Mrs Eddase." We were almost body to body,
close enough that I could feel the heat of her sex. My mouth

was two inches from hers. If she *really* wanted to be kissed, let her close the gap.

"I'm helpless," she said.

"Helpless," I agreed. When you say "helpless" your tongue touches the inside of your lower lip, twice. Mine didn't. It touched the outside. Hel – tongue out on the first "l", pl – tongue out on the second "l" – ess.

She said, "He-l-p-less" again, in the same fashion as I had.

My mouth moved a fraction closer. "He-l-p-less."

She craned towards me. "He-l-p-less."

I moved closer. As *I* said, "He-l-p-less," she said it too. The tips of our tongues brushed, twice.

"He-l-p-less," again in unison, closer, tongue flickering on tongue.

"He-llll-p-lllless." Tongues slithering, the flat of mine beneath hers, then the flat of hers beneath mine. We were still saying it when our lips sealed, muffling the sound as we spoke into each others mouths.

She arched against me. I pressed back. My right hand circled her left breasts, found her nipple, squeezed.

Her wet sounds could have been, "Can't stop you, no matter what."

I found the buttons of her dress, slowly released them one at a time, from her throat to her waist. Her skin was fevered and smooth. Her breast was soft but firm in my palm. Her nipple was rigid and pulsating. I teased it, stroking its slopes. Her hips bucked at me. My fingers closed.

"Hurt!" she moaned.

I told her, "Yes," and pinched harder. My fingers rolled and tugged. Her tongue tried to make words and attack mine at the same time. She moaned in time to the thrust of her hips and the swaying of her upper body.

I pulled back, leaving her with slack lips and a wet mouth, to inspect the morsel of flesh I was playing with. "You have two little dents in your nipple," I observed.

"They've been pierced, haven't they."

"Yes," she confessed. "Pierced. Right through."

"You enjoy pain," I accused.

"The right pain, inflicted by the right man," she admitted.

"A man like me?"

She shook her head, not denying, just coming back from an erotic daze into reality. "You were going to show me the rest of the things."

I released her wrists. She didn't adjust her gaping dress to cover her engorged left nipple so I assumed she wasn't done with her kinky games.

"How would you use that?"

"You must recognize it. It's a pillory."

"The head goes here? And the hands here?"

I closed the wooden beam with the half-circle cut-outs on her, trapping her wrists and neck. "Exactly."

"And I'm helpless again, aren't I? Silly me."

"Yes, you're helpless. You can't stop me from doing this." I undid the rest of her buttons, taking my time. When it hung loose I lifted it aside. She *was* wearing panties, nylon ones, transparent as her stockings, bikini style, with a little fine embroidery in a pattern like lace.

"I could take these off you," I said, one finger in the band, "and you couldn't do a thing to stop me."

"You wouldn't take advantage of a lady."

"Yes, I would." I pulled the skimpy garment down her long thighs, over her knees, down the suede curves of her calves, and lifted her feet out of them, one at a time. As I stood, my fingers ran up her boots, inside her knees, over the inner surfaces of her quivering thighs. They paused an inch below the backwards bulge of her sex.

"Don't!"

"Don't what?"

"Don't touch me there."

"Why not?"

"I – I want to see the rest of the things. Show me how they work, please, Markie?"

I slapped her naked behind. "Mark! Mark! I don't like 'Markie'."

"I – I'm sorry, Mark. Let me go? Please?"

"You'd make a run for it."

"No I wouldn't, honest. If I did, you're stronger and faster than me."

"And I'd punish you."

"And you'd punish me."

"Remember that."

She gave a delightful little shiver. "I will! I will!"

I showed her the four cuffs that could hold a woman spread-eagled against a wooden wall. That gave me ample opportunity to inspect her sex, but I didn't touch it. I stroked the taut skin of her belly; I drew a fingertip along the pale blue crease between her body and her thighs; my cupped fingers hovered an inch away from her mound, but I didn't touch her sex.

"What's the half drum for?" she asked. It was a semi-circle, two feet wide, as high as my waist.

"I'll show you. Stand close, with your back to it." I bent and fastened the floor-anchored cuffs around the ankles of her boots. My hands eased her back to lie, bent arched backwards, on the padded surface. Two more cuffs fastened her wrists to the floor on the other side.

"Helpless," she sighed.

"You like 'helpless', don't you."

"Perhaps."

"In this position, a man could use your mouth." I put my fingers to her lips. They parted. I stroked her lower lip, tugged it down, slid my fingers into the wet heat of her mouth. "A man could order you to suck him, and you'd have to."

She drew on my fingers. Her tongue danced on their tips. Her cheeks hollowed. Roughly, I explored the tenderness of her mouth, rubbing my fingers on her gums, prodding the insides of her cheeks. "A man could use you for his pleasure." I slid my stiffened fingers in and out of her mouth, demonstrating how a man could take advantage of her "helpless" position. My free hand mauled her breasts, leaving livid marks, distorting their perfect globes into obscene shapes. She nodded, encouraging my fingers to ravage her more savagely.

"Your sex is arched up," I told her. "A man could use that, too." I bent closer to her sex, much closer, close enough that it would feel my breath. It was bald, with fleshy engorged lips. Her clitoris was thick but its head hadn't emerged – yet.

I pursed my lips and puffed. She shivered and sucked harder on my fingers, almost slobbering as she tried to gobble them deeper into her mouth. I pulled them out and wiped her spit off on her belly.

"You love to suck, don't you?"

"Have to do what you say. Helpless."

"If you weren't helpless? Would you still suck?"

"Perhaps."

"You would. You're a slut, Mrs Eddase. What are you?"

"A – a slut. A helpless slut."

"I'm going to release you. If you are a real slut, you'll take your dress off."

When I unbuckled her wrists she sat up and rubbed them. I stooped to her ankles. "Your dress?"

"It's as good as off, already."

"But a good obedient slut would take it off completely, by herself."

"Yes, Mark." She shrugged out of the sleeves and laid the dress aside.

"I knew what you were from the moment I first saw you, Mrs Eddase. You have the heart of a whore."

"Yes, Mark. A whore. What're those for? In the corner."

"They are specially made for whores, to punish them."

"How? I don't see . . ."

"I'll show you if you like, but it's reserved for only the most depraved women, the totally debauched harlots. Are you sure you want to try it, no matter what, no matter how painful?"

"You told me I was a slut, Mark. Don't I deserve . . .?"

The device was simple. Two padded cuffs were attached to steel cables. The cables ran to two pulleys, set in opposite walls of a corner, about five feet above the floor, six feet apart. From there they went up to a box on the ceiling.

I put a small leather-covered stool in the corner, between the cuffs. "'Sit." She sat. I fastened a cuff around each ankle.

"I don't see . . ." she said.

I pushed a button on the wall. A motor hummed. The cables began to wind in, very slowly. Once the slack was taken, her ankles were pulled apart and raised.

"Lie back," I told her, "or you'll bump your head."

Wordless, she obeyed, resting her head on the floor behind the stool. The cables reeled in. Her feet were lifted. Her legs were spread. In a minute, her feet were above her head, pulled wide apart. The motor's whine changed to a deeper note as it took her weight. Her behind came up off the stool.

"I'm going to split!"

"No – not quite."

When just her shoulders rested on the floor, taking some part of her weight – when her legs were so taut and straight that she was doing a reversed splits, I hit the button.

"No," she moaned. "It hurts. I'm so far apart. I'm so exposed."

She was right. The tendons on the insides of her thighs stood out. The skin on her delta was stretched glossy. The lips of her sex had been tugged wide apart, exposing their tender inner pinkness.

"Exactly," I said. I cupped my palm over her gaping sex.

"This is what whores use, right? This is what they peddle. It's only right that this should be where they're punished."

"No – not there!"

"But yes." I compressed her oozy sex in my hand. "Here. I should be using a whip or a cane, but my hand will have to do, for now."

With two deft fingers I spread her lips. I could see into her, past the glistening, as deep as the convoluted shadows would let me. She'd leaked enough that her lips stuck there, open, inverted.

"You wouldn't!"

"I would." I folded my little finger and my thumb into my palm. My hand lifted . . . and slapped down. There were two noises – a wet "splat" and a moan from her mouth.

"Stop! Stop, and I'll do anything – please?"

"You'd do anything, anyway. That's why you are being punished, Mrs Eddase, for being a woman who'd do 'anything'." I slapped again. She was even wetter.

My victim whipped her head from side to side, denying the indignity and the shame as much as the pain. The lips of her sex puffed up, purple and thick. I slapped, and slapped.

"No, no, no, no, nooooo!"

I stopped and inspected my work. She was so wet that liquid was pooled in the cup of her sex. I dabbled my fingertips in it. "You had an orgasm, didn't you," I accused.

She confessed through her sobs, "Yes, I did. I came."

"A woman who gets pleasure from being humiliated and having her sex beaten? What kind of a woman is that, Mrs Eddase?"

"A slut; a whore; a harlot."

I hit "reverse". The motor started again, lowering her. "So – more punishment then, for enjoying your punishment. You owe me, Mrs Eddase. It's *your* turn to give *me* pleasure."

As I uncuffed her ankles she asked me, "Do you want me to suck you?"

"You'd enjoy that, wouldn't you? That's what your slutty mouth likes to do."

"Yes, Mark. I'd enjoy doing that for you."

"Then no. Come here." I jerked her to her feet and snatched two pairs of cuffs from a bench. "Bend over this." It was a horizontal padded bar, crotch high. She bent. I cuffed her right wrist and ankle together, then her left wrist and ankle.

"Helpless," she moaned. It seemed to be her favorite word. I ran cords from her cuffs to the iron legs of the bar and secured them with her feet off the ground, legs spread, her entire weight on her hips and tummy. I tossed my jacket aside. She heard me tug my belt from its loops and unzip my pants.

"My sex is sore," she said. "Let me make you happy with my mouth – please? I'm good with my mouth."

I knelt behind her. "Don't worry. I'm not going to touch your whorish sex." I squatted and looked between her legs. With her being bent double like that, her breasts hung, just a little. I wrapped my belt around my right fist, leaving about a foot of loop hanging, and flicked out once, twice, each blow just clipping the point of a nipple. She sucked air but didn't cry. I rocked back. My palms pressed on her buttocks, kneading and rotating.

"Then what? Oh no! Not that! Please, no. No, Mark, anything but that."

My thumbs parted her. Her sphincter was rosy, not brown, a deep pink ring around a tiny dark hole. I spat into it.

"Mark – Mark! Please? That's disgusting – what you plan to do. It's unnatural. You can't . . ."

"I can. I will." I stood up. My penis was eager, wagging and wet. I fit its head between her buttocks.

"Stop! Don't do it."

"I'm not going to do it. You are going to do it to yourself. Wriggle, Mrs Eddase. Impale yourself."

"No! Never!"

My belt cracked down across her right buttock. "Do it."

She clenched, gripping the head of my penis between her cheeks. I nudged just enough to part her ring a fraction. "Do it!"

"No!"

My belt came down again, crossing the weal that was blossoming on her rounded whiteness. She jerked, either deliberately or in reflex. It didn't matter. The result was the same, either way. My glans popped through the rubbery restriction, into the tight sleeve of her rectum.

"I'm going to beat you until I am satisfied," I said. "You can wriggle hard and make it sooner, or softly and make it last. It's up to you."

After the third blow she was writhing and jerking, trying desperately to bring me to a climax. Her "no"s had been insincere. This wasn't her first time. She was convulsing her rectum on me, massaging my glans in a frantic rhythm. A woman who can pulsate her internal muscles like that isn't an anal virgin. It's a skill that takes hours of practice.

It was a skill that worked. I hadn't laid more than a couple of dozen blows across her cheeks when my fierce pleasure overcame my willpower. I thrust juddering-deep and let the flow come, jerking out the after-shocks, jetting my fluids deep into her.

When I released her she could hardly stand. She sagged into my arms and soaked my chest with her tears. I lifted her head and kissed the sweet dew from her cheeks.

"Well, Mrs Eddase, what do you think? Do you like the house? Shall I write up an offer?"

She blinked wet eyes and dabbed at the mascara smears. Smiling up at me, she said, "I think so, Mr Eddase. Think what we'll save, buying a house that comes ready furnished with all the right toys. And thanks for the new boots. That was a nice touch."

"You can give me a proper thank you later, when you're recovered, darling."

"There's still my mouth." My dear wife sank to her knees before me. She hadn't lied. She *is* good with her mouth – very good.

THE MAN WHO LOVED WOMEN

Julian Rathbone

THE DISCREET ALARM on his wrist-watch woke him at half-past five. Sam turned it off, pushed feet out from under the duvet. Toes stubby, blotched ankles, varicose veins, sparse yellow hair, knobbly knees. He stood and pulled his night-shirt down so it covered them. The last of his early morning erection subsided beneath it. He went into the *en suite* and had a wee. His wife, Zoë, creamy, warm and nesty, shifted a little in the hollow he had left behind, allowed herself a tiny squeak of a fart.

"Going for your bike ride, then?"

"Yes, dear."

"Is it nice, dear? A nice morning?"

"Yes, dear."

"You'll enjoy it then."

"Yes, dear."

Already he had pulled on Lycra cycling shorts, cherry-red, that came down almost to the tops of his knees and hugged his thighs, a T-shirt, socks and deck-shoes. The shorts, without benefit of underwear, outlined a thin prick pushed to the side of his groin and two little egg-shaped swellings tight up against his pelvic floor. From behind his buttocks were narrow – their slightly floppy scrawniness held firm by the clinging, shiny material. His chest though was still deep, his waist narrow, his body compact, neat, powerful for all his sixty years.

In the kitchen he mixed fizzy mineral water with the day before's herbal tea and drank it off – not unpleasant, with a slightly hoppy after-taste which often reminded him of the days when he home-brewed bitter to a better standard than even the best of real ales. Stronger, too. Finally he pulled on a red baseball cap, a relic of the Nicaragua Bike Ride ten years ago.

He pulled his Ozark mountain bike out of the garden shed, and out through the side gate of their cottage, mounted carefully, while still stationary, adjusted the Shimano gears, and pushed off from his still grounded left foot. His spirits rose. They always did unless it was actually pissing down, but more especially today. It was the second week of a perfect June, the sun just showing through the trees, a mist lingering in the hollows on the heath, the swifts and house martins skimming the hedgerows, a distant cockerel, and a nearby lark. And what's more, it was Monday. Some days he did not bother. But on Mondays, yes, he usually did. They seemed really to want it on Mondays.

His usual route took him downhill across the heath and into the village of Birling. The sunlight strobed through the oak and beech leaves; a black tom trotted home, paused, gave him a glance and trotted on. The milk float hummed by, Jimmy Pond driving it, with his young brother Peter doing the deliveries. Sam gave them a wave and they waved back. His tyres purred on the tarmac, the chain ticked over the cogs, a rise before the drop to the war memorial produced a slight ache in his calves and he clicked down a gear or two. Outside the newsagents a van driver dropped heavy bundles of papers on the step. Sam turned into the Enclosure.

The Enclosure had once been private forest land: oak, beech and holly, with deer, badgers and foxes, but since about 1880 largeish red brick dwellings had gone up, with walled gardens, paddocks and latterly swimming pools and garages. Incongruous among them, a handful of small-holdings clung on round foresters' cottages. And still much of the forest remained, open and untouched apart from the gentle control of the Forestry Commission which was now in charge. Built for professionals and businessmen from the nearby conurbation, the larger dwellings were occupied by the seriously wealthy – even in a depressed market, most of them fetched half a million or more on the rare occasions they were up for sale.

The new rich work for their wealth. As Sam rose out of the saddle to avoid the intimate jarring caused by the potholes of the unadopted track and cruised down a slope where the lower beech boughs almost brushed his red baseball cap, a large black BMW slipped through electronically operated gates a hundred yards ahead. Exhaust smoke spun in twin streamers as it climbed the rise opposite, rounded a bend and was gone. Bob Pepper, mobile clamped to his ear, Dunhill between fingers that gripped the steering wheel, was already about his business, catching up with the twenty-four hour market. Tokyo closed three points up, Honkers remained steady. He would park the BMW twenty miles away and catch the 6.45 – the first commuter train of the day. Sam braked, turned, put both feet on the ground and with head on one side waited in front of the gates. He counted up to twenty and precisely then the gates swung silently open. Somewhere beyond the gravel and the big ornamental cherry tree on an island in the middle of it, from behind leaded windows and swags of pale lilac wistaria, a dog barked. Nearer a blackbird sang.

"You are kind, so kind," Zara murmured. She lay, in the

position of Boucher's Pompadour, spread on a dusty pink silk sheet chosen to set off the pale gold glow of her fading Cayman Island tan. She was on her stomach which, on account of a certain looseness above her mons veneris, the result of her one pregnancy, she tended to keep hidden as much as she could. But her elbows were pulled in and her creamy shoulders raised so she could glance behind and almost see him. Sam knelt between her legs and gently stroked the backs of her knees – such vulnerable innocent-looking places. Very slowly he let his hands slide up the outside of her thighs and then back again, allowing his nails occasionally to scratch – just enough to produce weals that faded immediately. Four minutes of this, then he spread his hands across the backs of her legs so his thumbs could track up towards and between her buttocks.

She pulled her knees in an inch or so, raising and spreading them for him. A moistness was now beneath the balls of his thumbs as they delved deeper, finding the rose-bud of her anus while his fingers spread across the smooth rounded globes, squeezing and kneading. The richness of the very best perfumes man can make or buy, and which she had presumably sprayed herself with as soon as Bob left, were undercut now by more bodily ones – musk and hawthorn blossom with a hint of the farmyard, too. Pushing deeper, one thumb gently tickled her between anus and the point where her nether labia began to open. A hair or two and a suggestion of the sea-side in the odours, sea-weed and shell-fish. His other thumb gently probed the rose-bud, encouraging the tight moist muscle to give a little.

She quietly sighed

"I wish you had four hands," she murmured.

"I wish I had six."

He leant forward over her back, rubbed the now very taut Lycra against her rump and ran his hands up her flanks and under, feeling for plump breasts and nipples as hard as

cherries but with the texture of raspberries. He rolled them
between thumbs and forefingers, making it almost hurt –
but not quite – till she twisted and moaned beneath him.
For a second or so he released one, just for as long as it took
to push swags of blonde hair up from the nape of her neck,
then back his hand went round and under her, while his
mouth, teeth and tongue roamed over her upper vertebrae,
scratching with his white designer stubble, nuzzling and
nipping.

At last she pushed up on the palms of her hands, arched
neck and back – Zara was a big woman and strong, played a
lot of tennis and swam – twisted and laughed. "Off, dog,"
she cried. "You know what to do."

And indeed he did. He pulled back a little, let her twist
round, one leg over the other, so she was on her back, her
head propped on a heap of pillows, her chin up so he
wouldn't notice the sag beneath, her breasts flopped sideways a little (already there was a small runnel of sweat
between them). Her chest and round tummy heaved a little
with the effort of shifting. She smiled wickedly from big
blue eyes beneath the mop of straw hair, bleached and
coarsened by tropical suns, and giggled through lips almost
as full as the paint that contoured them, through teeth as
neat and white as classy orthodontics could make them. She
cupped the top of his head in both palms and pushed down.
Obediently he shifted his knees and torso down the bed, up
came her knees then her shins so they squeezed his ears, and
her ankles met below his shoulder blades. He slipped his
hands beneath her buttocks and began to knead them again.

The angles were not ideal. He had to lift his head, strain
his neck so it ached a little, but her response as his tongue
played round the tiny cowl, teasing but not yet quite
touching, was more reward than he needed for the minor
discomfort. He relished the coarseness of her tufted hair,
the faint flat sourness of urine giving way to subtler
flavours.

She still had her hands behind his head and soon she was pushing him inwards, trying to swing him from side to side, but he'd have none of that, not yet; he tensed sinews to keep the pressure still gentle, minutely distanced. His tongue (the root of which now also ached a little, but what the hell) slipped down one side of her cunt and then up the other, and then the same in reverse and he could feel how the labia filled and began to throb. But while he kept his tongue movements controlled he allowed his fingers to probe and push from the root of her spine, up to the twin dimples and then down and round and under.

By now the channels ran with unguent juices and, not letting up with his tongue, he found only minimal resistance to the middle finger of his right hand (considerately he kept the nail well trimmed) and soon the first joint was easing through the sphincter which suddenly expanded then sucked, taking the whole finger in behind it. It roamed through crimson spaces, caressing the giving walls that closed round it like a loose glove.

And so at last he allowed his tongue to climb up to the taut little button of tumescence that now protruded like a tiny glans from its foreskin. He rolled the tip round and over it, began to give it quick firm flicks. He could feel the tension building now, all over her, sense it in places he could not see or reach, in eyes and teeth clenched tight, in heaving chest and pounding heart, in the strength of her thighs against his cheeks, in the fists that pulled and pushed and beat at his short-cropped hair, in heels that pummelled his back. Suddenly she went, back arching, a long, loud crow of delight, and his mouth filled with liquid silver as he sucked and sucked it all in and deepest, deepest of all he felt the muscles on her pelvic floor beat like squeezing pumps round his intrusive finger.

When she had her breath back she looked up at him and said: "Why the fuck don't you take off those stupid shorts?"

Even as she spoke, his taut thin prick which was pressed

up against his stomach began to shrink a little beneath the Lycra and a tiny dark patch formed above it. He smiled down at her, said nothing, but, reaching round for it, pulled his T-shirt back on over his head and shoulders.

He gave her painted toes a suck and was gone.

"Bastard," she murmured, then sighed slowly, voluptuously, pulled the duvet around her and, with one hand holding her cunt like an over-ripe fruit and with her other thumb in her mouth, Zara dozed off into a wonderful, warm, relaxed sleep.

Goat-milk hissed round the curve of a small, shiny aluminium bucket, held between her knees, and swirled rhythmically round to the bottom where it swung with the slight circular motion her rocking body gave it. Head on one side, ear cocked, Joan listened for the gate; meanwhile, she squeezed the soft full, almost rubbery udders, more like human breasts, those of an older woman anyway, than those of any other ungulate.

Five years earlier she had been a secondary school teacher, but had been sacked for laying a complaint against the headmaster: she had caught him in the stationery cupboard with his hand up the knickers of one of the sixth formers. Unfortunately the girl backed him up and it was Joan who got the sack. She already had a house, inherited from her parents, which she sold, and bought instead a small-holding on the edge of the Enclosure where she raised goats and sheep, from whose milk a local co-operative made a particularly pungent and very expensive cheese that retailed in posh outlets for a tenner a pound. She also grew mushrooms in heated bunkers – a cover for dope, her main source of income. She lived on her own, worked on her own, and nursed a deep scorn of men which, however, did not extend to sexual matters: she was not gay.

The five-bar gate squeaked, more of a rasp really, and the angled beam of sunlight (it was now a quarter to seven) was split as he stood in the doorway behind her, his shadow extending across the dusty russet dry wool of the nanny-goat's back.

"Is that you, Sam?"

"Of course it is, Joan."

She set the pail down between her legs, dipped her body to the left and came up with an over and under twin-barrelled Purdy. She swung round on the stool and, firing from the hip, blasted the medieval daub above and to the right of his head.

"Take your clothes off."

He did as he was told, the T-shirt over his head, kicking off his deck-shoes, peeling the Lycra shorts down over his knees, and stood there hands clasped over his genitals, shaking with a fear which, even though this was the eighth time they had been through this ritual, was not entirely assumed.

The first time he had dropped in he had been on his way home from Zara's and had spotted her notice advertising duck eggs at ten pence an egg. She had not expected buyers as early as that and had taken him for an intruder – that first gun-shot, though aimed to miss, had been in earnest.

"Hands by your sides."

Slowly she looked him over, keeping the shot-gun always pointing at his stomach and her finger lying along the trigger-guard. There was danger, even in this play-acting – they both knew it, and both relished it: like the taste of blood or iron on the tongue.

Short grey hair balding on either side of what had been a widow's peak, blue eyes with heavy slanting lids and bags beneath, a good nose but pink and not as sharp as it was, thick lips which his tongue licked moistly – either in anticipation or nervousness or a combination of both – a weakish chin, a long scrawny neck with old skin looped over tendons and a prominent Adam's apple, deep barrel chest with a sprinkling of white hair between the nipples, arms thin, scrawny, hands ditto. Tummy just a shade heavier and more rounded than it should be . . .

"Turn round."

Buttocks narrow but dimpled and saggy, legs quite well muscled, especially in the calves (all that cycling), ankles blotchy with purple marks, long feet with yellowish white toes, slightly crooked and misshapen (sixty years of the wrong shoes).

"Back again."

And that silly prick, long and thin, uncircumcised, swinging well to the left and small balls held tight in their wrinkled pale brown purse. Some white in the pubic hair here too – nothing so sad as white pubic hair. Joan's eyes narrowed and she lowered the muzzle of the gun an inch or two. Two things happened. His scrotum contracted even more but his prick lifted a little and swung out even further to the left before coming back again and reaching an almost horizontal plane. A tiny bead of colourless ichor formed on the tip which now showed pink and moist through the foreskin.

"Naughty," she murmured.

Sam felt the blood pound in his chest. He knew what would happen next.

She stood, laid the gun across the stool, crossed her arms and pulled her polo-collared top over her head and gave her brown short hair a shake before running her fingers through it. Her breasts were long, full behind pointed nipples which swung outwards, much like those of her goats. She stepped out of cut-down jeans and the tan briefs beneath them. The fingers of her left hand combed down through her glossy beaver, not seeking pleasure particularly, but in an absent-minded way, releasing the curls. Her body was lean and strong, in shade the colour of dark honey but golden where the sunlight splashed her. Sam's prick struggled up another degree or so.

"Naughty," she repeated and, reaching to her left, grasped the long haft of a hay-fork. Its two wicked, wide-spaced, curved tines were eighteen inches long, with needle-sharp points. She pushed it towards him so the points were only an inch or so from the tops of his thighs, on either side of that still swinging prick. Then she jabbed and he jumped back from the sharp pain.

"Run," she said.

He dashed out into the cobbled yard, stubbing his toes and hopping manically as she came after him, prodding, almost stabbing at his rump. He circled the duck-pond, feet struggling for a hold in the green slime of duck shit on the edge, falling forward on to his hands so his back was arched, his splayed bum in the air, his genitals now shrivelled, mere excrescences between his legs. She batted him sideways so he lost what balance was left and rolled into the filth and water on the edge. The ducks, tails waggling, clipped wings beating, scurried to the sides and climbed, half-flying, half awkwardly jumping, up on to the dung-heap where the big rooster, tail like the feathers on a colonial governor's topee, lifted his wattled throat and trumpeted defiance back at them. Dogs, collies, rushed round in circles like dervishes chasing their tails and yapped cacophonously, the swallows swooped between them chasing dragon-flies and a big tortoiseshell cat woke up on the barn's shingles, stretched, yawned and smiled.

Sam, grovelling in the mess he was wallowing in, came up with a huge handful of weed, heavy with duck-shit, and flung it at her – splat! – right across her breasts and midriff. She waded in after him, prodding, thrusting, up to their knees, their thighs. He turned to scoop up more of the scum on the surface and curtain it back at her. Then he turned and scampered back into the barn and up the ladder to the hay loft. The goats in their stalls, waiting to be milked, leaked cream from their weighty udders as they swung and pushed and bleated, and one of them let loose a shower of black droppings like large shiny black seeds.

She threw aside the fork and hauled herself up, hand over hand, reaching up as he got to the top and making a grab for the balls above her. She got a momentary grip and he let loose a howl, but the slime and wet was too much and they slipped out of her fist before she could get a proper hold. He tumbled onto his back half up against a looseish hay-bale. Dust and dry pollen billowed about him and he fell into a convulsive sneezing fit. She got him out of it by crouching astride his writhing body, with her backside over his face and lowering her ass-hole and her cunt into his face; she began to grind them against his nose and mouth. The smells were rich, the contrasts between the wiry ring that circled her anus, the hard but giving muscle of her sphincter, the smooth skin of her inner thighs and the moist softness of tumescent labia was a kaleidopathic maelstrom of sensation.

Steadily and not slowly she worked herself up into a frenzy which he did his best to push on with his teeth and his tongue and reaching up with his hands, dragging his nails down her flanks. Meanwhile, as she writhed and pushed and twisted, and rubbed his balls with one hand, she masturbated his long thin prick with the other, but savagely, roughly, making it hurt, until suddenly she came with a gush of sweeter, lovelier fluids than the sour and foetid ones he'd so far enjoyed.

With her orgasm the storm passed. Presently, and with a shy half smile now instead of the Amazonian snarl, she stood, offered him a hand, pulled him upright, followed him down the ladder. In the yard she turned on a hose already attached to an outside tap and in turn they sluiced each other down; she even had some soap – a big square yellow block of household stuff. Occasionally, when the water played over her breasts or up her bum she giggled at him, once indeed bending over and thrusting her buttocks

up at him. Then they sat in the sun, already hot, drank
goat's milk and shared a huge, fat turdish home-grown
joint.

Downhill, back past the war memorial and following the
curving road up the other side, he panted a bit, felt again the
strain on his calves, the heat on the back of his neck. He
shifted the cap round to protect it. The woods seemed to
float by, in spite of the climb and, high on the dope he'd
smoked, he relished the ache in his groin and balls, the
bruised sensation in his prick. Snatches of song and melody
floated from his lips, inaccurately remembered, about
wanting to ride a bicycle, and *Freude, Freude, Tochter
auf Elysium.*

At the junction at the top of the hill he took the right fork
away from the main road across the heath towards Daw
Hill. Spikes of marsh orchids bloomed in the still dormant
heather and three forest mares with russet foals paused
from cropping the coarse grass looked up at him. Nearby
the white stallion that was running with them arched its
neck and neighed – beneath its stomach its long black pizzle
curved away from its stomach. "I should coco," Sam
murmured to himself, enviously.

Another short climb brought him to a small copse of pine
trees and a large patch of tall green bracken by the side of a
pony path that circled a hillock and the highest spot for
miles around.

Virginia was waiting for him. Nearly six feet tall, an inch
or so taller than Sam, wearing a long brownish grey shift
that clung to her slim but well rounded body, head up so the
faint breeze at this height just stirred the curls of her red
and gold hair, with two English setters straining at their
leashes in front of her, pointing, with tails like auburn
panaches straight out behind them, she looked like Diana
the Huntress – a likeness she was no doubt conscious of. At
seventeen years old, girls tend to take themselves seriously.

Virginia Leighton-Smith. Cut a long story short. Her sexual experience had not been happy. Taken by a trio of Saudi princelings at a Belgravia cocaine party where they had been celebrating their victory in the Eton and Harrow cricket match. Sam had met her at her mother's fiftieth birthday party, a garden party with a marquee, where he had been playing bass in the Buddy Holden Seven. The party had gone on through to nightfall, by when skinny-dipping was taking place in the Leighton-Smiths' swimming pool. Sam had found himself standing near Virginia and watching. She had expressed deep revulsion at the whole sex business – "Bare bums and tits and male genitals, ugh!"

He had said, "Oh, it's not so bad if you do it right."

"I'd like to know how," she had said.

"I can show you," he had replied, a bit tight on all that Buck's Fizz.

"All right then, I take the dogs walking before breakfast most fine mornings up on Whitton Hill; meet you there."

This was lesson three, the one where theory was planned to move into practical.

They left the track and, walking between heather over tiny clumps of heath lobelia and the yellow stars of tormentil, came to a large expanse of bracken, which, watered by a tiny spring, had grown above waist height. They pushed through it, careful not to trample or even bend any of the long stalks supporting spreading fern-like leaves right into the middle where, a fortnight earlier, they had folded down thirty or so of them over the mossy ground and turf, short-cropped by rabbits, to make a sylvan bed. The dogs followed obediently, snuffling at rabbit scents, but not taking off after them, and, to a brisk command from Virginia, lay like the lions in Trafalgar Square at opposite ends of the clearing, heads up, tongues lolling over their liver-coloured jaws, tails rhythmically thumping the earth behind them.

Virginia knelt, pulled the hem of her dress above her knees and heaved the whole garment over her head.

Sam swallowed, gulped and shook his head, trying to clear it of the last of the fumes left by Joan's pot. He pulled off his T-shirt and his Nicaragua baseball cap with it, and knelt before her, ceremoniously touching his head on the spread and now drying bracken.

"I am not worthy," he murmured. "Indeed I am not worthy."

He meant it, too.

She leant back, putting her arms behind her, supporting herself on her hands, turning her feet out beneath her buttocks, spreading her knees, head thrown back, using the slight slope they were on to exaggerate the posture. Her eyes were closed against the sun, a slight smile playing on her young angel lips, through which the tip of her tongue just showed. Like that, her neck arched down to collarbones as delicate as a bird's above breasts that were full but taut, pushing upwards to rosy nipples puckered up with the slight chill of the air after the warmth of the fine wool of her dress or with excitement at being the object of so much adoration. His own tingled in empathy.

Beneath her stomach, hollowed as she pushed her breasts and pelvis forward, with its neat tummy button a purple shadow in the sunlight, her mount of Venus was thrust forward and almost up at him between her taut spread thighs. Through the triangle of dark red hair, pinker labia peeped and glistened. Perhaps attracted by her fragrance, a large peacock butterfly fluttered briefly above them and settled on her thigh for a second.

Sam came forward on his knees, between hers, and put his hands high upon her chest then, firmly, so as not to tickle, in her arm-pits, which were moist. His fingers came slowly down and spread across her breasts, squeezing, then teasing her nipples. He licked the base of her throat, then the cleavage he made by pushing her breasts together. She sighed with satisfaction, then, as he increased the pressure a little, a small giggle bubbled through her lips.

"You're making me feel very good," she murmured.

"You are. You're utterly adorable. Worshipful."

"You make me sound like a mayor." She laughed and added, in case he had misinterpreted her, "Lord mayor. Lady mayor, anyway."

He continued to caress her waist, her stomach, her thighs, occasionally stooping to slip his tongue between her labia, searching upwards for her clit. At last he sensed a response there, a tiny thickening.

She shifted, bringing her thighs quite hard against his temples. He pulled back, suddenly nervous that he had gone too far too soon.

"Pins and needles," she said, and pulled her legs in front of her, still with knees flopped out and the soles of her feet now together on the bracken between them.

"Do you really feel good?" he asked. "Really happy with yourself, with your body?"

"Yes; yes, I do."

He sat back on his haunches, held her eyes for a moment. She turned her head a little away from him. The smile remained on her lips but faded a touch from her eyes. Not yet then, he decided. Not yet.

"Then," he said, "you should play with yourself, make love to yourself, celebrate your own loveliness."

"What, frig myself?"

"Yes."

"With you watching?"

"Of course."

She was disconcerted, he could see that, but excited, too; at any rate very interested in the idea.

"Hang on," he said. He stood, peeled off the Lycra shorts. His long thin prick popped out and swung blindly to the left again.

"What are you doing?" Nervous now, almost frightened.

"Don't worry."

Stooping, keeping below the level of the bracken, he moved behind her. One of the English setters stopped panting, growled a little.

He sat behind, wriggling his buttocks and balls into the dry coarse bracken, spreading his knees so she could lean back between them with her head on his shoulder, her cheek against his. She wriggled back so the top of her bum pressed against his prick. He draped his arms over her shoulders so his hands could hold her breasts. Her back was sticky with sweat against his chest.

"Go on," he said. "Do it."

Peering down between his hands and her breasts he saw how her right hand, quite hesitantly at first, came over her thigh, spread across her bush and then quickly, too quickly began to rummage away there.

"Hang on, that's no way to go about it."

He felt her stiffen in his arms.

"Relax. Close your eyes. Pretend your hand is not your hand – mine neither. Pretend it doesn't know its way around, pretend it's exploring, it's never been there before. Just use your middle finger. Ever so gently on your clit." His own eyes were shut now, and though his hands were still on her breasts, gently kneading her nipples, rolling them between thumbs and forefingers, he could imagine as vividly as if it were his own finger what he wanted hers to be doing. "It's a little dry, isn't it? It could hurt almost, if you're not careful. Go down beneath it, move around between your lips, push in a bit. It's wetter there, isn't it? Moist, and crimson and warm and wet. Pull that wetness up with the ball of your finger, squeeze your lips around it as it comes back to your clit. Now that's better, isn't it? Slowly, though, slowly does it. Go back down for more wetness as soon as it feels dry." He felt his prick swelling and tingling now in the top of her natal cleft, and she gave a little wriggle to accomodate it better. Steady, now, he thought, steady.

"Slowly now. Let your finger relish your clit; let your clit relish your finger; curl that finger up into it and let the others get down there inside and outside and between those lips. Slowly, slowly; don't hurry." He let her go on like that for a bit, then, "How does your other hole feel? I bet it feels warm and tingling and spreading. See if you can get your other hand there, see if you can get a finger on it . . ."

"I've never done this before."

"Really? First time for anything."

Where has this girl *been*?

He murmured in her ear, his lips brushing it. "You know an ass-hole is no more there just for shitting that a cunt is there just for peeing. And it's just as beautiful as all the rest. Now, ever so gently, ease that other finger in, through the sphincter; let it hold, get a grip . . ."

Now things were really beginning to happen. She twisted a little, got herself more comfortable; her pelvis began to grind round and backwards and forwards. He shifted his right arm down so it was round her waist, holding her tighter now, supporting her, and spread his left hand so his little finger was still on one nipple, his thumb on the other. Her silky moist skin slipped against his chest, against his prick in her natal cleft and his inner thighs where they held her hips. The blood pounded between them as though it were one blood they shared, then shooting stars as he clenched his eyelids tighter and *whooooosh!!!* they came together; he could feel his spunk spreading up her back as it pumped out of his prick, and, "Yes, yes, yes, YES!" she cried as they both collapsed backwards, her hair in his mouth, her cries ringing in his ear. For a moment – he was, after all, sixty and had had an exhausting morning – he actually passed out. He came to before she realized, but with one English setter licking his face, the other apparently nibbling his toes.

"Next week," she sighed, "we'll do it properly."

Well, if you insist, he thought. But I doubt it'll be as

good. I'll have to remember to bring a johnny with me. Or two.

At a quarter past eight he made it back up the hill to the hamlet where their cottage was, meeting the milk-float as, empty now, it trundled down towards him. He managed to give Jim and Pete Pond a wave without falling off. They waved back, grinned too. Funny, he thought, with two of them on the round he'd have expected them to be through by now. He used the side gate, put his bike back in the garden shed, went in through the back door and found the milk bottles on the kitchen table. He peeled the top off one and drank half of it before putting the two bottles in the fridge. Then he went upstairs, first to the bathroom for a wee and a bit of a wash, then back to their bedroom.

"You were a long time." Zoë was still in bed.

"It takes a bit longer each time. Not as young as I was."

"Perhaps you shouldn't go so far."

"Maybe."

He peeled off the T-shirt, pulled on his night-shirt, pulled off the Lycra shorts and got in beside her. She hugged him briefly and then turned away, he hugged her broad back, let his hand wander a little.

"You've been playing with yourself," he said teasingly.

"Sort of," she said, and snuggled in closer. "No need to get up for a bit, anyway."

He felt sleep coming on. But something niggled. The milk bottles. Either she didn't go down when they were delivered, in which case they'd have been on the step still, or she'd have got them in and put them in the fridge. Funny. Almost as if someone else had brought them in for her . . . *Two* of them?

RAPUNZEL

Sue Dyson

"STEFFI!"

The Style Director snaps her fingers, and the girl with the bad bleach-job looks up from sweeping the floor. A strand of brittle hair has escaped from its plastic slide and hangs limply across her cheek. Do all hairdressers look like "before" pictures in a magazine makeover?

"What?"

"Cup of coffee for my lady. Small espresso, no sugar; what are you waiting for, Steffi? Get on with it."

She turns back to me, serrated scissors gaping expectantly in her left hand, styling comb in her right. I notice that every piece of equipment down to the last clip is marked with a proprietorial dot of varnish, matching the apple-green ovals of her fingernails. "Nikki" scrawls in embroidered letters across the small, hard, fist-sized swell of her left breast. A breast whose nipple is cheekily pert beneath the white polo shirt, coaxed awake by the over-enthusiastic air-conditioning perhaps, or is she turned on by the long, silky drape of my waist-length hair?

Her own hair is nothing to write home about: dry and spiky, standing out from her head in short, plum-coloured corkscrew curls, like the spines on a sea-mine. I smile to myself. Six months ago I probably wouldn't even have noticed.

"Complete restyle, is it?" she asks hopefully.

I flinch as the comb sweeps down through the back of my hair, tugging at my scalp and jerking back my head as it snags on a knot. I meet her gaze in the mirror as Steffi bangs a tin-tray of coffee down on the glass shelf in front of me.

"Just a trim."

You can see the disappointment in those hard green doll's eyes, the disdainful twitch at the corner of Nikki's mouth. At first sight it's a sensual mouth, but really it's faintly ridiculous, an exaggerated Baywatch pout drawn on with dark pencil and filled in with gloss the colour of a synthetic strawberry jam. The sort of mouth you might see moulded onto the face of a blow-up doll.

It purses in exasperation.

"Wouldn't you rather *do* something with it?"

I almost laugh in her face. Do something. If she knew the half of it, her toes would curl in their black patent mules.

"Just a trim," I repeat, and reluctantly she starts spritzing the back of my hair with tepid water. Where did you first find me, Mikhail? I can scarcely recall our first meeting now; it seems such a long time ago, part of another life. Someone else's life. Have I really changed so much? I never dreamed I would let my life drift along the tide of a lover's sensual imaginings. I'm not that kind of woman, you see – or at least, I never used to be.

It was at the art gallery; I remember now – that one on the river, the old converted chapel. It's supposed to be haunted, did you know? I was being bored rigid by Modigliani and you were far more beautiful than anything on the walls. I know that I was drawn to you instantly, that intriguing mix of East and West in you compelling my gaze and filling me with unspoken, half-conscious fantasies. I don't believe I could have put those fantasies into words even if I'd tried, but somehow I sensed that they lived in the secret depths of your *café-noir* eyes. I just couldn't take my eyes off you. In fact, I was so lost in contemplation of you that I didn't even hear you when you spoke to me.

"Do you like Modigliani?" you repeated. That threw me. And, to be honest, I've never mastered the art of lying.

"He leaves me cold," I heard myself confess.

You laughed; but not at me. And I noticed that your voice was like wild honey, crushed from the comb, drizzled over my skin in warm rivulets. I didn't so much hear it as experience it, like a caress; I could feel the fine, baby-blonde hairs on the back of my neck prickling to attention, as though your tongue were working its wicked way lazily down my spine, from the base of my skull to the hollow between my shoulder-blades and on, to the dark furrow between my buttocks, lightly teasing as it went. And then venturing deeper. Lapping up the wild honey that oozed at your touch . . .

"Me, too. I find him far too . . . restrained. Frankly, I'd much rather look at you."

It was the corniest of lines. OK, so I'm a good-looking woman – no classical beauty, it's true, but I have the kind of cool, pale, English looks that some men find . . . well . . . horny. I must have seemed as exotic to you as you were to me, with my blue-lilac eyes, clear complexion, naturally white-blonde hair. Yeah, it was a corny chat-up line and, believe me, I've heard them all, but half an hour later we're sitting in a taxi and I'm thinking, hey honey, what are you *doing* here? Where's this guy taking you? What's on his mind? What's behind that well-bred smile? What if . . . what if . . .?

Fear contracted in my stomach. If anything, it magnified the pleasure of being with you.

"Where are we going?" I asked, my voice dry and hoarse in my throat.

You turned to me and I saw the light from the sulphur-

ous-yellow streetlamps reflected in your eyes. They were
the eyes of a beautiful devil.

"Oh. Just a place I know. You don't mind?"

The shiver began at the nape of my neck and quivered
down through my whole body, tautening my flesh, erecting
every microscopic hair, turning my nipples to rock-candy
buttons. I imagined your teeth closing about them, your
tongue flicking, tasting, your lips sucking.

"Mind? No, why should I?"

Your hand brushed against mine, fleetingly, as you leant
forward to give directions to the driver. A silent voice
thundered inside my head.

He wants to fuck you. You know he wants to fuck you.

The fact is, even as I was telling myself, don't be crazy
girl, get yourself out of this weird situation right now; my
body was whispering to me hey, he's beautiful, he's six-
feet-four of perfection, sleek muscles moving elegantly
under *café-crème* skin . . . why shouldn't you want him,
too? And you do want him, don't you? Your pulse is one-
twenty and rising, your heart's thudding against your ribs,
you're hyperventilating, your palms are sticky with sweat.
And now you've started squeezing your thighs together,
you shameless slut, almost imperceptibly moving your
backside to and fro on the taxi seat, praying he doesn't
notice, but it's the only way you have to answer the pulsing
ache between your legs.

He's taking you home. In another ten minutes you could
be naked on his bed, sliding your body across his, letting
your kisses lead you oh-so-slowly down from his lips to his
cock, until mouth and cock meet and there is a blossoming
of joy in your throat. If you're enough of a cheap slut to let it
happen . . .

But you didn't lure me back to your flat; not that first
night. You were the perfect gentleman. I couldn't understand it; I was almost angry with you for not seducing me.
You took me to a club, classy and expensive but kind of

peculiar in a way I couldn't quite define. All the cocktail waitresses had really long hair . . . I didn't give it a second thought at the time, but then I'd never met anyone like you before.

"You're beautiful," you said, out of the blue.

"You think so?" I returned your smile but your eyes were distracted. They weren't looking into mine; they were tracing the smooth shimmer of my hair.

"And this . . . it's amazing . . ." You touched my hair, smoothing the flat of your hand lightly over it, from the crown to its end just above my waist. "An incredible colour. And so silky."

I blushed. "Thanks."

"It would suit you even longer. Right down your back, down to the floor, even. Like Rapunzel."

I laughed, flattered but faintly embarrassed. "Hey, I don't think so . . . It takes enough looking after as it is, I guess I'll have to get it cut, sometime."

You looked horrified. "Cut! No, you mustn't; promise me you won't ever do that."

I smiled at your intensity, like it was some kind of silly joke. "Well . . . It's just an idea."

We drank Moët and talked, about art, music, horses, dogs, food, clothes . . . about everything in the world except fucking. Frustration boiled inside me but I couldn't let it show.

You glanced at your watch and leant across the table. "When can I see you again?"

I tried to play it cool. "I'm not sure. I'm busy right now."

"Give me your number; I'll call you."

I wrote it down on the back of an old theatre ticket and you slipped it into your shirt pocket. At the door of the club, you hailed me a taxi. As the black cab glided towards me through the drizzle, my heart sank to my belly. It was cold outside; the dream was fading fast. "I'll call you." The polite lie. All at once I was certain I'd never see you again.

Then, when I had almost given up hoping, your hand snaked round my waist, pulling me close. So close that I could feel the muscle-hard perfection of your body, warm and hot beneath your linen shirt. Your mouth filled me with the taste of coffee and cinnamon and sambucca, and then you were kissing my chin, my brow, my closed eyes, devouring me with kisses. All the time your hands were stroking my hair and suddenly your face was buried in it and you were murmuring something into its pale, soft mass – nothing I could understand, just wordless sounds of pleasure like a stroked cat.

As you kissed my throat my hungry hands slid down to your buttocks and I pulled you closer still, savouring the musk-sweet scent of you and the wondrous hardness of your cock, its long line nestling into the long shallow groove of my pelvis. Savouring my triumph too, knowing that I had made you desire me.

"Ouch."

"Did I hurt you?" Nikki drags the styling comb through my hair, irritably tugging out the tangles. "Thick, isn't it?" It sounds like an accusation.

A man in black hipsters and a cut-off D&G white vest pauses, hairdryer in one hand, the other fiddling with the emerald stud in his bottom lip.

"Spiral perm, that's what she needs; nice spiral perm set on natural wood chopsticks."

"Shut up, Sven, she doesn't want to look like some Essex tart. Take no notice, love; he's perm-mad, that one. No, I tell you what'd suit you, just a good simple cut, really short, asymmetric across the front here . . ."

I'm not listening any more, just staring at our reflections in the mirror: Nikki's shiny pink mouth opening and closing like an absurd sea-anemone, Sven fussing about in the background, my hair hanging in a damp curtain about my shoulders as the comb drags and the scissors snip.

It's all so irrelevant. Nothing is real but the remembrance of you.

The pleasure. That's what sticks in my mind. Pleasure that grew in intensity until I wondered if I could bear it any more. With other lovers it has always been the law of diminishing returns, but not with you. This hunger could never be sated.

Tell me you remember, too.

I never found out very much about you; never felt the need to ask. You were a wealthy man, that much was obvious, though you never talked about it. To you, money was simply a tool for pleasure. You were an art collector, an aesthete, a connoisseur, a dilettante. A collector of experiences; I guess of women, too. Not that I cared, not about the others. I could have shared you with the whole world and I would still have been the only one you cared about. That, at least, was what I believed. I basked in the obsessive power of your desire, letting it enter me and grow inside like some monstrously radiant child.

Islands, cities, beaches, galleries – you took me everywhere, showed me a lifetime's adventures in a few short months. You took me from Sunset Boulevard to Montego Bay, from sleazy motels to exotic markets blistering in the noonday sun, where eyes undressed me from the shadows. Covetous eyes that followed the white-skinned girl with the long pale hair that swished across her back and the wrap-round skirt that parted as she walked, revealing a defiant flash of thigh.

Oh the games you taught me, Mikhail, the games I played for you. That time you sat me naked in your sports car, and drove me through the streets of Acapulco . . . That time I played the whore for you on the Bois de Boulogne . . . The gifts you showered on me, the jewels, the clothes, the silver pins for my hair . . .

You loved to bathe me, do you remember? Massaging my

backside with long, lazy circles of fragrant lather; kissing the softness of my breasts as I stood beneath the shower, and drinking the water as it dripped from my nipples. Rinsing my hair in chamomile and sweet-scented rose-water.

It was getting late. The air was hot and dry, and insects were singing in the lemon groves. The silver-backed brush moved in long, slow, rhythmic strokes down my back as you brushed out my hair. I watched you in the mirror, wondering what you were thinking. I knew you desired me; I could smell your desire, the faint acrid stench of it that catches in the throat. And I wanted you, very very badly. My cunt was sticky-wet with the badness of it.

My hair was barely paler than my skin. No matter what I do I always stay pale; I never tan. I used to hate the way my white skin shimmered in the heat, loathed the milky whiteness of my breasts, my ivory thighs, my plump white sex that opens up to reveal the squishy paw-paw-red flesh within. But you taught me not just to believe in my own beauty; you taught me to flaunt it, use it, control it.

"Wear it like this," you whispered. Setting down the brush, you clutched handfuls of my hair and piled it on top of my head. "Wear it this way tonight – for me." And you kissed the slope of my bare neck and shoulder as I pinned up my hair, the way you had shown me. I've come to accept that everything should be the way you showed me, the way you taught me, the way you wanted.

All these things you asked of me, the things I did with you and for you – they are things that I would never have done for anyone else. And there is one thing you must understand. I did not do these things because I was subservient to you, but because I knew so little about pleasure and you had so much to teach me. With you I felt the freedom to do anything, everything, to do whatever your imagination could dream.

Pleasure is the only thing that matters. Show it to me again.

It's night now. Very dark. In the gleam from the lamp on the dressing table my hair is like spun sugar, white cotton-candy piled on top of my head. A few fine strands curl down over my cheek and throat, lifted and shaken by the light breeze. I am proud of this sluttish, imperious beauty you have created in me. I am proud of my uncut hair, silky and strong; I'm not your poor little trapped Rapunzel, I'm your Lilith, your Delilah, I have ensnared you and captured your adoration. Why should I ever let you go? Beyond the open window the sea sparkles under a scattering of stars and the slash of a crescent moon. Whatever you may think, Mikhail, you are my prisoner now.

"Where are you taking me tonight?" I ask, gazing out at the far-distant lights of the town.

You silence me with a kiss on your fingertip, placed upon my lips. "Nowhere. I'm leaving you here."

You produce a silk scarf from your pocket. It's black, painted with silver, I can still picture it now – like a midnight-black night sky scattered with starry constellations.

"Leaving me? I don't understand."

Another kiss. "Always trying so hard to understand. That's not what I want you to do, I just want to make you feel."

And you do. More than I have ever felt before.

"Then what. . . ?"

"It's just another game; you'll see. Let me blindfold you."

"Mikhail, I . . ."

"You do trust me, don't you?"

You lift the scarf. I keep silent but my eyes question you. I can hear excitement trembling in your voice. I am excited, too, profoundly aroused by this new journey into the unknown . . . and yet . . . for the first time, perhaps, I feel a little afraid. And then the silk covers my face, binding my eyelids closed. I can see nothing. Your lips brush mine, and your voice is breathy with exhilaration.

"You know I adore you."

Tonight I am naked. The breeze from the open window ruffles my hair and dances over my skin, puckering my nipples, taking the powerful scent of my womanhood and floating it up into my face so that I catch it in faint gusts. I am wearing nothing at all, save your black and silver scarf and the silver stud I wear in the secret folds of my pussy, the mark of your favour and my body's devotion.

I wait. You have taught me a fakir's patience.

Do you remember that time in the Colorado mountains? How you lathered my pussy with handfuls of melting snow and with each stroke of the cut-throat razor brought me one long step nearer to gut-wrenching orgasm . . .?

I hear the door close softly and know that I am alone. I do not know how long it is before the men come. I can hear their breathing, shallow and fast, hoarse with excitement. I am excited too, in spite of my fear – or could it be because of it?

"Who are you?"

The question hangs on the air and then is gone, carried away on the night-wind. No one answers. How many are there? It is impossible to tell, and I no longer care. The only answers are touching hands and lips and tongues and penises and teeth and fucking; the only answers that mean anything to me.

Hands take me, strong hands. I don't resist, why should I? This is the lesson of your love and desire, Mikhail, and more than anything else in the world I want to learn it. Your pleasure is my pleasure; is that so absurd?

"Mikhail . . ."

That is the only other sound I make, whispering to you because I know that somewhere, somehow, you are watching. It fills me with joy to think of you watching me as I pleasure these nameless strangers. I cannot see their faces but all their faces are yours, Mikhail. The cock that enters my sex is yours, the fingers probing deep between my arse-cheeks are yours also. My throat is filled with the taste of you, the hot, hard saltiness of you, the desire that explodes into stars of ecstasy.

My sex throbs. I am on my belly on the cool stone floor, my body shaken by the mad rhythms of the fucking, and I scarcely notice the fingers free my hair from its silver pins and let it tumble. Its white-gold serpent slithers down and becomes a waterfall, a silky curtain spreading out into a shimmering pool. And then a tangle, a sudden shaft of pain as someone seizes it and starts to twist, to clutch, to possess.

Disorientated, my head swimming, I hardly know what is happening to me. Somewhere beyond the pleasure that engulfs and dominates me, I hear a cry. It is a cry of apotheosis, the kind of exquisite fulfilment that is ten times more unendurable than pain.

And then silence.

In the aftermath of orgasm, I lie slumped on the floor. Footsteps tap away into the distance, a door opens and closes. Somewhere beyond it a man is laughing. At last, someone unties the scarf and it flutters away from my eyes. I try to sit up but I cannot; something still grips the rope of my hair, clutches it fast, tethering me to the ground. I open my eyes. I am alone. All alone, save for you, Mikhail.

You are kneeling by my face, legs apart, your cock cradled in your hands; and twisted around it, matted and sticky with your semen, is the soiled white gold of my hair.

I understand now, Mikhail. I pull away, suddenly angry, and the tangled rope of hair uncoils from your dick, leaving behind a few fine strands; tumbles down, heavy with sticky gobbets of wetness. All at once you revolt me, nothing has ever disgusted me more. You've been fucking my hair. Not me, my hair.

You aren't even looking at me. You're looking at those

few fine strands of hair wound round your dick, so tightly that the flesh bulges. Your eyes are fixed on this parody of love, stroking, tightening, loving, adoring, lost in your own world of obsession. You can't see me, I might just as well not be here.

It took me a long time, but at last I understand. I always wondered, and now I know. All this time, you never desired me for myself. It wasn't me you desired at all.

Steffi is jabbering on about something and nothing while Nikki snips a ruler-straight line across my back.

"... an' then this bloke says, 'Ain't you never thought of gettin' it cut?' An' I say, 'Why's that then?', an' he says, ''Cause you look like bleedin' Morticia with that hair right down your back' ..."

You'd never have said that, Mikhail. You spent all your time making me promise never to have my hair cut. I must have been insanely naive. All those gifts – the silver ornaments, the clips, the pins, the silk snoods, the ebony combs. Hair fetishism, it's a harmless enough perversion; God knows, it shouldn't shock me. Does it matter what turns you on? Hair, shoes, rubber, leather, sexy underwear, it's all the same; it's not as if you were into anything illegal.

But you know what you did to me, Mikhail? You did the worst thing anyone has ever done; you objectified me, made me feel like a ... a *thing*. And that's what I can't forgive you. That's why I'm cutting you loose.

"There." Nikki straightens up. "Reckon that's about it. You want to take a look?"

"Wait a minute." I stop her as she picks up the mirror to show me the back. "I've changed my mind."

"What?" She gives me that "are-you-taking-the-piss?" look, but I just smile back as if I haven't noticed.

"I told you, I've changed my mind. Do what you like with it. Cut it all off. Short."

As she cuts, I watch my precious white-gold hair drop in

silent, silky hanks to the floor. Maybe when she's done I'll gather them all up, put them in a box and mail them to you. Second class.

Meantime, I have my eye on that cute-assed salon junior. What's his name? Edouard. He can't be more than sixteen years old and, as I recall, I have never had a sixteen year-old boy in my entire life. Well, Edouard, if you like, you can be the first. There's so much I've learned and so much more I want to teach you . . .

WORTH MORE THAN A THOUSAND WORDS

Lawrence Schimel

I HAVE NEVER been good at keeping a diary. It presupposes an audience, supposedly one's self, but I have never been comfortable with the idea. I am afraid someone will find it, and read it, and I will have bared my soul to a stranger, or worse, someone I'm close to. I am afraid because I have done this to others. Friends of mine. My sister. I have always been a voyeur.

Reading someone's diary is the thrill of the forbidden. The knot of worry in the stomach, the fear of being discovered. When I was younger, I read porn that way. I didn't need to. My grandfather kept stacks of porn magazines on top of the toilet in the bathroom of his apartment; I could have read them at leisure, in that small locked room, poring over the pictures. But I would go to a bookstore and sneak porn magazines from the rack, hiding them inside a copy of something innocuous like *Cats Magazine*. I would walk back to the middle of the store and stand in an empty section to flip through the pictorials. I hardly even looked at the pictures, glancing down for a second and taking a mental photograph, my heart racing as I quickly glanced back up to make sure no one was coming down the aisle where I stood, to make sure no one ever saw what I was doing. As soon as someone came near, or if I even thought they would, I closed the magazine and moved from Gardening to Humor, to wherever there wasn't anyone else.

My heart pounds the same way when I read someone's diary, even if there's no chance of my being discovered – they're away for the weekend and I have the only key to the apartment, whatever. It is forbidden, and I feel there is someone watching me as I reach for the slim, clothbound book that's hidden beneath the bed. I flip through the pages, scanning for any mention of myself, or anything else that catches my eye. I look for moments where the handwriting changes, clues to highly emotional scenes. I'm like a vampire, thirsting not for blood, but vicarious emotion. Thirsting furtively, at night, when no one else is around, lest I be discovered.

I am always careful to replace the diary exactly as I found it. If it were my own, I would notice if it had been moved, even if anything around it had been moved. I guess that's why I've never been able to keep a diary before. I'm too paranoid. Afraid of exposing myself. I've broken the trust of too many friends who left me alone in their rooms while they went to class or work, while they went on vacation for a week, trusting me to water their plants. Trusting me not to read their diary.

So I know someone else will read this. I can't help being aware of you. I feel as if I'm writing for you, not for myself. But I have something I want to write down, need to write down, so I don't lose it. So I don't forget. I know you're reading over my shoulder, so I'm going to fill in the background for you. After all, who knows what will happen? Fifteen, twenty years from now, the stranger who finds this book again, buried in an attic at the bottom of a box of books, might be myself. And my heart will begin pounding as I realize it is a diary, and I open it and read all the details I'd long since forgotten.

There are some who consider thirteen an unlucky number. Not I. But I've got reason; I have a lover thirteen years older than myself.

Not unlucky, but still witchy. She's definitely a witchy-woman. Enchanting seductress. It's almost impossible not to be drawn in by her. When we go out together I watch it happen to the men around her. And I, I was drawn in, as well, although it's harder for me to know what happened, trapped in her glamor.

I've wondered sometimes if it was a potion she made, something she wore. She's an aromatherapist, always using subtle essences of plants to influence mood. Lavender. Ginger. Scents I've never been able to identify. Her home is suffused with a rich aroma of comfort and warmth, an amnesiac to anxiety.

Yet each time a man is ensnared by her spell she is taken by surprise. It is perhaps that very aspect which is so appealing: she does not wield her sexuality like a weapon or tool, but is so familiar with it, so intimate, that it sits upon her as an integral part of her being, as simply as the features of her face. If you saw her, you would understand what I meant. If you saw her, you would be drawn in by her spell.

While she may not understand the effect she has, she is now aware of it. We met at a poetry reading in Boston, and exchanged business cards. Later that week, a story showed up in my mail, a piece entitled, "Desire." It was our first flirtation. I know not to assume that a first person narrator is the author, but I could not help noticing similarities, how men seemed drawn to the protagonist like moths to a porchlight on a summer's evening. The writing was in-fused with that same sensuality which surrounds her presence. Though the story wasn't full of explicit sex, it played a strong role, tantalizingly alluded to or glimpsed. And the writing itself was lush, like a flurry of caresses moving up one's thigh and across belly and chest.

A writer myself, I appreciated the sumptuousness of her prose. I was also very turned on by it. Words have always held strong sway over me. Perhaps she'd sensed this about me, and thus chose to make her first move in print. Subtly, yet relentlessly, working my weakness.

Perhaps because she understood this power words held over me, I was able to persuade her to let me read an erotic fantasy she had written for another lover of hers. Showering after the first night we spent together, I'd found her aromatherapy jars in the medicine cabinet. Later, I asked her if she ever used them in lovemaking. She said she had, and also mentioned this fantasy she had written. The moment she realized what she had confessed she said, "I can't believe I just told you that."

I begged her to let me read it.

I was curious. I wondered who he was, what he looked like, why she had chosen to write something for him. I wondered what it would reveal about her, her own desires, her fantasies.

And the idea of reading something meant for someone else thrilled me. I've always been a voyeur. In college, I would lie atop the window seat for hours, warmth on my stomach from the radiator underneath as I stared across the courtyard. I could never see much – the buildings were too far apart – but what I saw was never really the issue. It was the looking. Often I would spend an entire night staring at the yellow squares of light across the way, waiting for the brief shadows to cross their frame, unaware of how time was passing, lost in the act of watching.

Reading a fantasy for someone else held the same appeal. Already I could feel myself begin to grow hard with anticipation.

She relented. I'm still not sure why. She'd never shown it

to anyone but the man it was written for. But for some reason I convinced her to let me read it. Maybe because she had realized how powerful words were to me, and wanted to help me change, to grow.

I remember almost everything I read. It's as if I had a photographic memory, which I don't, since I only remember words. But eventually I will forget, or not be able to remember exactly. I'm sure that already I must have changed things, remembering what I would have found more erotic rather than what she actually wrote.

He was an actor who starred in horror films. Naturally, he lived in LA, across the country from her. Most of their relationship therefore took place in words, on the page or the phone. Once, it took place like this:

For Paul

I woke up this morning with the most luscious fantasy in my mind. Here, let me share it with you. Then we can both enjoy it.

We are in a luxury hotel; it is night. You sit on the bed in a white silk robe, gazing through the window at the panorama below: a city bejeweled with light. A muffled whisper of traffic filters through to your ears, almost as soothing as the surf.

Your back is to me. I can see from your reflection in the window that your eyes are closed in quiet contemplation, listening to the city sounds below. I ease onto the bed and move towards you, circle your chest with my arms from behind, rest my head against yours. Your hand lifts to caress mine; you smile, sigh, eyes still closed. A gentle squeeze, and I pull my arms away, letting my hands glide beneath the collar of your robe and slide the silk away like milk pouring from your skin. I knead your shoulders for a moment and am pleased to find you already so relaxed. My fingers wind through your hair, soft, like a spider sorting threads for her web. Your moan is barely audible until it evolves into another sigh. I am so happy to please you.

Knowing how much you enjoy it, I let my fingertips sneak down to your neck and feather your back with caresses. They play at your shoulder blades, tease your spine, explore your sides as you wriggle against them. I switch to a calmer touch, flat hands soothing nerve endings, then tickle once more, enough to bring delight, no more.

You turn to kiss me. Once, softly, then again. Our mouths open and we feel the warm moistness of each other's desire. I hear a tiny sound of surprise from you and you move away, smiling.

"What's that scent?" you ask, leaning forward to sniff and kiss again.

"Can you guess?" I ask.

"Let me smell that again." You turn yourself fully around to embrace me and kiss me deeply. "Flower, I think."

"Yes, flower. A special flower."

Another kiss. Another sniff. "Not roses. Not lilacs; not so sweet." Another kiss. "Ah! Lavender."

"Yes!" I smile. "Do you like it?"

"Love it. Did you put it on your entire body?"

"Nothing so dull as that, sweetie."

You are intrigued, guessing that there is more. I know the notion of impending discoveries excites you. I can feel your erection against my thigh as you guide me down onto my back. Your hands are delightfully warm; I feel heat through the wine-colored silk of my robe as they find my breasts. You whisper my name as your mouth reaches my neck. You kiss, and then you lick. "Lemon. That one's easy!"

I turn to bare more of my scented neck to you . . . take it. My fingers find your hair again as you clasp your hungry mouth to my neck. My turn to sigh now. A wave of passion crests inside me and I press you away and onto your back so I can devour you with hot, wet kisses on your neck and face. The fingers of one hand are still entwined in your hair. The other dances across your chest, down your stomach, finds you hard and holds as your hips push against me, a promise of delights to come.

Both hands move now to your face, learning the features with my fingers as a blind woman might. I close my eyes to enhance the sensation, resculpting the lines of your face. Your hands grab my wrists. You press them to your lips.

"Peppermint," you say. "Peppermint wrists."

"You're very good at his," I answer, kissing your hands. My tongue presses along the inside of your palm, spreads your fingers as it dances between them. "Have you done this before?"

"Never," you declare, tugging at me until I rest on top of you. You suck at my wrists like a child with a candy cane until the scent is gone. "But I sure hope to again." Straddling you in this way, I notice how very wet I am by the way you nearly slide into me without effort. But, ah, not yet, no.

I move forward, kiss the top of your head, rub my body along yours until my breasts are at your lips. Your lips part automatically and my right nipple stiffens in response to your tongue. You taste the left nipple before making your guess. They are both the same, but you are not sure you've got this one right. "Smells like . . . gin? Even tastes like gin." Determined to make your guess conclusive you taste once more, moving between my nipples, licking, sucking, thrilling me!

When I can find my voice, I tell you, "Yes. It's juniper berry. What they make gin from."

You release my breast long enough to grin and say, "Hmm, educational as well as nutritional," then return to sucking. Your right hand nudges between our bodies and finds me wet and wanting. One finger slips inside me and I press against it, moaning softly. Two on the next gentle thrust . . . oh, I could almost come right now! But, no, there are still discoveries to make.

Playfully, I push away, sitting up and pulling you with me. Our skin is flushed with passion, our breath quick, eyes sparkling. "I just want to make it last," I explain, "savor it."

"Savor it," you repeat, "I get it." You pass back through the familiar lavender garden, the lemon of my neck, and I lean back to let you revisit the juniper of my nipples. You brace me at the waist as I lean back further, resting on my hands as your tongue circles my navel. It's ticklish, and I giggle and squirm as you make up your mind what it is.

"Spicy. Hot."

"Like you," I say through my giggles.

You taste again, then declare, "Cinnamon!" triumphant.

"Go to the head of the class!"

With a raised eyebrow and a boyish grin you say, "I thought you'd never ask," and move lower still, to the final scented spot. This is the challenge, since you have to get past my own musk to find the herbal aroma.

The moment I feel your tongue probe the soft, moist folds between my legs I no longer care about herbs or slowness or anything except that you don't ever stop! How wonderful you are with your mouth; tongue tentative, yet firm. You move your head away, to make a guess at the aroma, I imagine, but I gently push you right back, moving my legs out from beneath me and letting you settle in. The heat and the wetness release the herbal scent into the air around us; amazing what a single drop can do. The earthy scent envelops us as your tongue carries me to an excruciatingly pleasant plateau, then coaxes me over the edge into the warm rolling ocean of orgasm.

As I begin to float back to the coherent world, I find my voice and say, "Paul, I want you inside me." I feel your weight and then I feel you push into me, a delicious feeling with the area so highly sensitized and flushed. My legs encircle your waist as your hips move, grinding against me in the realization of that earlier tantalizing promise. My arms come up under yours to hold onto your shoulders, bracing me for the thrill of each thrust. With one hand I grasp your hair, baring your neck where I smother my moans. I arch to let you reach further into me and orgasm again overtakes me. You move slowly, helping to prolong the delight. When I have settled back to earth once more, you let your passion have control, pounding against me with increasing lust.

"I'm so close," you whisper, your voice hoarse with pleasure.

I quickly turn you over so that I can be on top of you, sitting up. "Lay back and enjoy this," I tell you, as I match the rhythm we had a moment ago. You manage to smile broadly through your sighs, encouraging me with a word or two until eloquence deserts you altogether and your back arches and you buck and grunt and grasp my hips and hold me against you until you are spent. Keeping you inside of me, I bend forward to hold you and let you hold me as we catch out breaths.

After a moment of quiet, you ask, "Are you going to tell me what the final aroma was?"

"Won't you guess?"

"Something earthy, like the woods. Like you."

"It's Patchouli," I say. "From India."

"It's magical," you reply.

"You're magical, my dear."

We fall asleep there, in each other's arms, the moist fairies between us and the aromatic fairies watching over us.

With Love,
Laura

Writing it down, I found myself aroused again. Often, I paused and put down my pen, rereading the passage I just wrote as I took off my shirt and ran my hands across my chest and back, along the line of hair that runs down my chest. With my left hand, I undid my jeans and stroked myself through my underwear as I wrote. Slipping my hand underneath the brim, I avoided my cock, teasing myself, running my hand along the inside of my thigh and letting the backs of my fingers tickle my balls. And as I write this now I hold my balls in my hand, gently squeezing and rolling them, pressing deeply against the muscle underneath, the root of my cock, so hard. Enough of writing for now –

The afternoon I first read that piece stays firm in my mind. We woke at two in the afternoon. The house was quiet. Outside, the neighbors could be heard in the yard, as could the trills of birds in the dogwood which bloomed outside her bedroom. It felt like a lazy Sunday afternoon in spring as we reveled in the indolence of rising so late. Laura had called in sick earlier that morning, at dawn, when we decided finally to go to sleep.

The night had been spent in touch, a revelry of physical sensation. I'd had no idea what to expect, when she'd offered to put me up for the night after a poetry reading in New York. I'd figured it was likely I'd wind up on a couch in her living room. Instead she'd given me a massage, by candlelight, on her bed, since my back was sore from lying on floor cushions at the reading. I had injured my wrist, which was in a splint, and thus could only lean on one arm during the entire performance, cradling my injured hand in my lap.

She rubbed scented oils into the muscles, a soothing sensation I had never before experienced. The combination of smells, from the oils and candles, the lighting, the lingering sensation of her fingers along my back – it just seemed natural as we were lying next to each other, to reach out and pet her stomach over the satin of her chemise. Though my hand was in a splint, the fingers were still free and danced across the fabric, thrilling the skin beneath with the light friction. Later, our clothes off, we rubbed our bodies together simply for the exhilarating sensation of skin moving against skin. Crouching over her like a wildcat, I ran my torso over her body, pressing down on her breasts to knead them gently with my own, dragging my body down across her belly, her waist, her legs, then back again. I dropped my head down to let my hair, which I'd been growing out for more than a year now, dangle lightly against her skin.

That night was touch for its own sake. We explored each other's bodies until dawn, kissed once, briefly, and slept. We stayed in bed until mid-afternoon. At last, I got up and showered, where I found the oils in her medicine cabinet. Wrapped in a towel, I went back into the bedroom and asked her about them, thus discovering the erotica she'd written for Paul. She made tea while I read the piece, understandably nervous about being in the same room with me as I was reading, and soon returned to the bedroom with two steaming mugs.

"Tea?" she asked innocently, ignoring the fact that I'd been reading.

"Come here," I said, getting to my feet. I let my towel fall to the floor around my feet. I was very excited from her story; my erection throbbed, flushed with blood. I took the mugs from her hands and placed them on the nightstand, enfolding her in my arms. We kissed, and I drew her back onto the bed with me, running my hands along her back through the fabric of her robe. The neck of the robe hung wide, and I nuzzled her skin, running my tongue up to her chin, then back down to slide between her breasts. We rolled over, and she opened the belt of her robe, pulling the dark red fabric back slowly as if she were peeling an artichoke. I wanted to devour her. I leaned over her, bracing myself on my hands, when suddenly my right wrist gave out in a searing wrench of pain. I did not have the splint on, and the pressure of supporting myself had been too much. I bit back a cry, and collapsed on the bed next to her, cradling my injured hand under me, against my chest.

"I'm sorry," I said, "but I'm not up to this, it seems."

"Shhh," she said, rolling me over and sliding on top of me. "I don't want you to do anything that will cause you pain." She took my injured hand in hers and gently kissed it. She licked the palm, then ran her tongue down to my wrist, and slowly along my arm. When she reached my shoulder, she moved across to my nipple, teasing it with circles of her tongue and gentle bites. But she quickly slid backwards, dragging her body along mine as she kissed down my chest and stomach. The loose folds of the robe billowed about her like a butterfly's wings. Her breath was warm, exhilarating, as she explored my pubic area, rubbing her face against my hard cock as she tickled around my balls with her tongue. At last, her tongue met my shaft – a quick lick, a tentative probe. With her hands, she lifted my cock until it was perpendicular from my body, and slowly lowered her mouth over it, surrounding it, but not touching, not yet, only her warm breath. She held for a moment, and I burned with anticipation. Then her lips closed, and suddenly her tongue pressed against the length of my shaft, sliding up and down.

My breathing grew heavy as she drew her lips along the length of my shaft, teasing my balls with one hand as the other grasped the base of my cock and squeezed gently. I was so excited that it did not take long before her touch pushed me into orgasm. "I'm so close," I warned her, holding back to prolong the blissful sensation, and give her a chance to pull back if she did not want me to come in her mouth. She kept her lips firmly clamped, her head bobbing up and down furiously, and I could not hold back any longer. I let out a cry, which slowly faded into a sigh as I recovered from my orgasm. My lips and hands were tingling with bliss, and I held them against her body, whispering, once I got my voice, "Look what you do to me."

"How do your hands feel?" she asked, concerned.

"In ecstasy," I answered, with a smile. They tingled with pleasure.

Laura smiled as well. "I've found a new form of therapy for them, then. Something your doctor would never think to prescribe."

"They should make you a practicing physician," I said, hugging her close to me and kissing her. My fingertips reflexively began to caress her thigh, but she stopped me.

"I don't want you to do anything that will injure your wrists. Just lay there and enjoy yourself."

I was frustrated with my body's betrayal of me, but succumbed to the bliss it was currently feeling. I lay in the afterglow, feeling incredibly self-indulgent, and enjoying it. The phone rang. I tilted my head to look at her and smiled as she turned to looked back. Neither of us wanted to get up to answer it. After the fourth ring, the answering machine picked up. It was her lawyer, saying that at last he'd submitted the final papers for her divorce, and that soon, hopefully, everything would clear.

I'd known she had been married, but had not realized the divorce was not finalized. Suddenly a gulf loomed large between us as I thought of where she was in her life with regards to where I stood in mine. But curiously, despite the vast differences in our lives, the closeness between us as we lay entwined, her hand gently squeezing my leg, my fingers still caressing despite her protests, did not dissolve.

"Ah, adultery," I said with a grin as I turned onto my side to look at her.

"A new experience?" she asked, also with a smile. I hesitated, and knew she was suddenly wondering, having noticed. But she did not ask. "Don't worry," she continued, "we've been separated for over a year now."

I deliberated whether to tell her, wondering what would happen to our relationship once she knew. "It's not new," I say. "For the past two years, up until September when he moved back with his wife in Syracuse, I've been seeing Brian Coney."

I waited for a response, hardly daring to breathe, unsure whether to expect outrage, incredulity, or calm acceptance. She smiled, and after a moment said, "Well, at last I get to sleep with him, if only vicariously through you!"

I smiled, pleased that she was so accepting. I knew that I could share how special that relationship had been to me. "Only you and he have ever made me feel an orgasm like that," I said. "Make me tingle. Too often it's just an ejaculation." I looked at her, and said, "Thank you."

She ran her hands across my chest and said, "I'm glad. You deserve it."

I chuckled and asked her, "Remember when Jo Ann said I looked like a young Brian Coney at the reading in Boston? Right before you said he was so sexy that you couldn't talk in his presence? Oh, how I was biting my tongue!"

She was curious about everything, then, asking questions about him, and my relationships with men in general. The questions were never accusatory, rather pure curiosity. I believe the notion may have even excited her, especially when I spoke of Brian. She did not ask me which I preferred, making love to a man or a woman, but rather what I thought were the best things one could do with either sex, and what I enjoyed most from each.

I spoke of finally learning to receive pleasure with Brian, of how before I had simply been going through the motions of sex, with either men or women, without enjoying it. How sometimes a need for physical intimacy will well up inside me until it's unbearable. How I need to touch and be touched, the feel of skin and skin. How sometimes I have to go through other things I don't want, or enjoy, to get those. When it builds up inside me like that, I almost don't have a choice. And there's almost always a man who wants to get me into bed, and I go with him, for the brief moments of foreplay – before he has my pants off, and his own, his large erection pressing against me – and afterwards, as we lie together, our bodies touching.

I think what I like most is lying in a lover's arms afterwards. I can never fall asleep like that – I'm too sensitized to the feel of warm skin against my own – but I relish it for as long as I can. But one has to go through sex to get there. Even if I don't enjoy the sex along the way, I'll go through with it, for that luxurious sensation afterwards.

If you haven't noticed, I've been avoiding writing about the event which made me need to write this account. It's so much easier to wallow in the background, spewing forth endless, easy details. There's no emotional stake involved. Even talking about sex is easy, although revealing my desires and fantasies starts to get slightly uncomfortable. That's why I just realized, as I was writing the above, how much I'd been avoiding the issue.

Enough of cold feet.

Laura is a portrait photographer, by profession, and we began taking photos of me, to try and reveal my inner self. I've never been terribly awaare of what I look like, and a comment to this effect made Laura decide on this project. I readily agreed. I was curious what she could show me. I'd produced a body of work as a writer that was much more familiar to me than my own body.

I hadn't been photographed in a long time, and was very nervous as we began. For one thing, I truly had no idea what I looked like now. Until I had begun to grow my hair out a year ago, my image had not changed in the last seven, eight years. I'd shown Laura two photographs of me, one taken when I was thirteen, the other at twenty, and both looked identical. Now, with shoulder-length hair, and the start of a beard, I had no idea who I was. I'd still been using those photographs of my younger self as my mental image of myself. It's how I'd always defined myself, by the pictures I had of myself. That's how I imagined I looked to other people, and since I had no other way of seeing myself, that's how I looked to myself. Laura was going to show me who I was now.

The first session went awfully. I'd taken the train out to her place after work Friday, and after a quick dinner, we went upstairs to her home studio, on the second floor of the house. I was so tense that it made Laura nervous as well, and seeing that she was now nervous only made me more so. It fed on itself in a vicious cycle, until the air was thick with uncomfortable frustration, and we finally called it quits. We went downstairs, leaving the studio set up in hopes that tomorrow we'd manage a better session. We made love that night, tension dissolving as slow caresses gave way to deeper passion.

Waking the next morning, I felt contented as a cat as I stretched in her bed as she moved around me. "I wish you'd been this comfortable last night," Laura remarked.

"You should run get your camera," I teased. "Or rather, you can walk. I'm not going anywhere."

"Yes, you are, dear," she said, tugging me upright and kissing me on the lips. She dropped a white-terry cloth robe in my lap. I smiled as I noticed the Hilton insignia embroidered onto it, and wondered if it had been stolen after a tempestuous weekend with one of her previous lovers, like something from the story she'd let me read. I put the robe on and followed her upstairs.

She positioned me in front of a large free-standing oval mirror in her studio, and stood behind me. Reaching around my waist, she undid the sash of my robe, letting it fall open. "I want you to look at yourself, touch yourself, until you know what it feels like from the inside," she said. "Until there are no boundaries between the you in the mirror, and the you inside here." She tapped her knuckles against my chest, and squeezed me gently from behind. Then, taking my hand in her own, she began guiding my fingers across my chest, pushing the robe from my shoulders until it fell to the floor. She released my hand and stepped back as I continued exploring, running my fingers over my arms and torso. I watched myself in the mirror, studying my body as my hands passed over each area. I felt the double sensation of touch, in my fingers and skin, not trying to analyze but simply feeling it.

I explored every inch of myself, running my hands along the muscles of my neck, even exploring my scalp, the fingers running through my own long hair as they felt their way along the curves of my skull. I ran my hands down my chest and back, onto my legs, crouching down to reach all the way to my feet. I stood again, my hands always in motion, exploring new areas – my thighs, my buttocks. I caught sight of Laura in the mirror, noticing that both she and the camera were watching me. I smiled, and did not stop my exploration. I grew hard, reveling in the multiple voyeurism: looking at myself in the mirror, looking at Laura looking at me. I could tell she was turned on by our voyeurisms as well, and began tantalizing her, staring into her eyes through the lens as I moved my hands over my body, grabbing my erection with one hand as the other circled a nipple or explored elsewhere.

And suddenly, I turned and looked at her over my shoulder, directly, no longer through the mirror. The camera clicked, the shutter winking open and shut like the lips of her labia moving apart and together again in fast motion. She put the camera down and I went to her, almost giddy with desire. We kissed fiercely. I undid the sash of her robe, and she shrugged out of it so quickly, like from one of those tales sailors tell of seals who shed their skins and become women. As her hands explored all the areas where my own had just been, I thrilled at the difference in the feelings. I remembered the mirror and looked up, to see my hands running up and down her back. I snorted with amusement, and pointed to the mirror. Laura turned towards it, and in that moment I leaned down to kiss her neck, her breasts, the entire time watching myself perform these actions in the mirror.

I took the café chair she used for portraits and positioned it in front of the mirror. I sat down on it and held my arms for Laura to come to me. She eased my knees apart with her hips and kissed her way down my neck, her breast surrounding my erection. She licked my nipples, sucked on them, then began to drop lower, towards my cock. I stopped her, pulling her to her feet. "I want to be inside you," I said.

She looked at me for a moment, and I could sense what was going on inside her mind, her wondering, marveling. I ran my fingers over her nipples, pinching them slightly, and desire overrode any lingering concerns she held. I pulled her towards me and she climbed onto the chair with me, slowly lowering herself onto me. I moaned as I slid into her, watching in the mirror as she rocked her hips backward and forward. I threw my head back, reveling in the sensation, and no longer cared about the mirror or watching us. I no longer needed it. I could feel my entire body from the inside, knew it exactly, perfectly. I wrapped my arms around her waist, and stood from the chair, slowly lowering us to the carpet. I kissed her fiercely, and then, supporting myself on my elbows since my wrist would give out, began rocking my hips, pushing deeper into her. She moaned with pleasure, her fingers grasping my shoulders tightly. I began to build speed, exploring deeper inside her with each thrust, reaching for those spots which would thrill her most. I was quickly hurtling toward orgasm, but held back, an almost painful sensation as each thrust brought me closer and closer. And finally, just when I could not restrain myself any longer, she arched her back and cried out as we pushed over the edge into orgasm at the same time. We laughed, kissed once, and collapsed in each others arms, spent.

It's somewhat ironic that now, after she's pushed me from defining myself by words to showing me what I truly look like, I am writing about it. But in a way, it's exactly what I should do. It shows how I have grown so far. My body of work was much more familiar to me than my own body. Now, having explored my body by sight, by touch, to the point where I truly know it, from the inside, the only thing remaining was to explore it once again, in words, to make the two bodies one.

BLOW-OUT

Yseult Ogilvie

HE PUSHED OPEN the swing door with enough momentum for it to hover briefly before its return. For some reason this manoeuvre took him back to the science laboratory of his school years; the strange motions of chalk dust caught in the sun; mahogany surfaces, the grain raised in sharp spills by years of misuse, the double gas taps that left their taste on your fingers. The Laws of Motion.

"Three mousseline of scallops, two skate wings, one lamb, pink."

It was strange to be serving again, brought back the early days when they were just starting out, when he and Clare did everything, just the two of them together. Good times, working toward success. And now? In the office, opening new restaurants while trying to capture the excitement of the first. He married young, too young to consider a lifetime. What had happened to that energetic girl?

He'd employed Susan a fortnight before and hadn't really seen her in action, though the manager offered encouraging reports. She had been a school friend of his wife's and this small knowledge of her past led them to an unearned intimacy. At interview she had worn a grey linen suit, no

make-up, attractive, terse. He remembered little other than
her references; and her hands, cook's hands prematurely
aged by experience. Now she stood with hips pressed
against the robust gas cooker, her pale hair piled on her
head, the end secured with a twisted drying-up cloth. She
wore checked trousers, clogs and a lurid purple vest of
ribbed cotton. One black bra strap had fallen down her arm,
which was white and wiry, flexing with the effort of
removing a huge pan from the heat. She lifted the lid
and veils of steam rose, reddening her cheeks and conden-
sing on her upper lip. She dumped it under the cold tap in
the sink and moved to the sauce, whisking in a blob of
glistening butter, lifting strands to check consistency. He
collected the cutlery and sliced bread.

"Did you catch that order? Table eight."

"Oh yes. Oh, it's you! Hi. Sorry, I was busy with the
squid; they only need a couple of minutes at the most. How
long are you going to be working up front?"

"Just 'til Sam gets out of hospital. I'm enjoying it."

"Yeah, it's fun when you know it's going to end."

She stuck the lamb under the grill and put the ramekins
of scallops into a bain marie in the oven while she fetched
the skate wings from the fridge. She had a protruding arse
which was accentuated by the curvature of her spine.
Weighty breasts, not usually to his taste, hung from her
slight frame like a shelf. The effect was one of confinement.
He thought of the pleasure of pulling the thread on a
stitched sack of meal.

"How many skate portions left?"

"Nine, and those two lemon tart can go, table fifteen."

She did not look round. Her eyes were on the shelves that
toured the walls at head height, holding great stainless steel
cylinders, pans, colanders, skillets, cake tins; a long still life.

"I like to use a wok for these seafood salads; they really
need to be kept moving. Could the management acquire
one?"

She sliced up the lamb, arranged the pink lozenges in a crescent around the salad and grated shards of fresh turmeric over the olives.

"Whatever cook wants."

He swung out into the roar of the dining room.

The heat grew as the restaurant filled; steam lifting her scent and dispersing it through the room. It was like really seeing her for the first time. He found himself wandering into the kitchen for butter, candles, tapers, brown sugar crystals. No one seemed to notice. Conversations with customers seemed interminable. They arrived in a blunt wedge and orders piled. He watched her pivoting on the sharp edge of her heels; plates queuing the surfaces in various states of dress; running them up his arm in threes, hadn't done that in years. And then it subsides, the grills are turned off and she's washing the floor, moving the mop in slow arcs.

"Well, I'm glad that's over. It was a bit of a bottle-neck. I must have lost pounds in the heat."

"You don't look like you've got pounds to lose."

"We need more cream, by the way; I haven't been told about the ordering yet. And someone will have to knock out some sesame biscuits for cheese tomorrow, and now I'm off, for three whole shifts."

He looked so disappointed that she stopped her action and soothed, "Don't worry, Jeff's on; he's very able, taught me everything I know."

She withdrew to the staff room to change while he emptied the crumb drawer of the toaster; hadn't done that in years. She emerged, wrapped in a grey sarong, black T-shirt, clogs. "See you Friday." Striding out, heels down first, light infantry step. He stood propped against the unit, his arms folded across his chest. Outside the broken light fell through the trees and a faint smell of rotting vegetation rose from the bins. He heard her car door and then the continuous repeat of the ignition like the vigorous scratch of a dog.

"Can I help?"

"Bloody thing. It's due for a service. It just does this sometimes."

"I know nothing about cars, I'm afraid, but can I give you a lift?"

"Are you sure it's not too much trouble? You know I live quite a way out?"

"No, no, Clare's away, so I'm in no particular hurry to get back."

"Great. I'll get a lift in with the local mechanic in the morning. God, it's close."

She flapped the front of her shirt against her chest. A strand of hair had welded itself to the moisture of her temple, a perfect curl. Clouds were gathering as she got into the slither of leather seats. The door closed to the heavy sound of an expensive car, so silent that she kept thinking it had stalled.

"Now that's worth paying for."

"What is?"

"It's so quiet."

"Yes, it's good, isn't it? Particularly for long journeys; very discreet, no noise from outside."

They left the town to the north and the landscape seemed to spread itself beneath the weight of the cloud, its surface scored with channels of water. They were silent in the small, cool space of the air-conditioned car, furtive beneath the extent of the sky.

"I still haven't got used to this place yet; when those shafts of light come down through the cloud I keep thinking there'll be a parting and a pyramid with an eye will appear like on a dollar bill. The sky's so huge. I find it troubling."

"What a strange idea. I grew up round here so it's just, well, you know, home."

The road turned sharply right and then ran straight to the horizon, a slip of water running alongside to the left. A pale, pink crevice appeared in the cloud. It centred above them, trailing fronds of dense, grey vapour which sickened to a jaundiced yellow.

Suddenly there was a loud gun-shot; the car stumbled slightly, followed by the circular sound of a sharpening knife.

"Oh God! A burst. Sorry."

He drew the car to the roadside as a huge drop of rain struck the windscreen followed by a flock of others. He paused, hand on handle.

"I think I'll wait until the storm passes."

He turned to Susan. She was looking straight down the perspective of the road. Lightning was fingering the landscape up ahead, followed by the collision of thunder.

"They say the safest place to be is in a car. But I'm afraid this one has lost some of its insulation."

She didn't answer.

"Tell me about your school days. You know, with Clare."

She blinked repeatedly, as if summoning an equation.

"Well, we weren't very close. Or we were, early on, and then we managed to fall out over a boy. Silly, really. I can't even remember his name now, and we certainly weren't of an age when relationships are fully formed."

"When are we?"

"What?"

"Nothing."

He didn't really want to talk; listening was his strong suit.

"She was fun, popular, worked hard and went to university. She had a great sense of style; always looked a lot better than the rest of us, better turned out. Used to go to this second hand clothes shop that was run by the sister of the local undertaker, so she got a steady flow of stock. We were all far too provincial. Anyway, I was the wild one. After the bust-up, we went our separate ways. I ended up in California; she married you, and now, well, here we are."

"You married, didn't you?"

"Yeah, for a moment; it wasn't really what I wanted."

The car was warming up now the ignition was off. A pool of sweat gathered momentum between her breasts and trickled down to her navel. She parted her thighs, sealed in the damp, and a small pocket of air rose through space. It arrived, a strong chemical message in his mind. He breathed deeply. The grey cloth had ridden half way up her thigh, a mole on the pale skin, its edges slightly blurred as if floating on cream. The particularity of this mole, he felt he would be able to map its position always, just follow the cusp of the knee round to the right . . . The rain kept up a strong percussion on the car, glazing the windscreen with tides of water, the grey blur of the sky beyond. There was a loud crack of thunder breaking to the west and she jumped, involuntarily clutching his sleeve. He reached out, allowing his hand to hover briefly before it came to rest on her thigh. Fine dark hair grew in panels between the joints of his fingers, hands, strange, unfamiliar long after faces. She placed her hand on his and they folded to a kiss. Freed by fused mouths, she worked her way over to his seat and lowered herself onto him, her knee wedged by the door. She rose from the knee and he helped, gently cupping her ribcage in his palms as she moved to a gentle rhythm.

They sat for a long time with their temples pressed together while they recovered their breath. They did not know how to become individuals again. She clambered back to her own seat and smoothed her clothing impulsively. The sky was clearing and he looked to the wide horizon,

"Thank you."

"Look, I don't know what happened; that's never happened to me before. I don't want you to think . . . It's that I just don't want you to think . . ."

"I'm not thinking anything."

He was free, like an addict who can't decide whether or not to smoke; now he'd had one he could have a whole packet. He could just see her hair coming in dark at the roots and her nails bitten to the quick. Why did they have to talk at all . . .

"We have to talk."

He had noticed her silhouetted against the porch light as he drove up, tyres treading the gravel.

"I've been worried sick. Finally I phoned the restaurant and Fran tells me you'd given Susan a lift home. She'd seen you from the office window."

She threw her voice from the front door and he locked the car by remote as he walked towards the house. He had driven home with the window open and he felt hollowed by the passage of air, inclining his face slightly as he stooped to kiss her, worried there might be some scent remaining. On the new oak boards in the hall there was a pile of shopping, mainly boxed beneath the thick plastic: Giorgio, Joseph, names. She had been up to London.

"I'm sorry, darling. Susan's car broke down, so I offered to drive her home. And then we had a blow-out in the middle of this massive storm, so I waited for it to pass before changing the tyre. It all took much longer than I expected. I'm sorry. I would have phoned but I thought you were dining in London with Stella."

"Yes, well, she cancelled. Something to do with an American client in town for one night only."

There was a bottle of wine opened on the low table and he noticed two licks of red in the corners of her mouth, like an extended smile.

"Would you like a glass?"

"Yes, please. Have you anything in mind for supper? I'm starving."

"Sorry, I thought you'd have arranged something yourself, not expecting me back. I was just too tired to get into all that when I got home."

She refilled her glass and went to retrieve a package from the pile.

"I got you a present." She offered him a box from Hermès, obviously another tie, which he opened and put on; floral like the last one.

"So what did you talk about, you and Susan."

"Thanks, it's great. You mainly, and your mutual school days."

"And what did she tell you?"

"How hard-working you were. What a success. How stylish. All these things I didn't know."

"Very funny. You mean she didn't mention Will? Will Jameson."

"Was that his name? The name of the boy who caused the rift? She said she couldn't remember. I'm impressed."

"Couldn't remember! What rot! She spent weeks trying to lay claim to that boy, months. She was pernicious, like a weed . . . oh, I don't know . . . knowing you were out there with her, not knowing where you were, it got me all worried. Silly, really . . . after all these years . . . Stella said she was transformed but I don't know if people ever really change . . . Let's have another bottle."

She got up and went to the cupboard for more red.

"And you know she's not a natural blonde."

"Oh, really?"

It was about the only thing he did know. He was doing well, starting to relax. She refilled their glasses and sat in the tartan armchair. Back-lit by the light on the side table, her golden hair was like a halo. She had been so pretty. And now, the wine was scrambling her features.

They first started in cheap premises where with mismatched tables and salvaged goods she forged an image. Pre-war rugby caps from the local schools framed with hockey sticks and lacrosse rackets. It looked like a public school dining hall without the hammer beams. She found some scholarship listings in gold on oak panels and mounted them with the menu in similar format. They did all the cooking together, good school food, and the public flocked. Released by their wealth, she did nothing, as if it had removed all her confidence. She just went shopping for names.

"You mean you just sat in the car and talked? You don't like talking."

"No, no; of course not, we had sex. Come on, Clare, you think she clambered over to my seat and we did it with her arse resting on the steering wheel."

"All right, all right, it sounds ridiculous when you put it like that."

"Exactly. I have to go to bed now; I'm completely exhausted, not used to working up front."

"I'll be up in a minute; I'll just clear a few things first."

But she was finishing the bottle. The more she thought about it, the more possible it seemed, after the last time: walking back to catch Will on his way home and hearing them doing it under the arch of the bridge, the strange noise that couldn't really be anything else. To be sure, she ducked down and caught them locked together. Susan saw her and smiled from below Will's weight as she backed out of the darkness, feeling sick.

He could hear her sobbing through the floor, some wine-induced misery. He knew he should go down, gather her up, bring her to bed, but really he was too tired. She would be up soon enough and with any luck he would be asleep. Why did they have to talk at all?

TRESPASS

Lunar

ONCE, WHEN I was young, I didn't care about sex. But sex was rearing everywhere. Magazine nuddies littered *my* secret clearing in the bushes of Johnson Park. High school kids learning to smoke cigarettes claimed my turf theirs, chasing me away with threats of roping me upside down by my toes if I ever returned.

I kept sneaking back. Quietly hiding in the brush to catch a glimpse of teenage lust. Rubbing my crotch; growing . . .

I *wanted* one of those pretty *girls* – in her tight skirt and fishnets, popping gum in between sucking the breath out of her boyfriend with kisses that led to groping, petting and moaning – to catch me; tie me up.

Play with me!

After all, I thought of myself as their mascot. The kid always hanging out with them on the park bleachers. At a safe distance, of course. But they got to know me. Called me Dynamite.

One day, when I was crouched in the bushes, a huge, oily rat scurried across my feet. I gasped. Then *she* did. And *his* voice rose from whisper to roar: "Dynamite!"

I vamoosed like a steer on steroids, only to be rustled by a bunch of teenage boys who dragged my snarling scruff home to my parents, stating they had had it with me.

I had become their pest.

I never became the greaser those sweet tarts flash their lashes for. My silent brooding became my persona. I wanted what I could not have: an adventurous young female who'd take advantage of my willing vulnerability towards her.

In junior high I met Marla. We would sit in the cafeteria and flirt. I'd tell her my fantasies of submission. She would kick off one of her heels and slide her foot between my legs, heightening the provocation of my tales. After school Marla was carted off to the girls' reformatory on the other side of town.

The first time I hitch-hiked to see Marla I was picked up by a pervert. I hopped into the passenger seat and at the first traffic light this guy pretended to need something from the glove compartment. As he searched, his elbow squirmed in my crotch. Then he gave me a look of desire I'd never seen in a man before. Senses hightened, frightened as I was, I directed him to drive me to the girls' reformatory. I stood peering, over the stone wall, through the trees, to the mansion converted to "Girls' Town".

I wondered which room Marla slept in.

The next day, I sat in the cafeteria and told Marla all about my expedition. She was quiet, but her smile was pleasing, her contemplation obvious. "When can you come back?" she asked.

That night I had followed her instructions. I walked to the corner of Elm and Norwood, climbed over the wall and, at 9:30, I was perched in the oak tree left of the lamp-post. A light came on. Second floor. The shade came up. It was a bare room: just a dresser, twin bed and music (Steppenwolf) from a boom box on top the dresser. Then Marla's bare leg wrapped around the white curtain bordering the side of the window. Her face glowed as she slithered up and down the curtain, pirouetted, then stood in the window with hands on hips, dressed only in a tight guinea-tee, nipples pert, her triangular curlicue right there in front of me.

I was so excited: hand in motion, emitting musk, feeling faint, when suddenly my legs were grabbed and I was pulled out of the tree. I hit the lawn with a thud, knocking me out of breath. Before I could catch on to what was happening a girl pounced upon me, her small hand firmly covering my mouth. "Ssshhh! You're trespassing!"

Was it the fall or the fear and delight of actually being constrained by this girl that caused the dizziness which froze me into such passivity? Hands were on me! Someone else's flesh was touching mine for the very first time! Stripping me naked and rolling me in the grass. A sensual overload brought on by two girls; Marla and her girlfriend Gina. And I do mean girlfriend; Gina occasionally pouting, pissed, spouting, "We don't need him."

Both of them threatening, "Keep quiet!"

"What if the night guard catches you here?"

Whispering, "Ever see this?"

"Ever do this?"

"Feel this."

"Taste this!"

No. No, no, *no*! I had never done any of this before.

Giggling; they used me, maybe abused me, but I didn't mind. I loved every kiss, scratch, bite and the smells of our bodies smearing across each other with juices, blood and come. I was elated . . .

I had became their mascot!

This only happened two times.

Gina told other girls about our next rendezvous and they told other girls and other girls told the guards and I was half-way to the oak tree when the whistle blew and two flashlights beelined my retreat.

I scaled the wall and never returned.

Neither did Marla. Marla and Gina were transfered out of "Girls' Town". Accusations of lesbian activity separated them to different institutions.

I missed them both. Their scent faded from my body, then my clothes. The separation caused a wringing in my gut. I couldn't eat in such a state of unrequited desire. I lost a lot of weight.

Now, I'm a clerk, working the desk of the Triborough Motel, watching a voyeur sneak up to the window of room 8, open his coat and play with himself.

My indoctrination to sex with Marla might be as bizarre as this guy's actions, except ours was consensual, *somewhat*, and this guy's trip includes unwilling, unsuspecting paying customers. I pass judgment, feeling territorial. I can't have people jerking off outside the motel windows. I open the office door, deepen my voice and yell, "Hey!"

He doesn't stop. I start walking towards him with the big flashlight in my hand. "Hey, buddy, what the fuck's wrong with you?"

In the orb of my flashlight he stared like a startled deer, then raced away, his flight sphered by the light in my hand. I slowly stomped, allowing him to get into a dark sedan on the side street. As he pulled away with his lights out, my beam lit up his license plate. I yelled out the three letters and numbers on the plate.

He never returned . . .

HACK WORK

M. Christian

HIT HER, he said, his voice an inch from my ear, inside my skull. *Hit her now.*

The crop didn't feel like much, to me, but I knew it felt more real to him – wherever he was.

Hit her, dammit; his anger copper, his anger stars and then, FIRST WARNING scrolled by my eyesight, just outside my peripheral vision, sent straight into my optic nerve.

The crop was light, almost not in my hand at all. She was on the bed, on her stomach, ass ripe and full, plump and soot – all but steaming with excitement, already flexing and releasing in preparation.

Hit her now!

It wasn't my first, but I remember that one very well – better than all of them.

I was in New Orleans, dumped after my last fare's money ran out. I'd been stuck in a dingy French Quarter apartment with a lanky white trash asshole, a Bible-belt gigolo, his body greasy and alternately sagging and as hard as rock, as he fucked me. When I'd felt my fare start to come, ghostly quavers flickering up and down my spine and a phantom tightness in the crotch and balls I could feel but didn't have, I'd braced myself – predicting the fare to be a cheap bastard. Too true: as he came, so he went – clipping the connection as his cock, wherever it was, started to spurt. As he did, and his ghostly cock and balls vanished from my senses, I pushed the gigolo off and got as far away from his horribly bleached and spotted body, his sagging gut and his crooked spotted cock as I could.

I ignored his bass complaints, a mix of locally mangled English, Spanish, and Japanese spiced with a Tourette's Syndrome of *fucks*, *bitches*, and *motherfuckers* at not being able to show his "good fine loving" to me, "the pretty lady" to claim my clothes, efficiently climb back into them and leave – as fast as possible.

The day was pounding hot, a sauna that only New Orleans could be. I swam, struggling for breath, till I found the first cable bar I could find that didn't look like either a trap or too fucking expensive. In the back I found a lonely booth, paid the attendant – a piebald mulatto Korean kid with a cheap Russian prosthetic hand – and found the unit. Sliding my thumb over the id window, I charged up an hour of Blissful Oblivion followed by a chaser of Soulful Self-Examination.

Too soon, the lights of heaven faded, the angels put away their instruments, and the clouds broke up behind my eyes. Then I felt them turn deeply inward, looking hard and long at the face they were stuck in.

It wasn't a bad job. I've heard of worse, God knows: horror stories marionettes and jockeys have told me, sitting around company shops waiting for upgrades and maintenance, of wetfun, thrillkills, near-deaths, and even baby-wipes. Compared to being dumped in a box apartment somewhere with blood sticking everything to everything else (copper scent too strong in your nose) and most of a face staring back at you from the bed, being a simple hired hack was a good job.

Blame the "elegant facial structure" (as it says on my vid catalog entry), the "piercing blue eyes", "clean", "36–25–36", "long blond hair" and "fully compatible" but I hadn't had a day to myself, as myself, for almost three months. I was popular. I was busy, and I wasn't myself – most of the time.

When I was in the right mood, when I picked Sarcastic Self-Assessment rather than Soulful Self-Examination, I would say that I didn't really know who Rosselyn Moss was anymore – just who was in the back seat, screaming out directions.

The fare came on later that night, as I was stretched out in yet another room, in yet another coffin hotel. They all become one, after a point, the broken telephone in Tokyo, the broken vid in London, the smelly mattress in Seoul – all floated and combined to form one fuzzy box: a place to wait, and wait, till someone told me what to do.

Dispatch flickered the *Fare Waiting* yellow and black status bar across my eyesight, covering the static-fuzzy and rolling image of a local religious zealot spraying spittle as he and his topless "nun" begged for donations.

Then, the words. I had actually started to dream them – their tones and words warbling and waving as I flew through dreamscapes, even rented ones, warning me that soon, very soon, I wouldn't be my own man any more.

Thank you for selecting Express Taxi® service, the premier service for high class, quality, personal escorts. In just a few moments you will be connected to one of our expert and highly trained taxi personnel. You may feel some disorientation as your nervous system matches with our relay service. If you experience any form of discomfort or nausea, please summon the assistance of one of our monitors by patting your stomach, twice.

Please stand by while we interface with your bio-mate transmission system. Thank you again for selecting Express Taxi™ and we hope you have a pleasant trip!

Interface: the "falling over", the clean, crisp, disorientation as the fare matches with me, shakes hands with my cortical shunts and bioplast sensory nodes.

Then, just like that, I didn't feel quite like *myself* – my senses had been subverted, processed, compressed by black magic algorithms, zapped via the mono-wire antenna that ran along my spine to the nearest uplink and then to . . . wherever the fare was, laying back and enjoying the scratchy mattress, the chill of the box's air conditioning, and the slight cramp in my leg.

I got a little feedback from him, just enough to tell me he that he was, indeed, a "he", that he wasn't so short or tall as to screw up my balance – he got most of it, most of what I was feeling, tasting, seeing, hearing, smelling. From what I could figure, stretching myself with my usual series of slight exercises to orient him to my body's sensations – the way I feel things as opposed to the way he felt things – he was about my height, and near enough to my weight. Once again I felt the phantom sensation of a cock and balls. You can get used to anything, I suppose – walking was the hardest part: try putting one leg in front of the other sometime with a heavy and meaty sausage and meatballs between your legs (after you weren't born with them). Took me months of practice not to move without waddling like a damned duck.

When I was sure that he was comfortably settled in, riding piggy-back my senses, I introduced myself, as rote and familiar as brushing my teeth or tying my shoes. "Good evening, sir," I said to myself in the spacious confines of my pay-by-the-day aluminum coffin, my ears replaying the words to him. "My name is Rosselyn Moss, your taxi for this trip. I am a 35-year-old biological female in top physical condition, with no aches or pains that you need be aware of. May I ask your name, sir?"

Go to 1213 Flood Street, immediately. Take a cab, don't waste any time. British accent poured thinly over somewhere else, somewhere Eastern Europe, German, Russia: "immediately" and "Flood" sounding fluid and bubbling.

I'd been used to the cheap, where time is really money. I knew the drill, I knew the man: yet another vicarious fuck, yet another nameless pickup so he could feel it like a woman, me, felt it – I thought, at least.

I was wrong.

Be efficient, he added as I climbed out of my box, *I know this town. I know the way.*

Outside, the night was hot and sticky, a blanket wrapped around me – the day's legacy. People moved through it like underwater ferns and fish. I knew it must have been bad, sweltering, for me to feel it. For my fare, though, must have felt it like a steam bath.

He wasn't new at this, at being a taxi fare, so I didn't bother to warn him about the mark-ups on my expenses. I just walked out into the hard sodium lights and to the nearest call box and swiped my card. *Pay for a rush*, he said, the only thing he'd said since hiring me.

"Yes, sir," I said. "What, may I ask, is to be your pleasure tonight?"

He didn't respond so I leaned against the side of the call box, in the heavy, hot, New Orleans night, and waited.

Hey, what did I care? My meter was running . . .

She was beautiful. Stretched out on her huge bed, a midnight expanse that all but filled her bedroom, she looked up at me with huge, earthen eyes – lit by quivering desire, a pulse-pounding fever.

Her mouth was on my right nipple, painting it with the gleam of her wet lips, hard almost to the point of pain. I felt, ghostly, her rub it with the cool strength of her white, white teeth. Then she really sucked, and I felt my legs turn to rubber and my cunt get heavy, wet and hot.

In my hand, the crop was light, all but intangible.

We took a table near the back, in the soft shadows where the industrial lights around the stage didn't reach. There was a red biolight in the center of the diamond plate tabletop, making it an island of rich blood. On the stage, a woman was singing a meaningless song: canting her head back to rumble out a random handful of notes, a jumble of half-tunes, mostly lost above the chatting, drinking and laughing crowd.

We'd paid at the door, giving my card to a heavily modified doorman – his face all clear plastic, as best to show off the geometries of the circuits running underneath – then entered, pausing inside just long enough for my eyes to dilate against the shadows and the sanguine biolights.

To the bar: you can see well enough now.

"Sir," I said, "I do not know if you have been informed or not, but the consumption of consciousness modifiers of any form violates the terms of my hire – "

Not drink, just go.

I went to the bartender, a giant black man whose skin was much too glossy, too thick to be organic, who held his stare at me longer than usual when he saw the taxi mark on my forehead – used to hacks and having to wait till the fare gave the orders.

Ask for a crop. "I want a crop, please."

He smiled, showing teeth capped by .22 bullets, a tongue the color of tire rubber, and brought out a plastic and nylon riding crop.

Longer, smaller tip. I repeated my fare's instructions. His eyes were a brilliant red, as if filled with blood or wine, I noticed as the bartender brought out another.

Pay him. I did. He swiped my card with cool reflexes.

Take it to a table in the back. I did, and my fare and I sat down to watch the show: Sometimes she dropped an octave or two as she cut too deep, or just deep enough

Her.

There were many – the place was busy: Boys in paint and piercings and nothing else; blond warriors colored in bioglow circuits, primitive glyphs and signets. Men roped with amplifier cords, their glandular immenseness augmented by the matte coils. Girls whose bodies vanished and appeared in slices, from their fashionably designed, industrial plastic dresses. Women with anger-lit eyes, prowling the club and scratching the steel-plate walls with their charged nails, leaving cascades of sparks and a machine-shop howl.

Her. The black one, in the simple dress. Hair up. Choker of floptical cable, diamond-flashing eyes. The one that looks scared.

She did look that way, hunted eyes scanning – trying not to make contact with anyone. She looked like she was caught, trapped, like the whole nightmare club had descended on her. She'd just been walking home and the place had fallen on her. Despite the fevered dashes of her head, though, she didn't once step towards the door, towards EXIT.

I timed it just right: when she turned I caught her eye, gestured her towards our table.

Her.

I guess I was a lot less frightening than the others – outwardly. Inwardly, my fare was calm, patient; I didn't get anything from him but the dully flashing HIRED indicator just outside my range of normal vision.

She sat down, smiled a flash a pure white teeth, and didn't say a word.

Ask her what she's doing here.

I tapped the Taxi mark on my forehead, the tattoo that meant that I wasn't my own person and that my words, too often, were not my own. "What are you doing here?"

She shrugged. Her hair was curly, close-cropped dreads penned by a tight band of dimly glowing fabric, its soft blue light making her face appear to be hovering, immaterial, above her black-clothed, black body. "I was curious," she said, with a taste of a Southern accent, though not so strong as to peg her as being local, off the streets. "I heard about it from a friend. She told me some things. I wanted to see for myself."

Put the crop on the table. Ask her if she knows what it means.

I did as he told me, as I was hired to do. "Do you know what this means?"

"I do. I know what it means."

Does she really? "Do you really?"

"I do. I've been told. I want to."

Take her someplace. Hers, if it's closer.

"Do you want to go someplace?"

Nein! The voice, the force of it almost like a hard slap behind my ear, in my skull. *Do not ask, tell her. Say to her, "We are going now." Do it!*

She had seen the look of shock cross my face. She waited, patiently.

"We're going someplace. Now."

Better.

Hers was closer. A tiny apartment four blocks away. I got maybe twenty feet from the unnamed club when he said *Come up from behind her, take her wrists and put it behind her back. Do it!*

"Sir, it is against – "

Nein! Do you not understand yet? This is foreplay, this is before – do as I say or I will complain.

I did what I was hired to do. I reached over and grabbed her right wrist, put it behind her back, then her left. It was clumsy, with the crop still in my hand, but I managed –

thinking more of the act of juggling the nylon and plastic than of what I was going to do, might end up doing. She leaned back, into me, shocked by the move, the force (though I had been as gentle as possible), and tilted her head back.

Kiss her.

Wine, a tiny trace of garlic. Her tongue was strong, wrestling with mine. Her lips were fat, and full.

I broke when he told me to, said "fucking slut" when he told me to, and pushed her, hard, back down the street. She turned, flattening herself against an ancient brick wall – fear lighting her eyes.

I felt nausea boil in my guts.

Where? "Where?" I echoed, feeling my mind fall into the groove, retreat from my connection with what was going on. It wasn't a technical thing – I just didn't want to be there anymore, didn't want to be a part of what was bubbling up. I did as I was told: following her to her place, waiting while she scanned her thumb, climbing the steep steps with her, going inside.

The place was dark, so she clicked on a biolight that ringed her bedroom. A huge, black, wrought-iron bed. A Christ against the wall, also huge – looking like it might have fallen off some church, sadly watching over her bed.

He said, I did: grabbing her shoulder and turning her so that she faced away from me. He said, I did: putting my hand over her mouth, cupping it as I bit down into the thick muscles of the back of her neck.

He said, and, yes, I did: taking hold of the dress and pulling, hard, hearing and seeing the cloth tear all the way down to her ankles.

Throw her on the bed.

Her back was hot, like a pot left on the fire. I shoved, feeling myself pull back at the last, resist the feeling to shove her really hard, really *throw* her onto her expanse of black sheets, and turned black iron.

Turning, she looked back over her shoulder at me like a wild animal hearing the hunter thrash through the brush. She was gorgeous, body full and rich, rounded at ass, thighs and breasts – poured, overflowing, into purple bra, garters, hose. No panties, just a black fog of curly hair.

His voice, thundering:

Hit her.

Nein, wait, first – take her ankles, pull her towards you. Idiot! Put the crop down first, on the bed. Yes! Pull her towards you. Good, now turn her over, hard. Do it, idiot! Yes, yes – such a pretty cunt she has: such a pretty, pretty cunt. So black. She gleams, ja? She shines for us, for me. Tell her, speak to her, tell her she is wet. Tell her that she is a cunt, just a pussy for us. Tell her.

The words jammed in my throat and stammered, but they came. I felt my body break sweat from my feet to my face, a fever of fear and disgust that made everything waver in the hot room. I wanted to drop away, to give up completely and just let him have me, do what he wanted to do with her. I just didn't want to watch any more.

But I didn't think, not once, of cutting the connection. I didn't know then, and I don't know now.

Take off your blouse, take off your bra – I know they're hard because I can feel them. Do nothing, do not say anything. Just stand.

I do. She turns quick and wraps her lips around my right nipple, sucking with her strong lips, teasing it with her strong teeth. One hand, her right, reaches up to tickle my left.

Take her hair, force her back.

I do, drawing her off my nipple. Then she's free, panting like she'd been running, eyes fixed on, first, crinkled, hard, nipple and then, second, my face.

Draw her up, pull her up by her hair. Do it!

I lifted her by her hair and, with my other hand, her chin. She helped by climbing up onto her knees. Then she was kneeling in front of me. A nipple (like a drop of coal on her breast), I saw, mesmerized, had fallen free of her bra.

Tear it off.

I did, my arms following his directions – my mind disconnected, retreated into doing exactly what he said to do.

Her breasts were lovely, and as dark: large but not fat, bigger than mine – they barely fell as the bra snapped and tore in my hands (she almost falling forward by my earnest ripping). Two nipples out, then, both large and hard, blacker on black.

Tell her that if she makes a sound or moves away the game is over and we will leave. Tell her.

I do, his words falling from my mouth.

Take her nipples in your hands, thumbs and forefingers, and squeeze. Hard! Harder than that – you idiot, this is what she's here for. Do it!

I thought about reminding him of our contract, that I could have a case of cutting him for abusive treatment of me. I didn't though. I didn't. I couldn't say a word; I just took her nipples and captured them in my hot and sweaty hands (dimly aware of his cock, a phantom ache of hardness somewhere) and squeezed as hard as I could.

Her eyes got wide. She began to breathe, hot and heavy, like a horse after a race, sweat making her reflect the dim green light in the room – polishing her with pain and something else. I was aware of her smell, rich and strong, as I watched her pupils widened till she stared at me (at me?) – black walnuts quivering in pure cream.

Run your fingers through her cunt, get her juice on your finger tips. Hold them in front of her face. Say, "This is what you are."

I did, my body did, my mind in the back – shaking with fear and something else. She sucked my fingers, tasting herself and growling in heat.

Take her, turn her hard and throw her on the bed.

I did. Her ass was tight, hot, and glimmering on the bed. Her smell was even stronger. She rose up on all fours, the perfect globes of her ass parting, showing me herself, offering herself to me.

Hit her.

I held the crop and did not move, trapped between his bellowing voice and my own arm. I only do what he says I have to do. He does not have control. I will break the connection, pull myself in, zip myself up and leave.

I will.

Coward. You are afraid. Gott, you feel it, but you are scared. She wants this, she needs this as much as I need this. She wants the crop, idiot. She wants to feel your force, your power. That is why she is here, why I am here. Do it now, fool, or I will break and report you: we do this because we want to do this. I take nothing that is not offered.

Look at her, she wants it more than your body. Hit her, damn you, hit her and give us what we both want!

Anger was a vibrating wire in my guts, around my spine. The crop was light in my hand – but I knew he felt it more than I did, my senses rerouted to my fare.

Hit her now! His anger was an echoing copper taste in my mouth. He must have complained, VRslanged with one hand to transmit his dissatisfaction to Dispatch because FIRST WARNING scrolled by. Hacks were allowed only two.

Anger. At him, her, or me I didn't know then; don't even know now. I hit her, clumsy and inaccurate.

Good – but aim better, hit her light at first, get her used to your hand, the toy. Tap her. Aim for the sugar spot, there – between her tailbone and the top of her thigh, parallel with her cunt. There. Hit her there.

I did, my hand light at first but with growing frustration and anger (him, her, me, him, her, me) – soon my hand and the crop were a vibrant blur, its plastic tip slapping on her rich black ass. She quivered and shook, moaned and jumped. She made noises no lover before or since has made for me, or any of my fares.

She leaned back to get closer to each blow, then jumped forward at the crack of it. Flexing, knotting her magnificent black ass, she echoed the impact with the clenching of her muscles: her thighs, her cunt.

Good, good! Now you understand. Feed her the crop, use it to make her moan and beg, cry and scream! Use it: make it hard and fast and mean! Yes!

His cock was hard, a ghostly ache that I couldn't touch – somewhere – distantly, shamefully, I knew my own cunt was steaming, aching to be touched, licked, satisfied.

The crop went from a blur to a humming *whack*! as I used it – faster and harder, harder and faster – more and more. She wasn't just moaning, towards the end; she was crying and screaming with each sharp impact.

Then: *Fuck her*.

I didn't have a real one, and his was wherever he was, but I knew, and he knew exactly what he meant: I climbed up on the bed and sank my right hand into her – feeling the burning heat of her ass, of the furnace of her cunt with first one, then two, then three, then four fingers. It was only an aftermath, though, and he came as she came – from something our quick fist couldn't touch: the whip.

Then he was gone, pulled out and away. AVAILABLE flashed across my vision.

She was quivering, shaking from the crop and, maybe, from my hand – just a little. Sadness dropped over me and I felt like crying. Her ass was burning, so hot from the beating we – no, *I* – had given her. She didn't seem able to relax. Even as I wiped my hand of her wetness, carefully pulled the bedclothes up and over her, and put a pillow under her loose-rolling head, she jumped and quivered still from the crop.

I tucked her in and kissed her forehead. Her face seemed to be on fire and her breath was quick and hot. I wanted to cry, the tears heavy in my eyes, making the room seem submerged.

I went to leave then, but she called from the bed, a small voice. I went over to her, knelt down and said, "Sorry?"

Then she said, then she said, then she said, "Call me. Please. Call me."

I smiled, and patted her head, almost, almost saying I would, but then I knew, totally, then and there, that she didn't mean me, didn't mean Moss.

She meant *him*.

THE END OF THE RELATIONSHIP

Will Self

"WHY THE HELL don't you leave him if he's such a monster?" said Grace. We were sitting in the Café Delancey in Camden Town, eating *croques m'sieurs* and slurping down *cappuccino*. I was dabbing the sore skin under my eyes with a scratchy piece of toilet paper – trying to stop the persistent leaking. When I'd finished dabbing I deposited the wad of salty stuff in my bag, took another slurp and looked across at Grace.

"I don't know," I said. "I don't know why I don't leave him."

"You can't go back there – not after this morning. I don't know why you didn't leave him immediately after it happened . . ."

That morning I'd woken to find him already up. He was standing at the window, naked. One hand held the struts of the venetian blind apart, while he squinted down on to the Pentonville Road. Lying in bed, I could feel the judder and hear the squeal of the traffic as it built up to the rush hour.

In the half-light of dawn his body seemed monolithic: his limbs columnar and white, his head and shoulders solid capitals. I stirred in the bed and he sensed that I was awake. He came back to the side of the bed and stood looking down at me. "You're like a little animal in there. A little rabbit, snuggled down in its burrow."

I squirmed down further into the duvet and looked up at him, puckering my lip so that I had goofy, rabbity teeth. He got back into bed and curled himself around me. He tucked his legs under mine. He lay on his side – I on my back. The front of his thighs pressed against my haunch and buttock. I felt his penis stiffen against me as his fingers made slight, brushing passes over my breasts, up to my throat and face and then slowly down. His mouth nuzzled against my neck, his tongue licked my flesh, his fingers poised over my nipples, twirling them into erection. My body teetered, a heavy rock on the edge of a precipice.

The rasp of his cheek against mine; the too peremptory prodding of his cock against my mons; the sense of something casual and offhand about the way he was caressing me. Whatever – it was all wrong. There was no true feeling in the way he was touching me; he was manipulating me like some giant dolly. I tensed up – which he sensed; he persisted for a short while, for two more rotations of palm on breast, and then he rolled over on his back with a heavy sigh.

"I'm sorry – "

"It's OK."

"It's just that sometimes I feel that – "

"It's OK, really, please don't."

"Don't what?"

"Don't talk about it."

"But if we don't talk about it we're never going to deal with it. We're never going to sort it all out."

"Look, I've got feelings too. Right now I feel like shit. If you don't want to, don't start. That's what I can't stand, starting and then stopping — it makes me sick to the stomach."

"Well, if that's what you want." I reached down to touch his penis; the chill from his voice hadn't reached it yet. I gripped it as tightly as I could and began to pull up and down, feeling the skin un- and re-peel over the shaft. Suddenly he recoiled.

"Not like that, ferchrissakes!" He slapped my hand away. "Anyway, I don't want that. I don't want . . . I don't want . . . I don't want some bloody hand relief!"

I could feel the tears pricking at my eyes. "I thought you said — "

"What does it matter what I said? What does it matter what I do . . . I can't convince you, now can I?"

"I want to, I really do. It's just that I don't feel I can trust you any more . . . not at the moment. You have to give me more time."

"Trust! Trust! I'm not a fucking building society, you know. You're not setting an account up with me. Oh fuck it! Fuck the whole fucking thing!"

He rolled away from me and pivoted himself upright. Pulling a pair of trousers from the chair where he'd chucked them the night before, he dragged his legs into them. I dug deeper into the bed and looked out at him through eyes fringed by hair and tears.

"Coffee?" His voice was icily polite.

"Yes, please." He left the room. I could hear him moving around downstairs. Pained love made me picture his actions: unscrewing the percolator, sluicing it out with cold water, tamping the coffee grains down in the metal basket, screwing it back together again and setting it on the lighted stove.

When he reappeared ten minutes later, with two cups of coffee, I was still dug into the bed. He sat down sideways and waited while I struggled upwards and crammed a pillow behind my head. I pulled a limp corner of the duvet cover over my breasts. I took the cup from him and sipped. He'd gone to the trouble of heating milk for my coffee. He always took his black.

"I'm going out now. I've got to get down to Kensington and see Steve about those castings." He'd mooched a cigarette from somewhere and the smoking of it, and the cocking of his elbow, went with his tone: officer speaking to other ranks. I hated him for it.

But hated myself more for asking, "When will you be back?"

"Later . . . not for quite a while." The studied ambiguity was another put-down. "What're you doing today?"

"N-nothing . . . meeting Grace, I s'pose."

"Well, that's good; the two of you can have a really trusting talk – that's obviously what you need." His chocolate drop of sarcasm was thinly candy-coated with sincerity.

"Maybe it is . . . look . . ."

"Don't say anything, don't get started again. We've talked and talked about this. There's nothing I can do, is there? There's no way I can convince you – and I think I'm about ready to give up trying."

"You shouldn't have done it."

"Don't you think I know that? Don't you think I fucking know that?! Look, do you think I enjoyed it? Do you think that? 'Cause if you do, you are fucking mad. More mad than I thought you were."

"You can't love me . . ." A wail was starting up in me; the saucer chattered against the base of my cup. "You can't, whatever you say."

"I don't know about that. All I do know is that this is torturing me. I hate myself – that's true enough. Look at this. Look at how much I hate myself!"

He set his coffee cup down on the varnished floorboards and began to give himself enormous open-handed clouts around the head. "You think I love myself? Look at this!"

(clout) "All you think about is your own fucking self, your own fucking feelings." (clout) "Don't come back here tonight!" (clout) "Just don't come back, because I don't think I can take much more."

As he was saying the last of this he was pirouetting around the room, scooping up small change and keys from the table, pulling on his shirt and shoes. It wasn't until he got to the door that I became convinced that he actually was going to walk out on me. Sometimes these scenes could run to several entrances and exits. I leapt from the bed, snatched up a towel, and caught him at the head of the stairs.

"Don't walk out on me! Don't walk out, don't do that, not that." I was hiccupping; mucus and tears were mixing on my lips and chin. He twisted away from me and clattered down a few stairs, then he paused and, turning, said, "You talk to me about trust, but I think the reality of it is that you don't really care about me at all, or else none of this would have happened in the first place." He was doing his best to sound furious, but I could tell that the real anger was dying down. I sniffed up my tears and snot and descended towards him.

"Don't run off, I do care. Come back to bed – it's still early." I touched his forearm with my hand. He looked so anguished, his face all twisted and reddened with anger and pain.

"Oh, fuck it. Fuck it. Just fuck it." He swore flatly. The flap of towel that I was holding against my breast fell away, and I pushed the nipple, which dumbly re-erected itself, against his hand. He didn't seem to notice, and instead stared fixedly over my shoulder, up the stairs and into the bedroom. I pushed against him a little more firmly. Then he took my nipple between the knuckles of his index and forefinger and pinched it, quite hard, muttering, "Fuck it, just fucking fuck it."

He turned on his heels and left. I doubled over on the

stairs. The sobs that racked me had a sickening component. I staggered to the bathroom and as I clutched the toilet bowl the mixture of coffee and mucus streamed from my mouth and nose. Then I heard the front door slam.

"I don't know why."

"Then leave. You can stay at your own place – "

"You know I hate it there. I can't stand the people I have to share with – "

"Be that as it may, the point is that you don't need him; you just think you do. It's like you're caught in some trap. You think you love him, but it's just your insecurity talking. Remember," and here Grace's voice took on an extra depth, a special sonority of caring, "your insecurity is like a clever actor, it can mimic any emotion it chooses to and still be utterly convincing. But whether it pretends to be love or hate, the truth is that at bottom it's just the fear of being alone."

"Well, why should I be alone? You're not alone, are you?"

"No, that's true, but it's not easy for me either. Any relationship is an enormous sacrifice . . . I don't know . . . Anyway, you know that I was alone for two years before I met John; perhaps you should give it a try?"

"I spend most of my time alone, anyway. I'm perfectly capable of being by myself. But I also need to see him . . ."

As my voice died away I became conscious of the voice of another woman two tables away. I couldn't hear what she was saying to her set-faced male companion, but the tone was the same as my own, the exact same plangent composite of need and recrimination. I stared at them. Their faces said it all: his awful detachment, her hideous yearning. And as I looked around the café at couple after couple, each confronting one another over the marble table tops, I had the beginnings of an intimation.

Perhaps all this awful mismatching, this emotional grating, these Mexican stand-offs of trust and commitment, were somehow in the air. It wasn't down to individuals: me and him, Grace and John, those two over there . . . It was a contagion that was getting to all of us; a germ of insecurity that had lodged in all our breasts and was now fissioning frantically, creating a domino effect as relationship after relationship collapsed in a rubble of mistrust and acrimony.

After he had left that morning I went back to his bed and lay there, gagged and bound by the smell of him in the duvet. I didn't get up until eleven. I listened to Radio Four, imagining that the deep-timbred, wholesome voices of each successive presenter were those of ideal parents. There was a discussion programme, a gardening panel discussion, a discussion about books, a short story about an elderly woman and her relationship with her son, followed by a discussion about it. It all sounded so cultured, so eminently reasonable. I tried to construct a new view of myself on the basis of being the kind of young woman who would consume such hearty radiophonic fare, but it didn't work. Instead I felt quite weightless and blown out, a husk of a person.

The light quality in the attic bedroom didn't change all morning. The only way I could measure the passage of time was by the radio, and the position of the watery shadows that his metal sculptures made on the magnolia paint.

Eventually I managed to rouse myself. I dressed and washed my face. I pulled my hair back tightly and fixed it in place with a loop of elastic. I sat down at his work table. It was blanketed with loose sheets of paper, all of which were covered with the meticulous plans he did for his sculptures. Elevations and perspectives, all neatly shaded and the dimensions written in using the lightest of pencils. There was a mess of other stuff on the table as well: sticks of flux, a broken soldering iron, bits of acrylic and angled steel brackets. I cleared a space amidst the evidence of his

industry and, taking out my notebook and biro, added
my own patch of emotion to the collage:

> I do understand how you feel. I know the pressure that you're
> under at the moment, but you must realize that it's pressure
> that *you* put on *yourself*. It's not me that's doing it to you. I do
> love you and I want to be with you, but it takes time to forgive.
> And what you did to me was almost unforgivable. I've been
> hurt before and I don't want to be hurt again. If you can't
> understand that, if you can't understand how I feel about it,
> then it's probably best if we don't see one another again. I'll be
> at the flat this evening; perhaps you'll call?

Out in the street the sky was spitting at the pavement.
There was no wind to speak of, but despite that each gob
seemed to have an added impetus. With every corner that I
rounded on my way to King's Cross I encountered another
little cyclone of rain and grit. I walked past shops full of
mouldering stock that were boarded up, and empty, derelict
ones that were still open.

On the corner of the Caledonian Road I almost collided
with a dosser wearing a long, dirty overcoat. He was
clutching a bottle of VP in a hand that was blue with
impacted filth, filth that seemed to have been worked
deliberately into the open sores on his knuckles. He turned
his face to me and I recoiled instinctively. It was the face of
a myxomatosic rabbit ("You're like a little animal in there.
A little rabbit, snuggled down in its burrow"), the eyes
swollen up and exploding in a series of burst ramparts and
lesions of diseased flesh. His nose was no longer nose-
shaped.

But on the tube the people were comforting and worka-
day enough. I paid at the barrier when I reached Camden
Town and walked off quickly down the High Street.
Perhaps it was the encounter with the dying drunk that
had cleansed me, jerked me out of my self-pity, because for
a short while I felt more lucid, better able to look honestly at

my relationship. While it was true that he did have problems, emotional problems, and was prepared to admit to them, it was still the case that nothing could forgive his conduct while I was away visiting my parents.

I knew that the woman he had slept with lived here in Camden Town. As I walked down the High Street I began – at first almost unconsciously, then with growing intensity – to examine the faces of any youngish women that passed me. They came in all shapes and sizes, these suspect lovers. There were tall women in floor-length linen coats; plump women in stretchy slacks; petite women in neat two-piece suits; raddled women in unravelling pullovers; and painfully smart women, Sindy dolls: press a pleasure-button in the small of their backs and their hair would grow.

The trouble was that they all looked perfectly plausible candidates for the job as the metal worker's anvil. Outside Woolworth's I was gripped by a sharp attack of nausea. An old swallow of milky coffee re-entered my mouth as I thought of him, on top of this woman, on top of that woman, hammering himself into them, bash after bash after bash, flattening their bodies, making them ductile with pleasure.

I went into Marks & Sparks to buy some clean underwear and paused to look at myself in a full-length mirror. My skirt was bunched up around my hips, my hair was lank and flecked with dandruff, my tights bagged at the knees, my sleeve-ends bulged with snot-clogged Kleenex. I looked like shit. It was no wonder that he didn't fancy me any more, that he'd gone looking for some retouched vision.

"Come on," said Grace, "let's go. The longer we stay here, the more weight we put on." On our way out of the café I took a mint from the cut-glass bowl by the cash register and recklessly crunched it between my molars. The sweet pain of sugar-in-cavity spread through my mouth as I fumbled in my bag for my purse. "Well, what are you going to do now?" It was only three-thirty in the afternoon but already the sky over London was turning the shocking bilious colour it only ever aspires to when winter is fast encroaching.

"Can I come back with you, Grace?"

"Of course you can, silly; why do you think I asked the question?" She put her arm about my shoulder and twirled me round until we were facing in the direction of the tube. Then she marched me off, like the young emotional offender that I was. Feeling her warm body against mine I almost choked, about to cry again at this display of caring from Grace. But I needed her too much, so I restrained myself.

"You come back with me, love," she clucked. "We can watch telly, or eat, or you can do some work. I've got some pattern cutting I've got to finish by tomorrow. John won't be back for ages yet . . . or I tell you what, if you like, we can go and meet him in Soho after he's finished work and have something to eat there – would you like that?" She turned to me, flicking back the ledge of her thick blonde fringe with her index finger – a characteristic gesture.

"Well, yes," I murmured, "whatever."

"OK." Her eyes, turned towards mine, were blue, frank. "I can see you want to take it easy."

When we left the tube at Chalk Farm and started up the hill towards where Grace lived, she started up again, wittering on about her and John and me; about what we might do and what fun it would be to have me stay for a couple of nights; and about what a pity it was that I couldn't live with them for a while, because what I really needed was a good sense of security. There was something edgy and brittle about her enthusiasm. I began to feel that she was overstating her case.

I stopped listening to the words she was saying and began to hear them merely as sounds, as some ambient tape of reassurance. Her arm was linked in mine, but from this slight contact I could gain a whole sense of her small body. The precise slope and jut of her full breasts, the soft brush of her round stomach against the drape of her dress, the infinitesimal gratings of knee against nylon, against nylon against knee.

And as I built up this sense of Grace-as-body, I began also to consider how her bush would look as you went down on her. Would the lips gape wetly, or would they tidily recede? Would the cellulite on her hips crinkle as she parted her legs? How would she smell to you, of sex or cinnamon? But, of course, it wasn't any impersonal "you" I was thinking of – it was a highly personal *him*. I joined their bodies together in my mind and tormented myself with the hideous tableau of betrayal. After all, if he was prepared to screw some nameless bitch, what would have prevented him from shitting where I ate? I shuddered. Grace sensed this, and disengaging her arm from mine returned it to my shoulders, which she gave a squeeze.

John and Grace lived in a thirties council block halfway up Haverstock Hill. Their flat was just like all the others. You stepped through the front door and directly into a long corridor, off which were a number of small rooms. They may have been small, but Grace had done everything possible to make them seem spacious. Furniture and pictures were kept to an artful minimum, and the wooden blocks on the floor had been sanded and polished until they shone.

Grace snapped on floor lamps and put a Mozart concerto on the CD. I tried to write my neglected journal, timing my flourishes of supposed insight to the ascending and descending scales. Grace set up the ironing board and began to do something complicated, involving sheets of paper, pins, and round, worn fragments of chalk.

When the music finished, neither of us made any move to put something else on, or to draw the curtains. Instead we sat in the off-white noise of the speakers, under the opaque

stare of the dark windows. To me there was something
intensely evocative about the scene: two young women
sitting in a pool of yellow light on a winter's afternoon.
Images of my childhood came to me; for the first time in
days I felt secure.

When John got back from work, Grace put food-in-a-
foil-tray in the oven, and tossed some varieties of leaves.
John plonked himself down on one of the low chairs in the
sitting room and propped the *Standard* on his knees.
Occasionally he would give a snide laugh and read out
an item, his intent being always to emphasize the utter
consistency of its editorial stupidity.

We ate with our plates balanced on our knees, and when
we had finished, turned on the television to watch a play. I
noticed that John didn't move over to the sofa to sit with
Grace. Instead, he remained slumped in his chair. As the
drama unfolded I began to find these seating positions quite
wrong and disquieting. John really should have sat with
Grace.

The play was about a family riven by domestic violence.
It was well acted and the jerky camerawork made it grittily
real, almost like documentary. But still I felt that the basic
premise was overstated. It wasn't that I didn't believe a
family with such horrors boiling within it could maintain a
closed face to the outside world; it was just that these
horrors were so relentless.

The husband beat up the wife, beat up the kids, got
drunk, sexually abused the kids, raped the wife, assaulted
social workers, assaulted police, assaulted probation officers, and all within the space of a week or so. It should have
been laughable – this chronically dysfunctional family – but
it wasn't. How could it be remotely entertaining while we
all sat in our separate padded places? Each fresh on-screen
outrage increased the distance between the three of us,
pushing us still further apart. I hunched down in my chair
and felt the waistband of my skirt burn across my bloated

stomach. I shouldn't have eaten all that salad – and the underdone garlic bread smelt flat and sour on my own tongue. So flat and sour that the idea even of kissing myself was repulsive, let alone allowing him to taste me.

The on-screen husband, his shirt open, the knot of his tie dragged halfway down his chest, was beating his adolescent daughter with short, powerful clouts around the head. They were standing in her bedroom doorway, and the camera stared fixedly over her shoulder, up the stairs and into the bedroom, where it picked up the corner of a pop poster, pinned to the flowered wallpaper. Each clout was audible as a loud "crack!" in the room where we sat. I felt so remote, from Grace, from John, from the play . . . from him.

I stood up and walked unsteadily to the toilet at the end of the corridor. Inside I slid the flimsy bolt into its loop and pushed the loosely stacked pile of magazines away from the toilet bowl. My stomach felt as if it were swelling by the second. My fingers when I put them in my mouth were large and alien. My nails scraped against the sides of my throat. As I leant forward I was aware of myself as a vessel, my curdled contents ready to pour. I looked down into the toilet world and there – as my oatmeal stream splashed down – saw that someone had already done the same. Cut out the nutritional middlewoman, that is.

After I'd finished I wiped around the rim of the toilet with hard scraps of paper. I flushed and then splashed my cheeks with cold water. Walking back down the corridor towards the sitting room, I was conscious only of the ultrasonic whine of the television; until, that is, I reached the door:

"Don't bother." (A sob.)

"*Mr Evans . . . are you in there?*"

"You don't want me to touch you?"

"*Go away. Just go away . . .*"

"It's just that I feel a bit wound up. I get all stressed out during the day – you know that. I need a long time to wind down."

"*Mr Evans, we have a court order that empowers us to take these children away.*"

"It's not that – I know it's not just that. You don't fancy me any more; you don't want to have sex any more. You've been like this for weeks."

"*I don't care if you've got the bloody Home Secretary out there. If you come in that door, I swear she gets it!*"

"How do you expect me to feel like sex? Everything around here is so bloody claustrophobic. I can't stand these little fireside evenings. You sit there all hunched up and fidgety. You bite your nails and smoke away with little puffs. Puff, puff, puff. It's a total turn-off."

(Smash!) "Oh, my God. For Christ's sake! Oh Jesus . . ."

"I bite my nails and smoke because I don't feel loved, because I feel all alone. I can't trust you, John, not when you're like this – you don't seem to have any feeling for me."

"Yeah, maybe you're right. Maybe I don't. I'm certainly fed up with all of this shit . . ."

I left my bag in the room. I could come back for it tomorrow when John had gone to work. I couldn't stand to listen – and I didn't want to go back into the room and sit down with them again, crouch with them, like another vulture in the mouldering carcass of their relationship. I couldn't bear to see them reassemble the uncommunicative blocks of that static silence. And I didn't want to sleep in the narrow spare bed, under the child-sized duvet.

I wanted to be back with him. Wanted it the way a junky wants a hit. I yearned to be in that tippy, creaky boat of a bed, full of crumbs and sex and fag ash. I wanted to be framed by the basketry of angular shadows the naked bulb threw on the walls, and contained by the soft basketry of his limbs. At least we felt something for each other. He got right inside me – he really did. All my other relationships were as superficial as a salutation – this evening proved it. It was only with him that I became a real person.

Outside in the street the proportions were all wrong. The block of flats should have been taller than it was long – but it wasn't. Damp leaves blew against, and clung to my ankles. I'd been sitting in front of the gas fire in the flat and my right-hand side had become numb with the heat. Now this wore off – like a pain – leaving my clammy clothes sticking to my clammy flesh.

I walked for a couple of hundred yards down the hill, then a stitch stabbed into me and I felt little pockets of gas beading my stomach. I was level with a tiny parade of shops which included a cab company. Suddenly I couldn't face the walk to the tube, the tube itself, the walk back from the tube to his house. If I was going to go back to him I had to be there right away. If I went by tube it would take too long and this marvellous reconciliatory feeling might have soured by the time I arrived. And more to the point there might not be a relationship there for me to go back to. He was a feckless and promiscuous man, insecure and given to the grossest and most evil abuses of trust.

The jealous agony came over me again, covering my flesh like some awful hive. I leant up against a shopfront. The sick image of him entering some other. I could feel it so vividly that it was as if I was him: my penis snagging frustratingly against something . . . my blood beating in my temples . . . my sweat dripping on to her upturned face . . . and then the release of entry . . .

I pushed open the door of the minicab office and lurched in. Two squat men stood like bookends on either side of the counter. They were both reading the racing form. The man nearest to me was encased in a tube of caramel leather. He twisted his neckless head as far round as he could. Was it my imagination, or did his eyes probe and pluck at me, run up my thighs and attempt an imaginative penetration, rapid, rigid and metallic. The creak of his leather and the cold fug of damp, dead filter tips, assaulted me together.

"D'jew want a cab, love?" The other bookend, the one behind the counter, looked at me with dim-sum eyes, morsels of pupil packaged in fat.

"Err . . . yes, I want to go up to Islington, Barnsbury."

"George'll take yer – woncha, George?" George was still eyeing me around the midriff. I noticed – quite inconsequentially – that he was wearing very clean, blue trousers, with razor-sharp creases. Also that he had no buttocks – the legs of the trousers zoomed straight up into his jacket.

"Yerallright. C'mon, love." George rattled shut his paper and scooped a packet of Dunhill International and a big bunch of keys off the counter. He opened the door for me and as I passed through I could sense his fat black heart, encased in leather, beating behind me.

He was at the back door of the car before me and ushered me inside. I squidged halfway across the seat before collapsing in a nerveless torpor. But I knew that I wouldn't make it back to him unless I held myself in a state of no expectancy, no hope. If I dared to picture the two of us together again, then when I arrived at the house he would be out. Out fucking.

We woozed away from the kerb and jounced around the corner. An air freshener shaped like a fir tree dingled and dangled as we took the bends down to Chalk Farm Road. The car was, I noticed, scrupulously clean and poisonous with smoke. George lit another Dunhill and offered me one, which I accepted. In the moulded divider between the two front seats there sat a tin of travel sweets. I could hear them schussing round on their caster-sugar slope as we cornered and cornered and cornered again.

I sucked on the fag and thought determinedly of other things: figure skating; Christmas sales; the way small children have their mittens threaded through the arms of their winter coats on lengths of elastic; Grace . . . which was a mistake, because this train of thought was bad magic.

Grace's relationship with John was clearly at an end. It was perverse to realize this, particularly after her display in the café, when she was so secure and self-possessed in the face of my tears and distress. But I could imagine the truth: that the huge crevices in their understanding of each other had been only temporarily papered over by the thrill of having someone in the flat who was in more emotional distress than they. No, there was no doubt about it now, Grace belonged to the league of the self-deceived.

George had put on a tape. The Crusaders – or at any rate some kind of jazz funk, music for glove compartments. I looked at the tightly bunched flesh at the back of his neck. It was malevolent flesh. I was alone in the world really. People tried to understand me, but they completely missed the mark. It was as if they were always looking at me from entirely the wrong angle and mistaking a knee for a bald pate, or an elbow for a breast.

And then I knew that I'd been a fool to get into the cab, the rapistmobile. I looked at George's hands, where they had pounced on the steering wheel. They were flexing more than they should have been, flexing in anticipation. When he looked at me in the office he had taken me for jailbait, thought I was younger than I am. He just looked at my skirt – not at my sweater; and anyway, my sweater hides my breasts, which are small. He could do it, right enough, because he knew exactly where to go and the other man, the man in the office, would laughingly concoct an alibi for him. And who would believe me anyway? He'd be careful not to leave anything inside me . . . and no marks.

We were driving down a long street with warehouses on either side. I didn't recognize it. The distances between the street lamps were increasing. The car thwacked over some shallow depressions in the road, depressions that offered no resistance. I felt everything sliding towards the inevitable. He used to cuddle me and call me "little animal", "little rabbit". It should happen again, not end like this, in terror, in violation.

Then the sequence of events went awry. I subsided sideways, sobbing, choking. The seat was wide enough for me to curl up on it, which is what I did. The car slid to a halt. "Whassermatter, love?" Oh Jesus, I thought, don't let him touch me, please don't let him touch me, he can't be human. But I knew that he was. "C'mon, love, whassermatter?" My back in its suede jacket was like a carapace. When he penetrated me I'd rather he did it from behind, anything not to have him touch and pry at the soft parts of my front.

The car pulls away once more. Perhaps this place isn't right for his purposes, he needs somewhere more remote. I'm already under the earth, under the soft earth . . . The wet earth will cling to my putrid face when the police find me . . . when they put up loops of yellow tape around my uncovered grave . . . and the WPC used to play me when they reconstruct the crime will look nothing like me . . . She'll have coarser features, but bigger breasts and hips . . . something not lost on the grieving boyfriend . . . Later he'll take her back to the flat, and fuck her standing up, pushing her ample, smooth bum into the third shelf of books in his main room (some Penguin classics, a couple of old economics text books, my copy of *The House of Mirth*), with each turgid stroke . . .

I hear the door catch through these layers of soft earth. I lunge up, painfully slow, he has me . . . and come face to face with a woman. A handsome woman, heavily built, in her late thirties. I relapse back into the car and regard her at crotch level. It's clear immediately – from the creases in her jeans – that she's George's wife.

"C'mon, love, whassermatter?" I crawl from the car and stagger against her, still choking. I can't speak, but gesture vaguely towards George, who's kicking the front wheel of the car, with a steady "chok-chok-chok". "What'd'e do then? Eh? Did he frighten you or something? You're a bloody fool, George!" She slaps him, a roundhouse slap – her arm, travelling ninety degrees level with her shoulder. George still stands, even glummer now, rubbing his cheek.

In terrorist-siege-survivor-mode (me clutching her round the waist with wasted arms) we turn and head across the parking area to the exterior staircase of a block of flats exactly the same as the one I recently left. Behind us comes a Dunhill International, and behind that comes George. On the third floor we pass a woman fumbling for her key in her handbag – she's small enough to eyeball the lock. My saviour pushes open the door of the next flat along and pulls me in. Still holding me by the shoulder, she escorts me along the corridor and into an overheated room.

"Park yerself there, love." She turns, exposing the high, prominent hips of a steer, and disappears into another room, from where I hear the clang of aluminium kettle on iron prong. I'm left behind on a great scoop of upholstery – an armchair wide enough for three of me – facing a similarly outsize television screen. The armchair still has on the thick plastic dress of its first commercial communion.

George comes in, dangling his keys, and without looking at me crosses the room purposively. He picks up a doll in Dutch national costume and begins to fiddle under its skirt. "Git out of there!" This from the kitchen. He puts the doll down and exits without looking at me.

"C'mon, love, stick that in your laugh hole." She sets the tea cup and saucer down on a side table. She sits alongside me in a similar elephantine armchair. We might be a couple testing out a new suite in some furniture warehouse. She settles herself, yanking hard at the exposed pink webbing of her bra, where it cuts into her. "It's not the first time this has happened, you know," she slurps. "Not that George would do anything, mind, leastways not in his cab. But he does have this way of . . . well, frightening people, I s'pose.

He sits there twirling his bloody wheel, not saying anything and somehow girls like you get terrified. Are you feeling better now?"

"Yes, thanks, really, it wasn't his fault. I've been rather upset all day. I had a row with my boyfriend this morning and I had been going to stay at a friend's, but suddenly I wanted to get home. And I was in the car when it all sort of came down on top of me . . ."

"Where do you live, love?"

"I've got a room in a flat in Kensal Rise, but my boyfriend lives in Barnsbury."

"That's just around the corner from here. When you've 'ad your tea I'll walk you back."

"But what about George – I haven't even paid him."

"Don't worry about that. He's gone off now, anyway he could see that you aren't exactly loaded . . . He thinks a lot about money, does George. Wants us to have our own place an' that. It's an obsession with him. And he has to get back on call as quickly as he can or he'll miss a job, and if he misses a job he's in for a bad night. And if he has a bad night, then it's me that's on the receiving end the next day. Not that I hardly ever see him, mind. He works two shifts at the moment. Gets in at three-thirty in the afternoon, has a kip, and goes back out again at eight. On his day off he sleeps. He never sees the kids, doesn't seem to care about 'em . . ."

She trails off. In the next room I hear the high aspiration of a child turning in its sleep.

"D'jew think 'e's got some bint somewhere? D'jew think that's what these double shifts are really about?"

"Really, I don't know – "

"'E's a dark one. Now, I am a bit too fat to frolic, but I make sure he gets milked every so often. YerknowhatImean? Men are like bulls really, aren't they? They need to have some of that spunk taken out of them. But I dunno . . . Perhaps it's not enough. He's out and about, seeing all these skinny little bints, picking them up . . . I dunno, what's the use?" She lights a cigarette and deposits the match in a free-standing ashtray. Then she starts yanking at the webbing again, where it encases her beneath her pullover. "I'd swear there are bloody fleas in this flat. I keep powdering the mutt, but it doesn't make no difference, does it, yer great ball of dough."

She pushes a slippered foot against the heaving stomach of a mouldering Alsatian. I haven't even noticed the dog before now – its fur merges so seamlessly with the shaggy carpet. "They say dog fleas can't live on a human, yer know, but these ones are making a real effort. P'raps they aren't fleas at all . . . P'raps that bastard has given me a dose of the crabs. Got them off some fucking brass, I expect, whad'jew think?"

"I've no idea, really – "

"I know it's the crabs. I've even seen one of the fuckers crawling up me pubes. Oh gawd, dunnit make you sick. I'm going to leave the bastard – I am. I'll go to Berkhamsted to my Mum's. I'll go tonight. I'll wake the kids and go tonight . . ."

I need to reach out to her, I suppose, I need to make some sort of contact. After all she has helped me – so really I ought to reciprocate. But I'm all inhibited. There's no point in offering help to anyone if you don't follow through. There's no point in implying to anyone the possibility of some fount of unconditional love if you aren't prepared to follow through . . . To do so would be worse than to do nothing. And anyway . . . I'm on my way back to sort out *my* relationship. That has to take priority.

These justifications are running through my mind, each one accompanied by a counter argument, like a sub-title at the opera, or a stock market quotation running along the base of a television screen. Again there's the soft aspiration from the next room, this time matched, shudderingly, by the vast shelf of tit alongside me. She subsides. Twisted face, foundation cracking, folded into cracking hands. For some reason I think of Atrixo.

She didn't hear me set down my cup and saucer. She didn't hear my footfalls. She didn't hear the door. She just sobbed. And now I'm clear, I'm in the street and I'm walking with confident strides towards his flat. Nothing can touch me now. I've survived the cab ride with George — that's good karma, good magic. It means that I'll make it back to him and his heartfelt, contrite embrace.

Sometimes — I remember as a child remembers Christmas — we used to drink a bottle of champagne together. Drink half the bottle and then make love, then drink the other half and make love again. It was one of the rituals I remember from the beginning of our relationship, from the springtime of our love. And as I pace on up the hill, more recollections hustle alongside. Funny how when a relationship is starting up you always praise the qualities of your lover to any third party there is to hand, saying, "Oh yes, he's absolutely brilliant at X, Y and Z . . ." and sad how that tendency dies so quickly. Dies at about the same time that disrobing in front of one another ceases to be embarrassing . . . and perhaps for that reason ceases to be quite so sexy.

Surely it doesn't have to be this way? Stretching up the hill ahead of me, I begin to see all my future relationships, bearing me on and up like some escalator of the fleshly. Each step is a man, a man who will penetrate me with his penis and his language, a man who will make a little private place with me, secure from the world, for a month, or a week, or a couple of years.

How much more lonely and driven is the serial monogamist than the serial killer? I won't be the same person when I come to lie with that man there, the one with the ginger fuzz on his white stomach; or that one further up there — almost level with the junction of Barnsbury Road — the one with the round head and skull cap of thick, black hair. I'll be his "little rabbit", or his "baby-doll", or his "sex goddess", but I won't be me. I can only be me . . . with him.

Maybe it isn't too late? Maybe we can recapture some of what we once had.

I'm passing an off-licence. It's on the point of closing – I can see a man in a cardigan doing something with some crates towards the back of the shop. I'll get some champagne. I'll turn up at his flat with the bottle of champagne, and we'll do it like we did it before.

I push open the door and venture inside. The atmosphere of the place is acridly reminiscent of George's minicab office. I cast an eye along the shelves – they are pitifully stocked, just a few cans of lager and some bottles of cheap wine. There's a cooler in the corner, but all I can see behind the misted glass are a couple of isolated bottles of Asti spumante. It doesn't look like they'll have any champagne in this place. It doesn't look like my magic is going to hold up. I feel the tears welling up in me again, welling up as the offie proprietor treads wearily back along the lino.

"Yes, can I help you?"

"I . . . oh, well, I . . . oh, really . . . it doesn't matter . . ."

"Ay-up, love, are you all right?"

He's a kindly, round ball of a little man, with an implausibly straight toothbrush moustache. Impossible to imagine him as a threat. I'm crying as much with relief – that the offie proprietor is not some cro-magnon – as I am from knowing that I can't get the champagne now, and that things will be over between me and him.

The offie proprietor has pulled a handkerchief out of his cardigan pocket, but it's obviously not suitable, so he shoves it back in and, picking up a handi-pack of tissues from the rack on the counter, he tears it open and hands one to me, saying, "Now there you go, love, give your nose a good blow like, and you'll feel better."

"Thanks." I mop myself up for what seems like the nth

time today. Who would have thought the old girl had so much salt in her?

"Now, how can I help you?"

"Oh, well . . . I don't suppose you have a bottle of champagne?" It sounds stupid, saying that rich word in this zone of poor business opportunity.

"Champagne? I don't get much of a call for that round here." His voice is still kindly, he isn't offended. "My customers tend to prefer their wine fortified – if you know what I mean. Still, I remember I did have a bottle out in the store room a while back. I'll go and see if it's still there."

He turns and heads off down the lino again. I stand and look out at the dark street and the swishing cars and the shuddering lorries. He's gone for quite a while. He must trust me – I think to myself. He's left me here in the shop with the till and all the booze on the shelves. How ironic that I should find trust here, in this slightest of contexts, and find so little of it in my intimate relationships.

Then I hear footsteps coming from up above, and I am conscious of earnest voices.

"Haven't you shut up the shop yet?"

"I'm just doing it, my love. There's a young woman down there wanting a bottle of champagne; I just came up to get it."

"Champagne! Pshaw! What the bloody hell does she want it for at this time of night?"

"I dunno. Probably to drink with her boyfriend."

"Well, you take her bottle of champagne down to her and then get yourself back up here. I'm not finished talking to you yet."

"Yes, my love."

When he comes back in I do my best to look as if I haven't overheard anything. He puts the bi-focals that hang from the cord round his neck on to his nose and scrutinizes the label on the bottle: "Chambertin demi-sec. Looks all right to me – good stuff, as I recall."

"It looks fine to me."

"Good," he smiles – a nice smile. "I'll wrap it up for you . . . Oh, hang on a minute, there's no price on it, I'll have to go and check the stock list."

"Brian!" This comes from upstairs, a great bellow full of imperiousness.

"Just a minute, my love." He tilts his head back and calls up to the ceiling, as if addressing some vengeful goddess, hidden behind the fire-resistant tiles.

"Now, Brian!"

He gives me a pained smile, takes off his bifocals and rubs his eyes redder.

"It's my wife," he says in a stage whisper. "She's a bit poorly. I'll check on her quickly and get that price for you. I shan't be a moment."

He's gone again. More footsteps, and then Brian's wife says, "I'm not going to wait all night to tell you this, Brian, I'm going to bloody well tell you now – "

"But I've a customer – "

"I couldn't give a monkey's. I couldn't care less about your bloody customer. I've had it with you, Brian – you make me sick with your stupid little cardigan and your glasses. You're like some fucking relic – "

"Can't this wait a minute –?"

"No, it bloody can't. I want you out of here, Brian. It's my lease and my fucking business. You can sleep in the spare room tonight, but I want you out of here in the morning."

"We've discussed this before – "

"I know we have. But now I've made my decision."

I take the crumpled bills from my purse. Twenty quid has to be enough for the bottle of Chambertin. I wrap it in a piece of paper and write on it "Thanks for the champagne". Then I pick up the bottle and leave the shop as quietly as I can. They're still at it upstairs: her voice big and angry; his, small and placatory.

I can see the light in the bedroom when I'm still two hundred yards away from the house. It's the Anglepoise on the window-sill. He's put it on so that it will appear like a beacon, drawing me back into his arms.

I let myself in with my key, and go on up the stairs. He's standing at the top, wearing a black sweater that I gave him and blue jeans. There's a cigarette trailing from one hand, and a smear of cigarette ash by his nose, which I want to kiss away the minute I see it. He says, "What are you doing here; I thought you were going to stay at your place tonight?"

I don't say anything, but pull the bottle of champagne out from under my jacket, because I know that'll explain everything and make it all all right.

He advances towards me, down a couple of stairs, and I half-close my eyes, waiting for him to take me in his arms, but instead he holds me by my elbows and looking me in the face says, "I think it really would be best if you stayed at your place tonight, I need some time to think things over – "

"But I want to stay with you. I want to be with you. Look, I brought this for us to drink . . . for us to drink while we make love."

"That's really sweet of you, but I think after this morning it would be best if we didn't see one another for a while."

"You don't want me any more – do you? This is the end of our relationship, isn't it? Isn't that what you're saying?"

"No, I'm not saying that, I just think it would be a good idea if we cooled things down for a while."

I can't stand the tone of his voice. He's talking to me as if I were a child or a crazy person. And he's looking at me like that as well – as if I might do something mad, like bash his fucking brains out with my bottle of Chambertin demi-sec. "I don't want to cool things down, I want to be with you. I need to be with you. We're meant to be together – you said that. You said it yourself!"

"Look, I really feel it would be better if you went now. I'll call you a cab – "

"I don't want a cab!"

"I'll call you a cab and we can talk about it in the morning – "

"I don't want to talk about it in the morning, I want to talk about it now. Why won't you let me stay; why are you trying to get rid of me?"

And then he sort of cracks. He cracks and out of the gaps in his face comes these horrible words, these sick, slanderous, revolting words; he isn't him anymore, because he could never have said such things. He must be possessed.

"I don't want you here!" He begins to shout and pound the wall. "Because you're like some fucking emotional Typhoid Mary. That's why I don't want you here. Don't you understand, it's not just me and you, it's everywhere you go, everyone you come into contact with. You've got some kind of bacillus inside you, a contagion – everything you touch you turn to neurotic ashes with your pick-pick-picking away at the fabric of people's relationships. That's why I don't want you here. Tonight – or any other night!"

Out in the street again – I don't know how. I don't know if he said more of these things, or if we fought, or if we fucked. I must have blacked out, blacked out with sheer anguish of it. You think you know someone, you imagine that you are close to them, and then they reveal this slimy pit at their core . . . this pit they've kept concreted over. Sex is a profound language, all right, and so easy to lie in.

I don't need him – that's what I have to tell myself: I don't need him. But I'm bucking with the sobs and the needing of him is all I can think of. I'm standing in the dark street, rain starting to fall, and every little thing: every gleam of chromium, serration of brick edge, mush of waste paper, thrusts its material integrity in the face of my lost soul.

I'll go to my therapist. It occurs to me – and tagged behind it is the admonition: why didn't you think of this earlier, much earlier; it could have saved you a whole day of distress?

Yes, I'll go to Jill's house. She always says I should come to her place if I'm in real trouble. She knows how sensitive I am. She knows how much love I need. She's not like a conventional therapist – all dispassionate and uncaring. She believes in getting involved in her clients' lives. I'll go to her now. I need her now more than I ever have.

When I go to see her she doesn't put me in some garage of a consulting room, some annex of feeling. She lets me into her warm house, the domicile lined with caring. It isn't so much therapy that Jill gives me, as acceptance. I need to be there now, with all the evidence of her three small children spread about me: the red plastic crates full of soft toys, the finger paintings sellotaped to the fridge, the diminutive coats and jackets hanging from hip-height hooks.

I need to be close to her and also to her husband, Paul. I've never met him – of course, but I'm always aware of his after-presence in the house when I attend my sessions. I know that he's an architect, that he and Jill have been together for fourteen years, and that they too have had their vicissitudes, their comings-together and fallings-apart. How else could Jill have such total sympathy when it comes to the wreckage of my own emotions? Now I need to be within the precincts of their happy cathedral of a relationship again. Jill and Paul's probity, their mutual relinquishment, their acceptance of one another's foibles – all of this towers above my desolate plain of abandonment.

It's OK, I'm going to Jill's now. I'm going to Jill's and we're going to drink hot chocolate and sit up late, talking it all over. And then she'll let me stay the night at her place – I know she will. And in the morning I'll start to sort myself out.

Another cab ride, but I'm not concentrating on anything, not noticing anything. I'm intent on the vision I have of Jill opening the front door to her cosy house. Intent on the homely vision of sports equipment loosely stacked in the hall, and the expression of heartfelt concern that suffuses Jill's face when she sees the state I'm in.

The cab stops and I pay off the driver. I open the front gate and walk up to the house. The door opens and there's Jill: "Oh . . . hi . . . it's you."

"I'm sorry . . . perhaps I should have called?" This isn't at all as I imagined it would be – there's something lurking in her face, something I haven't seen there before.

"It's rather late – "

"I know, it's just, just that . . ." My voice dies away. I don't know what to say to her; I expect her to do the talking, to lead me in and then lead me on, tease out the awful narrative of my day. But she's still standing in the doorway, not moving, not asking me in.

"It's not altogether convenient . . ." And I start to cry – I can't help it, I know I shouldn't, I know she'll think I'm being manipulative (and where does this thought come from, I've never imagined such a thing before), but I can't stop myself.

And then there is the comforting arm around my shoulder and she does invite me in, saying, "Oh, all right, come into the kitchen and have a cup of chocolate, but you can't stay for long. I'll have to order you another mini cab in ten minutes or so."

"What's the matter, then? Why are you in such a state?"

The kitchen has a proper grown-up kitchen smell, of wholesome ingredients, well-stocked larders and fully employed wine racks. The lighting is good as well: a bell-bottomed shade pulled well down on to the wooden table, creating an island in the hundred-watt sun.

"He's ending our relationship – he didn't say as much, but I know that that's what he meant. He called me 'an emotional Typhoid Mary', and all sorts of other stuff. Vile things."

"Was this this evening?"

"Yeah, half an hour ago. I came straight here afterwards, but it's been going on all day, we had a dreadful fight this morning."

"Well," she snorts, "isn't that a nice coincidence?" Her tone isn't nice at all. There's a hardness in it, a flat bitterness I've never heard before.

"I'm sorry?" Her fingers are white against the dark brown of the drinking-chocolate tin, her face is all drawn out of shape. She looks her age – and I've never even thought what this might be before now. For me she's either been a sister or a mother or a friend. Free-floatingly female, not buckled into a strait-jacket of biology.

"My husband saw fit to inform me that our marriage was over this evening . . . oh, about fifteen minutes before you arrived, approximately . . ." Her voice dies away. It doesn't sound malicious – her tone, that is, but what she's said is clearly directed at me. But before I can reply she goes on. "I suppose there are all sorts of reasons for it. Above and beyond all the normal shit that happens in relationships: the arguments, the Death of Sex, the conflicting priorities, there are other supervening factors." She's regaining her stride now, beginning to talk to me the way she normally does.

"It seems impossible for men and women to work out their fundamental differences nowadays. Perhaps it's because of the uncertainty about gender roles, or the sheer stress of modern living, or maybe there's some still deeper malaise of which we're not aware."

"What do you think it is? I mean – between you and Paul." I've adopted her tone – and perhaps even her posture. I imagine that if I can coax some of this out of her then things will get back to the way they should be, roles will re-reverse.

"I'll tell you what I think it is" – she looks directly at me for the first time since I arrived – "since you ask. I think he could handle the kids, the lack of sleep, the constant money problems, my moods, his moods, the dog shit in the streets and the beggars on the tube. Oh yes, he was mature enough to cope with all of that. But in the final analysis what he couldn't bear was the constant stream of neurotics flowing through this house. I think he called it 'a babbling brook of self-pity.' Yes, that's right, that's what he said. Always good with a turn of phrase, is Paul."

"And what do you think?" I asked – not wanting an answer, but not wanting her to stop speaking, for the silence to interpose.

"I'll tell you what I think, young lady." She gets up and, placing the empty mugs on the draining board, turns to the telephone. She lifts the receiver and says as she dials, "I think that the so-called 'talking cure' has turned into a talking disease, that's what I think. Furthermore, I think that given the way things stand this is a fortuitous moment for us to end our relationship, too. After all, we may as well make a clean sweep of it . . . Oh, hello. I'd like a cab, please. From 27 Argyll Road . . . Going to . . . Hold on a sec – " She turns to me and asks with peculiar emphasis, "Do you know where you're going to?"

A TALE OF INNOCENCE
Cree Fox

WE STOOD AWKWARDLY by the ticket machine. He already had his travel-card and I didn't have the sense of possession to fiddle around with change and buy a ticket for myself. We looked at each other shyly, as if we hadn't spent the last three or four hours talking together. A current of commuters rushed past.

"Well," he began, "I suppose I'd better be getting back home."

"Me too. Relieve Grandma. See if the kids missed me."

"What do you think?" He wasn't talking about the kids, his or mine. I didn't know what I thought or if I was thinking at all. Maybe I had just spent this last afternoon in a daze. He had changed. So had I, although he seemed not to see it. Said only my hair was different. Didn't like it short, much; he was an old-fashioned kind of guy.

"We turned out all right, didn't we?" he grinned. And he went, still smiling in that boyish way of his, through the turnstile, on to the train and back to his wife.

How old am I now? Thirty-six and still travelling. I can still see my ex-husband and kids standing at the airport, looking

anxious because I'm so nervous. My armpits are damp and
sweaty already. They know how I hate planes, the interminable monotony of crossing the globe in a cramped space.
How I always feel guilty when I go through Customs or
Immigration – something to do with their fierce looks and
all those forbidding signs. Still that inner wrestling with
authority. The kids in a funny way are unconcerned
because they don't know where I'm going and they trust
I'm coming back. Which is more than I do. I know I'm
going to New York, but that's all. I know I'm staying near
Times Square for six days in a hotel with antique furniture.
But I haven't told them I'm going to spend that time with
someone I've never met.

"I'll miss you," Tony tells me with a rueful smile.

"Yes. You'll miss having a co-parent around."

"No – I'll miss having you to talk to."

"Oh spare me, Tony. I'm not the only one you can tell
your troubles to. Besides, I'm not your wife any more and I
don't have to do that." Tony pulls me to him for a quick
kiss. He's nervous, too. In that husbandly proprietorial
style, he's still worried that no one will treat me as well as he
did. Ha!

"It's all right," I tell him. "If it doesn't work out, I'll be
back. And if it does work out . . . I'll still be back." The
kids are impatient with goodbyes and go scampering off,
heedless. And I leave their father with a rather crooked
smile on my face and a guilty thumping heart.

There was one summer when I was sixteen years old that the
sun shone almost every day and I worked up a glorious
golden tan. This was England, mind you. People didn't
believe me when I said I had never been abroad. I fostered
this tan lovingly, pre skin cancer days, by the public outdoor
pool in the middle of town. Every morning, I wore my
favourite black bikini (nothing more than triangles held
together by little gold chains), pulled on a pair of white

shorts and lacy top and, armed with the bare essentials for serious sunbathing, cycled furiously down the hill to the pool, pedalling, I suspect, in some kind of hormonal spin.

That summer, I met sixty-one people, most of them men, but not one of them compared with David. He worked at the pool. He was that most blessed of people, a lifeguard. It was his job to shamelessly observe everyone who came to the pool and check on their safety. It was he who lifted his sunglasses one day in early July and met my gaze with his cool blue eyes and asked me curiously, flirtingly, "Why are you always surrounded by a retinue of men?" I fell in love with him on sight.

I cycled home that day in a frenzy to look up "retinue". Any man who knew a word I didn't was halfway to my heart already. It was one of those soft, lingering nights when the sun seems never to set. My family and I had strawberries and cream in the garden and I felt as if my body would burst with this golden river that flooded my veins.

My parents thought he was too old for me. As it turned out, they should have been grateful. At twenty-one, he was one of the youngest I ever had. From the moment he lifted his sunglasses, I was irrevocably changed. He took over every waking moment. He was the focus of every word in my teenage diary. Every song on the radio proclaimed my desire. He was my gorgeous obsession. So the day he invited me to the pub with his best friend, I heard angels singing in heaven and hurtled down the hill on my bicycle with the fever of a thousand burning my tanned skin. I locked my bike against the fence, walked in and there he was, waiting for me. And I knew at that moment, I had never looked more beautiful.

"What will you have to drink?" he asked me, his dimples deepening with his heart-wrenching smile.

"Dry martini," I answered, trying to sound worldly and over eighteen.

"I'm quite sure you'll get away with it," he observed. "You're a very mature young lady."

"People always say I seem older than I am."

"You're lucky. You've got the brains of an older woman and the body of a starlet." I hoped fervently my blush got lost behind the fresh rose of my new tan. I gripped the martini with trembling fingers. He looked right into my eyes steadily, with the look of a man who has claimed his prey but means to tease her, play with her, until at last he tosses her in the air and swallows her whole.

It was February. The tan had faded, but my passion for David was intense. There is nothing like the boiling, pent-up desire of a woman who is resolutely virgin. Seventeen years of religious strait-jacketing had done its work. I had not yet given myself to a man. I was proud of that. And I was a seething mass of sexually frustrated hormones, yearning for David.

Unlike me, David went where his body took him. I watched him with the strawberry blond lifeguard at the pool and jealousy racked my mind from morning till night. One evening, we were in the pub together. I was drinking more martinis than usual.

"Watch out; you'll get drunk," he warned.

"I want to."

"Better be careful, little girl. You might do something you regret."

"I hope I do."

"Meaning?"

"I'd like to stop being so sensible for a change."

He looked at me with those heart-stopping eyes and smiled with the arrogance of a man who knows his own power. "You know I want to make love to you. All you have to do is ask."

"Oh, David." I started to stare at his knees, terrified to meet those eyes that seemed to strip me bare with one glance. He took hold of my chin and lifted my face gently so I had to face him with all my passion paraded for him to see.

"You're too young for me," he murmured. "Oh, why do you have to be so sexy? My beautiful young girl. I want you." And he kissed me lightly on my mouth.

I was hot metal, melting into the floor. This is what men do, I thought. I never forgot it. I embraced him clumsily and he held me very softly, like a frightened child.

Sitting on the plane between a middle-aged woman and an apparently gay man, I pick at yet another tray of unappetizing food. I lost my appetite about eight hours into the trip. Fatigue holds me in its fuzzy grip. I have already read an entire novel and listened to two rounds of the jazz and contemporary music channels. The gay man has told me he's going to visit his friend but won't say the pronoun. I can't be bothered to tell him that I've been married to a gay man for the last fifteen years. The woman watches the movie, reads *Woman's Weekly* and popular romance novels. And with all this, my mind races, invents, conjures the trip to New York. How can I tell either of my fellow passengers that I'm going to spend six days with a man I've never met?

I scribble in my journal the latest ramblings of my adventurous and fearful heart. *What am I doing on this plane? What if we can't stand each other? Supposing I fall violently in love with him? Supposing he turns out to be a total nut and straps me to the bed for six days? And what if, at the end of six days, we decide we never want to be apart again? Fevered thoughts. Now I know I'm truly crazy. Another perilous journey. Why can't I be happy with two weeks on the Gold Coast, like everyone else?*

"Are you a writer?" The man on my right has a strong English accent.

"No. Yes. I hope!"

"I write children's stories. Odd, really; I've never had any children. Not likely to."

"I suppose it takes the ability to get inside a child's mind."

"I think I've got a child's mind. I've worked with children all my life. Never really grew up, I suppose. In some ways it's an advantage."

"I think I'd rather see the world through a child's eyes." He smiles at me. We make a connection. I don't mention the gay husband until much, much later and by then the woman is asleep and I know I won't offend her sensibilities as I seek the comfort of a stranger.

Time zones pass, and with the steady roar of the engine my mind continues its reel of imaginings about New York. New York, New York. The Big Apple. I try to imagine his black and white photograph on my board at home by my desk. He's older than me: greying wild hair, glasses, fingers inside his belt loops, legs crossed. Will I recognize him in colour? What will we say? Will we be shy? Or will three months of daily electronic correspondence give us the natural ease of intimate friends? I am strangely wary of revealing these circumstances to the man beside me. As if, somehow, the details he has shared of his affair with a much younger man pale beside the momentous fact of my visit to New York to see a stranger. Ashamed, perhaps. Of what? Ashamed of my impetuousness? My willingness to risk? The man I write to every day understands this. He burns with the same fuel. And so we fall towards one another like two comets colliding.

Another journey. David moved to London to be a croupier. I couldn't bear to think of him moving away and yet I knew this was our opportunity. He wrote to me, soon after he'd found a bedsit in Goodmayes: *Do you think your parents would let you visit me this Sunday? I'll meet you at the station*

*and deliver you back safely. It will be nice to see you. I work
late and will probably sleep in on Sunday but after 11 o'clock
should be OK. Ring me at work on this number if you can . . .*

"Mum, is it OK if I go and see David this Sunday? He's a
bit lonely up there and he said we might go to a matinée
together. I've got the timetable. There are plenty of trains.
And I won't be home late. He has to work at eight o'clock."

"I suppose so. What does Dad say?"

"Oh, you know him. Mumbles something about keeping
myself out of mischief and making sure I don't do anything
stupid. As if I would. You've taken care of that, all right."
My voice sounded mildly aggressive and I changed my tone
to stay on her good side. "Anyway, the train trip will be a
good opportunity to catch up on my reading for college."

On Sunday I wore a pair of jeans and a tight black T-
shirt. I left home with a shoulder bag and a heart full of love
and fear. The halo was still in place. I had convinced myself
that no matter what, I would remain chaste. Standing on
the draughty platform, my hair newly curled under a
headscarf, I was convinced that I looked irresistible and
I would resist him. This potent combination took its place
in my gut.

I sat on the swaying train, trying to read *The Sunday
Times*, feeling utterly nauseated. I couldn't bear to eat a
thing. This didn't bother me. I decided that the thinner I
looked, the better I would be for him. He once told me he
loved me in jeans. I remembered everything he said and
agonized about it later. Then I would repeat things he had
told me to flatter his ego. This was part of my sexual power,
although I didn't know it then. Sweet seventeen and still a
virgin. I bore my innocence proudly and, when the man
opposite me in my carriage lasciviously caught my eye, I
looked at him squarely, secure in the chastity belt of my
own making.

Because it was Sunday, I had to change at Ilford. This
was frustrating, as Goodmayes was only two more stops. I

hovered restlessly on the platform, unable to read, or eat or go to the toilet because it was closed due to vandalism. The churning in my belly turned my body to mush. I wondered how I'd be able to even speak to him. I was so nervous, I thought a newspaper blowing rapidly along the platform in the corner of my vision was a dog. The smell of train fumes made me want to vomit. It began to rain. London took on a thousand shades of grey, but inside I was burning volcanic orange and red.

The last part of the journey found me curled in the seat, barely daring to breathe in case I vomited. When I saw the sign, *Goodmayes*, my belly churned as if I had been tossed upside down. I was a wreck. When I saw the familiar generous sweep of David's nose, his wide, square shoulders and his smart trench coat, I turned to human putty. If he had asked me at that moment to throw myself under the train I would have. It was like meeting God. When he took me into his arms, I was complete.

There is only one hour left to go. Our seat-belts are fastened and we're losing altitude. My belly feels as though it's dropping through the floor. I haven't been able to eat for the last six or seven hours. I've snatched sleep, grasped on to it like a drowning child. But most of the time it has eluded me. My mind is racing into overdrive, veering dizzily round the track across old ground at new speeds. Suddenly this whole thing seems like a nightmare and I scream inwardly that all I want now is to be at home in the familiarity of my futon, threatened by nothing more than an entire wet weekend with my children.

"Are you feeling nervous?" the man asks. He obviously is, judging by the waver in his voice.

"Nervous?" I laugh. "I'm bloody suicidal." My belly lurches again. I swear I'm going to be sick. I wish to God I would be sick and perhaps I could feel normal again. But nothing happens. The nervousness, fear and glorious anticipation stick resolutely in my gut. I start manically taking in details, like the pattern of fingerprints on the window, the tattered front page of the in-flight magazine on the back of the seat in front, the way my toes arrange themselves in my sandals. I don't listen to anything the flight attendant says to me but I seem to make the right moves. I look at my watch. I want to throw up, piss and shit all at the same time. And most of all, impossibly, I want to shake off jet lag and fear and be beautiful. I'm going to meet the man I have never met. As I walk guiltily through Customs, I feel like I'm being led like a fattened calf to my death.

David wanted to eat. He took me to the pub. Since the very thought of eating had me on the verge of throwing up, I told him that all I wanted was a lemonade. He tucked into a ploughman's lunch with the enthusiasm of a late night croupier who had had no supper. He talked cheerfully about his new job. How his mental arithmetic had improved no end in the last three weeks. How exciting it was to be surrounded by so many classy people. I listened, since I was dumbstruck by his extraordinary handsomeness. Being this close to him was intoxicating. I imagined myself like this for days on end, unable to eat or sleep. But enraptured by his physicality, his mesmerizing blue eyes. The dazzling daylight of his smile. I had never loved like his, nor would again.

"Are you sure you don't want anything to eat?"

"No, I don't. I feel slightly sick. I think it's something I ate."

"You look OK. Gorgeous in fact. I like your hair." He reached out momentarily to touch my hair. A current ripped through me. "I like you in jeans. Very sexy. Some women can't wear jeans, but you have such a good figure. You must take care of it, you know. You've got the kind of body that could put on weight when you're older." His words ripped through me. I envisaged months and months of semi-starvation to maintain my hips in perfectly curvaceous condition for his eyes. I was too young to protest against media images of skinny women. I didn't even know about them.

"Why don't you wear make-up?" he wondered.

"I don't like it much. I prefer the natural look."

"You should wear some, you know. It would suit you. Especially those full lips of yours."

He unsettled me so much with this that I had to go to the bathroom. I peered myopically at myself in the mirror (I wasn't wearing my glasses) and wondered if I was beautiful enough for him. Was I fooling myself? Was he really in love with the strawberry blonde? I tried retching in the toilet but nothing happened. I brushed my hair, licked my finger and traced the saliva along my eyebrows to make them tidy. *You really are pathetic*, I told myself. *You should wear make-up*. I walked back towards him and he was at the bar paying the bill. I hadn't finished my lemonade; nor could I.

"Let's go home," he said. I followed him along the gloomy streets; it was still drizzling and he had an umbrella which he held over us. Rows and rows of terrace houses lined the rain-lashed street. It was ugly, but I didn't see it. When he opened the door to his little bedsit, all I saw was the light in his eyes. If you had told me the floor was pure marble instead of faded lino it would have been all the same to me.

"Would you like some coffee?" he asked politely. He went over to the cassette player and flipped the play button. An acoustic guitar filled the room. It was Leonard Cohen, whom I loved. I watched him making coffee to the sound of that velvet voice and my heart was as wide and as open as it had ever been. My love for him filled the room as surely as the sound of rain. My love was the rain. I would shower him with it. I would give him everything, except my virginity. Yet, when he turned to me, two coffee cups in his hand, a smile dancing playfully on his handsome visage, he said two words I will remember for ever.

"Let's frolic."

At that moment, I knew I was lost. He led me to his bed. I remember the sound of the heater whirring away below Cohen's soulful poetry. I remember David removing my clothes with that look of mischief dancing in his eyes, lightly kissing me where the fabric revealed my skin. He kissed me gently. He was relaxed. I wondered why he couldn't hear the roar in my blood as he pulled me down onto the bed.

"It's all right. I'll be very gentle with you," he reassured me.

I was mute. I was terrified. Would it hurt? Would it feel good? Would I get pregnant? Would it be like the other girls said it was? I couldn't ask him. My overwhelming thought was: *I have to get this right*. He found my nipples with his cool fingertips and began to squeeze them softly. He kissed me on my hair. Fear and desire flooded my veins.

"Touch me," David urged.

I was afraid to look. That part of him which until now had always been a hard lump in his trousers was lying there, small and kind of defenceless. I put my hand around it, not really knowing how to touch it. I was used to them being big and upright. His was curled and barely hard and, as I caressed him, seemed not to respond.

"Harder," his voice told me. His fingers were doing something between my legs which felt strange but sweet. He reached down to his penis and pumped it with his hand, cupping my hand as he did so. It began to grow, terrifyingly so. Then he climbed on top of me. I began to panic.

"What about condoms?" I whispered.

"I haven't got any. I've run out. Aren't you on the Pill?"

"No."

"It's all right; I'll pull out."

"No. No, you can't do that. It's too risky." I reached down and thrust my hand between my thighs. He looked at me cheekily.

"Oh, come on. You can't stop now. I'm hard. It's all right. Believe me, I know how to pull out in time."

My head swam wildly. I knew it was risky. But I loved him. My God. Would I come this far and not have the man I loved more than any man in the whole world?

I felt him push against my vagina. He was gentle, but it hurt. He pushed a little harder. The pain was sharp.

"You OK?" he asked.

"It hurts a little," I told him. Not wanting to admit that it hurt a lot. Wanting to be a woman of the world and a virgin both at once. He pushed again. I felt myself open up, felt the fullness of his penis inside me and the pain spreading as I stretched open to accommodate him. It didn't feel good, but it was a sensation like nothing else. As he moved inside me, and I saw the grimace on his face, I thought: *This is it. This is sex. I'm not a virgin any more.* His thrusting became faster. The fullness was almost unbearable, mixed with pain.

"You mustn't come inside me!" I cried out.

"I won't!" he muttered. His cheeks were flushed. There were droplets of sweat on his forehead. Suddenly, he began to breathe heavily. He pulled rapidly out of me and fell across my belly, eyes shut. I felt the warm trickle of sperm across my hip and belly and smelled its tart milkiness.

"Were you in time?" I asked.

He barely heard me for a moment. Then he said gently, "It's all right, baby. I was in time." And he lay there for what seemed a very long time, breathing deeply, his eyes shut, one leg over mine, and I didn't know if he even knew that I was there, waiting to be acknowledged for this gift I had given him.

Eventually, after what seemed like an eternity, I ventured, "Was I OK?"

He smiled without opening his eyes. "Yes, of course. You were fine. Next time, you'll be even better."

When we got up, I put on his blue denim shirt. He, a T-shirt, and got out his guitar to sing to me. His voice was good, if a bit flat sometimes. He played chords using a capo and strummed the strings rather clumsily. But to me, he was giving me the gift of his soul. I gave him the gift of my sexual innocence that day and, to my knowledge, he still has it.

Newark Airport. I'm pushing the trolley through the "nothing to declare" corridor, my clothes sticking to my skin like plaster. There's a crowd out there waiting for us to emerge from the chrysalis of flight, still new and crumpled. I look for Henry. My tired eyes look for only Henry, wondering if each grey wild-haired man is him. I see blond, red, old, young men who could all be Henry. Perhaps he sent me the wrong photograph. Perhaps he's sixty. Perhaps he has dyed his hair. My brain plays tricks on me and in my exhaustion I hardly notice someone standing there holding a placard which says, misspelled, my name.

There is a woman holding the placard. She is short, petite, blonde, wearing a black jacket over a pair of jeans. She looks foreign, something about the shape of her nose and the cheekbones. My first thought is, *Henry prefers blondes*. I approach her and she smiles.

"Ah yes, you fit the description," she says sweetly, with an accent. "Henry always notices the most minute details, even from photographs. How are you? Exhausted, I suppose. Look, I must explain. Henry isn't here. He got held up in London. I'm sorry. He sent me to take care of you. I'm Olivia."

"What's happened? Is he ill?"

"Oh, no. Something came up in the business. I'm so sorry. You must have been looking forward to this moment so much. Henry, to be honest, is absolutely devastated. I've never heard him ranting and raving so much. But he promises he will be on the next flight. He faithfully promises. And I promise you that Henry wants to be here more than anything." She pauses. Her mouth is perfectly painted with lipstick and her hair falls in a gentle sweep from her forehead to her shoulders. I want to hide. Her beauty in the face of my disappointment and my bedraggled appearance. It is too much. I want to cry.

She seems to sense my fragility.

"You poor thing. I'm going to drive you to the hotel. You don't have to do anything. Henry has told me to take care of you. I'm sure all you want is to fall into bed." I follow her out of the terminal, pushing the trolley, unable to think and process what is happening. Her car, a grey BMW, is waiting in the car park close by.

"Henry, I must tell you, will be here the very second he can. He's not a man to be kept waiting. And I'm sure you are desperate to see him." She looks at me, right in the eyes, as if assessing me. "I'm a literary agent. Henry uses my services, from time to time. This is one of my more unusual assignments. But I'm willing to help him out because he helps me. As I think you know, he's a generous man."

"I appreciate you doing this. Do you think he'll be here in the morning?"

"As I said. The second he's able to, he'll be here." Olivia drives assuredly, weaving in and out of the traffic. She sounds Italian. Her jewellery looks expensive. I am more acutely aware of my crumpled state and all images of my first meeting with Henry fall away. Our tender drive in the taxi to the hotel has turned into a journey by BMW escorted by a gorgeous woman who is or probably was Henry's lover. Jealousy twists inside me. She puts on some music and Puccini fills the car. She sings softly, between curses at other drivers. At the hotel she leads me to my room. Suddenly I long to be alone. But when we enter the small room, it is full of flowers, vases of graceful tulips of all hues.

The beauty of it stuns my tired eyes.

"Henry. Ever the romantic," Olivia sighs. "I'll call you first thing in the morning. But here's my number if you need anything. Anything. As you can see. Henry will give you whatever you need. But for now, I'm your fairy godmother." She kisses me on the cheek, leaving me in a cloud of her perfume. I wonder fleetingly why Henry can't call me, but then fatigue takes me over. I look at myself in the mirror and wonder if it's me, then I shower the sweat from my body and fall gratefully between white sheets on an impossibly wide bed which has only me in it.

My dreams are colourful and tortured. I keep meeting Henry at the airport in all kinds of guises. First he's my father: taller, but I know it's him because of the way he purses his mouth. Then he becomes my English teacher, or at least how I'd imagine him to be, now that I'm way past school age and he has endured more years of marriage to his paraplegic wife. Finally, he's David. Of course. Why am I meeting him again? To reclaim my innocence?

But when I wake, there's a knock on the door and it is not David or Henry.

"Hello; it's Olivia. Are you awake? Are you OK? Can you open the door?" I sigh, climb out of bed, cursing her for waking me so early, but the clock says 11.10 a.m. My eyes are puffy with sleep. I look for a dressing gown but settle for a large T-shirt from the top of my suitcase. I find myself frantically brushing my hair. She is no doubt looking beautiful. I open the door.

"You have slept in," she observed. "How are you?" She was wearing a tiny transparent sleeveless cream top with a pair of jeans. Her hair was up in a pony tail. I noticed for the first time how green her eyes were.

"I feel good, I think. I don't know. Where am I?" I laughed.

"New York, New York. It's a beautiful day. You don't know how much. It's hot, sunny, blue sky. It will remind you of Sydney. Please get dressed. Henry says I must show you around."

"Have you spoken to him?" My heart quickens.

"No. But he left a message on my mobile. He expects to be here tonight. So. We don't have much time. Have a shower. Get dressed!" Olivia has that cryptic Italian style. I realize that now. She doesn't mean to be rude. It's just the way she expresses herself.

"I'll wait for you downstairs. Don't worry about your clothes. Henry wants me to take you shopping." She leaves with a smile. I watch her sassy walk down the corridor. My heart quickens again. It's as if my life has been taken over by someone else and all I have to do is follow.

We're sitting in a café near Central Park eating mountainous salads with fresh orange and pineapple juice. Olivia talks. She is full of stories about all the authors she works with, the books that have failed, the books she loved. In her spare time, she translates books from Italian, Russian and Greek. She lives alone. Has one lover, who is married. She had a daughter by her former husband who is now fourteen and lives with him in Rome in the summer.

"Do you miss her?" I ask.

"I miss her too much," Olivia murmurs. "We are like sisters. I don't have many friends in New York although I know lots of people. As you can imagine. It's the nature of my work. But in the end, all I want is to stay at home and read a book."

"And Henry?" I am hesitant. Wanting to know more. Not wanting to hear the truth.

"Henry is a very old friend." Olivia sighs, looks straight into my eyes. "We used to be lovers, a long time ago, and it was beautiful. He is a wonderful lover. But we both have a terrible temper! Over time, we became friends. It happens, sometimes. I like it now the way it is. Henry comes to New York, we spend lots of time talking, lots of debating. You know how he can talk! I do admire you, doing this. It is so brave. Coming to see a man you have never met. I wouldn't do it."

"But you seem so capable and so worldly. Your career. Your writing. Are you telling me you wouldn't go to Sydney to meet a stranger?"

"I would like to. But I'm not sure. Strange as it may seem, I am still quite innocent." She pushes her hair behind her ear, crosses her legs again. The sun catches the ring on her finger. I look in her eyes briefly and catch her watching me. Looking for something perhaps.

"Have you ever been with a woman?" I ask. Her laugh is loud and her cheeks flush.

"Of course not! As I told you. I am still quite innocent." She stands up. She doesn't ask me the same question. "Let's go shopping!" she announces.

Olivia brings me piles of clothes to the dressing room. She may be a bit abrupt at times, but she has an eye for beautiful fabrics. She stands beside me at the mirror, assessing the cut, the way the material falls on my body. She says Italy is the home of fashion and I believe her. I've long forgotten jet lag or children or Sydney. Her Italian modulations, the elegance of the surroundings, and the excitement in my blood have taken over.

"You see," she tells me. "This looks beautiful on you. You are tall, you see. You have wonderful legs. I knew this would be the right thing. You must have it. Do you like it?"

"It looks lovely, Olivia, but . . ."

"No buts. Henry will love it. Now take it off and try this. These soft layers will show off your breasts. You are so lucky to have breasts. Mine are so small. The only time I had breasts was while I was breast-feeding Sophie. Then they were so nice. I even used to wear a bra. Now, it seems silly. I'm like a girl who keeps wanting to ask her mother when she will be big enough to wear one."

"How can you say that? You're a gorgeous woman. When Henry does come, I shall tell him he has wonderful taste in women." I laugh, realizing what I have said. Wondering, as I look at myself in the mirror of a New York boutique, if that is me. We leave with two large bags full of garments wrapped in pale turquoise tissue. Henry, in the guise of Olivia, pays for them all. And I wonder, for a fleeting moment, if Henry is Olivia.

We take a ferry to the Statue of Liberty. My kids want a picture of it and it's a perfect late afternoon for breathing the warm sea air and looking back at the gold sunlight flashing off the windows of Manhattan. Olivia and I chatter as if we have known each other for a long time. She asks me about my marriage, and I hers, and we seem to understand each other. Then she makes me laugh with more stories and we end up giggling uncontrollably. By the time we get back to the hotel, night has fallen. I am exhausted and she is, too. We lie on my big, wide bed, looking at the ceiling. I can hear the endless muffled rush of traffic outside and the sound of people moving around in the building, each one in their own rhythms.

"Olivia. Is Henry really coming?" Olivia giggles quietly.

"Nothing could keep him away," she asserted. "Supposing he never came? Would you be terribly disappointed?"

"Yes, of course. He'd stay a fantasy, I suppose. Someone I write to, but not flesh and blood. He'll always be a ghost of my imagination. But you. You'll be real."

"Yes. I'm very real. I can smell myself. I need a shower!"

"Let's have a bath!"

"You mean together?"

"If you like."

"You are a very cheeky woman. I can see why Henry likes you."

"Henry doesn't know me. I'll run the bath." I get up and

turn on the taps. I pour in some bubble bath which smells of jasmine. I catch sight of myself again: this time eyes sparkling, cheeks flushed, and something inexpressible moving underneath my skin, the slow sweet spreading of desire. I take off my clothes and stand looking at my soft blue bra and pants. I like the way they mould to my shape. I see my nipples poking through the lace. I walk out to the room. Olivia smiles.

"You have a beautiful body," she tells me. "Henry will love you."

"Ah. Henry. Where is he?" At that moment, the phone rings. Olivia picks it up.

"Henry!" she exclaims. Suddenly, strangely, I feel shy. I go back to the bathroom, pretend to adjust the taps, move the bubbles around. I can hear her talking and I can tell by her tone of voice that Henry is not far away. He must be calling from London, just before he leaves. I take off my underwear. I examine my body, wonder how he will touch me. Will he enjoy the slope of my pubic mound the way my lover does? Will he enjoy the taste of me when he buries his head between my legs? And at that moment, I imagine the gentle lapping of Olivia's innocent tongue. I walk out again, in all my nudity, and my desire.

"Henry's here!" she tells me. "He's at Newark. He's coming in a taxi now. I have to leave. This is the moment you've both been waiting for." She suddenly sees my body. I'm standing there for her, in all my femaleness. She's still fully dressed, her thin top clinging to her small frame. I can see her nipples and it makes me ache.

"Olivia . . ." I start to say. She is up from the bed before I can speak. "Don't say any more," she says. "You are lovely. But I have to go." She comes towards me, kisses me on both cheeks and then, quickly but fully, on my mouth. My body shivers. She heads for the door. I'm sure she doesn't want to go but all she says is, "Please call tomorrow, if Henry allows. And have a good night. For me."

I let my body sink into the warm soapy water and watch the bubbles move around over the surface of my skin. I am trembling. My cunt feels so warm and moist that I have to push my fingers into it and feel the soft pillows of my insides. My other hand roams around over my belly and skims my nipples. I imagine Olivia licking them now, her soft, blonde hair brushing my breasts as she moves across me. I begin to skate gently across my clitoris, enjoying the electric rush that radiates from it, my fingertips penetrating the opening of my cunt. Feeling the heat rise. Ripples fill the bath from my movements. I start to breathe heavily, whispering to myself, my fingers doing their erotic dance, knowing just how to touch me, just how to make me come with that sweet, hot, spreading pleasure.

"Oh God!" I call out. I lie there for a while, basking in the glow of my orgasm, and then reality taps on the edges of my consciousness. Henry will be here soon. I get up, dress in a small, lacy top and a long, soft, leonine skirt. I brush my hair. My eyes are unnaturally bright with desire. I spray my neck and cleavage with CK. This is the moment, I tell myself. This is the moment you've been waiting for for three months and all you can think of is Olivia.

I lie on the bed. I get up and try to find some music on the radio. I cut my nails. I lie down again. My heart is thumping noisily. I try to write in my journal. It is 8.30 p.m. when there is a knock on the door.

"Who is it?"

"I think you know." I know that voice. I've heard it so many times across the wires of long distance, as if he were in the next room. I get up, terrified, elated, and open the door.

"Cree Fox, I presume," he says.

"And you must be Henry," I say. "I've heard so much about you." He stands there looking at me in wonder, his brown eyes taking in every detail of me: my eyes, my mouth, my breasts, my belly, my toes. He looks tired.

"Come in," I tell him. "Please come in. Sit down. Tell me about your trip." The way Olivia would.

Henry and I look at one another. He is seated on the chair. I am on the bed, cross-legged, with the advantage of familiarity with this room. We smile stupidly, laugh suddenly. In this moment there is nothing much to say.

He says kindly, "You're not what I expected. Taller, thinner. Your hair's longer. Your eyes are bluer. What can I say? You're lovely."

I blush slightly. I'm being scrutinized and not for the first time today. "You are much taller too," I declared. "And younger than I imagined. You don't do justice to yourself."

"Thank you. But I don't like to present myself as something I'm not."

"Well, present yourself as something you are. And who's Olivia?"

Henry smiles. His face becomes softer and cheeky when it creases. His brown eyes crinkle. "Olivia is an old friend," he smiles. "Didn't she tell you?"

"I must admit I thought for a while that Olivia was Henry."

"You do have an oblique mind. Who was doing the deep voice on the phone for the past three months?"

"Anyone, really. Anyone who wanted to have a joke with me. I thought maybe Henry was a *nom de guerre* for a little old man with a mad sense of humour."

"Well. Meeting you seemed mad. But it doesn't any more. I can't quite believe how lovely you are. Did Olivia take you shopping? I think I detect her impeccable Italian taste in your clothing." I stand up and let my skirt fall along my legs. Part of me wants to take it off. To stun him with the stirrings of my desire for Olivia. But I want to increase the tension.

"Perhaps you'd better have a shower," I suggest. "Get

into some clean clothes. Are you hungry? Do you want to go out?"

"I'm actually exhausted," he admits. "Something came up. I've hardly slept in two days. I don't think I can even eat. Can you?"

"Not really. I'm too nervous. Too excited."

"Uhuh. So what shall we do?"

"Perhaps we could just talk to each other. Discover each other. I feel terribly shy all of a sudden. In a strange kind of way you are so familiar and yet . . . Talking to Olivia was fairly revealing, too."

"Oh yes? What did she say?"

"It was more a matter of what she didn't say."

"Yes?" He brushes back his curly hair. Gives me a questioning look that turns into that grin again. "Christ, I need a shower. Wait for me. I'll be back." He looks at me straight in the eyes. "I can see you and Olivia got on rather well," he says shortly. And disappears into the bathroom.

I find myself gazing out of the window absently, my mind racing. My hands are cold with nerves. There is a pleasant fluttering in my stomach. As I hear the swish of the shower, I reach for the lace top Olivia has chosen and pull it over my head. I look down at my breasts in the cream satin bra. They invite me to touch them. I unzip the skirt, letting it fall lightly to the floor. I let my hand rest between my legs, feeling the smooth satin over my pubic hair. I push them down and step out of them. I reach for the catch of my bra and my breasts escape its hold. My nipples stiffen in the air.

The shower is still running. I lie down on the bed on my belly and rest my head on a large plump pillow. I suddenly feel very sleepy. My legs fall apart slightly. I tuck my arms underneath the pillow and enjoy the way it cushions my heavy head. I can feel the dampness between my legs. The expectancy that is already opening me and making me ready. Still the shower runs. I begin to dream that Olivia is slowly sucking my toes then flicking her tongue teasingly up the backs of my legs. I quiver slightly as if in a breeze.

I hear the new silence. The movements of a man towelling himself, taking the comb out of his bag and sliding it through his hair. The sound of teeth being brushed. I am impatient now. I am so tired of waiting. The tension no longer titillates but torments me. Then the sound of a door being opened. I catch my breath. Footsteps across the carpet, so slowly it seems they will take forever. One foot in front of the other. One moment inexorably following another.

A light moan. Or did I imagine it? Did I imagine the lightest feather on the soles of my feet or the tentative wet tongue exploring the inside of my leg? I lie very still, not daring to move in case I should be jolted out of my dream. Warm breath on my buttocks. Fingertips in the small of my back. I can feel every hair on my body lifting and sending tiny waves of sensory delight through my body. A tongue making circles on my back and around my arse. I make a sound, just to let the person know that I am here. That I'm not sleeping. That I'm not dreaming any more.

The tongue licks me slowly from my neck to my ankles. My cunt throbs, longing to receive its texture and insistent rhythm. I raise my buttocks slightly to meet it. The tongue finds its way to my lips, slightly open already. The longing sends a tremble through me. There is a gentle nibbling on my clit. I start to moan and open myself further. Heat floods me. I begin to drown in the warm river of sensation. The tongue penetrates me, dances around my clit then darts inside, finding that perfect place where I hover on the brink of orgasm until it overwhelms me. I cry out. He breathes deeply.

Then warm skin pressing on my lips, nudging the folds away. The gentle pushing of a man's cock at the entrance to my cunt. I cry out again. The longing to be penetrated is so strong, I almost thrust my buttocks up towards him to make him do it now. But he knows. He plays with me, making teasing circles with the head of his cock around my labia. Kisses on my spine, hair brushing my shoulder blades.

Suddenly he plunges inside me. I groan with the force of it and he fills me right up. Then slowly moves in and out, careful to slide over my vulva before sinking deeply inside me and thrusting a few times, until my clitoris sings. I still don't dare to look, penetrated as I am by this man I still don't know. I hear his breathing, the gasps of pleasure. Feel the tension of his muscles as he teeters on the edge of exploding.

Suddenly I turn over. There is a moment there when neither of us knows what to do. I search his eyes for some clue but they are glazed with lust. Faced with him, all I want right now is to be fucked. He slides his cock forcefully into me, grimacing, and pumps me, in and out, groaning with each thrust. He tenses. I arch my back, lift my mound towards him to receive him. He yells loud enough to wake the sleeping. I feel the hot orgasmic energy pounding through his body penetrate mine. He falls on top of me, his hair fanning across my face.

There is a long, sweet silence. Our bodies seem to quiver together. Then, just when I think he's about to slip into slumber, I pluck up the courage to ask. "Who's Olivia?" I whisper.

I can feel his mouth smile on top of mine.

"I think you know," he mumbles.

"Do I?"

"Who would you like her to be?" he teases.

The warmth of our bodies pressed together begins to melt me down, eases me towards sleep.

"Your wife?" I ask.

There is no sound. Then, a gentle almost imperceptible snore. I can't see his eyes but they seem to be closed. The weight of his body on mine begins to feel heavy. Slowly, I ease out from under him. It is past midnight. I want to sleep, too, but my mind is sizzling. It is as if orgasms have set my brain on fire. I get up. Wander around the room. Gaze in wonder at this man who is sharing my bed, who I still do not know.

I sit in the chair looking out of the window. The moon is quite full, and bathes me in its foxy white light. I begin to breathe more gently. The sounds from the street rock me. After a while, I can feel my body relax, the tension draining from my muscles. I rest my head on the arm of the chair. Tiredness overtakes me. Climbing back into bed beside Henry, I fall into the deep and knowing sleep of the innocent.

ENTERTAINING MR ORTON

Poppy Z. Brite

London, 1 August 1967

"HAVE YOU BEEN reading my diary?"

Kenneth looks up from the baboon's head he is pasting onto the madonna's body. He is standing on the bed to reach the upper part of his collage, which covers most of the wall, and the top of his bald cranium nearly brushes the pink and yellow tiles of the flat's low ceiling. They have lived together in this tiny space in Islington for eight years.

"No, I have not been reading your diary," Kenneth lies.

"Why not?"

"Because it would drive me to suicide."

"Right," says Joe with an edge of impatience in his voice. He has heard this threat many times before, in one form or another, and Kenneth realizes dimly that his lover either doesn't believe it or just doesn't care. That doesn't mean Kenneth can make himself stop saying it, though.

"But if you won't read my diary and you won't talk to me," Joe continues, "what's the point of remaining in this relationship? You're always telling everyone how I make your life miserable. What keeps you hanging about?"

Kenneth wipes glue from his fingers onto his pants, then turns and sits heavily on the bed. He took a number of Valium earlier in the day, but something in Joe's voice pulls his brain out of its pleasant half-numb fog. They can still listen to each other, and even talk seriously when they really try.

Of course, most of the serious talk these days is about writing. Writing Joe's plays, to be precise. The very same brilliant and successful plays that have made Joe's name synonymous with decadence, black wit, and tawdry glamour as far as London was concerned. If the talk isn't about Joe's plays, it is about what they should do with all the money Joe's plays are making. Joe spends most of it on toys: clothes, Polaroid cameras, holidays in Morocco.

"What surprises me," Joe continues, "is that you haven't killed me. I think you don't leave or top yourself because you can't stand the thought of anyone else having me."

"Rubbish. All sorts of people have you."

"Ah! You *have* been reading my diary."

Kenneth rises up suddenly in one of his outbursts. "When you come home reeking of cheap aftershave, I don't need your diary to tell me where you've been!"

Joe waves this away. "I mean, of anyone else having me permanently. And I can't conceive of it either, honestly. It's as if we've become inextricable."

Suspicion flares in Kenneth's mind. "Why are you talking about me killing you? Are you setting me up for something?"

Joe throws back his head and brays laughter, a sound which usually lessens Kenneth's tension but now induces a smouldering rage. "What did you have in mind? Me setting you up for murder and slipping back off to Tangier? My family gets your fat arse thrown in prison and you do your *De Profundis* bit again? Oh, Ken . . ." Tears are spilling out of Joe's eyes now, tears of laughter, the kind he used to cry in bed after a joyous orgasm. Kenneth remembers how they tasted, salt and copper on his tongue like blood.

"I think I *could* kill you," he says, but Joe doesn't hear him.

Tangier, 25 May 1967

Five English queens stoned on hash and Valium and Moroccan boy-flesh, sipping red wine on a café terrace against a blood-orange sky. Two American tourists, an older married couple, sitting nearby eavesdropping on the conversation and making their disapproval evident. Joe Orton lets his voice rise gradually until he is not so much shouting as *projecting*, trained Shakespearian actor that he is.

"He took me right up the arse, and afterward he thanked me for giving him such a good fucking. They're a most polite people. We've got a leopard-skin rug in the flat and he wanted me to fuck him on that, only I'm afraid of the spunk. You see, it might adversely affect the spots of the leopard."

"Those tourists can hear what you're saying," one of the entourage advises. (Not Kenneth Halliwell; though he is present, he wouldn't bother trying to curb Joe even if he wanted to.)

"I mean for them to hear," Joe booms. "They have no right to be occupying chairs reserved for decent sex perverts . . . He might bite a hole in the rug. It's the writhing he does, you see, when my prick is up him, that might grievously damage the rug, and I can't ask him to control his excitement. It wouldn't be natural when you're six inches up the bum, would it?"

The Americans pay for their coffee and move away, looking as if they've had it considerably more than six inches up the bum – dry.

"You shouldn't drive people like that away," says the sensitive queen. "The town needs tourists."

Joe sneers. He has practised it in the mirror. "Not that

kind, it doesn't. This is *our* country, *our* town, *our* civilization. I want nothing to do with the civilization they made. Fuck them! They'll sit and listen to buggers' talk from me and drink their coffee and piss off."

"It seems rather a strange joke," offers another member of the entourage timidly.

"It isn't a joke. There's no such thing as a joke," says the author of the most successful comedy now playing in London's West End.

Leicester, August 2, 1967

Joe leaves his father's small threadbare house and walks two miles up the road to an abandoned barn, where a man he met in town earlier that day is waiting for him. He is in his home town, which he mostly loathes, to see a production of his play *Entertaining Mr. Sloane* and fulfil family obligations. Just now he has some obligations of his own to fulfil.

Joe often likes to have one-off trysts with ugly men, men he finds physically appalling, but this one is a beauty: tall and smoothly muscled, with brown curly hair that tumbles into bright blue eyes, a thick Scottish accent, an exceedingly clever pair of hands, and a big-headed, heavily veined cock.

In the late afternoon shafts of sunlight that filter through the barn's patched roof, they take turns kneeling on the dusty floor and sucking each other to a fever pitch. Then Joe braces himself against the wall and lets that fat textured cock slide deep into his arse, opening himself to this stranger in a way that he never can to Kenneth – not any more, not ever again.

London, 8 August 1967

Conversation after the lights are out:
  "Joe?"
  ". . ."

"Joe?"

"What?"

"Why did you ask me if I'd kill you?"

"I don't know what you're on about."

"Do you want to die, Joe?"

"Do I . . .?" A sudden bray of laughter. "Hell, no! You twit, why would I want to die?"

"Then why did you bring it up?"

"Hm . . ." Joe is already falling back asleep. "I suppose I just wondered whether you were that far gone."

His breathing deepens, slows. Joe is lying on his left side, his face to the wall. The collage spreads above him like a fungus, its components indistinguishable in the street-lit dark. Kenneth sits up, slips out of bed, maybe planning to take a Nembutal, maybe just going to have a pee.

But he freezes at the sight on the bedside table: Joe's open diary and, balanced atop it carelessly, as if flung there by accident, a claw hammer. Joe hung some pictures earlier in the day, so the hammer has every reason to be there. But the juxtaposition of objects hypnotizes Kenneth, draws him.

He extends his hand cautiously, as if he is afraid the hammer will disappear. Then it is in his palm, heavy, smooth wooden handle, a comfortable fit. He raises it.

"Joe?"

Slow breathing.

"Joe?"

I suppose I just wondered whether you were that far gone . . .

And the knowledge that he *is* that far gone, that Joe must know that or be blind, sweeps over Kenneth like a dark sea. All the years he has invested, his work, his talent, his whole existence subsumed by Joe. The infidelities lovingly recorded in the diaries, literally under Kenneth's nose (the flat is only sixteen by eighteen feet). In that moment the dam overflows, the camel's back breaks, the shit hits the fan, and life as Kenneth Halliwell knows it becomes intolerable.

Without allowing himself to think about it further, he lets the hammer fall.

Nine times.

The amount of blood on his collage is staggering. Even in the dark Kenneth can see that most of the cutout figures are spattered if not obscured entirely. The thing on the pillow is no longer Joe; it is like a physician's model, an example of a ruined cranium. And yet he still imagines he can hear that slow breathing.

After undressing (Joe's blood is sticky on his pajama top) and scrawling a brief, unremarkable note, Kenneth goes for the bottle of Nembutal and swallows twenty-two, washing them down with a tin of grapefruit juice. He is dead before his considerable bulk hits the floor.

Joe's sheets, however, are still warm when the bodies are found the next morning.

London, 8 August 1996

"Harder! It's not going in! *Lean* on it . . . Oh bloody fuck, Willem, get out of the way and let me do it!"

Clive shoulders his way up the narrow staircase and pushes Willem away from one end of a large sofa upholstered in royal purple velvet. The other end of this venerable piece is stuck fast in the doorway of the tiny flat. Clive leans against it and gives a mighty shove. Wiry muscles stand out on his neck and shoulders. Willem mutters something in Dutch.

"What?"

Willem points at a spot just below his navel. "What do you call it when the intestines come out?"

"Hernia? No, look, you push with your knees bent. Like *this* . . . Ugh!" The paint on the door-frame surrenders several layers, and the sofa is in the flat.

Back outside, they struggle to get an antique steamer trunk full of Clive's photography equipment up the granite steps of the stoop. The staircase looms above them. Everything seemed much lighter in Amsterdam, probably because they had two friends helping. Now that they are here, their possessions appear enormous and unmanageable.

A young man passing on the street stops to watch their efforts. Clive is annoyed until the man, who is distinctly rough-trade, says, "Need a bit o' help wi' that there?"

They accept too gratefully, and he asks for forty pounds. They bargain him down to thirty-five. A bargain it is, for they could not have done it alone. By the time their things are in the flat, they feel sufficiently comfortable with the young man to ask if he knows where to get weed in Islington. The young man exclaims that he lives right around the corner and knows a guy who had some good stuff coming in today. They pay him the thirty-five pounds, give him an additional twenty toward the weed, and say goodbye, half-expecting never to see him again.

Of course, they never do.

"Fucking London," Clive grumbles over Indian takeaway that night. "Fucking welcome home. Forgot why I left, I did."

On the verge of thirty, Clive has received glowing reviews for his art photography, but couldn't get the lucrative portrait work he needed to live well in Amsterdam. He has decided that Dutch people don't care for having their pictures taken nearly as much as the English do. Even Willem, in all his scruffy blond loveliness, is a lousy model, always fidgeting, wanting a cigarette, wanting a joint, saying he is cold. Willem is a writer (some of the time) and can work anywhere (or not), so they have decided to relocate to Clive's home city. Willem is excited about the move; he is twenty-five and has never lived outside the Netherlands. Clive hopes it will be temporary.

"We'll get it somewhere else," Willem consoles.

"You're in England now, luvvie dear. You can't just wander down to the corner coffee-shop and ask to see the menu. Anyway, I don't care about the weed." Clive makes an expansive gesture ceilingward. "It's the attitude of this place I loathe."

"The flat?" Willem looks around in alarm. He selected their new home, and particularly likes the pink and yellow tiles on the ceiling, though he wondered at the wisdom of bringing the purple sofa.

"No, no . . . London. Filthy place, innit? Always somebody ready to rip you off, from the drug dealer on the street to the poshest restaurant in the city." He looks up at Willem. "Don't you think so?"

They have visited London twice in their three years together, and Willem has been coming here on his own since his teens. He loves the grand spaces and vistas, the whirl of traffic, the diversity and dazzle. "No. I find it glamorous."

Clive smirks. "Wait 'till you've lived here a while."

Willem finishes his rice, sops up the last of the lamb vindaloo with half a chapati, and begins to clear away the containers. "Shall we do some unpacking tonight," he asks, "or are you too tired?"

"I think I'm too tired for unpacking."

Willem stops on his way to the kitchenette and looks at Clive. Clive is still smirking, but in a wholly different way.

"Only for unpacking?" Willem inquires.

"Well, the bed's already unpacked, innit?"

The first sex in a new home is unique, preserved somehow in the watching walls that have already seen so much. It marks the space as your own, and you are conscious of this during the act. It also awakens things in the space that may have lain dormant for years – currents, if you will, or points of energy, or electromagnetic impulses. Or ghosts.

Clive and Willem don't know anyone has been murdered here. Clive has heard of Joe Orton and his famous death, though he would be hazy on the details if asked. Willem has seen two of Orton's plays produced in Rotterdam, but knows little of the author's life in London. He found the plays very clever, had admired their facile wit. Now here he is, all unknowing, sucking his lover's cock on the spot where that wit met its end.

Admittedly, it is the obvious place for a bed, against one of the longer walls under the big window. Thirty years' worth of paint, the latest coat a semenesque oyster-white, covers the bloodstains and nightmare collages. Clive lies sprawled on the bed, his back arched, his fingers tangled in Willem's hair. Willem's mouth is hot and smooth on his cock, tongue teasing the head, lips slipping down the shaft. The soreness and tension of moving day begin to drain away, and Clive lets himself relax into a stupor of equal parts bliss and exhaustion.

What the FUCK . . .

This is Joe's first thought, and he suspects that it is not particularly original. But the feeling is too much to describe: the memory of the hammer blows, the sensation of leaving his body slowly, so slowly, trying to wrench himself free of the mangled meat like an animal chewing off its paw in a trap. Kenneth nearby, but maddeningly cold and dead, having taken the easy way out. Having gotten the last word. Kenneth was not bound to this place; he could have died anywhere.

After that, nothing. It might have been a second or a century since the first blow fell. There was no heaven, no hell, absolutely nothing at all. Just as Joe had always expected. Until now. Until he finds himself not only sentient, but in the middle of an orgasm.

"Willem!" he hears himself gasping. The name is unknown to him, but the sensations are deliciously familiar.

The young man who has just finished sucking his cock looks up, smiling. His face is square, honest, and beautiful, his eyes china-blue, his full lips still glistening with traces of come.

"Please, will you fuck me now?" he says.

"Well–well, all right."

"You're not too tired?" Willem has a charming little accent, German or Dutch; could be Hottentot, for all Joe cares.

"Absolutely not." As he gets up onto his knees, he takes stock of this blessed body he has found himself in. Its build is much like his own, smallish but solid. It has a big uncircumcised cock already swelling back to half-mast as Willem kisses his mouth, strokes his chest, bites his nipples. It feels young, healthy, glorious.

He turns Willem around and rubs his cock between the younger man's ass-cheeks. The crack of Willem's ass is lightly furred with gold. He groans as Willem pushes back against him. Willem passes him a tube of lubricant and a condom. Joe applies the lube to his erect cock and Willem's pretty ass, gently sliding a finger in, then two. He tosses the condom away, having no idea what else he is supposed to do with it.

Willem feels Clive entering him unsheathed, which is strange but not entirely without precedent; each of them has tested negative three times, and since the third time they've gone condomless once or twice. It feels so good that he doesn't protest now. Clive's naked cock slides way up inside him, faster and harder than Clive usually puts it in. Clive's hands are clamped on Willem's hips, pulling Willem onto him. Clive has always been a wonderful fuck, but Willem cannot remember the last time he felt so thoroughly penetrated.

It seems to go on for hours. Just when he's sure Clive is going to come, *must* come, Clive stops and catches his breath and kisses the back of Willem's neck for a bit, then starts fucking him again. At one point he pulls out, flips Willem over with no apparent effort, pushes Willem's legs up to his chest, and re-enters him. They settle into a slow, deep rhythm. Clive is nuzzling at Willem's mouth, not just kissing him but inhaling his breath, sucking hungrily at his lips and tongue. Hungrily. That's how Clive is making love to him, like a man starved for it.

At last Clive whispers, "I'm going to come now." His cock seems to go deeper yet, and Willem feels it pulsing inside. Then Clive is holding him ever so tightly, pushing his face into Willem's neck and (Willem could almost swear) sobbing. His sperm sears Willem's insides, hot and effervescent, melting into Willem's tissues and suffusing them with something Willem has never felt before. It is a little like an acid trip, if all the hectic color and strange splendor of an acid trip could be folded into the space of two sweating, shuddering bodies.

"Thank you," says Clive, kissing him. Willem sees that Clive *is* crying, and when he kisses back, the tears taste of salt and copper on his tongue.

Clive knows *something* happened while Willem was sucking his cock, but he can't say just what. It was the sex of his life (both his cock and Willem's ass are satisfyingly sore for days), but there was something detached about it, almost as if he'd been watching himself fuck Willem instead of actually doing it.

Never mind, he tells himself. They were both exhausted from moving; that's why it was a bit odd. Not bad, though. He wouldn't actually mind if it happened again.

Within days of their arrival, Clive's entire Amsterdam portfolio is taken on by a posh London gallery for a handsome commission. He won't be doing any portrait work for a while. On the way home to give Willem the good news, Clive buys a Polaroid camera.

When he enters the flat, he is surprised to see Willem banging away on his old electric typewriter. As far as Clive knows, Willem hasn't done a lick of writing since the move.

But now a sheaf of pages has accumulated on the desk beside him.

"I wasn't thinking of anything in particular," Willem explains, "and then suddenly I had an idea for a play."

"A play?"

"Yes, I've never written one before. Never even liked the idea." Willem shrugged. "I don't know what's gotten into me, but I hope it stays."

THE HUNGRY HOUR

Lucy Taylor

SOMETHING HEAVY ON my chest. Mashing me down. Making it hard to breathe.

I woke up feeling the way I used to feel as a child, empty and scared, wondering what the night would bring. I remember starting to roll over and reach for Mark.

Then I heard the sounds – soft sighs and the swishing of sheets. Tiny guttural grunts and the wet smack of flesh.

I thought Mark was having a nightmare.

Or jerking off.

For a moment, I lay there, hoping this was a continuation of the nightmare, willing whatever was happening to go away, to leave me alone.

It went on. Sex sounds. Whimpers and whispers, throaty growls. The creak and sag of the bedsprings.

Two voices moaning in the night. Neither of them mine.

I opened my eyes and saw Mark up on his knees, fucking a woman doggie-style. The woman was leaning forward, braced to take his thrusts. Head back, lips parted. Mouthing *Oh God, oh God!*

Her skin was one shade darker than albino, her lids as fiercely painted as the wings of a macaw. Sweat like beads of

tallow glistened on her breasts. Her dark auburn hair was a
ratty, tortured nest, and there was come in it, clotted and
slick. A breeze came in the window and I got a whiff of her –
an odor old and flowery, like rotting blossoms or the cloying
sweetness of a sick room. A scent I'd smelled before.
Frightening and familiar.

"What the hell –?"

Like a porn star going through a choreographed routine,
he slid out of her. Wet, slurping sounds. Hiss of air leaking
out of her pussy as he flipped her over, got her on her back.
Legs up over his shoulders.

Reinserted himself.

Commenced again.

While I looked on, with a frozen, rabbit-caught-in-
headlights horror, mesmerized and traumatized in equal
parts.

Under any circumstances, it's an odd, bizarre intimacy,
watching one's lover make love to someone else, because
you get to see how the things you've both done together
appear from the point of view of an observer; and sometimes, I realized, they're erotic and elegant, sometimes
ridiculous and clumsy. I'd never before seen how the
muscles in his buttocks bunched and knotted; and that
his toenails, which sought purchase in the sheets, were
ragged and in need of cutting; or how his penis angled
slightly to the left as it thrust into the woman's cunt, almost
withdrew, then punched her open again, disappearing root-
deep in her pink furry folds.

I realized I was watching them as if I'd come upon their
performance on some late-night TV channel – enthralled by
them in a perverse way that left me confused as to which I
found more revolting, their performance or my reaction to
it. But now I came back to reality – this was Mark, *my* lover,
in *my* bed.

"Goddamn it, stop!"

In the silence that followed my scream, all I heard was

the slick, in-out rhythm of Mark's cock in the unknown
woman's pussy, the slurp and grunt of their union and
Mark's breathing, short and sharp, as though the air were
full of tiny spurs that hurt his lungs.

"Mark!" I leaned forward and whacked him in the head
with the heel of my hand. He reeled sideways. His cock slid
out and the woman pitched face-first into the pillow.

He blinked and squinted in a befuddled way. "Jesus,
Dru, I'm sorry. You were supposed to be asleep."

At that moment I didn't know if I was relieved or sorry I
wasn't one of those people who keep loaded guns around
the house. If I did, I surely would have used it.

"You fucking bastard. Go to hell. Get out of here." I
turned to the slut he'd been screwing. "You, too. Get out!"

The woman slithered off the sheets and started dressing –
unhurriedly, her movements languid, indolent, like one
performing a striptease in reverse. Furious, I snatched
her rumpled T-shirt off the floor and hurled it at her.

For the first time, she seemed to really notice me. *Looked*
at me. Her eyes were small and almond-shaped, some
murky shade of blue or green, her lips soft and full, but
asymmetrical, the upper one wider and darker than its
mate. But her gaze – it was liquid, cool and moist and
hungry. Like love, I thought, if you could reduce love to a
substance the color and consistency of honey and then lace
it with poison.

After she'd gone, I went down to the kitchen and sat
there, shaken and dumbstruck, while Mark made coffee.

"I don't understand. You fucked her in the bed with me
in it? You had to know I'd wake up. If you wanted to cheat
on me, there were a hundred smarter, kinder ways to do it.
You did this to hurt me. To humiliate me."

"I was an asshole. It was stupid. I agree."

"But you did it anyway. Why?"

"I–I don't know. Honestly. She needed me and I–I
wanted to help."

"A mercy fuck. I see. Who is the bitch? What's her name?"

"Tilly."

"Tilly who?"

"Just Tilly."

"What does she do?"

"She's – she models."

I thought about the ratty hair and garishly made-up eyes, the sensuous but irregular features and thought: for what, *Outlaw Biker Monthly?*

"How did you meet her?"

The tiniest of winces flickered across his features. Desire, longing, need.

"I knew her in my drinking days – before you and I got together. It was right before I went to jail for that DUI. I was stupid enough to believe her when she said she'd wait for me. She didn't, of course. She moved on. I told myself it was better that way. She was too reckless and unstable – seeing other men, disappearing for days at a time, coming back with no explanations. Always needing something from me – drugs, rent money, sex. But still she seemed to know me better than I knew myself. Always one step ahead of me, always knowing what I wanted. Then when I ran into her the other day – "

"Ran into *her?*"

"All right, what happened was she tracked me down. She showed up at the job site. She's living in an awful place . . . I couldn't, I didn't have the heart not to at least buy her a meal. One thing led to another and – I knew it was stupid. I knew I should stay away from her, but – "

" – your dick said otherwise."

"It's not that simple."

"Of course it is. Your cock commands. Your brain kowtows. It's old as time, encoded in male DNA. But with me in the bed – "

"That was her idea. To see if we could do it in the bed without waking you up."

"What is she, one of these people who gets off having sex in outrageous circumstances? Giving blowjobs in confessionals, fucking on ferris wheels, that kind of thing?"

"She's – different," he said. "She used to joke around and say she was a sex witch. Sometimes I half believed her. I mean, she isn't beautiful. Her tits are too small, and I hate her freckles. But when I have her, I feel ten feet tall and bulletproof. Like I used to feel when I drank and did cocaine."

"What about us? I thought we loved each other?"

"We *do*. Look, I know this sounds crazy, but – "

"Try me."

"I thought that if I had her – just one more time – then I could let go of her once and for all. Get her out of my system. Forget about her. Be free."

"And did you accomplish that?"

He slumped down and put his head in his hands, contrition and defeat in every motion. "It was a stupid, unforgivable thing to do. I don't even like her. Oh, God, it kills me to see you look at me that way." He reached across the table, tried to take my hand. I pulled away. "Please give me another chance. Everything will be all right. I promise."

After Mark left, I went back to bed and lay on the side where the sheets still smelled of her cunt, his come, their rutting. On the pillowcase I found some of her hairs – long and wavy, a soiled and sooty red. I picked them off and held them to the light like evil talismans and felt the hole in my heart enlarge from a wound the size of a bullet to one as ugly and gaping as a hollowpoint's exit route. A hunger great as Calcutta.

A feeling that used to come to me in the night.

The hungry hour, I called it when I was a child.

That endless, lightless time of night when the dark seemed alive and carnivorous, and I lay alone, listening to the silence, knowing that something vital was missing from me – stolen, lost – my life was leaking out in sips and whispers and I was powerless to staunch the flow.

When I got older and sex became my drug of choice, I discovered that what filled the hole between my legs could satisfy my soul as well, but the effect lasted no longer than my partner's hard-on. To fill the void, I sought out allies. Male ones. Virile and robust. Fuck freaks with dicks as hard as their hearts.

When I met Mark, I saw in him that urgency and hunger. I felt it in the way he tried to penetrate more than just my pussy – my heart, my mind, my soul. And isn't that, I'd thought, the very definition of soulmates, two beings who share the same disease, the same deficiencies, the same death wish . . . isn't that what leads to love, what forms the ties that bind?

"It will never happen again," Mark promised me.

And it didn't, of course – until the next time.

We'd made love on the sofa and fallen asleep, me with my head tucked into his shoulder, him on his side, legs intertwined with mine.

Except when I woke up, he wasn't there with me but on the floor with *her* and they were –

– making love, I want to say, but it was both more and less than that. They were fighting, struggling. There was a swelling under her right eye and bloody cuts along his cheek. *She's evil and he's killing her*, I thought, with a horrid sort of glee.

He rolled on top and pinned her down, forcing hard kisses on her. She let her arms fall to her sides and gave a little moan of such exquisite surrender and desire that I felt as though I'd been slit open throat to gullet.

I snatched up the ceramic ashtray off the coffee-table and lifted it to smash across her face, but before I could complete the motion, she turned away from Mark and looked at me.

Her gaze was cool, remorseless, metallic in its beauty and its hardness. The tip of her pink tongue flicked out across her lower lip and moistened it in a familiar gesture.

"You bitch!" I screamed, but as I brought the ashtray down, Mark grabbed my wrist and twisted it. The ashtray tumbled to the bed.

"Christ, what are you doing?"

As though I were the crazy one, the guilty one.

Although we were in Mark's apartment, he didn't tell me to go. Instead he left with Tilly.

To hell with him, I told myself. *He's sick. Except he won't die quickly. What's eating him alive won't kill him for a long, long time.*

Easy to say. But watching him leave with Tilly only drove the hook of shame and longing deeper into my heart.

So began that sad, familiar cycle of obsessive love. Rupture followed by reconciliation.

We broke up.

Got back together.

Broke up again, but kept on finding ways to meet, to fuck "just one more time," then go our separate ways. Him back to Tilly, me to hell.

I borrowed a girlfriend's clunker car and parked around the corner from Mark's apartment. What did they do? Where did they go? How often did he fuck her?

I could see how she was aging him. I'd spy on him at work and see how wearily he pounded nails and lifted beams, how loosely the heavy toolbelt hung on his lean hips. I'd note the twitchy agitation of a muscle in his cheek, the haggard eyes and desperate way he sucked on cigarettes.

He gave up on his sobriety and went back to the bars. The sleazy ones, with greasy-looking bouncers and at least one fight per night serious enough to call the cops. Usually he drank alone. Once I saw Tilly loitering outside the bar that he'd gone into. She glided past the window, small and urchin-like, serene. The kind of woman men want to keep away from other men, the kind they treat like daughters.

The first time I caught her leaving Mark's apartment, I followed – in my car at first, and then on foot. She was wearing ripped jeans and a slithery white top whose spaghetti straps kept sliding off her shoulders, and sometimes she'd pluck the straps back up and sometimes not. In the dark, the material glowed with the shimmery incandescence of a gigantic lightning bug. She walked rapidly, passing from Mark's genteelly low-rent neighborhood to one of outright squalor, plunging heedlessly into darkened streets a sane person wouldn't walk in broad daylight. Rape bait, but she showed no fear. As though she knew no one would touch her. Or didn't care.

She reached an abandoned duplex beneath an overpass and went inside by ducking under a crumbling staircase, descending into what must have been a basement.

Crash pad? Crack house? What?

I steeled myself and followed her inside. Inhaled the sour stench of rot and food gone bad and something else, an unexpected note of sweetness, perfume that hinted at decay and ancient, wilted corsages.

I heard the scuffling of her feet and then her murmur, soft and rumbly, electric as the air before a thunderstorm. "I know it's you, Dru."

"I want to talk to you."

"Come here," she said, and stepped out of the shadows behind a staircase that must have led to the first floor. Lips pouty, petulant, eyes heavy-lidded, slitted-down. Smelling of sex, of sweat, of come.

"I know what you want. You haven't changed."

She ran her fingertips between my lips, along the edge of my teeth.

Before she kissed me, I had the chance to hit her, take her soft lips between my teeth and make her bleed. Instead I kissed her back. Then I felt a rush of loathing and desire – I craved whatever Mark possessed, to run my hands and tongue and mouth wherever his had traveled. Everywhere. Milky skin, so soft and bruisable. I could smell her flesh, her cunt, her dampness. And she was right: I wanted her. To gorge myself on her nipples and feast at her crotch, devour her like a banquet of pink lips and pale, freckled flesh laid out in front of me.

I kissed her brutally, mashing my teeth into her soft lips, digging my nails into the flesh of her hips as I tugged down her jeans. Her pubic hair was downy, blonde. I wished for a dick to ram into her, to make her scream, but, failing that, I used my hand. She bucked and whimpered, made those little sighing sounds that reminded me of a patient going under anaesthesia, of a swimmer drowning in the sea, while I inserted finger after finger and finally closed my hand. I pressed my other hand against her belly just above the line of pubic hair and felt the hard ball of my fist moving up and down her birth canal.

And for a little while, making love to her, lapping, sucking, kissing, fist-fucking her, the emptiness and fear retreated. It didn't haunt me any more. I didn't feel alone. I felt powerful and calm and loved. Shame was banished, need dissolved. There was no Dru and no guilt for a little while – there was only Tilly, and she knew what I wanted.

Afterwards, I sprawled on the filthy floor, afraid of what I'd done, of what I'd set in motion.

I shut my eyes and heard her zipper going up, the closing of the outer door, and when I overcame the paralyzing despair sufficiently to try to leave, I found that I could not. She'd locked or somehow blocked the door. She'd left me a prisoner in the dusty gloom of that basement, with the sound of freeway traffic passing overhead, rumble of trucks, screech of cars, but nothing louder than my own heart, nothing louder than the emptiness and desolation.

I climbed onto a chair and broke a window. I slashed my leg on the glass; blood oozed through the leg of my pants.

Some men, ashen-faced and derelict, passing a bottle back and forth, stopped guzzling long enough to stare at me. One of them made a lewd gesture. Another lifted up the bottle of Everclear.

"Hey, sister, wanna drink?"

I looked down at myself, dirty and bleeding. They thought I was one of them. I started running and made it back to my car. I sat shivering and panting with the doors locked, trying to calm down. Sniffing the cunt-smell on my fingertips to see if it was real.

I went back to Mark's place. I didn't tell him how I'd gotten so shaken and disheveled, that I'd fucked Tilly, too.

We lay in bed together, just the two of us, but it was as if she lay between us still. We touched each other, but were lifetimes apart.

"I'm through with her, you know," he said. "I can't stand the way I let her use me. I don't want her any more. It's over. Done."

"Then prove it. Fuck me like you used to."

He turned me over, grabbed my breasts and thrust against the crack of my ass. He got me up onto my hands and knees and fucked me like a freight-train. He fucked me till my brain went black. All was sensation, impact and friction; my arms ached from taking his thrusts. I dissolved into sex and heat. Obliterated.

"I love you," I moaned while he rammed into me. Over and over, as if by repetition I could make it true. Make it reciprocal.

But later on, once he had fucked me, the old craving returned. He grew restless, antsy, unable to sleep. Getting up to use the bathroom, drink a beer, adjust the stereo, put the TV on mute and channel surf through silent images of late-night movies, talk shows for insomniacs and the sexually unsated.

Finally he muttered, "I need to go somewhere." A

minute later, I heard the Harley kicked to life. I knew he was going to find her, to search the vacant buildings that she haunted, the after-hours bars and backstreets, the way the owner of a rutting cat goes searching in the night. Alleys and fenceposts and places to yowl.

Mark didn't come back that night.

Which meant he found her, I suppose.

Found something, anyway.

"I haven't seen her," Mark told me on the phone. "Yeah, I'm by myself. I'm settled back with a movie and a six-pack."

I pretended to believe him, then drove to his place. I unlocked the front door with the spare key and slipped into the bedroom. And saw them there, entwined like snakes, him on top of her, slapping her face while he fucked her and she whispering, "More. Please more."

My vision blurred red with rage.

I don't remember going to the kitchen and picking out a knife, but that's what I must have done, because the next thing I remember is pushing the blade into Tilly's chest, opening a red river between her freckled breasts.

But when I turned the light on, Tilly was gone and there was only Mark, his blond chest hair streaked with scarlet, wet and hot.

"You crazy bitch, what have you done?"

The wound, though it produced a terrifying amount of blood, was really minor – or so the paramedics said. Mark got stitched up in the ER, spent one night in the hospital, and came home.

He walked in the door and backhanded me so hard that comets pin-wheeled behind my eyes, and I fell to the floor. "I'll teach you to pull this shit," he said. He unzipped his pants and took his cock out, kicked my legs apart and pinned my arms while he forced himself inside me. I tried to scream, but he put his hand across my mouth and nose, and I stopped struggling.

When he was through, he said, "You're lucky. I'd planned to press charges. You could have gone to jail. But Tilly talked me out of it. She says that we should try again. That you deserve another chance."

"Is that all?"

"She also said that I should treat you differently. That I've been too nice to you."

"And you believed her?"

"I like being rough sometimes. She reminded me of that."

"What if I lose control again? What if I kill you next time? Or you kill me?"

"There won't be a next time." he said. "Tilly said she's going away. She won't get between us any more, so nothing like this ever has to happen again."

Oh, no, of course, it will never happen again.

Oh, God.

He pulled me close. "I'm sorry that I had to hit you. But I know you wanted it."

The hungry hour. My insides ache with craving deeper than my empty pussy, vaster than my hollow heart.

The ticking clock, the creak of bedsprings, the swish of sheets.

Across the ocean of a bed, I see Mark's pale hair, moonlit, quicksilver on the pillow. The darkly tanned triangle of his back, languid glow of moonlight licking shoulderblades and spine.

I reach for him. My hand brushes softly pliant skin. A hot tongue licks my wrist and palm. Tilly's long hair, sticky with come, falls across my face.

Across the bed, Mark stirs and tries to kiss me, but his mouth finds Tilly's breast instead. His hand, reaching for me, penetrates her pussy. "You want this, don't you?" she is whispering.

Don't, I think, *Just this one night, let Mark and me make love. Just for tonight, let us be alone together. Let us touch.*

But she is merciless, implacable, unmoved.

I have no other choice.

Later on, after I watch Mark make love to her, she follows me when I go into the kitchen and select a knife. Puts her cool hand on my shoulders, nibbles at my neck. Reminds me what I knew so many years ago: *Oh, yes, I want to do this. And this I know. He wants it, too.*

THE PRESENT

J. P. Kansas

WE HAD BEEN together just over one year. I was thirty-three; she was just thirty. Julie had been married for a few years in her early twenties; I had never been married, although I had once lived with the same woman for almost six years. Neither of us had any children.

I was a production manager for a large printing company on Hudson Street. Julie worked for a medical supplies company in midtown. I had finished three years of college, and had had enough. Julie had her BA, and was pursuing a Masters degree in hospital administration. Julie had a moderately large apartment in a fashionable neighborhood in Brooklyn known as Park Slope. I had a small apartment in an unfashionable part of Manhattan once known as Hell's Kitchen, now renamed Clinton Hill. I played handball and bicycled and used to play trumpet in a jazz band. Julie sewed and went to a gym. We'd met when her company was having something printed and she had hand-delivered some last-minute changes. We often joked that if her boss had trusted a messenger service, we would never have gotten together.

It was not a troubled or troublesome relationship. It was

not fraught with deep emotional undercurrents. We enjoyed each other's company, each other's sense of humor. We liked the same restaurants, the same movies, the same music. We even could occasionally tolerate each other's friends and – more rarely – each other's relatives.

I'm nothing special to look at, with very dark, curly hair, a face scarred from a bad case of adolescent acne, and dilute blue eyes. Julie is pretty but not strikingly so, with light brown hair, hazel eyes, and a straight nose she told me she had always wished was a little smaller. We're almost exactly the same height, and often borrow each other's clothes.

There'd been an immediate attraction between us. Even though the papers she'd brought were entirely self-explanatory, Julie went over them with me carefully. Even though she'd told me she had to get back to the office, I'd given her a tour of the entire plant, explaining the operation of the computer-controlled presses in far more detail than she could possibly have absorbed. It was obvious that the subtext of our conversation was entirely unrelated to printing a medical supplies brochure. She had had to call her office to make excuses for her long absence.

We went to bed for the first time on our third date – later we both admitted we were ready on the first date, but hadn't wanted to seem too forward or too eager. After the movies, I invited her back to my place. Inside the door, we began to kiss even before we'd gotten our jackets off. We were in the bed and naked within two minutes. I could not believe how sweet she smelled. I couldn't wait to feel my cock inside her. Even with the latex of the condom between us, I could feel how wet her pussy was. We fit each other perfectly.

There's nothing like going to bed with someone for the first time. It can be the most wonderful experience, or the worst. For me, with Julie, it was the best. It had all the novelty of discovery without any of the awkwardness. It was if we'd been going to bed with each other for years, but every sensation was new.

That first time we fucked, we confined ourselves to the missionary position. Julie, who later told me that she sometimes had some difficulty reaching orgasm without a finger on her clit, came easily, and I came as soon as she did. The second time that night, Julie straddled me, and the third time, in the morning, we lay on our sides, spooning, and I fucked her from behind.

Julie kept her apartment, but began spending more and more time at my place. By the second weekend, she'd brought over enough clothing that she could dress for work for an entire week without once repeating an item of clothing.

We had sex almost every night, and occasionally during the day on weekends. Gradually, we widened our palette of sexual activity. I went down on her, sometimes as foreplay and sometimes making her come. Julie went down on me, sometimes making me come – in a condom, of course – in her mouth. Sometimes, we went down on each other at the same time, which I found almost overwhelmingly exciting. Sometimes while we were fucking, she would sneak the tip of her finger into my ass, which would always drive me crazy. Sometimes, I'd do the same to her – which I think got me even more excited than it got her.

Sometimes, when she was tired, Julie offered her body to me, and I rubbed my cock against her breasts or in the crack of her ass until I came, or used my hand on myself while mouthing her breasts. More than once while I was using her body like this, Julie would find herself getting hot, and we'd end up having to scramble to get a condom so we could fuck. Once or twice, Julie found herself still hot after I'd come, and I used my fingers to make her come again – we always called that her "extra" orgasm.

The company I worked for bought a small printer in England and offered me the job of overseeing the installation of some new equipment, training its personnel, and generally revamping its operations in our procedures. The six-month assignment came with a substantial increase in pay and the possibility of even greater responsibility in the future. The only thing it didn't come with was Julie, who couldn't take a half-year leave of absence from her job, and couldn't disrupt her career by taking a temporary assignment overseas.

In the week I had to decide, Julie and I had many long late-night conversations that usually ended with tears or sex or both, and in the end we recognized that I was going to take the assignment and that we'd either live through it or we wouldn't. We agreed I'd come home for the weekends as often as I could.

Julie threw a going-away party for me that Saturday in June just before I left. After I'd unwrapped the half-dozen or so presents, Nancy took another gift-box out of her handbag and said, "And here's one for Julie. A Mike-going-away gift."

Julie reached across the coffee table and took the white cardboard box from her friend. It was a little smaller than a shoebox but of about the same proportions, tied with a purple ribbon and finished with an elaborate bow. Julie took the bow and the ribbon off the box and lifted the lid. Sitting next to her, I had a good view of its contents, but all I could see was a layer of white tissue paper.

She lifted the tissue paper. Nestled in more white tissue paper was an extremely realistic dildo – an artificial cock, complete with a fully-equipped scrotum.

I heard Julie take a sudden breath, and there was a moment of surprised silence from the group. None of us were prudes, but there was something startling and rude about its literalness, laying on the pure white of the tissue paper. And it wasn't anything I expected from Nancy. I glanced over at her, and saw that she was grinning and blushing.

In the next moment, the jokes and the laughter began.

"Is that meant to be an exact replacement for Mike?"

"Just the important parts," Nancy said, but giving me a friendly wink.

"It's much smaller," I said, because I thought it was expected. In fact, it looked about seven inches long – a little longer than mine, I'm sorry to admit – and somewhat thicker, too.

"Is that true, Julie?"

Ostentatiously, I nudged her with my elbow.

"Yes, much smaller," Julie said, in a jokingly insincere voice.

"Don't throw out the box," Nancy told Julie in a more serious voice. "It's comes with a little booklet."

"I don't think Julie needs instructions on how to use it!"

"No, it's got stuff about how to keep it clean, stuff like that," Nancy said.

There was another awkward silence, as people seemed to realize that Nancy was not entirely joking: she seemed really to expect Julie to use it.

Julie cleared her throat. "Thanks, Nancy. I can always count on you in emergencies," she said lightly, and put the cover back on the box.

I thought it was interesting that everyone wanted to see the presents I'd gotten – the guidebooks and the electronic organizer and the travel wallet – and passed them around; no one expressed any such interest in this present.

Julie put the box on the table, and it seemed to me that she tried to push it under some of the crumpled wrapping paper already there.

"Who's ready for coffee?" Julie asked in the next moment, rising from the couch. The party moved on to other activities and other matters, but it seemed to me that people – including me – were giving Nancy strange looks for the rest of the night.

*   *   *

The subject of Nancy's present didn't come up again that night, or in fact at all, for some time. She'd already cleaned up from the party when I woke up the next morning, and had put all my presents in a neat little pile near where I'd accumulated some of the other things I'd intended to bring with me. After breakfast, after I finished my last-minute packing, Julie and I spent a pleasant Sunday, and we had a sweet if somewhat subdued love-making Sunday afternoon, just before the car came to take me to the airport.

By the time it was late enough in New York to call, I was already halfway through my first workday. Julie and I had a brief and hurried conversation, and I promised to call her again from my furnished suite just before I went to sleep, by which time she would be back home from work. Fighting jetlag and the exhaustion of my first day there, I held out until 11:30 London time, 5:30 New York time, calling her from my new, unfamiliar bed.

The phone rang several times, and I was about to hang up to avoid the answering machine when she finally picked it up. "Hello?" she said, sounding rushed and annoyed.

"Julie, it's Mike,"

"Oh, hi, honey. I'm sorry. It was so hot out, I jumped into the shower as soon as I came home. I didn't hear the phone ring. I'm standing here in my robe dripping wet."

"I was about to hang up."

"I'm glad you didn't. How was the trip? Tell me everything."

I told her how the trip had gone, what my office was like, who I was working with, and what my accommodation was. She told me about how her work day had gone, and how much she missed me. There was an awkwardness in the conversation that I couldn't quite account for. We'd lived through separations before. I reminded her that I was already scheduled to come back for a weekend in two weeks.

"Listen, honey," I said after we'd been on for nearly

twenty minutes, "It's almost midnight here, and I'm falling asleep."

"I'm sure you are," she said. I heard a hesitation in her voice.

"What's the matter?"

She paused. "I have a little confession to make."

She didn't sound too guilty, so I wasn't too alarmed. "What confession?"

"You know Nancy's present?"

I had a quick, vivid image of the white box and its startling contents. "Sure."

"Well . . . I . . . I used it last night."

I felt a confusing mixture of feelings, and saw a confusing jumble of imaginings. "Yeah?"

She spoke hurriedly, as if to get it over with. "I was straightening things up after you'd left for the airport, and I saw the box. I didn't really know what to do with it or where to put it. I decided I'd just put it in the bedroom closet, on the shelf, and forget about it. But as I took it into the bedroom, I began to wonder what it was made of, what it felt like when you touched it. So I sat down on the bed and opened the box and looked at it. I think I was afraid of it or something. I didn't even touch it. I just sort of dumped it out on the bed. And then I noticed the booklet Nancy had mentioned. Most of it was just a catalog of other products – and, my God, they have some weird stuff, Mike! – but it also had a section that talked about things like how to take care of it – using lubricants with it, washing it, stuff like that. That's was when I decided I'd better wash it. That sort of made it all right, and I picked it up. I kind of pretended to myself that it was no different from picking up anything else – like a vegetable or, I don't know, a flashlight or something, and I took it into the bathroom and started washing it with soap and water."

She spoke more slowly now. "It got me incredibly hot. I can't tell you how real it feels, particularly when the water warms it up. Suddenly I saw my own hands on the thing in the mirror, and I was almost dizzy. I met my eyes in the mirror and I knew that something strange was happening."

In my imagination, I saw exactly what she was describing, and under the covers I was as hard as stone.

"I finished washing it off, and I lifted it up to look at it more closely. Except for the eye at the top, which was just sort of a shallow dimple, it was incredibly realistic. It looked like it had been cast from a mold of a real penis. And the outer layer even felt a little loose, like real skin. I don't know – maybe I was imagining that part.

"Mike, it was like I was possessed. I was shaking with excitement and, I guess, fear. It was almost as if the thing had a life of its own. As I examined it, it got closer and closer to my face. At first it just brushed against my lips, but then it was pressing against them, almost forcing them apart. I looked into the mirror and of course I saw that I was holding the thing up, but I had no conscious control over my hands. I watched as my lips opened and my tongue came out and licked it, and I almost fainted, my heart was beating so hard. The next thing I knew, my mouth was wide open and it was all the way in, as far as it could go, almost choking me, and then it was going in and out, like it was fucking my mouth, and it was like I could feel it between my legs.

"It was like I had no will of my own – it came out of my mouth and sort of dragged itself down my body – down my neck. I was still in my robe, and as the thing moved down, the robe parted and opened. The thing brushed over one nipple – and you know how sensitive my nipples are, it almost made me come, right then – and then it went over the other nipple, and I watched in the mirror, and that just made it even more exciting.

"And then, it parted my robe a little further and made me open my legs just enough, and I was already so wet and open, it slipped in immediately – all the way in.

"It was almost too rough with me. Every time it came out

and then went back in, I must have taken a little step back, because I ended up against the bathroom door, and then I just watched in the mirror as it just fucked me until I came."

There was a silence. I could hear her breathing. "Mike? Are you okay?" she asked. "Are you mad at me?"

"I'm not mad at you," I said. "I'm fine." In fact, I'd been holding myself – stroking myself – as she described what had happened. I was close to coming myself. But I had the sense that there was more. "Then what?"

She hesitated. "Then I took it to bed," she said huskily.

I swallowed hard. "Are you in the bedroom right now?"

"Yeah."

"And where is it?"

"It's in the drawer in the end table, right here."

"Why don't you take it out?"

"Right now?"

"Yeah, right now."

"Mike, I'm embarrassed. Do you really want me to?"

"Very much. Please do this for me."

"Okay," she said slowly. After a moment she said, "I've got it."

"Tell me what you did with it last night. Show me."

"Well, after I came in the bathroom, I took it out of me and I came in here. I lay down on my back and I put it on my chest, between my breasts."

"Is that what you're doing now?"

"Yeah."

"Then what did you do?"

"For a few minutes I just lay there, just kind of stunned at what had happened. I kind of went over it in my mind."

"Where were your hands?"

"They were kind of resting on it, holding it between my breasts."

"Are you doing that now?"

"Yeah."

"Then what?"

"Well, as I was thinking about what happened, my hands started moving a little bit, letting it brush against my breasts, rubbing it against my nipples."

"Are you doing that now?"

"Yes. And it got me very hot again. I rolled onto one side so I could squeeze it between my breasts and let it fuck my breasts, the way you like to do sometimes."

I rolled onto my side and imagined it was my penis between her breasts.

"And I bent my head down so I could lick the head." She paused, and I thought I could hear her licking. "I could taste myself on it, and I sucked it all the way into my mouth again."

"Do that now," I told her. I listened to the wet sounds. I imagined the dildo in her mouth, my penis in her mouth, and stroked myself. "Then what?" I asked.

"Mm," she said. I imagined her taking it out of her mouth. "Then I got onto my knees and my shoulders. I reached down between my legs and put it inside me again."

"Now. Are you doing that now?" I was up on my knees, cradling the phone against my shoulder, both hands on my penis.

"Yes. Oh, yes. Oh, God, yes. And I fucked myself with it until I came."

"Let me hear what that sounds like."

And she did. There were no more words. We came at the same time.

After that, she called me from the bedroom every day as soon as she'd come home from work and taken off her clothes. In bed, naked, already fully erect, I waited each night for her call.

I didn't get to come home until the end of the second week. My plane left Friday morning, London time, and arrived early afternoon, New York time. I called her at the office from the airport, and then found the limousine driver waiting for me.

I was a little surprised when I got to the apartment, because the front door wasn't double-locked, as it usually is when it's empty. Then I saw Julie's keys on the little table in the vestibule, and I understood. I dropped my bags and almost dashed into the bedroom.

She was in bed, under a single sheet. Her hair looked a little wet, as if she'd just showered. She was smiling her wonderful impish, innocent, suggestive smile, and almost by magic I found myself sitting on the edge of the bed; her naked breasts pressed against my chest as we kissed so hard I was having trouble breathing.

With even more than the usual frenzy, we managed to remove or at least open most of my clothes, and with almost no preliminaries I had a condom on and was inside her. Even though, in some sense, we'd been having sex each night – and that trans-Atlantic telephone sex had been extremely exciting – my body had been missing hers achingly, and now it felt like I was truly home. Effortlessly, the excitement climbed and peaked, and I came hard.

I could tell that I'd left Julie behind, but I had to hold her still. I was in that state just after orgasm where stimulation is so uncomfortable as to be almost painful.

"Hey," Julie said. "Not fair."

"It just shows how exciting I find you."

"That's flattering, but not satisfying."

"Give me a little while."

"That's what you always say – just before you fall asleep." She wiggled her hips suggestively.

I'd already passed the stage of oversensitivity, but my erection was also quickly disappearing, and it was time to withdraw from her, before the condom slipped off and we risked an accident. With my finger on the base of the condom, I lifted myself off her and turned to fall onto my back beside her.

"I'm exhausted," I admitted, as I removed the condom with a tissue and threw it away.

"Not fair," Julie repeated, playing but serious.

"Why don't you use your little friend?" I asked as I used another tissue to clean myself off. 'Isn't that what it's for?"

"Maybe I should," she said.

"Go ahead." She turned to look at me with a quizzical expression, trying to read whether I meant it or not. I met her eyes and gave her a smile and a nod.

Quickly, she turned away from me, opened the drawer of her end table, and removed the device. I turned on my side to watch her. She lay on her back. I saw the profile of a self-conscious smile.

The sheet was down to her waist. She held the dildo on her chest in both hands.

"Go ahead," I said again. "You've told me about what you do with it so many times. I want to see it now."

Julie took a huge breath, making her chest expand and her breasts rise wonderfully. She brought the artificial penis up to her left breast, the one nearer me, and rubbed its head against her nipple. I heard a soft sudden outbreath and glanced up at her face. Her eyes were closed and her mouth was open. And although only a few moments earlier I'd been ready to drift off to sleep, I was now fully awake and erect again.

I knew she had not forgotten that I was lying beside her, watching her, that this was all in some sense a show for me, but this didn't make her excitement any less real – nor mine.

Her eyes still closed, she turned on her side, bringing her arms together to force her breasts together. She pulled the penis back and forth between her breasts, occasionally moving it to one side or the other to caress a nipple with the head of the penis, each time sighing more and more deeply. A barely audible vocal sound joined her sighing.

She bent her head, and as the head of the penis neared her mouth, she stuck out her tongue and gave it a lick.

She took the penis deeply into her mouth, and then slowly withdrew it and brought it down her body. I sat up to watch as she raised her upper knee, rubbed the head of the penis between her lips and slowly pushed it into herself.

The sight of the woman I loved fucking herself with a dildo was far more exciting than I had even imagined. Not quite knowing how I was going to participate, I reached behind myself and groped for another condom. Never once taking my eyes from Julie's hand as it guided the penis in and out of her, I opened the foil packet and unwrapped the condom onto my cock.

I knew that Julie had opened her eyes. I looked at her. Taking one hand from between her legs, she reached for my cock, gently grasping it, pulling it up toward herself.

Sensing what she wanted, I lay down on my side upside down relative to her, my face opposite her pussy. With one hand, she guided my cock into her mouth, as she worked the dildo from behind. I grabbed her ass with both hands and stuffed my face against her, finding her clit with my tongue.

It was very exciting, and very weird, to have the dildo moving in and out, right in front of my eyes. It was somehow as if there was a third participant in bed with us – as if the two of us were having a three-scene – something we had never done, talked about, or even imagined – at least I hadn't, especially one involving another guy, rather than another girl. Suddenly, although the sensation of Julie's mouth on my cock was wonderful, I was envious of the dildo. I pulled away.

There was the usual momentary confusion as the two of us sorted ourselves out and, without talking, agreed what to do. I ended up on my back and Julie ended up sitting on my cock, rocking back and forth.

Our gazes were locked together. She raised the dildo to

her face, staring at me as she licked it and mouthed it. I stared, fascinated. She let her hand drop, making the head of the dildo rub against one nipple and then the other.

She drew the dildo down her chest, down her belly, down to her pussy, and rubbed it against her clit. It poked against my cock, as if wanting to go back where it had been, to unseat me. I stared.

With a small laugh, Julie turned the dildo around and held it against her bush. The sight of Julie masquerading as one of those so-called she-males was almost incomprehensibly shocking and exciting.

But she didn't give me more than a moment to consider that strange sight. She leaned forward to press her breasts against my chest, and I felt the incongruous sensation of a cock other than my own pressed between us. She moved her hips more quickly, bringing me almost unbearably close to coming.

It must have been awkward, though, because her arm was also caught between us. She raised herself up enough to free her arm, and then moved her hand away as she lowered herself to me again, this time pressing her mouth to mine. I opened my mouth to her tongue, and we kissed deeply. I put both hands on her waist, and then moved them down to cup her ass, guiding her up and down on my cock.

I felt a strange sensation near my lips, and at first I thought Julie had brought her hand to my face, but I smelled the strong odor of her pussy juices and realized what it was. Julie raised her head up slightly. Our eyes met again. Almost before I even knew what was happening, she guided the dildo into my open mouth, and I came with a shudder so intense that it frightened me. Julie moved quickly, and followed.

Soon after that, Julie ordered the harness – the contraption that straps around a woman's waist and her thighs and holds the dildo in position, just where a real cock would be.

SEX IN LITERATURE

Geoff Nicholson

FOR A LONG TIME I used to be the manager of the paperback
department in a large bookshop. I realize this is not the
sexiest opening line anybody has ever read. And I admit it
wasn't exactly the sexiest, most exciting work anybody has
ever done. Bookshops are not, in general, places of great
eroticism, much less of sexual abandon. Occasionally there
may be mild flirtation between staff and customers, or
romance may blossom between a couple of shop assistants
– in which case there may be stolen kisses between the
shelves of Travel and Reference, and we did once catch a
strange old man masturbating in the Health section – but,
let's face it, it was always fairly tame stuff.

A lot of women came into the shop and I always thought
it should have been quite easy to talk to them, to fall into
conversation with them about books. But there was a
problem. It seemed to be a law of nature that the better-
looking the woman, the worse her choice of reading matter.
The really glamorous pussycats, the ones in high heels and
Spandex and leather, were always the ones who wanted
nothing more than cheesy, down-market, shopping and
fucking novels.

Now I'm not against shopping and fucking *per se*, and I'm not too much of an intellectual snob, but I couldn't understand why these good-looking women couldn't get into Tolstoy, Shakespeare, James Joyce. I still can't.

But in truth I didn't spend too much time worrying about it. I just tried to get on with my job. The days were long but the work wasn't arduous and it was easy to drift off. I spent a lot of time in my own head. Sometimes I thought about sex, but more often I just thought about books.

It was a long, hot, midsummer afternoon. I was doing a stock check of the Biography section when an old lady approached me with some hesitation and said, "I think you ought to see this," and she handed me a photograph. She passed it to me face down and I turned it over as casually as you like; I got the shock of my life. The old lady had given me a photograph of a naked woman – at least, part of a naked woman. The area shown began a little way below the neck and ended a little way above the knees. It was a very attractive area, curved, full, shapely, well worth looking at, well worth showing off. The legs were open slightly and amid a thick tangle of pubic bush there was a tantalizing hint of pinkness.

I looked at the old lady in some alarm. Why was this apparently sweet old dear giving me dirty pictures? She could see what I was thinking and she started to explain rapidly.

"I found it here in this book," she said. "Someone, some pervert, obviously put it here inside this book, hoping to cause offence. Well, I'm offended."

I saw the book she was holding. It was *The Shorter Pepys*. Whoever had put it in there had good literary taste, even if, arguably, a somewhat juvenile sense of humour.

"I'm sorry about that," I said. "It's never happened before."

"Well, do try to make sure it doesn't happen again."

I said I would, but it was easier said than done. The paperback department was large. There were many thousands of books in stock, with new ones coming in all the time. Trade was brisk and large numbers of people passed through the bookshop all the time. How could you be absolutely sure there wasn't a dirty photograph lurking in one or two of the books? You couldn't check every single volume every single day, even if you had nothing better to do, and I liked to think I *did* have something better to do. So I told myself it was just an isolated piece of craziness, just something that someone had done as a practical joke or as a dare. I thought it wouldn't happen again. But I was quite wrong.

Nude photographs started popping up all over the place. In *Utopia*, in *The Way of All Flesh*, even in Darwin's *Voyage of the Beagle*. It was always a photograph of the same woman, although there were considerable variations in the pose. Sometimes she would be seated, or reclining; sometimes her hands would be on her hips; sometimes her legs would be open and one of her hands would be reaching down between them. Sometimes she'd be completely naked, but other times she'd be accessorized with stockings or elbow-length gloves. But one thing didn't vary. Whatever the pose, whatever the props, the face always remained well outside the frame of the picture.

It became a regular occurrence for customers to find these photographs and hand them in to me. The customer might be male or female, and they might be disgusted or angry or amused. I suppose one or two may even have been aroused. Other bookshop assistants would find them too, and duly told me about them, and I'm sure there must have been people who came across them and liked them enough to take them home without reporting them at all.

The odd thing was, they were only ever found in the paperback department, my department. I tended to think it was a fairly harmless activity as sexual peculiarities go, but it clearly wasn't going to stop. It was a little embarrassing sometimes but, more than that, it suggested that things were going on in my department that I wasn't able to control. It was all very well to make a joke out of it, but if one of my bosses found out about it – and I had quite a number of bosses, none of whom liked me very much – it wasn't going to do my working life any good at all. It was going to make me look like a complete idiot.

So it appeared I would have to do something. It didn't seem that ultimately I would have to do very much, just find the culprit, politely ask them to stop, and if that didn't work deliver a few threats about calling the police. That would surely be enough. The problem, of course, was finding the culprit.

For me, the first question that needed answering was whether it was a man or a woman planting the nude photographs. The idea that it might be a man who simply wanted to display nude photographs of his wife or girlfriend was dreary beyond belief. It smacked all too strongly of the "Readers' Wives" syndrome. On the other hand, if it was a woman doing it, then it was a very interesting form of exhibitionism indeed. The idea that a woman might want to flash bits of her photographed anatomy at an unsuspecting, book-buying public was one that I found quite horny. I sincerely hoped this was the case, and I rather looked forward to meeting the woman in question.

One of my assistants said we should get a big blow-up of one of the photographs and put it in the shop window with a sign saying, "Have you seen this woman?" The theory was that this would embarrass the person into stopping. However, it seemed to me that even if this absurd course of action had been possible, it would only have been taken as a sign of encouragement to the culprit.

By now I had quite a collection of nude photographs in my desk. I would get them out from time to time, in moments when business was slack, and study them carefully. If anybody had asked, I might have said that I was looking for clues, that there might be something in one of the pictures that revealed the identity of the woman. That wasn't an absolute lie, but, of course, it was only half the story.

I'm prepared to confess that I like looking at nude women. I'm even prepared to confess that I like looking at *pictures* of nude women. But the truth is, I like to know who I'm looking at. I like to see the whole personality, the real woman. Arty shots of bottoms and backs are all very well, but I like to see their faces.

I had got to know this particular body very well from the photographs. I had observed, for instance, a wicked little mole on the inner left thigh and I had come to feel great affection for those hard, dark nipples, the small, hard breasts, the artful way the pubic bush had been trimmed. And I couldn't help speculating about what kind of face belonged with this body. I was intrigued, I was attracted and I was prepared to be turned on; but would I feel the same way when I saw the face? Could I even guess what that face might be like? I tried, but I really couldn't. Then I had an idea.

Now, I'm no amateur psychologist but it occurred to me that the joy of exhibitionism must be two-fold. There must be the simple thrill of exposing yourself, but then there must be the extra, more complex thrill of seeing how other people react to that exposure. I thought it was quite possible that whoever was planting the photographs might also be hanging around the shop to see how other customers reacted to finding them. So I kept my eye out for anyone behaving suspiciously, and I didn't have to wait long.

One day, it all seemed to fall into place. I had discovered a new batch of nude photographs slipped inside the novels of Anthony Trollope, and I had deliberately left them there. The classics section was right next to the counter and I was able to watch as a dapper, distinguished-looking old boy in pinstripes browsed through the books. I knew that sooner or later he was going to find one of the photographs and he looked the sort of man who might react dramatically to the discovery.

I looked around the department. There was only one other person there; a young dark-haired woman whose size, shape and physique more or less fitted the bill as seen in the pictures. Even her face conformed generally to my idea of what our mystery nude ought to look like, although frankly not quite as appealing as I'd hoped, and there was no doubt that she definitely kept looking in our direction.

That was good enough for me. I pounced. I dashed across the department and grabbed her by the wrist. "All right," I said, "the game's up."

She looked at me in a resigned, helpless way, and said resignedly, "Okay, it's a fair cop."

I saw then that she was carrying a large rucksack and she opened it and started hauling out piles of paperback books.

"You look like a decent bloke," she said. "You can have all your stock back. Just don't call the police, okay?"

The plan had gone dramatically wrong. I had caught not a phantom, female exhibitionist, but a common or garden shoplifter. There was some satisfaction in this, but not quite the sort I was looking for.

The situation could only get worse, and it did. The nude photographs seemed to be breeding and multiplying. I found at least one a day, inside *Lord of the Flies*, inside *Our Mutual Friend*, inside *To the Lighthouse*. I wondered if somebody was trying to tell me something.

I got bizarre complaints from customers. One man had bought his father a copy of *The Decline and Fall of the Roman Empire*. It had contained a nude photograph that I hadn't managed to spot and extract. The customer wouldn't have minded particularly, except that his father now assumed the son was having an affair and was demanding to meet the "beguiling little creature".

Then things took an even stranger turn. I was on the bus going home from work. I was reading *Middlemarch* and it was slow going. I could only manage a few pages a day. I opened it at the page I'd got to and found, not my usual bookmark, but a brand new nude photograph, one that I hadn't seen before. How had it got there? The book had been lying around on my desk at work, so it wouldn't have been so very difficult to tamper with it, but there was something rather special about this particular photograph. You may have guessed, though I must say it would never have occurred to me: the face was visible.

It was a great face: the face I'd been looking and hoping for. The features were strong: big deep eyes, sweeping eyebrows, a full red mouth. But it was not a face I'd ever seen before. I supposed I had expected that seeing the face would solve everything. I assumed it would belong to a someone I recognized, a regular customer. I was devastated to find that this revelation had solved nothing. The woman in the photographs was as elusive as ever. Serious action was called for and, after much serious thought, I hit on a wild but ingenious plan.

On my next day off I went out and bought myself a Polaroid camera with a self-timer. I took it home and spent a lot of time and effort composing myself into tempting nude postures before shooting off a roll of film, and I made sure the photographs only showed the area of my body from neck to knee. I took the results into work next day and distributed them among some of our more literary volumes.

I waited all day. Remarkably, nobody bought any of the books I had put my Polaroids in. Nobody even browsed through them and found the photographs. Closing time arrived. I cashed up, put my coat on, and was ready to call it a day. I was about to leave the department when a voice behind me said, "I'd like to buy these, if I'm not too late."

I'd thought all the customers were long gone and I was about to say yes, it *was* too late, that the till was closed, the shop was closing and I had a home to go to. But I turned round and saw that my lone, late customer was indeed the woman in the nude photographs. What's more, the books she wanted to buy were all the ones containing the nude photographs of me. She had taken all the Polaroids out and was tapping them on the counter like a pack of cards.

She nodded towards the photographs and said, "It's fun, isn't it?", and I'm afraid I had to agree.

We went back to her place, where she had a whole photographic studio set up. I undressed her, peeled off her clothes to reveal the familiar body that I knew so well from the photographs, and she did the same for me.

We started to make love in the middle of her studio and I noticed that she was holding a cable release in her hand. Whenever we got into a position that she considered photogenic, she'd press the release, a shutter would clank open and shut, and a bank of flash-light would explode over us.

It could have been off-putting but somehow it wasn't. I felt extremely good. I felt like a model, a star. I felt strong and athletic and we were able to get into some wild and complex positions. And when it was all over, I felt pleased to know that we'd have a photographic record of the happy event.

Afterwards, she told me she'd been coming into the bookshop for years and had always wanted to fall into conversation with me but I'd never seemed to notice her. It was undeniably true. I still couldn't remember ever having seen her before. I asked why she hadn't taken the initiative and asked me a question about books, and she said it was because she was shy.

Next day we took the best of the photographs, the ones where the faces didn't show, and slipped them into numerous great works of literature in a local bookshop – but somebody else's bookshop, not the one where I work. I wanted it to be somebody else's problem from now on.

And that's been the pattern ever since. We fuck, we take photographs, we show our snaps to the world. Of course, we never show our faces. I'm sure there are those who would say it's all a bit sick and kinky and not what a real relationship should be all about, but it works pretty damn well for us.

Besides, there's more to our relationship than sex. There are many evenings when we just sit together and read books, books like *Madame Bovary*, Boswell's *Life of Johnson*, Mary Wollstonecraft's *Vindication of the Rights of Women*. Sometimes we find there isn't enough sex in them. And that's when we give in, lower our aesthetic standards and read the occasional shopping and fucking novel.